T0129250

*From spirited young woman to reckless widow, the beautiful Marchioness of Hadley remains a force to be reckoned with. But beneath her antics lies a broken heart . . .*

Since her husband's tragic death, Lady Charlotte Hadley has embarked on a path of careless behavior and dangerous hijinks from which no one can divert her . . . until suddenly, her first—and only—true love reenters her world. Their fiery romance was so scandalous Charlotte had no choice but to marry another, more suitable man. Surely now they are both free to pick up where they left off . . .

Julian West has returned to London a hero after making a name for himself in battle at Waterloo. Every woman is vying for his attention—except the one who stole his heart. No matter, Julian has other obligations. But when Charlotte's sister, Eleanor, charges him with protecting the widow from ruin, what ensues is another kind of battle—one that leads a chase from London's bars and brothels to the finest country estate as Julian and Charlotte untangle a host of secrets, regrets, and misunderstandings. For could it be that the love they've forced themselves to forget is exactly what they need to remember? . . .

# Books by Anna Bradley

LADY ELEANOR'S SEVENTH SUITOR

LADY CHARLOTTE'S FIRST LOVE

TWELFTH NIGHT WITH THE EARL

**Published by Kensington Publishing Corporation**

# Lady Charlotte's First Love

*The Sutherland Sisters*

## Anna Bradley

**LYRICAL PRESS**
Kensington Publishing Corp.
www.kensingtonbooks.com

LYRICAL PRESS BOOKS are published by

Kensington Publishing Corp.
119 West 40th Street
New York, NY 10018

All Kensington titles, imprints, and distributed lines are available at special quantity discounts for bulk purchases for sales promotion, premiums, fund-raising, educational, or institutional use.

Special book excerpts or customized printings can also be created to fit specific needs. For details, write or phone the office of the Kensington Sales Manager: Kensington Publishing Corp., 119 West 40th Street, New York, NY 10018. Attn. Sales Department. Phone: 1-800-221-2647.

Lyrical Press and Lyrical Press logo Reg. U.S. Pat. & TM Off.

First Electronic Edition: October 2017
eISBN-13: 978-1-5161-0518-2
eISBN-10: 1-5161-0518-4

First Print Edition: October 2017
ISBN-13: 978-1-5161-0519-9
ISBN-10: 1-5161-0519-2

Printed in the United States of America

*To my sister Liz*

*My deepest thanks to my agent, Marlene Stringer, my editor, John Scognamiglio, and the talented, creative team at Kensington.*

# Chapter One

*London, July 1816*

A scandalous wager, a marchioness in disguise and a notorious London brothel. Julian couldn't deny it had all the makings of an excellent farce.

Off stage, it was rather less amusing.

*Bloody hell.* One would think a marchioness who gambled with her reputation would choose an anonymous brothel in a quiet part of the city for her whorehouse romp. Instead, the Marchioness of Hadley had chosen this one.

*Devil take her.*

He peered into the dimly-lit parlor. Despite the muted light and the haze of acrid smoke, he could see the place was crowded with fashionably dressed gentlemen. A man might tend to ignore everything else when he cupped a plump breast or a shapely thigh in his hand, but if one of these drunken dandies happened to recognize him, he'd have a glorious headline in the scandal sheets tomorrow.

Triumphant Hero Returns to London, Frolics with a Whore.

A dark haired doxy sidled up to him and gave his arm a flirtatious tap. "In or out, guv. Wot will it be?"

Julian raised an eyebrow. "In *or* out? Must I settle for one or the other?"

The doxy blinked at him, then broke into a hoarse cackle. "Aw right then, luv, how's this? In or out, or *in and out.*" She punctuated the feeble jest with a rude hand gesture.

Julian's lips quirked. Ah, there it was. A quick-witted whore. It was something new, anyway.

Encouraged, the doxy rose to her tiptoes, put her mouth to his ear and whispered in what she no doubt imagined to be a seductive voice, "It's wot ye came fer, innit?"

It stood to reason. If a man wanted ale, he went to an alehouse. If he wanted to shoe his horse, he went to a blacksmith. If he wanted a woman and one wasn't readily available, he went to a whore. It was a simple enough matter.

Except it wasn't. Not this time. "No. I came for a marchioness."

The doxy flashed a gap-toothed grin. "'Course ye did. Dinnit I tell ye, guv? I'm a duchess, I am."

Julian rolled his eyes. No doubt this duchess was much like every other—more trouble than she was worth, but he couldn't hover in the entryway all night waiting to snatch a wayward marchioness. He needed a prop, and a doxy in the hand was worth two anywhere else.

Well. Not quite *anywhere* else, but he wouldn't be here long enough to maneuver her into a more satisfying location. Damn it, it was just like his cousin, Cam, to send him off to a whorehouse in pursuit of a marchioness instead of a whore. But it could be hours before Lady Hadley deigned to appear, and in the meantime…

He let the dark-haired doxy drag him across the threshold into a shadowy corner of the parlor. The gentlemen around him lounged on sumptuous red velvet divans, glasses of port or whiskey in their hands, many of them with women in various stages of undress perched on their laps. The low, continuous buzz of conversation was occasionally punctuated by a high-pitched squeal or giggle.

"There now," his doxy cooed, "not so hard, was it, luv? Don't ye worry, though," she added with a smirk. "It will be once the duchess gets ahold of it."

Julian felt an embarrassingly quick surge of interest in his lower extremities. He hadn't had a woman in…well. He couldn't quite recall how long it had been, but long enough so even the doxy duchess held a certain appeal. Every other part of him might rebel at the thought, but his body demanded a woman. The need was like a flea crawling under his skin, and the more he tried to ignore it, the more pressing it became.

He'd have to mount something other than his horse, and soon, so he may as well scratch the itch here and now. It insisted on being scratched, and it would have its way whether he willed it or not. If he tried to return to his old life with such a burden of lust in his loins, there was no telling how he'd be tempted to satisfy it.

The doxy ran her hands up the front of his chest, unbuttoning his waistcoat as she went. "That's it. Just relax, now, luv."

The burden in question began to swell insistently against his falls, much to the doxy's approval. Her eyes widened with appreciation. "Coo. Yer a duke right e'nuf, eh, guv? Naught but a duchess will do fer that bit—but wot's this, now?" She dove for his waistcoat pocket, her fingers as deft as any thief's, and held up a round, flat object.

Julian grabbed her wrist, hard—much harder than he'd intended to—and held on until her hand fell open. "Don't touch that." He snatched it away from her.

She gave him an indignant look. "I wasna going ter take it, guv."

He stared down at her thin fingers, dumbfounded, a wave of confused shame washing over him. *Jesus.* He hadn't meant to grab her like that. She'd only reached into his pocket, but he'd reacted as if she'd put a blade to his throat.

"Well, what it is, then?" the whore demanded. "The crown jewels? Must be, fer ye to take on so."

He opened his palm to reveal a pocket watch in a plain, gilded case. He hesitated for a moment, then flicked it open and turned the watch in her direction. "It belonged to a friend of mine, and it's… Well, I don't like anyone to touch it."

Her nose wrinkled with disdain. "Wot, that's all? Wrong time too, innit?"

Julian snapped the case closed. "Yes. It doesn't tell time anymore. The winding key is gone. Lost for good." The watch was useless now, but he didn't have it to keep the time. Ridiculous, to believe time *could* be kept. A man couldn't keep it any more than he could catch the sun and balance it on the horizon. He might keep a coach and four, hounds, a mistress—but he didn't keep time.

It kept him.

The whore made a disgusted noise, released her grip on his waistcoat, and turned away from him to screech into the parlor. "Mrs. Lacey! I got's a jumpy one here fer ye." She gave Julian one last offended look, stuck her nose in the air, and flounced away.

Well. Maybe she was a duchess, after all.

A female shape detached itself from a knot of people in the parlor and materialized out of the gloom. A woman, tall, with generous white breasts spilling from the top of a tight bodice sank into a low curtsey in front of him. It was the kind of curtsey that invited a gentleman to ogle her bosom, and Julian obliged.

"Good evening, sir. I'm Mrs. Lacey."

*Red.* Her hair, her lips, her scarlet-colored gown—everything about her was red except her eyes, which were a watery green. She was attractive in that hard, painted way the better-looking prostitutes were attractive.

She assessed him with a practiced eye and then held out her hand, a small smile on her full lips. "You're a pretty one, aren't you? What's your name, luv?"

"Does it matter?" She might recognize his name. He'd been mentioned in the papers more than once since his regiment returned to England.

She chuckled. "Not in the least. You may call me Evie. What shall I call you?"

He shrugged. "Call me whatever you want."

She gave him a curious look. "I don't want anything, luv. Gentlemen come to me to get what they want. So. What do *you* want?"

*One marchioness.* Was it possible she'd already come and gone and he'd missed her? "I'm looking for a woman."

The red lips curled upward. "Are you now? Imagine that."

"No, that is, not a woman, but—"

"Sorry, luv." Mrs. Lacey shook her head. "This isn't that kind of house. Try Fleet Street."

*For God's sake.* He was going to strangle Cam. "A lady, Mrs. Lacey. I'm looking for a *lady.*"

"A lady?" Her brow furrowed as if she couldn't imagine why he'd want such a troublesome thing. "This isn't Almack's, luv. The gentlemen here don't have much use for ladies. They come for a tumble, not a quadrille. So, do you want a tumble or not?"

The knot in Julian's lower belly tightened and hope creaked to life inside him. Mrs. Lacey looked as if she knew a great deal about fleshly desires. He'd promised Cam, but there was no sign of Lady Hadley yet, and well, this *was* a brothel.

"Such a fine, strapping young buck you are." Mrs. Lacey's green gaze lingered for a moment on his shoulders and chest, then moved lower, and lower still. "It's not healthy, luv, for such a vigorous gentleman to deny his urges."

*Urges. Yes.* He did have those. "No, not at all healthy."

Mrs. Lacey's eyes gleamed in the muted light. "That's right. Now come with me, luv, and we'll find you just the right lady to satisfy those urges. What do you fancy?"

*Anything in skirts.* "Blond with blue eyes." It was as good a choice as any.

"Ah. That's easily done." Mrs. Lacey glanced around the room, then crooked a finger at a young woman who stood by the fireplace, chatting up a scrawny lad with a lopsided cravat. "Mary. Come here, my dear girl."

Mary abandoned her young man without a backward glance and hurried across the room to Mrs. Lacey's side. "Yes, mum?"

Mrs. Lacey urged the girl forward into better light so Julian could get a look at her. "This gentleman would like a companion for the evening. Do you suppose you could entertain him?"

Mary's eyes went wide when she got a close look at Julian. "Oh yes, indeed, mum." She gave Mrs. Lacey a sidelong glance that made the older woman chuckle, and added, "Thank you, mum."

Julian studied the girl. She was young, but not too young, with fair-skin, light yellow hair, and dainty lips, faintly pink. Everything about her was pale and indistinct, like the sun hidden under layers of haze and London smog, pretty in its way, with a wan kind of beauty.

She wasn't perfect, but she was here, and that was good enough for him. He nodded once at Mrs. Lacey. "She'll do."

Mrs. Lacey smiled. "Then I wish you an enjoyable evening."

Julian watched her go, her lush, wide hips swaying, then turned back to Mary, his eyebrows raised expectantly.

"Fancy a drink before we go up?" Mary jerked her head toward a group of gentlemen who staggered about the center of the parlor, groping at females and guffawing loudly. Julian watched with distaste as one man stumbled to his knees and grasped at a whore's skirts to try and drag himself back up. "Sometimes the gentlemen like a drink or two first. To relax, I s'pose."

Julian shook his head. There was only one thing that would relax him, and it wasn't drink. "No, I don't care for—"

His words were drowned out by a sudden explosion of catcalls and whistles behind him. Gentlemen who were still lucid enough to stand lurched to their feet and crowded into the front of the room, craning their necks to see what fresh new mayhem was on offer. Whatever they saw caused the low din of conversation to rise until it reached a fever pitch of male voices raised in shouts of approval.

Julian growled with frustration as sweaty bodies surged against him. He took Mary's arm and tried to disappear up the stairs, but men pressed against him from all sides and blocked his path to the second floor. *Jesus.* He'd anticipated sweaty body parts pressed together, but his fantasies hadn't included foul male odors and coarse body hair.

*Anna Bradley*

After a great deal of scuffling and good-natured shoving the crowd parted, and four ladies in masques swept into the room, emerging from the chaos of eager male bodies.

"Come here, love, I've got something special for you!" One of the gentlemen made a clumsy grab for the lady closest to him—a tall, slender blonde with a jeweled black masque obscuring the upper part of her face. She dodged him, stepping neatly out of the way of his groping hand.

The crowd roared with laughter. "Looks like she doesn't want what you've got, Dudley!" shouted one delighted onlooker.

"Can't say I blame her," yelled another. "All the doxies in London know what you've got, my lord, and there's nothing special about it!"

The crowd erupted with laughter again. The four ladies took no notice of the heaving herd of rogues on either side of them, but made their way down the center of the room as if they were on a promenade through Hyde Park with the pink of the *ton*, not in a west end whorehouse with shrieking men ogling them from all sides.

They were rather too much like the pink of the *ton*, in fact.

Julian watched with narrowed eyes as the ladies made their way through the crowd to a corner of the room and settled gracefully onto two divans near the fire. A footman leapt forward to attend them, and one of the ladies—another blonde, this one petite and curvy—spoke to him. He rushed off at once to do her bidding, leaving the four ladies alone.

There was a brief silence—a breathless pause, the room frozen in a ludicrous tableau as everyone waited to see what they'd do.

The petite blonde waved a casual hand at the lady across from her, this one a redhead, her fair skin an unearthly white in the dim light. The entire room seemed to hold its breath as the redhead reached into the reticule in her lap. She took out a lacquered case, slid it open, and drew out—

"Cor," Mary breathed at his side.

Four cheroots.

She offered one to each of her three companions. The other ladies accepted and held the thin, brown cheroots between gloved fingers as they turned to their fourth companion.

And she… Julian went still, every muscle in his body drawing tight. Mary giggled nervously at his side, but he ignored her, his gaze fixed on the fourth lady.

She wore tight elbow-length black gloves and carried a tiny bag on a string around her wrist. She dipped her long, satin-covered fingers into the bag, took out a small bundle, smoothed the wrappings aside, and withdrew a bit of cloth. Every eye in the room was on her as she rose, crossed to the fireplace, and knelt down to touch the cloth to the fire. It caught at once, and more than one man in the crowd drew in a quick, sharp breath, as if the sight of that tiny flame had snapped them from a collective trance.

The lady held the lit cloth to one end of her cheroot and sucked gently on the other end until the tip glowed red in the dim room; then she tossed the cloth into the fire, resumed her seat, and handed her lit cheroot to the petite blonde next to her. One by one, each lady passed their lit cheroot to the next, until all four tips burned like identical red eyes.

"The way's clear now, guv."

Julian started, then turned to Mary in surprise. "What?"

She jerked her head in the direction of the stairs. "Don't ye want to go up?"

"Not yet." Julian let his gaze wander back to the fourth lady. "I think I'd like a drink, after all."

Mary shrugged. "All right, then."

He led her to a dark corner of the room, to another red velvet divan where they were cast in shadows, but which still afforded a clear view of the four ladies, who now sat, as prim as a quartet of governesses, sipping at the whiskey the footman had delivered and occasionally touching their cheroots to their lips. No one approached them despite the earlier burst of excitement at their arrival, for by this time it was obvious they weren't here for the gentlemen's amusement.

Why precisely they *were* here—well, that was anyone's guess. They weren't whores. They were ladies—*ton*, if one could judge by their fine gowns and jeweled masques.

Julian's lips stretched into a mocking smile. Four bored aristocratic ladies out on a whorehouse adventure. It wasn't unheard of—more than one titled lady had set out to test the *ton*'s limits for scandal—and yet a clandestine visit to a west end whorehouse was more than enough to leave a lady's reputation in tatters. Nothing but four silk masques stood between these four and social ruin.

Quite a risk for a bit of fun.

Julian leaned back against the divan, let a healthy swallow of whiskey burn a trail of fire down his throat and studied the fourth lady. Her masque covered the entire upper part of her face, just as the other ladies' did, and yet…

A masque couldn't cover everything.

She had dark hair, coiled into a mass of heavy curls at the base of her long, slender neck, red lips, an elegant body, too slim, but still curved where a man wanted curves. No wan, indistinct beauty here, but a lush, glorious explosion of warmth and color, like a blazing sun in a pure blue sky.

The kind of sun it hurt to look at.

Masque or no masque—it made no difference. He'd have recognize her anywhere.

*Charlotte Sutherland.*

No, not Sutherland. Not anymore. She was the Marchioness of Hadley now.

Now what would make a marchioness abandon her grand country estate for a Covent Garden whorehouse? Wilted roses in the flower gardens, perhaps, or lazy servants? Whatever it might be, it hadn't anything to do with him. She looked perfectly content to stay where she was. Despite his promise to Cam, Julian decided he'd leave her here, teetering on the edge of scandal.

He tipped the rest of his whiskey into his mouth and turned to Mary. "I'm ready. Shall we go upstairs?"

She rose to her feet. "Whatever you say, guv."

He was halfway to the stairs when it happened.

Charlotte laughed. Soft—a titter more than a laugh. No one else in the noisy room noticed it. Well, no one would, would they? No one, that is, who hadn't heard that laugh before, low and suggestive, her red lips pressed to his ear. Her laugh pulled him back at once, back into the dimly lit room, away from Mary and the sweet release her body promised.

As little as a year ago he'd dreamed of that laugh, dreams of such exquisite yearning he couldn't tell whether they were dreams at all, or nightmares. Odd, how much could change in a year. Dreams faded. A man traded one nightmare for another. Brides became widows, and widows became whores.

*What the devil was she doing here?* She should be tucked away in Hampshire like a proper little widow, mourning her late husband, not in some whorehouse in the west end, drinking whiskey and blithely courting ruin with every draw on her cheroot. Courting ruin and laughing about it, as if her family's reputation were of no consequence. As if Cam and Ellie weren't at this very moment torturing themselves with visions of her disgrace.

Julian dropped his empty glass onto the table with a dull thud. Very well, he'd escort the marchioness out of here just as he'd promised he would, but he'd be damned if he'd be a gentleman about it. After all, a marchioness who entered a whorehouse shouldn't expect to be treated like a lady.

"Here. Take this." He took Mary's wrist, turned her hand up, then reached into his pocket, grabbed a fistful of coins, and dropped them into her open palm. "I won't need your company tonight, after all, but I do need a room. Which one is yours?"

Mary gaped at the pile of coins in her palm for a moment; then her hand snapped closed. "Top of the stairs, last room on the left."

"Stay out of it for a time, until you see me leave the house. Can you do that for me, Mary?"

She gave him a curious look, but she knew better than to ask questions. "Whatever you say, guv."

"Good girl."

Julian walked back across the parlor and resumed his seat on the divan. He signaled to the footman for another glass of whiskey and settled in to watch and wait.

# Chapter Two

Red velvet divans, flocked silk paper on the walls, a fine Axminster carpet in shades of red, black and gold on the floor—if it weren't for the cheroot and the whiskey, she might have been in Lady Sutton's drawing-room.

The cheroot, the whiskey, and the half-naked whores, that is.

Charlotte blew a thin stream of smoke through her lips and tried to imagine the expression on Lady Sutton's face if she found out her drawing-room resembled the inside of a whorehouse. A laugh bubbled up in her throat, trapped the smoke in her lungs, and sent her into a coughing fit that had her gasping and wiping her eyes.

Wretched things, cheroots.

"My goodness, Charlotte." Lady Annabel gave her a disapproving look and drew expertly on her own cheroot. "Do be quiet. You'll attract attention."

Lady Elizabeth snickered. "It's a bit late for that, Annabel. We gave up being inconspicuous when we strolled into a whorehouse."

"Don't inhale the smoke, Charlotte. Like this." Aurelie Leblanc, the Comtesse de Lisle, touched the thin cheroot to her lips for a moment, then lowered it again without drawing on it. "See? No coughing."

Lady Annabel frowned. "That's cheating, Aurelie. The wager is—"

"Cheating?" Lady Elizabeth snorted. "What nonsense. The wager is we light the cheroots and stay in the brothel long enough for them to burn to the end. We never said we'd smoke the awful things."

"That's splitting hairs, Lissie." Lady Annabel took another draw on her cheroot to emphasize her point. "It's the spirit of the thing that matters, and I never cheat on a wager."

Lady Elizabeth gave her an arch look. "Honor among thieves, Annabel?"

"No. Honor among wicked widows." Lady Annabel adopted a virtuous tone. "After all, my dears, if we don't have our reputations, we don't have anything at all."

A moment of stunned silence greeted this statement; then all four ladies laughed appreciatively.

"A bit late for that as well, I'm afraid." Lady Elizabeth downed the rest of her whiskey in one swallow, then indicated their surroundings with a wave of her empty glass. "Have you forgotten where we are?"

Lady Annabel shrugged. "We're wearing masques. If no one recognizes us, it's just as if we weren't here at all."

Aurelie giggled. "A convenient sort of morality, is it not?"

"My dear." Lady Annabel smiled through a thin curl of smoke. "Is there any other kind?"

Charlotte studied her cheroot. It looked as long as it had when she'd first lit it, the blasted thing. "As far as the spirit of the wager is concerned, Annabel, I think our honor is safe, regardless of whether or not we smoke the cheroots. Lord Devon wagered we wouldn't enter the whorehouse. The cheroots and whiskey are incidental."

Aurelie downed her whiskey and stubbed out her cheroot in the empty glass. "*Certainment.* We've won the wager already, and here's the proof." She held up the cheroot for their inspection, then threw the remains of it into her reticule. "Just as well, too, because that dreadful cheroot is staining my glove."

Lady Annabel continued to smoke her cheroot with every appearance of enjoyment. "Lord Devon is terribly wicked, is he not? Imagine his challenging us to enter a whorehouse! We should cut his acquaintance, my dears."

"He's no wickeder than we are." Charlotte had no intention of cutting Lord Devon. Wicked or not, he'd proved most diverting at a time when she badly needed the distraction. "In any case, I confess I've always wanted to see the inside of a brothel."

Lady Elizabeth nodded. "Oh, I have, as well. I thought it would be different, though—more exciting, somehow."

Charlotte glanced around the room. "More exciting than bare-bosomed ladies being pawed at by sotted gentlemen? Yes, there's nothing so unusual in that, I'm afraid." One could see the same thing in many aristocratic ballrooms in London, though the *ton* did their best to hide their sins under a thin veneer of respectability. Failing that, they hid in secluded alcoves and behind the shrubbery in dimly lit gardens.

"No. It looks rather like Lord Harrow's ball last week." Lady Elizabeth sounded disappointed. "Even the same people are here. Look, there's Lord

Dudley. Oh dear. I'm sorry for that poor woman he's groping, for I suppose she has to have him, doesn't she?"

Aurelie observed the couple for a moment. "Not to worry, *ma petite*. He doesn't look as if he's in any condition to, ah...perform."

Lady Annabel snorted. "No, he doesn't. With any luck he'll lose consciousness. I hope she fleeces his pockets if he does."

Charlotte said nothing, but reached up to make sure her masque was securely tied. She hadn't noticed Lord Dudley before. She scanned the room again to see who else she'd overlooked. For pity's sake, half the *ton* was here. The male half. She knew, of course, that aristocratic gentlemen spent more time with whores and their mistresses than they did their own wives, but good heavens—weren't there other bordellos in London?

If any of these gentlemen were sober enough to focus, they'd recognize her easily, even with her masque on. Charlotte chewed on her lower lip. No, it wouldn't do at all for Ellie and Cam to discover this latest escapade. She never should have promised her sister she'd give up her mad frolics, for she'd known even as the words left her mouth it was a promise she couldn't keep.

Wretched things, promises.

She'd take care to avoid them in future. It was one thing to be a scandal, but quite another to be a scandal *and* a liar. She rose to her feet. "This was amusing enough for a time, but it grows dull. Shall we go find Devon?"

Annabel took a final draw on her cheroot. "Dear me, Charlotte. Bored in a bordello? How jaded you are."

Charlotte shrugged. "Perhaps it's more amusing for the prostitutes."

"Perhaps," said Lady Elizabeth. "But I draw the line at finding out. Besides, I believe the cheroot has made Aurelie ill." She held out a hand to help the Comtesse rise from the divan.

Lady Annabel jumped to her feet. "Oh, dear. She looks quite green. We'd better hurry."

Every eye in the room turned in their direction as they made their way to the door, but this time the men's scrutiny felt more ominous. No one said a word to her and no one approached, but Charlotte's flesh prickled in warning. The sooner they rejoined Devon, the better—

*Oh, hell and damnation.* She still had the blasted cheroot clutched between her fingers. It had burned to the end at last and now it threatened to singe her glove. She hurried back to the fireplace and tossed it into the flames. If some leering scoundrel got a peek under her masque because of that dratted cheroot, she was going to have Annabel's head—

"Leaving so soon, sweet?" A strong, muscular arm snaked around the middle of her body and jerked her to an abrupt halt. "But we haven't yet been introduced."

For a moment Charlotte froze with shock—only a moment, but that was all it took for her friends to vanish into the crowd. "Unhand me, sir," she ordered in the haughtiest, most marchioness-like tone she could muster.

"Unhand you? Oh, no. I don't think so." The voice was low and so close she felt his breath tickle her ear. "What fun would that be?"

He spoke pleasantly enough, but underneath the amusement was a thread of ice that made Charlotte squirm in his grasp. "Release me this instant. How dare you?"

He jerked her back against a chest as hard and unyielding as a stone wall. "How dare I claim a whore in a whorehouse? I assure you, sweetheart, it takes no daring at all."

Charlotte could tell by the width of his chest and the hard muscles bulging in his forearm it would do no good to struggle, so she went still and tried to collect her wits. No doubt her friends thought she was right behind them. They'd return for her when they realized she wasn't, and—

"Not much of a challenge, I admit, to bed a whore," he went on, "but sometimes a man wants his pleasures to come easy." He ran a caressing hand over her hip and around the curve of her bottom, then pulled her tighter against him. "And you, sweetheart, are easy."

Charlotte's eyes widened. *Oh, no.* His chest wasn't the only hard thing pressed against her back. He was becoming...engorged. He'd soon lose all use of his mental faculties and she'd never be able to reason him out of this madness. She took a deep breath and forced herself to speak calmly. "Sir, you can't possibly think to—"

"Take you right here in the parlor, with every drunken scoundrel in London gaping at us? Tempting thought, but I'm a gentleman, sweetheart. I have a room upstairs."

*Upstairs?* Oh, for pity's sake. Where were her friends? Why hadn't they come back for her yet? If they returned and couldn't find her...

Charlotte gave an experimental kick and managed to land a blow to his shin. She heard a pained grunt behind her, but instead of loosening his grip he hitched her higher against his chest, so only the tips of her slippers touched the floor.

"Come now, sweet," he crooned into her ear. "I promise I'll take good care of you."

Charlotte was rather alarmed by this point, but somehow his low rasp penetrated the fog of panic in her brain. *His voice.* For one wild moment she thought she recognized it, had heard it before, whispering in her ear, promising *something*. She stilled, trying to place it, but the memory danced just outside her grasp.

"That's better," he murmured. "You don't really want to give all these fine gentlemen a show, do you?"

*Fine gentlemen.* Of course. She was in a whorehouse, wasn't she?

She was in a whorehouse, her friends had abandoned her and this large, amorous gentleman—who thought, quite reasonably, she was a whore—was about to drag her upstairs. The other fine gentlemen in question—all of whom also believed her to be a whore—ogled her with ill-concealed excitement. A number of them had staggered to their feet and edged closer to get a better look at the struggle, so she and her tormentor were now surrounded by a circle of drooling scoundrels.

Any of whom could decide at any moment to tear off her masque.

She let her body go limp against her captor's hard chest. Her best alternative by far was to let him take her upstairs and then try to reason with him in private. If that didn't work, she could always bash him over the head with the washbasin. Whorehouses did have washbasins, didn't they? One would think they'd need them—

"Wise choice, love." The arm wrapped around the middle of her body eased a fraction when she made no move to flee. "You won't regret it."

*You will.* Best not to say so aloud, though. She'd need the element of surprise to escape unscathed this time. She permitted him to maneuver her across the room toward the stairwell and up the stairs in front of him, his hand heavy against her lower back. Once they reached the second floor he hurried her down the hallway to the last door on the left and thrust her through it.

The door thudded closed behind him and she heard the unmistakable scrape of the key as it turned in the lock.

Charlotte scurried away from him before he could grab her, toss her onto the bed and…well, do whatever gentlemen did with whores, which was, she guessed, not the same thing they did with their wives. She wasn't certain, having never been mistaken for a whore before, but she had a vague notion gentlemen tended to skip the preliminaries where prostitutes were concerned, and she'd rather not reason with him while flat on her back.

"I haven't got all night, love." His boots rang on the wooden floor and she felt the heat of his body close behind her, though he didn't touch her. "Take off your clothing and lay down on the bed."

Charlotte took a quick survey of the room. *Ah.* There, on a table by the far side of the bed—a washbasin, old and chipped, to be sure, but if she couldn't make him see reason it would do the job. She took a stealthy step toward it, drew a steadying breath into her lungs, and turned to face him. "I'm afraid, sir, you've made a rather unfortunate mistake—"

She got no further. The words lodged in her throat and her sentence ended on a choked gasp. Every limb in her body went numb with shock, and for one horrible moment she was paralyzed, unable to think or do anything other than stare up at him.

Oh God, she'd dreaded this moment—dreaded it and longed for it since his regiment returned to England. Now the moment was here. *He* was here. *Julian.*

"It's you who's made the mistake, sweetheart, not me."

His voice. She *had* heard it before, soft in her ear, his whispered promises—*he loved her, his heart was hers, always*—and, oh, she'd believed him, she'd treasured his every word, and trusted him with the absolute trust of first love. It made her chest ache even now, more than a year later, to think of such a love.

Maybe he had loved her. Maybe he'd meant to keep his promises, but it hadn't made any difference then, and it made even less difference now.

"Do you like what you see?"

She jerked her gaze from his face and shoved the memories back into their secret places in the darkest corners of her mind. Such a question needed no answer. It was like asking if she preferred a sky obscured by thick, black clouds where once there'd been nothing but stars.

His face, that handsome face, once so dear to her. He was handsome still—more so, even, now that life had filled in the hollows of youth and etched faint lines of experience into the corners of his eyes. He had the same dark waves falling in a silky drift across his forehead and the same wide mouth with the full, sensuous bottom lip. She'd spent hours tracing his lips with the tips of her fingers.

But his eyes… They were wrong. They were still dark and liquid, with a slight upward tilt at the corners and a long, thick fringe of sooty lashes, but there was no joy in them. No kindness. They were suspicious. Watchful.

At one time she'd thought his eyes the very essence of him. Perhaps they still were.

Her silence didn't seem to matter to him.

"I'm afraid it makes no difference whether you like it or not." He eased his coat over his shoulders and tossed it onto a bench at the end of the bed. "It matters only that I like what I see, and I do, sweet. I like it very much, and I've paid to see all of it, so remove your clothing."

His tone was bland now, nearly inflectionless. If she hadn't known every nuance of his voice, hadn't heard it echo in her dreams, she might have missed the subtle note of challenge. But she heard it, and as soon as she did, she knew. Her masque hadn't fooled him. He knew who she was. He'd known from the first moment he saw her. She was sure of it. How could he not? He'd brought her up here on purpose then, so he could…

What? Teach her a lesson. Put her in her place.

Her breath caught on a strange, grim little laugh. Did he really believe there was a lesson she hadn't yet learned? Did he truly think she hadn't been shoved into her place, again and again, and with such brutal force it had taken every shred of strength she could muster to crawl out of it?

"Remove your clothing."

Charlotte crossed her arms over her chest. "Why are you doing this?"

"Doing what, sweet? Getting what I paid for?"

If he felt any remorse—or any emotion at all—it didn't show in his face. He was utterly composed, in perfect control of himself. Bored, even, like a lazy cat who held a mouse's tail under his paw and was biding his time until he slashed a claw through its belly.

Bored, yes, but not so bored he was ready to end his game. Very well. She'd end it for him.

Charlotte reached behind her head to untie the silken cords of her masque, but Julian grabbed her wrists to stop her. "*No.* I said remove your clothing, not your masque. I'm not interested in your face. Leave the masque on."

*Oh, yes. He knew who she was.*

Charlotte stared up into his hard, dark eyes. He thought she wouldn't do it—he didn't even *want* her to do it. He wanted her to admit she'd been a fool to risk her reputation by entering a whorehouse, to crumple at his feet and beg his forgiveness so he could refuse to give it to her.

But she was done begging for forgiveness. His, or anyone else's.

So instead she did the one thing she could think to do under the circumstances. She curled her lips in a slow, seductive smile and turned around to present him with her back. "Aw right, guv, if ye say so. It's yer coin, right enough. Help wif my buttons, won't ye, luv?"

Oh, how she wanted to see his face then, to read his expression as she gave him just what he asked for.

*But not what he wanted.*

He made a faint sound, an angry, strangled word or a harshly exhaled breath. "Do you think I won't?"

He would, or he wouldn't. It didn't matter which. Either way he'd lose, because this wasn't what he wanted. "Aw, come on, luv. Why should I think that? Ye've got a right lusty look about ye, ye do, and ye did say you liked what ye seen. Or mayhap," she added, her voice as smooth as silk, "Ye don't like it as well as ye thought ye did, eh?"

She felt his hands against the back of her neck, his fingers twisting the top button of her gown. "Or maybe I like it even better."

Cool air touched her skin through the flimsy material of her shift as he worked her buttons one by one until her gown was open all the way down to the small of her back. He settled his hands against her waist, his fingers stroking over the soft flesh there before he eased her hips back against the front of his falls.

A tremor passed through her, but otherwise she didn't move. He was calling her bluff? Surely he wouldn't—

"What's the matter, *luv?*" He grazed his teeth over the sensitive skin under her ear. "You haven't changed your mind, I hope? It's a bit late for that. Once a man's desires are roused, there's only one way to satisfy him. I would think you'd know that, being a prostitute."

Anger stiffened her spine and her resolve. "A woman don't get ter change 'er mind no matter what, prostitute or not. I'd a thought ye'd know *that*, being a man."

A low chuckle was his only answer, but he gripped her shoulders, his palms hot, heavy. She braced herself to resist him, to dive across the room for the washbasin, but his touch turned gentle as he slipped his fingers under the edge of her shift to stroke her bare shoulders. She sucked back a gasp as he moved closer, so close his warm breath drifted over her skin. Her eyes fell closed, but just when she thought he'd put his mouth on her, he grasped her shoulders and turned her around to face him.

Charlotte caught her breath.

His perfect impassivity was gone. His eyes were no longer cold, his face no longer composed. His cheekbones were flushed with color and his breath came fast and hard. "Unbutton my waistcoat."

"No need fer that, luv." Her voice wasn't quite steady. "If ye'll just strip off yer breeches—"

He made a harsh sound in his throat and caught her wrists to press her hands against his chest. She could feel the thud of his heart through the silk of his waistcoat. "Do it. Unbutton my waistcoat."

He held her wrists until she worked the buttons loose; then he dragged her hands up his chest and pressed them tight against his neck. He stared down at her, his dark eyes burning. "Take off my cravat."

The command was low and hoarse, almost inaudible, but his voice throbbed with an intensity that brooked no argument. His words echoed inside her, and this time Charlotte didn't think to resist him, but untied the knot, unwound the long piece of linen, and drew it away from his neck.

He took the cravat in shaking hands, and let it slip through his fingers and flutter to the floor. "Put your arms around my neck."

She stared at the smooth olive-tinted skin left bare by the loose neck of his shirt, and a sense of unreality swept over her, as if time had somehow shifted, reversed, and they weren't here at all, in a whorehouse, with long months of bitterness and unanswered questions between them, and suddenly she wished it were so, longed for it with an ache so deep she staggered under it.

She closed her eyes and slid her arms around his neck, but even as she sifted the soft waves of his hair through her fingers, she knew it was hopeless. No matter how brief, how fleeting that sweet, perfect first love might be, one only ever got a single chance at it.

She'd had her chance, and she'd lost it. She'd never get another.

# Chapter Three

She did as he bid her and twined her arms around his neck. For a single, baffling moment her touch felt like home, but with his next breath the strange sensation dissipated on a wave of panic.

*She thinks to send me to my knees again...*

No. Not this time. He hadn't survived blood and battles and chaos only to be brought to his knees by her. "Open your eyes."

Fear made his voice harsh, but she didn't seem to notice. Her eyelids lifted on command, as if he'd jerked a string, but somehow her compliance only made him angry. "So obedient. But what now, sweet?"

"Wot? Ye mean ye don't *know?* Aw, well, don't worry, guv. I'll help ye along."

"Will you? Very well, then. Go to the bed and hike up your skirts." *There.* That should earn him a slap to the face. One sharp crack and they could end this farce.

Without a word she turned, marched over to the bed, lay on her back, and reached a hand down to lift her skirts.

He almost laughed. Some things hadn't changed, then. Charlotte had never been one to settle for a farce when she could have a drama. Julian crossed the room in two long strides, took her by the arm, and drew her to her feet. "How far do you plan to take this?"

She ran a teasing finger down his arm, but her eyes narrowed to dark slits. "Why, as far as you will, luv. Further."

"You'd let me bed you?" His laugh was harsh, incredulous. "Do you have so little regard for yourself? Or are you a whore now, after all?"

As soon as the ugly words left his mouth Julian flinched away from them, as if someone else had said them. How had they gotten to this point?

He'd only thought to bring her upstairs and show her how foolish she was to trifle with her reputation, and now he was calling her a whore?

*Jesus.* He had to calm down, to go easier. "I beg your—"

"'Course I'm a whore." Her eyes flashed, and an echo of it reverberated in his belly, the feeling both strange and familiar at once. He'd seen that spark before. He'd always thought her more glorious than ever when she was in a passion. So much passion, as if she carried a flame inside her. But as quickly as the flame sparked to life it was gone, and she regarded him with cool, dark eyes. "That's what ye paid for, innit?"

*Ah.* So that's what this was. Not a farce or a drama, but charades, and she'd continue to play until he removed her masque, and once he did, neither of them would be able to hide anymore. *Pity.* Charades were much more entertaining than reality. More truthful, too, because they didn't pretend to be anything other than what they were.

He didn't want to see her face, but it was inevitable, this moment between them. It wouldn't be cheated, and masked or not, her face would never cease to haunt him. It was printed indelibly inside his eyelids, waiting there to torment him every time he closed his eyes.

For months after he left London, every dark-haired woman he happened across was *her.* Every red lip, every long, white neck, every husky, teasing laugh—*her.* There were days when he thought he'd go mad from it, and yet still it was her, always, even after she'd tossed him away without a thought, much as she'd tossed her cheroot into the fire when she'd finished with it this evening—tossed it away to never think on it again.

*Remove the masque, and end this.*

He watched his hand reach for her as if he were trapped in a nightmare. The masque's silk tie was slippery under his fingers and he struggled with the knot, but then the scrap of jewels and ribbon fell to the floor at their feet, the black silk stark against the white linen of his cravat.

He caught her chin in his fingers and turned her face up to his. So soft and warm still, her skin so fine, so smooth. The perfect curve of her cheek, the wide dark eyes tipped with those feathery lashes—in another lifetime they'd made his chest ache with want, and her lips, so full and red, had made his knees buckle.

"Do you like what you see?"

She stood before him, her loosened gown slipping off her shoulders. He'd unfastened every button, all the way down to that sweet spot at the arch of her back. He knew it was sweet because he'd tasted her there, had trailed his lips over that fragrant arch again and again...

But he'd been gone for months—no, for a lifetime, and everything inside him had gone so jagged, so sideways he didn't recognized himself anymore. He was no longer the same man who'd been taken in by the promise of those eyes, those lips, and on a stab of inexplicable loss he thought some part of him must despise her now, in her fine gown and her elaborate jeweled masque, with her lovely face and hard eyes.

"No. Not quite the same, after all." He released her chin to trail his fingertips down her cheek. His touch was gentle, deceptively so, for his words were cruel. "Beautiful still, of course, but I find myself curiously unmoved, Lady Hadley."

He waited for another flash of temper in her eyes, but she might have been a marble statue or a porcelain doll, for not a ripple of emotion disturbed her blank face. "Ah, well. It's for the best, I suppose. It didn't end well for me when my face did move you, did it, Captain West?"

His hand dropped away from her cheek. "Have you rewritten our history, my lady? As I recall it didn't end well for either of us—"

"Charlotte!" A loud thump at the door made them both jump. "Are you in there?"

"Hush, Aurelie!" another voice hissed. "Or you'll have dozens of whores and their bare-arsed lords out here with us."

Someone rattled the handle, but the door remained firmly shut. "That devil has her locked in there with him!"

Another thump, this one followed by an incredulous laugh. "Lissie! Do you intend to knock down the door with your slipper?"

"I suppose you have a better idea, Annabel?" This question was accompanied by another dull slap on the door, then a shockingly unladylike curse.

"Well, yes. We'll have Charlotte let us in."

"But that devil must have restrained her," wailed the first lady, "or she'd have answered our knock by now! He likely has her secured to a chair, or worse, to the bed!"

There was a brief pause, then a smothered laugh. "That could be worse or better, depending on what he looks like. Did either of you see him?"

"That is *not* amusing, Annabel. Charlotte! Can you hear us? Maybe he has her gagged."

Julian raised an eyebrow. *Gagged?*

"Hush!" snapped the one called Annabel. "I think it far more likely we have the wrong room."

"But the blond-haired doxy said it was the last door on the left."

*Thud.* This time the door shuddered in its frame. The one wielding the slipper—Lissie—must have exchanged her shoe for her fist. "She must have lied. No doubt he paid her well to do so. Aurelie, go back down and give her a guinea."

There was another pause, then, "Oh, dear. I don't have a guinea. Do you suppose she'll take a crown and a half-smoked cheroot, instead?"

"What's a whore going to do with a half-smoked cheroot, for heaven's sake?"

"I don't know. Smoke the other half?"

Julian retrieved his cravat from the floor and looped it around his neck. "You'd better let your friends in." He plucked his waistcoat from the bench at the end of the bed and withdrew the key from his pocket. "Quickly, before they tear down the door."

He handed Charlotte the key, donned his waistcoat, snatched his coat up from the bench and braced himself for the inevitable uproar as all three ladies tumbled into the room at once.

"Charlotte! Oh, *dieu merci!*" The petite blonde rushed forward and clasped Charlotte in her arms. "We thought you were right behind us earlier! We would have missed you sooner, but when we got outside Lord Devon was waiting for us, and what do you think? The wicked man tried to argue we hadn't won the wager because Lissie didn't smoke her cheroot, and—"

"I bloody well did smoke it! Let Devon sniff my breath if he doesn't believe me."

The tall, slender blonde closed the door behind them, strolled into the room, and stopped in front of Julian. "Shall we discuss it later? I'd like to be introduced to this, ah, gentleman first."

The redhead, Lissie, placed her hands on her hips. "Right. Who the bloody hell are *you?*"

Julian shrugged and began to button his waistcoat. "Isn't it obvious? I'm the devil who locked the door, secured Lady Hadley to the bed, and gagged her."

"I *knew* it!" Aurelie crowed.

Charlotte glared at him, then turned to Aurelie. "For goodness' sake. You can see for yourselves that's *not* what happened."

The taller blonde continued to eye Julian. "I see. Was yours a random attack, sir, or do you often force your attentions on unwilling ladies?"

"*Ladies?*" Julian gave her a bland smile. "Need I remind you you're in a brothel? Generally speaking, whores are willing to receive a gentleman's attentions."

The redhead snorted. "*Gentleman?* I hope you don't refer to yourself."

"And this lady isn't a whore," the blonde added. "Anyone can see that, and I'd wager you knew it well enough when you brought her up here."

"Another wager?" Julian waved a hand around the room. "You're still in a brothel, madam. Perhaps you should conclude your last wager before you undertake a second one. After all, I may have rope and gags enough for all four of you."

"It wouldn't surprise me in the least if you did," snapped the redhead. "We're not afraid of *you*, and we'll have an explanation for your infamous behavior at once."

He shrugged. "Very well. The marchioness and I are…acquaintances."

"*Acquaintances?*" The little blonde grasped Charlotte's shoulders, turned her around, and began to fasten the back of her gown. "Are you in the habit of ripping your acquaintances' clothing from their backs?"

"Ah. Well. That depends on the acquaintance."

A corner of the tall blonde's mouth twitched. "Indeed. What is your name, sir?"

Julian tugged the ends of his cravat into place and began to tie it with smooth, precise movements, but he remained silent. He'd answered enough of her questions, and since he meant to stay far away from Charlotte after tonight, her blonde friend didn't need to know his name.

"Perhaps it's just as well," she murmured, when it became clear he wasn't going to reply. "All buttoned up again, Charlotte? Ah, very good. Then I see no reason to linger. Let's be certain we all leave together this time, all right, my dears?"

Julian pulled his coat on. "No. I don't think so."

All four ladies turned to him, but it was Charlotte who spoke. "What do you mean, you don't think so?"

He leaned down and scooped up her black masque from the floor. "You're coming with me."

Charlotte crossed her arms over her chest. "Not without rope and a gag, I'm not. I'm leaving with my friends."

"I don't think so," he said again. "For all I know your friends are on their way to another whorehouse. You'll come with me, as it's the only way I can be certain you're delivered safely to your door."

"How gallant. Rather surprising, given the circumstances. I've no need for an escort, however."

"You mistake the matter indeed if you think my concern is for *you*."

Somehow in the midst of this bizarre evening he'd forgotten why he dragged Charlotte upstairs in the first place. Because bloody Cam had cozened him into it, and because Ellie had made it clear she'd rather her younger sister *didn't* spend her time in a whorehouse.

"Such admirable family loyalty." Charlotte gave a short, mocking laugh. "But perhaps I can be persuaded to accept your escort after all, as long as we agree no one else needs to know about this."

*Too late.* But then Charlotte obviously hadn't caught on to that fact, and he wasn't about to enlighten her. The lie fell smoothly from his lips. "If you come with me now, no one need be the wiser."

"Good. After all, no harm was done tonight."

*No harm yet.* They still had to escape a crowded whorehouse with her reputation intact. A tricky business, that. Cam and Ellie could be the least of Charlotte's worries. By tomorrow everyone in London might know about her whorehouse escapade.

"I have your word on this?" Charlotte pressed.

"Of course." The promise was broken before he even made it, but she'd given up any right she had to the truth when she'd strolled into a whorehouse. He'd do whatever it took to get her out the door.

She studied him for a moment, then turned to her friends. "It's all right. He'll take me straight back to Grosvenor Square."

The redhead slid Julian a measuring look, then frowned. "I don't like it, Charlotte."

"I don't, either." The petite blonde looked as if she were on the verge of tears. "What proof do we have he'll see you home safely? Why, he could drop you in the middle of Seven Dials and leave you to the mercy of the footpads!"

"I assure you, madam, I have no such intention. Why should I play such a nasty trick on the footpads?"

The tall blonde's mouth twitched again; then she came forward and kissed Charlotte's cheek. "Alas, straight back to Grosvenor Square, just as if you were a naughty child. Rather a dull end to an otherwise promising evening. But no matter." She threw Julian a provoking smile. "There's always tomorrow night. Now, ladies, are your masques secured? We have to make our way through that pack of shrieking villains again."

The other two ladies kissed Charlotte, tightened the ribbons on their masques and followed the tall blonde out the door, leaving the room far quieter than it was before they'd entered.

Julian thrust the black masque into Charlotte's hands. "Here. Put this back on."

She didn't argue, but silently donned the masque and tied the ribbon.

He cracked open the door to check the hallway. It was empty. "Follow me, but don't come into the parlor. Stay out of sight while I secure a hack."

There was no sign of Charlotte's friends downstairs, but their departure must have caused an uproar, because he found Mrs. Lacey soothing a group of disgruntled young bucks with promises of exotic fleshly pleasures Julian knew to be illegal in England. She was more than happy to secure him a hack, shove him and his troublesome companion toward the door, and be rid of them.

Charlotte sat across from him in the carriage on their way to Grosvenor Square, her masque in her lap and a shaft of moonlight teasing pale fingers across her face. To look at her now, he'd never guess she'd spent her evening in a whorehouse, dangling her reputation from the end of a silken cord. She appeared every inch the grand marchioness.

Neither of them spoke until the carriage drew to a halt in front of Charlotte's house, and then Julian cleared his throat. "I'll remain in London for a short time only. A few weeks at most."

"Indeed? I suppose you have plans to return to Hertfordshire."

Considering the night of passion they'd shared at his home in Hertfordshire it should have cost her an effort to mention it, but if it did, she hid it well. "Anxious to be rid of me, are you, Lady Hadley?"

She smoothed her hands over her skirts, then folded them in her lap. "I can't think of any reason why I should be. Can you?"

Julian stared at her. She stared back with an air of polite enquiry, as if she were waiting for him to hand her a cup of tea. "As I said, I have business in London, and as my cousin is rather inconveniently married to your sister, we're bound to be thrown into each other's company. Not more than necessary, I hope."

"Oh? And how much of my company would you deem necessary, Captain?"

*So bloody composed.* "The less, the better. I'm staying with Cam, Ellie, and Amelia in Bedford Square, and you, well…" He gestured toward the carriage window. "You have a grand house in Grosvenor Square, don't you?"

Julian let this sink in and waited for something, anything to indicate she wasn't as unaffected as she pretended to be.

He was disappointed. She only tilted her head to one side to study him, then, "Oh. I see. You're warning me away from my sister's house."

He shrugged. "Not forever, but it would be easier while I remain in London, yes."

She considered this as if she thought it a perfectly reasonable demand. "And should your business keep you in London longer than you anticipate? What then?"

"Would that bother you?"

"Are you asking me, Captain, if it would bother me not to see my family?"

Her cool poise was beginning to nettle him. "I can't imagine you see much of them now, with your friends and your whorehouse romps to keep you busy. You can't be that fond of Amelia, especially. She's only your half-sister."

He leaned back against his seat and waited. If a shadow of Charlotte Sutherland hid under the marchioness's cool facade, he'd see her now. From the moment she'd discovered their connection, Charlotte had been fiercely protective of Amelia.

"I don't do things by halves, Captain West." Her tone was pleasant. Conversational.

"Don't you? That's not how I remember it."

"Memories are deceptive things, aren't they? I do beg your pardon, but I will make you no promises, as I may find I have an inclination to visit my family in between whorehouse romps."

"You forget, my lady, I've heard your promises before. Even if you did promise, I wouldn't believe you."

The coachman came down from the box and held the door, waiting for Charlotte to alight. She descended from the carriage, but hesitated on the street for a moment. "No," she said. "I don't suppose you would."

The moon had retreated behind a cloud and Julian could no longer see her face, but her gaze was fixed on… He didn't know what, but something he couldn't see. She closed the carriage door with a quiet click and mounted the stairs to her grand house, the entrance half lost in shadows.

# Chapter Four

It was late when Julian returned to Bedford Square, but Cam was still awake, pacing in the entrance hall. He jerked the front door open before Julian could reach the top step.

"Well, cuz." Julian shoved his hands into his breeches pockets and slouched against the doorframe. "If I'd known you'd answer the door dressed only in your banyan, I would have gone through the servant's entrance."

Cam opened the door wide and stood aside so Julian could enter. "I expected you back hours ago."

Julian followed him into the entryway. "You've had hours to dress and you still answered the door wearing *that*? A bloody frightening sight. I suppose Mrs. West chased you from her bedchamber?"

"What do you mean? Ellie adores the sight of me in my banyan."

"Does she? It's true love, then."

Cam turned down the hallway and entered his study. "It is, indeed."

Julian dropped into one of the leather chairs in front of the fire—*his chair*—and accepted a glass of whiskey from his cousin. "Is Ellie asleep?"

Cam poured himself a measure and settled into the chair next to Julian's. "Yes. She went to bed hours ago. You can speak plainly, Jules."

"All right, then. Plainly speaking, you sent me on quite an adventurous chase this evening."

Cam gave him a hopeful look. "A chase? Does that mean she wasn't there, after all?"

"No. Sorry, cuz. She was there. I have quite a whorehouse tale for you, but I'm not sure you'll find it amusing."

Cam sighed, but he didn't look surprised. "Go on, then. Let's hear it."

Julian took a swallow of his whiskey. "It was a strange bit of business—"

"*Christ.* That kind of place, was it?" Cam leaned forward in his chair. "I've heard stories, of course."

"Bloody hell, Cam. Not *that* kind of strange. I didn't think the marchioness was going to appear, after all, so I was on the verge of disappearing upstairs with a little blonde wench—"

"For God's sake Julian, whatever for?"

"*What for?* Think hard, Cam. I'm sure you'll figure it out."

Cam dismissed this with an impatient wave of his hand. "Of course I know *what for.* I've just never known you to frequent whorehouses, that's all. But let's have your tale, amusing or not."

"As I said, I was on the verge of disappearing upstairs, eager to conclude my business when I was prevented by a sudden uproar."

"An uproar? Was it one of those performances, where the ladies—"

"No! I told you, it wasn't *that* sort of strange, though now you say it, there was a performance of sorts, and it did involve ladies. Aristocratic ladies."

Cam's grin faded. "Aristocratic ladies?"

"Yes. There were four of them. Two blondes, one petite, the other tall and slender, and a fair-skinned redhead. I didn't recognize those three, but the fourth—"

"Let me guess. Dark hair? Tall, too thin, and known to you?"

"I'm afraid so. My God, Cam. I didn't truly think she'd be there, but you don't look shocked."

Cam shot to his feet, went to the sideboard, and poured himself more whiskey—a hefty measure this time. "I'm not. What happened?"

"They strolled in, seated themselves on a divan, pulled out four cheroots, and sat there and smoked them, as cool as you please."

Cam downed his whiskey in one swallow. "Jesus. What else?"

Julian came to his feet and joined Cam at the sideboard. He felt a sudden need for another drink, as well. "Charlotte had touch papers with her to light the cheroots, so they obviously planned the entire thing." He held out his glass and Cam poured him a measure. "You were right about it being a wager. The petite blonde mentioned someone named Devon."

"Ethan Fortescue, Lord Devon." Cam smiled grimly. "Yes. He was undoubtedly involved. Did anyone recognize them?"

Julian shook his head. "I can't be sure, but I don't think so. They wore masques. As soon as I discovered Charlotte I bundled her into a carriage and took her home."

That wasn't all he'd done, but it didn't seem a good time to confess he'd dragged her upstairs to a private bedchamber, nearly stripped her gown from her back, and told her to hike her skirts. He doubted his cousin would find that information reassuring.

"Thank God." Cam released a long breath. "At least the worst didn't happen. Not this time, at any rate."

"This time? Does the marchioness make a habit of frequenting whorehouses?"

Cam ran a hand through his hair. "This is her first whorehouse, but not her first brush with scandal. She hasn't been herself since she returned to London for the season. You know Hadley died not even four months after they wed, and that in itself was an awful enough business—"

"No." Julian held up a hand. "I don't want to know the details, Cam." The Marchioness of Hadley wasn't his concern, and he would keep it that way.

Cam gave him a measuring look, but he didn't argue. "Ellie's going to go mad when she hears of this."

"Don't tell her, then."

"Spoken like a naive bachelor, cuz. I don't keep secrets from my wife. Even if I wanted to, I couldn't. Wives always find out. Besides, if I don't tell her, Sarah will."

"Who's Sarah?"

"Sarah is Charlotte's lady's maid. Earlier this season when it became clear Charlotte wasn't, well…wasn't herself, Sarah agreed to keep an eye on her and report anything of concern back to Ellie."

*Keep an eye on her?* For God's sake. Cam spoke as if Charlotte were a rebellious child. "Tell Sarah to keep it quiet, then. It might be better if Ellie didn't know."

"It might be better if Ellie didn't know what?"

Julian whirled around, and his whiskey sloshed over the edge of his glass. "Good Lord, Ellie. You've made me spill whiskey all over myself. Where did you come from?"

Ellie stood by the door, one eyebrow raised and her arms folded across her chest. "The hallway, and not a moment too soon, it seems. It might be better if Ellie didn't know about what, Julian?"

Cam chuckled. "I told you, Jules. There's no point in trying to hide anything from them. They always find out. What are you doing awake, love?"

"I couldn't sleep until I knew the worst about Charlotte, and from what I just overheard, I gather the worst is awful, indeed."

"If by awful you mean I found her in a brothel with nothing but a flimsy mask standing between her and ruin," Julian said, "Then yes, the worst is awful."

Ellie paled. Cam crossed the room to her at once, took her arm, and led her to his chair. "Sit down, love."

"She takes it further every time, Cam." Ellie gripped his arm as he leaned over the chair. "Dear God. I shudder to think what she'll do next."

Cam took her hand and sat down on the chair's arm. "Perhaps there won't be a next."

Ellie shook her head. "There will be. We've tried everything we can think of to stop this, but she won't listen."

"Not everything." Cam fixed his gaze on Julian. "We haven't tried Jules."

Julian froze. *Tried Jules?* He didn't like the sound of that.

"Ellie, Alec, and Robyn have exhausted themselves trying to rein Charlotte in," Cam said. "Nothing they've said has made any difference, but tonight you managed to coax Charlotte from a brothel and deliver her safely to her door. You've had more success in one night than the rest of us have had in months."

*Coaxed her? Certainly, if lying and blackmail could be called coaxing.*

"What of her mother? Surely Lady Catherine can make Charlotte see sense."

"Our mother has been in Bath all season with my aunt, who's taking the waters there for a chest complaint," Ellie said. "Mother has written to Charlotte again and again, but a letter is easy enough to ignore, and it's done no good."

"How unfortunate," Julian murmured.

"It would be unfortunate indeed if Charlotte became a scandal," Cam said. "But thankfully you're here now."

"No, I'm not. Not for that."

Ellie regarded him steadily. "But it's so perfect. You're a single gentleman. You can follow her about London without attracting any attention, and—"

"Follow her about London? I can't think of anything worse than trailing about after a wild, spoiled marchioness—"

"And you're a Captain in the 10th Royal Hussars, London's most gallant regiment," Ellie rushed on, as if Julian hadn't spoken. "A hero—"

"Hero?" Julian made a disgusted face. "Hardly."

"But we've heard such stories. All of London's heard them." Ellie's mouth turned down at the corners. "I do hope you're not going to say they aren't true."

"All right." Julian dropped back into his chair. "I won't say it."

"The gossip has it you carried mangled bodies on your back across raging battlefields, saving men in your regiment from certain death despite the great risk to your own safety."

"Rot. I helped a few wounded men to a field hospital. That's all."

Cam sipped at his whiskey. "Ah, yes. Well, I can certainly see how that's different than what we heard."

"Damn it, Cam." Julian reached out a stiff arm and set his glass on the sideboard. "I'm sorry. I can't help you."

"It's well past the end of the season, Julian." Ellie's voice was quiet. "But Charlotte refuses to leave London. Unfortunately, a good many of the *ton* linger as well, hoping for a grand scandal, and it's only a matter of time before they get one."

"I'm sorry," Julian said again. "But I don't have time to chase Lady Hadley from one London whorehouse to the next. I'm in London for a few weeks only, to… Well, you'll know soon enough, I suppose. I'm betrothed."

Cam stared at him, his mouth open. "You're *betrothed*? How can you be betrothed? You've just returned home. Who is she?"

Julian frowned down into his glass. "Her name is Jane Hibbert. Her brother, Colin, was a Lieutenant in my regiment, and one of my friends. My best friend."

Cam searched his face. "Was?"

"Yes. Was." Julian drew in a quick breath. "He was killed at Waterloo."

Cam ran a hand down his face. "Julian—"

"Jane is Colin's younger sister. Their mother died years ago and their father passed away unexpectedly while Colin was in France. Now that Colin's gone she's alone, aside from an elderly aunt."

Cam seemed not to know what to say to this. "I see," he managed after a long hesitation. "Is she—what's she like?"

Julian shrugged. "I've never met her."

There was a shocked silence, then Ellie said, "I don't understand. You're betrothed to a lady you've never met?"

"I wrote to her, after Colin…" Julian cleared his throat. "It wasn't proper, of course, but Colin made me promise I'd write to Jane if the worst should happen, and I couldn't bear for her not to know how he spent his final days. In any case, we struck up a correspondence. She's a kind, decent young lady, and I doubt she'd understand if I became entangled with a notorious marchioness."

Ellie gazed at him for a moment, her expression unreadable, then, "Does Miss Hibbert know you're in London?"

"Everyone in England knows I'm in London, thanks to the newspapers."

"Have you called on her since your return?"

"No," Julian admitted. He could see where this was going, and he didn't like it.

"Well, then. Write her and explain you have urgent family business to attend to, and you'll come to her when it's concluded."

*Damnation.* "But I *don't* have urgent family business to attend to."

"This situation with Charlotte is urgent, Julian," Ellie said. "We travel to Bellwood at the end of this week, with or without her."

Julian raised an eyebrow. "You can't be as concerned for her welfare as you pretend, then, if you'll leave her in London alone."

"We don't want to leave her," Cam said, "but we haven't any choice."

"There's always a choice."

"Not this time. Ellie's increasing, Julian."

Julian fell silent for a moment as Cam's words sunk in, and then he smiled. "I can't think why I didn't guess it. You're glowing, Ellie, and Cam, you look smugger than I've ever seen you."

Ellie smiled. "The doctor confirmed it just this week. Sometime in mid-March, he says."

"Ah. Well, that explains why Cam's wandering the house at midnight in that ridiculous banyan."

"I can't sleep. Ellie is fatigued and I don't like to keep her awake, but I also don't wish to be denied my wife's bed until March."

"Seven months is a long time to sleep alone." Julian grinned. "And it will feel longer for us all if you plan to haunt the house in that banyan the entire time."

Cam looked worried. "But my sleeplessness will pass, won't it?"

"You're not asking me, I hope. I can regale you with the usual bachelor's tales—drink, wagering, brothels and the like—but ladies who are increasing? I haven't the faintest idea there, cuz."

"Well, I don't either, damn it."

Ellie laughed. "You will soon enough, and it's no good grumbling about it, because I have the hardest bit by far."

"I won't grumble to *you*, my love, but Julian is another matter. How fortunate that you should arrive home just in time to comfort me in my distress, Jules."

"I draw the line at sharing my bedchamber with you."

Cam grinned. "We'll see."

Julian crossed to the sideboard and helped himself to more whiskey. "What does Amelia say?"

Ellie smiled. "We just told her this evening, and she's thrilled, of course. It's a very grown up thing to become an aunt."

"She's grown a great deal while I've been gone." Julian couldn't quite suppress a wistful sigh. "She's almost a young lady now."

"Not to worry." Cam gave him a reassuring grin. "There's still a good bit of the little girl about her, for all that she's nearly thirteen years old. There are some things a child never outgrows, thank God."

"And since we're back on the subject of growing children..." Ellie began.

"Yes. I fail to see what this"—Julian gestured vaguely at Ellie's belly with his whiskey glass—"has to do with the marchioness."

"Ellie's exhausted, Jules. The ordeal with Charlotte, the heat and grime of London—it's unhealthy for her in her condition. I don't want to leave Charlotte here alone, but Ellie and Amelia and my unborn child are my first concern. We need to leave the city before Ellie becomes truly ill."

Ellie reached forward and took Julian's hand. "Lord Devon is a dangerous man, Julian. Certain of the *ton* even whisper he murdered his elder brother so he'd be first in line to inherit the fortune and title when his father died, and now he's dangling after Charlotte. If the worst should happen, if Charlotte should be hurt, I'll never forgive myself."

Julian opened his mouth to tell them for the third time he was sorry, he couldn't help them, but then Ellie squeezed his hand, and he fell silent. If Charlotte should engage in further antics...

What had that tall blonde lady said? *There's always tomorrow night.*

Oh, there would be further antics. Judging by the devilish gleam in the blonde's eye, they'd come sooner rather than later, and now there was a murderous earl to consider.

*There was Ellie to consider.*

He owed her.

Ellie loved Cam with all her heart—she'd loved him even when he'd tried to blackmail her into marriage. Even when his behavior toward her had been nothing less than barbarous, she'd loved him against reason, against logic, and against self-preservation. She'd saved him, and now...

Julian owed Ellie a rescue.

*One sister.*

Christ. Maybe he was a bloody hero, after all. "What do you want me to do?"

Cam rose to his feet to pace the room. "Persuade her to leave London. She'd be safe at Hadley House for the winter, or Bellwood, if she prefers it. We think she stays here for Devon. Get in his way. If you can make it difficult for him to get access to her—"

"He'll give up," Ellie said. "Then she'll have no reason to stay in London."

*Christ.* What an ungodly mess. A drama worthy of a cold, selfish marchioness. Or a cavalry captain, for it seemed the mess was about to be dumped in his lap, whether he liked it or not. "One week. That's all. I'll do what I can to see Lady Hadley is at Bellwood by the end of it."

Ellie clasped his hand tightly in both of hers. "Oh, thank you, Julian!"

Cam stopped pacing. "How will you do it? I warn you, Julian, it won't be easy—rather like chasing an extremely clever fox down every alleyway in London." He gave Ellie a fond look. "The Sutherland women are wily."

*But Charlotte wasn't a Sutherland anymore.* "I'll think of something."

Ellie rose to her feet and kissed Julian on the cheek. "You're a wonderful cousin, Julian." She turned to Cam. "I think I can sleep again now."

"I'm going to stay up with Jules for a while." Cam pressed his lips to her forehead. "Good night, love."

After the door closed on Ellie, Cam and Julian returned to their chairs and stared into the fire until Cam roused himself. "What's the truth about your heroics on the battlefield, Jules?"

Julian gave a bitter laugh. "Let's just say the truth doesn't make for a pretty headline, and leave it at that."

Cam considered this, then shook his head. "Even the most exaggerated story contains a thread of truth."

"Not this one. There was nothing so grand in it. Any other man would have done the same thing I did."

"Perhaps, but it wasn't any other man. It was *you*."

"Oh, yes, it was me." Julian downed his whiskey, but the bitterness still burned his throat. "And while I was running about the battlefield that day, dozens of men were slaughtered in my place. But London doesn't seem to care much about who was left behind."

"Who *was* left behind?" Cam's voice was quiet.

Julian shrugged, but his fingers tightened around his whiskey glass. "It doesn't make any difference now, does it? One rotting corpse looks much like another."

"It sounds as if it makes a great deal of difference to you." Cam placed his own glass on the table with a careful click. "But as tragic as those deaths are, you aren't responsible for them. You couldn't save them all, Julian."

*Not all. One. I should have saved one.*

But he wouldn't tell the rest of that story tonight. It was hardly a bedtime story. He rose and set his glass on the sideboard. "I'm for bed."

"Jules?"

Julian was halfway out the door, but he turned back. "Cuz?"

Cam cleared his throat. "I'm damned glad you're home at last. I can't tell you…" His voice grew thick, and he trailed off into silence.

"I'm damned glad to be home." God knew he owed a debt of gratitude to whatever higher power had kept him alive this past year. He shuddered to think how many times he wouldn't have wagered a farthing on his own life. "I don't care for the idea of *my* corpse rotting away on some battlefield."

Cam flinched. "No. But here you are, not a whiff of rot about you, and it's as if you'd never left."

Julian stiffened. Is that what Cam thought? That he was the same man he'd ever been?

He gazed at his cousin. Cam's legs were stretched out before him, his feet close to the fire as he sipped at his whiskey. He and Cam had sat in these same chairs in front of this same fireplace more times than Julian could count, and yet the moment felt strangely foreign to him, as if he'd slipped through a tear in time, or as if he were watching the scene unfold from a great distance.

No matter how much he wanted it to be the same as it always was, he hadn't been home more than a day before he felt like he'd stolen this life from the man he used to be—the man who *should* have it. The old Julian would never have grabbed a woman the way he had that dark- haired doxy, and he'd never have treated Charlotte like a whore, no matter how angry he was. This man he'd become—he had a dark, ugly thing living inside him, and there was no telling when it would get loose, or what it would do when it did.

It never could be the same as it had before, because *he* could never be the same.

But he couldn't explain it to Cam. He wouldn't even know where to begin. "Yes. It's just as if I never left. Good night, cuz."

He left Cam to finish his whiskey alone, mounted the stairs to his old bedchamber, and fell across the bed, too exhausted to remove his clothes.

*God, I'm tired. So tired.*

As his eyes began to close an image crept into his mind of long, dark strands of hair against the white skin of a woman's back, but then the picture dissolved and he fell deeper into the darkness that lured him with lies, with promises of a peace that never came. He struggled against it before he let it take him, but then he stopped fighting and collapsed into it, because there was nothing else he could do....

*Bodies, the twist and tangle and heave of them. Missing hands, fingers. Pieces of men half buried in gluts of blood and mud. He tries to make sense of the pieces, but no one can make sense of them because there are too many hands, an impossible number of them, and so many arms without hands, and hands without fingers, but if he can only put them together again, the fingers with the hands and the hands with the arms and the arms with the torsos... If he can fit all the pieces back together like a puzzle, the bodies will be whole again, but there are too many and there's too much mud and too much blood and he can't find all the hands or all the fingers dear God, there aren't enough fingers—*

Julian jerked awake with a gasp and shot straight up in the bed, icy sweat pouring down his back. *Jesus.* He ran a trembling hand down his face. Had he screamed? He must have. He always did. The scream was what tore him from the dream. For all the good it did, he screamed at the end.

*Colin's watch.* Julian clawed at the bedclothes around him in a sudden panic. Where—?

His fingers closed over the hard metal, still in his waistcoat pocket; then he fell back against the pillow until numbness stole over him. He lay there with his eyes open for what was left of the night, the watch clutched in his palm.

# Chapter Five

"I'm going to ask you once again, Sarah, and I'll have the truth this time, if you please. Are you a spy?"

Charlotte kicked her legs out in front of her, slumped back against the plush carriage seat, and waited for her vulgar pose to hurl Sarah from her icy silence headlong into the blistering scold that hovered on the tip of her tongue.

The scold was inevitable, so they may as well get it over with.

She didn't need to wait long. Disapproval rose from Sarah like thick clouds of smoke from a conflagration. "If I'm a spy, I'm not going to tell you so, am I? What kind of spy admits she's a spy, my lady?"

"That sounds like a confession."

"It's nothing of the sort." Sarah gave a haughty sniff. "I haven't anything to confess."

"Ah, now I know you're lying. Everyone, dear old thing, has something to confess. We all have at least one secret sin."

Sarah pressed her lips so tightly together they became indistinguishable from the rest of her face. "Sins now, is it? There's some as has a great deal more than one, and not so secret as they should be, neither."

Ah. There it was—the scold Charlotte knew was coming since Sarah dragged her from her bed an hour ago. Despite her rigid sense of propriety, Sarah had a tongue like a striking adder, and she never could hold it for long.

"How dull it would be if everyone kept their sins to themselves." Charlotte hid a yawn behind her gloved hand. "Thank heavens the *ton* doesn't think as you do, Sarah, or we'd never have any amusement. Public sins are far more diverting."

Sarah drew herself up, her spine rigid against her seat. "Surely you didn't just thank *heaven* for shameless sins, my lady?"

Charlotte laughed at the maid's scandalized look. "Why yes, I believe I did. But really, Sarah, I begin to think all this talk of sin is your attempt to divert me from the question at hand. If you're not a spy, then how does my sister, Eleanor, always know when I set a toe over the line of propriety?"

Sarah snorted. "A toe, indeed. It's a whole foot for you every time, or nothing at all, and Lady Eleanor knows it as well as I do."

"That's precisely the issue at hand, Sarah. *How* does she know it?"

It was no great mystery, of course. Charlotte knew very well Sarah had been whispering in Ellie's ear almost from the moment they'd arrived in London. She should dismiss Sarah at once for such blatant disloyalty, of course, but she was perversely fond of the impertinent creature.

"One of your widow friends told her, most like." Not a blush stained that guilty cheek, and Sarah's gaze never wavered. "Probably that little French one."

*She was blaming Aurelie? Shameless.*

Until now Charlotte hadn't been terribly concerned about Sarah's tattling. She didn't like to upset her sister, but she was a widow, not a debutante, and a widow of independent means, at that. She could do as she wished.

But now—*now* she was concerned, and had been since Julian West dragged her out of that brothel last night. Well, perhaps dragged wasn't quite the right word. He'd taken advantage of her foolishness to *maneuver* her out. She'd been so shocked to see him it hadn't occurred to her his presence at that particular brothel couldn't possibly be a coincidence. Cam and Ellie knew she'd be there last night, because Sarah had told them. They'd sent Julian to retrieve her, and she'd helped him finish the job by being fool enough to bargain for his silence.

It wouldn't happen again. Sarah couldn't tattle if she had no tales to tell, and Charlotte would take care in future to see she didn't.

She yawned again. "Honestly, I don't know why we indulge Ellie's whims in this ridiculous way, rushing over to Bedford Square at the crack of dawn as if we'd been summoned by the queen herself."

"Dawn? It's one o'clock in the afternoon, my lady. It'll do you good to be up and about before the sun sets. The fresh air will put color in your cheeks."

"One o'clock?" Charlotte's heart plummeted from her chest to her stomach with a sickening thud. *Only one o'clock. Too early.* She'd meet her friends again at the theater tonight, but that engagement was hours away.

The day loomed ahead of her, silent and empty.

*Think of something else.*

She yanked her skirts over her knees with an agitated jerk, pressed her nose against the window, and tried to focus on the blur of horses and carriages, the sound of their wheels against the cobblestones, the clatter punctuated by the cries of the costermongers.

But it was too late. The familiar panic rose in her throat. She squeezed her eyes closed as the dread began to claw at her—

Sarah plucked the crumpled folds of silk skirts from Charlotte's clenched fist. "Maybe Lady Eleanor will let Miss Amelia come back to Grosvenor Square with you this afternoon."

Charlotte turned from the window. "Won't she—" She cleared her throat, but her voice sounded small nonetheless. "Don't you suppose Amelia has lessons today?"

"Like as not, but you could hear how she does with her pianoforte, and then take her for a ride in the park afterwards. A little holiday won't hurt the child."

Charlotte relaxed her fists with an effort. "Well, it won't do any harm to ask, I suppose."

"No harm at all. Go on with you then," Sarah added as the carriage stopped in front of Cam and Ellie's townhouse and a footman appeared to hand Charlotte down. "Lady Eleanor's note arrived over an hour ago. She must wonder what's kept you so long."

Charlotte paused a moment to steady her breath.

*For pity's sake, get ahold of yourself.*

She fixed what she hoped was a convincing smile on her lips and swept up the townhouse stairs. "Oh, good morning—ah, that is, good afternoon, Phipps," she said to the butler. "I've been summoned to an audience with your mistress. Would you be so good as to tell me where I might find her?"

Phipps bowed. "Of course, my lady. She's in her bedchamber."

Charlotte handed him her gloves. "Ah. The royal bedchambers. Where else? Thank you, Phipps." She mounted the staircase to the second floor and entered Ellie's rooms after a cursory tap at the door. "Eleanor?"

Ellie was seated on the window seat watching something in the garden below, but she turned when Charlotte entered. "Ah, Charlotte. Good morning. What took you so long?"

Charlotte studied her sister. No—there was no froth at Ellie's mouth. A good sign, that. Some of the trapped air eased from Charlotte's lungs. "Well, let me see." She sank down onto a chaise, tucked her legs up underneath her, and attempted a light, teasing tone. "I had to sneak out of my bedchamber without waking my two lovers, and then I stopped on the way over here to gamble away all of Hadley's family jewels. I do apologize for the delay."

Eleanor raised an eyebrow. "Two lovers?"

"I think there were two. Perhaps there was a third burrowed under the counterpane at the foot of the bed."

"My." Ellie rose from the window seat and joined Charlotte on the chaise. "Such an excess of lovers. No wonder you look exhausted."

Charlotte held up three fingers. "I look exhausted because Sarah forced me from my bed not three hours after I collapsed into it, and that makes three times in the past two weeks. Three times, Eleanor! Whatever can you mean, dragging me from my bed at such an ungodly hour?"

There. She'd hit just the right note of mock outrage. Now Ellie would laugh, or smile…

But Ellie didn't laugh. Instead she began to tick points off on her own fingers. "Earlier this week it was Lord Fothergill's rout, which, if the scandal sheets have the right of it, was not so much a rout as a high-stakes card game. Lord Essex's son lost thousands to Lord Devon, didn't he?"

*For God's sake.* Sarah's wagging tongue was as good as a crystal ball. "What of it? I came away from the tables a hundred guineas richer."

Ellie ignored this and held up a second finger. "Then there was Lady Atwood's dinner last week. I believe you attended. Quite a debauched scene, if rumor is correct. Miss Grainger is ruined beyond redemption, you know. Her family has banished her. They bundled her off to the country the very next day."

Charlotte didn't quite meet Ellie's eyes. "Well, who told the chit to disappear into the library alone with a rake like Mr. Jermyn? Anyway, the rumors are nonsense. I saw Miss Grainger emerge from the library myself, and she was fully clothed—"

"That brings us to last night, and Lady Tallant's soiree."

*Soiree. Not whorehouse. Was there a chance Ellie would let the brothel incident pass?*

Charlotte forced a casual shrug. "Annabel Tallant is my friend, Eleanor. I could hardly refuse to attend her soiree."

"Perhaps not, but you could have refused to end your evening at a west end brothel."

*No chance, then.* Charlotte jerked to her feet in an agitated whirl of silk skirts. "I didn't end my evening there. Didn't Captain West tell you? He made quite a point of escorting me home. Kind of him, wasn't it? How convenient it must be for you to have him back in London."

Ellie paused, then, "You could hardly expect him to leave you there, Charlotte."

"I don't expect anything at all from Julian West, though now I think on it, perhaps I should." She stared hard at Eleanor. "Perhaps I should expect him to be forever at my elbow from now on? I grant you he'd make an admirable hound. Have you set him on my scent, Ellie?"

Ellie avoided her eyes. "How dramatic you are, Charlotte."

*That was a yes.* It was always a yes when Ellie gave an answer that wasn't really an answer.

Well. Julian may have failed to extract a promise from her last night, but he'd succeeded spectacularly this morning. As long as he remained in London she'd take care to stay away from her family and Bedford Square, just as he'd demanded.

After a long silence, Ellie heaved a sigh. "You've dragged out the season to the bitter end. The respectable half of the *ton* has already left London. Don't you think it's time you made up your mind to go back to Hadley House? It will be quiet in Hampshire, and you can rest."

Charlotte turned toward the window, away from Ellie. Quiet. Yes, there was plenty of quiet to be had at Hadley House, but precious little rest.

"Bellwood then, instead of Hampshire," Ellie said when she didn't answer. "Alec and Delia are already there, and Robyn and Lily leave London at the end of the week. You can stay through Christmas."

*Bellwood.* The place of all her girlhood dreams. It was the one place in the world even lonelier than Hadley House. "Soon. I'll go soon. Perhaps at the end of this month, or the start of the next."

Ellie remained silent. She wanted more than that, of course, a promise Charlotte would cease her wild escapades, retire to the country, and behave in a manner befitting a proper widow. Vows and assurances rushed to Charlotte's lips, but she choked them back down. *No.* She wouldn't make any promises she knew she couldn't keep.

"We're leaving London at the end of next week, Charlotte—Cam, Amelia, and I, and we won't return until next season."

"Leaving?" Charlotte's head buzzed as all the blood drained from it at once and then came back in a nauseating rush. They'd be off to the country before Julian left London. A few weeks without her family was one thing, but—dear God, it would be months before she saw them again. *Months.* It felt like a lifetime.

Ellie nodded. "Yes. The doctor was here this week, and he confirmed what we've suspected for several weeks now. I'm increasing."

Charlotte's heart squeezed in her chest, but she forced herself to turn back to Ellie with a smile. She took her sister's hands. "How wonderful. I know you've been hoping."

Ellie smiled back, but her face was anxious. "Yes. Cam is thrilled, but he insists we leave London at once for the healthier climate in the country."

"Yes. Yes, of course. Very wise."

Ellie squeezed her fingers. "We want you to come with us, Charlotte. There can be nothing keeping you in London this late in the season."

*Nothing but a wish to hold on to my sanity.*

She dropped Ellie's hands. "My friends are here."

"But your family is at Bellwood, and we want you with us. Don't you want that, as well?"

Such a lovely thing, to be able to do what she *wanted*. Such a wealth of choices. But she had only two choices left now—the things she could bear to do, and the things she couldn't. To go to Bellwood, to spend the winter with her besotted siblings, their equally besotted spouses and their happy, growing families...

No. She couldn't bear to do that. Not yet. Perhaps not ever.

She forced another smile to her stiff lips. "Soon. The end of next month, perhaps." It wasn't quite a lie. Maybe by the end of next month—

"I hope so." Ellie regarded her with a kind of hopeless resignation. "But if you must remain in London, will you promise to stay away from Lord Devon? I don't like to have you spend time with him. At best he's no gentleman, and at worst he's dangerous."

*No promises I can't keep.*

Charlotte laughed, but there was no humor in it. "You don't mean to say you believe all that gossip about Devon, Eleanor? You know how the *ton* exaggerates. He's as harmless as a kitten."

Ellie frowned. "He's no kitten, Charlotte. He's far more like a hound about to tear into a fox."

"Ah, but you forget, Eleanor, how clever the fox is."

Ellie's lips went tight. "Julian said it was a wager with Devon that led to the bordello escapade. Devon knows how dangerous such a wager is, but he's happy enough to risk your reputation for his own amusement."

*Damn it. Bloody Julian West.* Had he kept any of the details from last night to himself? "We all agreed to the wager. Lord Devon is no guiltier than any of us."

"Perhaps not, but then he doesn't have as much to lose, does he?"

An incredulous laugh rose in Charlotte's throat. Did Ellie truly believe she had anything left to lose? "I promise you I'll be as circumspect in my choice of company as I possibly can be."

Ellie wasn't fooled by her vague promise. She made her way across the room and sank wearily down on the bed, her face pale and set.

Charlotte couldn't look at her sister's pinched face, not if she wanted to keep her composure, so she turned her back on Ellie and retreated to the window. Amelia was on the lawn below playing at bowls, the sun's rays sifting through her fair hair. She rolled the ball, then jumped in the air with an excited shout as it struck the jack.

A smile tugged at Charlotte's lips. Such a pure, simple, childlike joy. How would she ever do without Amelia until next season? She turned back to Ellie. "Do you suppose Amelia could spend the afternoon with me?"

Ellie opened her eyes, then closed them again. "She was out all morning riding with Julian, and she hasn't finished her lessons—"

"Just a few hours, Eleanor? I'll have her back right after tea."

Ellie struggled up onto her elbows with an exhausted sigh. "Oh, very well. I suppose she can have a holiday today. She's too excited about the baby to concentrate, in any case. But do make sure she practices her pianoforte. She doesn't do nearly as well with her music master as she does with you."

"Yes, yes. I will." Charlotte flew toward the door, her heart already lighter.

"See she has a proper tea, as well!" Ellie's voice followed Charlotte into the hallway. "Not just lemon ices, like last time!"

"Of course not!" Charlotte called back as she bounded down the stairs, her skirts billowing out in a blue cloud behind her. Phipps opened the door and she sailed outside, rounded the corner of the house, and emerged at the edge of the lawn just in time to see Amelia toss the bowl with such enthusiasm it rolled past the others, off the edge of the lawn, and into the rose garden.

"Awful throw!" Charlotte called.

Amelia gave her a sunny smile, and waved from across the lawn. "Charlotte! Shall we have a game?"

*Oh, why not?* She hadn't played bowls in years. "Yes, one game, and then I'll steal you away for the rest of afternoon."

"Truly?" Amelia clapped her hands together with delight. "Will you take me to Gunter's for an ice?"

"Of course. As many as you want. Whatever you like."

"Hurrah!" Amelia darted across the lawn toward Charlotte, a wide grin on her face.

"After you've practiced your pianoforte, that is."

Amelia's grin faded a little at that. "Oh, all right. I'd much rather practice with you than that dusty old music master, anyway."

"Only because I let you play bawdy Irish songs. Go and fetch the other bowls and I'll find the one in the rose garden."

"All right." Amelia darted back across the lawn. "You'll lose, you know. I'm very good at bowls!"

The roses were in full bloom, the leaves clustered thickly on the canes. Charlotte strolled down row after row looking for Amelia's ball, but the dratted thing seemed to have disappeared. She was about to give up and leave it when she caught sight of it peeking out from under a particularly thorny yellow rose. "Blast it," she muttered, dropping down onto her knees. She stuck her hand under the rose, careful not to prick her fingers, and reached around until she felt the smooth surface of the ball against her palm. "Come on out, you devil."

"Not quite the greeting I expected, my lady, but then you never were one to fulfill expectations."

Charlotte froze, her hand still cupped around the ball, and turned her head to find a pair of black Hessians planted on the path next to her feet, their shine blinding in the afternoon sun. She didn't rise, but let her gaze travel upward over long legs encased in tight, buff-colored breeches, narrow hips, a lean waist, and wide shoulders under a beautifully fitted dark blue coat.

Captain West, looking every inch the handsome, valiant hero London so admired, right down to the halo of blurred sunlight framing his dark hair. Her breath caught in her throat at the sight of him. *Drat the man.* Why did he have to be so devastating?

"Don't rise on my account, my lady." He tapped the tip of his riding crop rhythmically against his boot. "I quite like you where you are."

Charlotte ignored this and rose slowly to her feet, Amelia's ball cradled in her palm. "So much so you plan to keep me there. Isn't that right, Captain West?"

"Oh, I don't think you need me for that. You're doing an admirable job of it on your own. I did, after all, come across you in a whorehouse last night."

Charlotte pressed her fingers into the smooth, hard surface of the ball. "That's not quite true, Captain."

He arched one dark eyebrow. "No? There were a surprising number of whores about if it wasn't a whorehouse."

She gave him a thin smile. "What I mean is you didn't *come across* me at all. That implies you stumbled upon me by accident, but that was no chance encounter last night, was it?"

"Oh, that." He gave a careless shrug. "Yes, if you want to quibble over words, I suppose that's true."

She hefted the ball in her hand. Heavy. Quite heavy enough to inflict damage to a skull. "I find it helpful to be precise. Lies often hide in ambiguities, you see."

A corner of his mouth turned up in a mocking smile. "I never lied to you last night. You made an assumption, and I didn't correct you."

Ah, yes. Julian always had been able to manipulate situations to his advantage, to withhold information while stopping just short of lying, and she'd do well to remember it instead of mooning over the way the sunlight framed his hair. "That's a convenient distinction, Captain. Surprising, for a man like you. Not so heroic, after all?"

His expression didn't change, but he stiffened, and something dark flickered in his eyes—something that made her heart shift uneasily in her chest before she shoved it back into place. "But call it a misunderstanding if you like. Tell me, do you anticipate future misunderstandings? I wonder, you see, if I should expect to *come across* you again?"

"Who can tell? London is a small city, Lady Hadley."

"No, Captain. It isn't." A flush of anger heated her cheeks. "Last night you expressed a wish that we spend as little time as possible in each other's company, and this morning I find myself more than willing to accommodate you while you remain in London."

He indicated the garden with a sweep of his hand. "You're doing a poor job of it so far, for here you are."

She squeezed the ball in her hand until her palm began to ache. "My sister was disturbed by the news of my adventure last night, and she summoned me here today. I could hardly refuse to see her, could I?"

Another faint smiled drifted across his lips. "I don't see why not. She'd rather you kept away from whorehouses as well, and you've refused her that."

"Yes, and how convenient for us all you were there to rescue me." She bit down hard on her bottom lip to control her temper. "However did we manage, I wonder, before the heroic Captain West returned to London to call me to account for my many sins?"

His gaze shot to her mouth, but he tore it away at once, his jaw going hard. "Are your sins so legion, Lady Hadley? I can only guess you managed poorly if you've committed such a prodigious number of them."

A tiny shiver darted down her spine at the look in his eyes, but she managed a casual shrug. "Oh my, yes. It's a great pity I've become so wicked, but then we can't all be heroes, can we?" She smiled as his face darkened with anger. How satisfying it was to tweak the righteous, especially the smug, heroic ones.

He stepped closer to her, so close the tips of his boots nearly touched her slippers. "So you've chosen to be a scandal, instead? If you were my sister, I'd haul you off to the country and keep you under lock and key until you learned proper behavior."

"Would you? How barbaric." She gave him a taunting smile. "Why not just turn me over your knee and be done with it?"

His lips parted, and he dragged the tip of his riding crop over his palm. "Don't tempt me."

Heat surged through her and sent her pulse skittering madly, but she ignored it and stepped into him until they were toe to toe. "I'm not your sister, Captain West, or indeed anyone at all to you, and as that is the case, I'll thank you to stay out of my affairs."

"Affairs. Liaisons. Scandals." He moved closer still so he towered over her, his broad shoulders shutting out the sun. "You did say you prefer precise words, my lady."

"Oh, I do." She wetted suddenly dry lips with the tip of her tongue. "Here are some other words, Captain. Widow. Wealthy. Marchioness."

His gaze dropped to her lips again, and his eyes burned. When he spoke, his voice had roughened. "With such words at your disposal, you can't imagine a mere captain in His Majesty's service is a threat to you, can you?"

"I confess it did cross my mind last night when you dragged me upstairs and ordered me to hike up my skirts under pretense of thinking me a whore." She caught her breath, stunned both by her own words, and the sudden heat in his eyes.

His blistering gaze raked over her. "I doubt I'm the first."

Charlotte went still, sure she must have misheard him, but the words echoed in the silence, their meaning unmistakable. The heat pulsing though her body vanished and she shivered in the sudden chill, but she forced herself to lift her chin and meet his eyes. "You don't give yourself enough credit, Captain."

The tremor in her voice made her furious. Why should it matter to her what he thought? He'd only said aloud what everyone in London was thinking—that she was a scandal, an embarrassment to her family, a disgrace to her dead husband's name, and very likely a whore into the bargain.

Julian's face had gone white. "I shouldn't have said...I didn't mean—"

"Of course you did," she said, as coldly as she could, because she didn't want his regret, and she didn't want to think about the trace of fear she'd seen in his eyes when those hateful words left his mouth. "Now, Amelia and I are going to have a game of bowls. Once we've finished, I give you my word I will not appear at Bedford Square again."

He seemed to make an effort to gather himself together. "As I said last night, Lady Hadley, you'll excuse me if I don't rely on any promise of yours."

"You may rely on it or not as you choose, but I don't make promises I can't keep." She managed a cool smile, but she couldn't quite resist one parting shot. "You see, Captain? Even a whore can have a code of honor."

*Ah, yes.* There it was—the flush of shame she'd hoped for.

But oddly, it didn't make her feel any better.

# Chapter Six

Charlotte edged a black-silk covered finger under the amethyst choker around her neck. It was one of her favorite pieces, but tonight it felt like a fist wrapped around her throat. The blasted thing was too tight, the jewels too heavy. To make matters worse, Sarah had tugged at her stays with ruthless zeal, as if she believed tight stays could contain Charlotte's wickedness.

Dear, foolish old thing.

Charlotte reached behind her neck and released the clasp. The heavy choker fell into her palm in a pile of glittering purple stones, and she tossed it into her reticule. Ah, much better. If she could fit her corset in there, she'd shove that in as well, but as it was she'd have to make do without the use of her lungs tonight. A pity, for she'd quite like to be able to breathe when she faced the *ton* this evening.

Once she stepped into her box, every head would turn in her direction. Every eye would fix upon her, silence would reign for one awful moment as every conversation ceased. Then the whispers would begin, just as they always did. Before she'd even taken her seat, her name would be on the lips of every gossip in London.

In other words, it would be very much like every other night this season.

With one difference. *He* was here.

Well, what of it? She'd already surrendered Bedford Square to him. Surely she wasn't about to give over Drury Lane, too? *No.* She would march into her box and take her proper place as society's most notorious widow since Mrs. Fitzherbert. Perhaps she hadn't set out at the start of the season to become a notorious widow, but she didn't deny she'd earned those stares, those whispers. Scandal was a small enough price to pay for distractions that served her well.

*Julian West could go to the devil, and the rest of the* ton *right along with him.*

"For goodness' sakes, Aurelie." Lady Annabel's voice carried into the hallway from Charlotte's theater box. "You'll give Lord Ambrose an apoplexy if you continue to lean over the edge of the box in that lewd manner. He's staring so intently at your bosom he'll need a surgeon to remove his opera glass from his eye socket."

Aurelie gave a Gallic sniff. "He's the lewd one, not I, darling. It's nothing to do with me if he chooses to behave like an over-eager stallion. Let him stare."

Charlotte tiptoed closer to the entrance to her box, a grin curving her lips. The *ton* might gawk and shake their heads over her tonight, but that was no reason to hover here in the corridor like a timid rabbit. She wouldn't have to suffer the stares alone. Her friends were waiting for her.

The wicked widows had arrived.

"I don't believe Lady Ambrose is as understanding as you are, Aurelie," Lissie said, a laugh in her voice. "She looks ready to do him an injury."

Lady Annabel snickered. "Only because he doesn't stare at *her* bosom. At least, not with such pointed admiration."

"Well, my dear," Aurelie drawled. "Can you blame him?"

"If one can judge by the look on Lady Ambrose's face," Lissie said, "He'll need a surgeon no matter what Aurelie does. Carry on, my dear Aurelie."

"I shall, indeed."

Charlotte swept into the box in a rustle of dark purple silk, her chin high. "Bosoms and surgeons already, ladies? The first act hasn't even begun."

Lady Annabel turned to her with a smile. "Ah, Charlotte. There you are. I thought perhaps you'd changed your mind and joined your sister in her box, after all."

"What, and forgo the pleasure of being gawked at by Lord Ambrose? Oh, good heavens, no. Besides, there's no room for me in Ellie's box tonight."

*Or any other night while Julian remained in London.*

Aurelie lifted the glass to her eyes and pointed it in the direction of Cam and Ellie's box. "It does look as if the whole of London is in your sister's box, Charlotte. *Mon dieu*, there are a great many Sutherlands, Somersets, and Wests, are there not?"

Lady Annabel raised a delicate blond eyebrow. "Yes, and bound to be more every year, for they keep multiplying. It's almost indecent, but one can hardly blame the ladies. The Sutherland gentlemen are rather devastating. Don't you think so, Lissie? And Mr. West is delicious—"

She was interrupted by an excited cry from Aurelie. "Indeed, my dears, *both* Mr. Wests are delicious! But I think you already know that, don't you, *ma petite?*" She gave Charlotte an impish grin.

"What other Mr. West?" Lissie asked. "Oh my goodness, you don't mean—"

"Captain Julian West." Charlotte sank into her chair and twitched her skirts into place around her. "Yes, yes—that's what she means, Lissie. For goodness' sake, Aurelie. Stop staring at him."

Lissie's eyes widened. "What, the gallant Captain West? Why, they've been raving about him in the papers. Something about how he single-handedly beat back three French dragoons and saved half his regiment."

Charlotte rolled her eyes. "That wasn't a newspaper, dear. It was a scandal sheet."

Lissie ignored this. "Even better, he's said to be devastatingly handsome. Give me those glasses, Aurelie. I want to get a look at him."

"No need for you to stare, as well." Charlotte snapped open her fan. "You've already had a look at him, Lissie, and a good long one, at that."

Lissie made a grab for the glasses. "Nonsense. I believe I'd recall it if I had."

Aurelie slapped Lissie's hand away. "Indeed you have, my dear. He's the devil!"

Charlotte smothered a laugh. That was one way of putting it.

Lissie rolled her eyes. "No, Aurelie—I said *hero*, not *devil*. They're not the same thing in English. Or in French, come to think of it."

Aurelie dismissed this comment with an impatient flick of her fingers. "No, no. He's *Charlotte's* devil! The man from the brothel. The one who tied her to the bed, yes?"

"For God's sake. He didn't tie me—"

"It's him, I tell you. See for yourself." Aurelie held out the glasses.

Lissie made a grab for them, but Annabel was closer. She seized them first and raised them to her eyes. The ladies watched her silently, waiting for the verdict—all except Charlotte, who knew very well her friend would find Captain Julian West at the other end.

At last Annabel lowered the glasses and held them out to Lissie, who peered through them, then nodded. "One and the same. His isn't a face a lady forgets, is it?"

"No. His figure, either." Annabel gave Charlotte a sly look. "Quite a dashing example of manhood from every angle, in fact."

All three ladies turned to Charlotte, and three pairs of eyebrows rose simultaneously. Charlotte gave her fan a casual flick, but when she remained silent, Lissie held the opera glasses out to her. "Would you care to have a look, Charlotte?"

No, she would not, and she would have preferred they didn't either, though of course it was inevitable they'd discover the truth sooner or later. Charlotte shook her head. "That won't be necessary. You're quite right. Captain Julian West is, indeed, the devil."

Annabel leaned forward. "Well, this is an interesting new development. Why didn't you say so at once?"

Charlotte shrugged. "Because it's far less interesting than you'd imagine. Captain West is my brother-in-law's cousin, and of course that means he's also my sister Amelia's cousin as well, though she's always called him uncle because of the disparity in their ages."

Aurelie hovered so close to the edge of her seat she was in danger of toppling off her chair and into Lord Ambrose's lap below. "And?"

Charlotte blinked innocently. "And what?"

Lissie threw her hands up in the air. "And what else, of course! Don't try and tell us he went to the trouble of dragging you upstairs, gagging you, and tying you to a bed because he's your sister's husband's niece's uncle. Or cousin! Or whatever it was you called him."

"For pity's sake." Charlotte scowled. "If you must know, there's a bit of a...history between us."

Annabel's eyes widened. "Oh, we must know, and a great deal more than that, my dear. What kind of history?"

Charlotte studied the three rapt faces before her and pinched her lips into a prim line. "A lady never tells."

Lissie snorted. "Perhaps not, but what has that to do with the four of us?"

*Damnation.* She may as well have it out now, for they'd never cease teasing her until she did. "Oh, very well. It's a sordid history, of course. What else? I thought myself in love with him at one time; then I found out he'd lied to me, and he wasn't the man I thought he was."

Annabel sighed. "They never are, are they?"

Charlotte's chest tightened. Hadley had been, for all the good it had done him.

"Yes? You were *amoureux* and then he wasn't the man you thought, and then what?" Aurelie was pouting like a child whose bedtime story has been interrupted. "What did he lie about?"

"Well." Charlotte hesitated. "It's rather complicated."

"Ah. Even better." Annabel twitched her fan back and forth. "Well, go on with it. You don't suppose we're here to watch the play, do you?"

"Oh, very well." Charlotte chewed her lip and tried to think of a way to explain it without sullying Cam's good name. "My sister's courtship with Mr. West was a bit...unusual."

"Indeed?" Annabel asked. "Unusual *how*?"

There really was no flattering way to say it. "Well, you see, Mr. West, he, ah, that is to say, he—well, he tried to blackmail my sister into marrying him."

Three mouths dropped open, and then Aurelie gave a little screech of glee. "*Blackmail?* Why, how delicious."

"It's all right now, of course," Charlotte hastened to add. "They're very much in love."

"Anyone can see that. But dear me, blackmail." Lissie looked impressed. "Mr. West is much naughtier than he looks. What of Captain West? Is he as wonderfully wicked as his cousin?"

Charlotte gazed at her friends' curious faces and all at once she couldn't speak. Her story wasn't what they wanted. It wasn't wonderful or romantic, or even particularly wicked. It was a dull old story—a man pretends to love a woman and breaks her heart, and she turns around and breaks someone else's—someone who doesn't deserve it.

*And then he dies. The end.*

The same story had been told a thousand times before.

A satin-swathed hand covered hers, and she looked over to find Annabel's thoughtful blue eyes fixed on her face. "Captain West, Charlotte?"

"Ah, well." Charlotte forced a smile. "You can imagine the rest. He pretended to care for me to forward his cousin's plot to marry Eleanor. I discovered the truth—the heroine always does, you know—and I sent him away."

"My goodness." Aurelie's eyes were huge. "What happened then?"

"You know what happened, Aurelie. I married Hadley and became a wife; then Hadley died and I became a widow, and now I've met the three of you, and I've become a wicked widow. Captain West went off to France and became a hero, and there's an end to it."

Lissie cocked her head to one side. "The Wicked Widow and the War Hero. That could be the title of a scandalous novel, couldn't it?"

Annabel laughed. "Oh, it could. I'd read it."

"But why read it, dearest, when you can watch it unfold before your eyes?" Aurelie plucked the opera glasses from Lissie's hand and resumed her study of Ellie's box. "Charlotte is here, and Captain West is just there, and so another chapter begins."

Charlotte closed her fan with a firm snap. She'd put an end to this here and now. "I don't like to disappoint you, Aurelie, but that story ended long ago. Captain West is only in London temporarily, and while's he's here you can be certain he'll stay well away from me."

Lissie gave her a measuring look. "He didn't stay away from you in the whorehouse the other night. What about that little drama? It has the makings of a rather exciting chapter, if you ask me."

Charlotte pressed her lips together. "In a novel, perhaps, and a bad one, at that. It's far less diverting in real life."

Lissie smiled. "Less diverting? I should think it was just the opposite."

"In a novel with a different hero and heroine, perhaps. But you're mistaken, my dear Lissie, if you think the brothel episode had anything to do with me. He acted on my family's behalf, not out of any desire to save me from my wickedness."

"But he's a hero, isn't he?" Aurelie waved the opera glasses for emphasis. "Why shouldn't he save you?"

"A war hero, yes, but I doubt he equates a whorehouse with a battlefield. No, I can assure you he acted for Cam and Ellie's sakes alone. No doubt he won't do so again, and just as well, for I don't wish to be saved by Captain West, or indeed by anyone."

*It was far too late for that.*

"Do you mean to say he'll ignore you while he's in London?" Aurelie asked. She was peering at him through the glasses again.

"Yes. Just so."

Annabel rolled her eyes. "Come now, Charlotte. Are you telling us he'll sit on the other side of the theater in your sister and brother-in-law's box and never acknowledge you? That's rather a pointed snub, is it not?"

"Quite. Captain West's intention is just that—to make it a point not to notice me."

"Hmmm. You say he doesn't notice you." Annabel caught and held Charlotte's gaze. "I can't agree, my dear. He's fixated on you even now."

"Fixated? What nonsense. You see him with your own eyes, Annabel. The entire theater is gaping at us, but he hasn't glanced this way once."

"Not that you care, of course," Lissie interrupted, green eyes twinkling with mischief.

"Oh, I see him, all right. I see a gentleman determined *not* to notice you," said Annabel. "That is in itself a particular kind of attention. Why bother to snub a lady one cares nothing for?"

"You try to make it sound romantic, but it's a snub, Annabel, not a bouquet of hothouse flowers and a waltz. Indeed, I believe he quite despises me."

Annabel smiled. "Oh my. That *does* sound promising. There's nothing more passionate than a man's hate, Charlotte."

"And nothing more implacable. Even his love."

*Dear God.* How maudlin she sounded. Annabel would never cease teasing her now.

Annabel didn't hear her, however, for Lord Devon entered the box at that moment, and the ladies were immediately diverted. For all Annabel's talk of cutting his acquaintance, the widows delighted in Devon. They adored a rake, especially a debauched, handsome one, and Devon was all three.

"My lord!" Aurelie clapped her hands with delight. "At last. We expected you earlier, you know."

Devon laughed, then bowed to each lady in turn. "Good evening, ladies. I would have paid my respects sooner, but Lady Hadley's brother-in-law was glaring at me from the other side of the theater. He's rather bearish—have you noticed? I was afraid he'd leap upon me if I attempted to move toward your box."

"Don't tell us you're afraid of Mr. West, Devon." Lissie gave him an innocent look as he bent over her hand.

He grinned. "Terrified. Have you seen the size of him? I hear he's a crack shot too, though it's difficult to imagine how those bear-like paws could pull a trigger."

Lady Annabel held out a hand to Lord Devon. "He *is* very large."

Devon brushed his lips over Annabel's glove. "Indeed he is. Can't you do something about that, Lady Hadley?"

Charlotte laughed, and the tension began to ease from her shoulders. Devon talked a good deal of nonsense, but he did it with such charm it was impossible not to be amused by him. "What shall I do, my lord? Hide his boots?"

"No, no. That won't suffice, for he'll still be too tall, even without his boots. I'm afraid you'll have to hide his legs."

Charlotte laughed again, and Devon's bright blue eyes moved over her with open appreciation. He took her hand and raised it slowly to his mouth, then held her eyes as he brushed her glove with slightly parted lips. "You, my lady, are worth the risk. How lovely you look this evening."

Charlotte felt a trickle of warmth in her lower belly. Devon hadn't made any secret of his interest in her. He was pursuing her, and she… Well, she hadn't made up her mind yet, but of all the scoundrels London had to offer, a lady could do far worse than Lord Devon.

He released her hand. "But I didn't come here to discuss Mr. West's boots or his legs, as diverting as they are. I came to see if you ladies might enjoy further entertainment after the play tonight."

Annabel glanced at the other ladies. "Indeed? What kind of entertainment would that be, my lord?"

"Nothing terribly interesting, I'm afraid—just a visit to a gaming hell."

"Need I remind you, Devon," Lady Annabel said, "That ladies aren't welcome at gaming hells?"

Devon smiled. "You will be at this one. It's not a proper hell—more like a private one."

Lissie's eyes narrowed. "Is this another west end wager, Devon? How dreadful you are to keep tempting us. We were almost caught out during the last one."

Charlotte raised an eyebrow. She *had* been caught out, and rather thoroughly at that.

"Now, my lady, no money changed hands between us the other night, so it wasn't a true wager, and it's nothing so scandalous tonight— just a little harmless entertainment between friends."

Charlotte hesitated. Her family wouldn't like it if she left with Devon, of course. Even now Cam was eyeing him with a murderous expression, but that was nothing new, and she had no intention of retiring early again this evening. "A private gaming hell, my lord? That sounds entertaining."

"More so if you'll accompany us, my lady." He smiled down at her. "Shall I give the direction to your coachman?"

The other ladies murmured their assent, and Charlotte smiled up at him. "By all means."

Lord Devon bowed, then pressed his lips once more to Charlotte's glove. "Wonderful. Until then, Lady Hadley."

# Chapter Seven

Julian peered over the edge of Cam's box at Drury Lane and swept his gaze over the crowd. "What the devil is everyone staring at?"

A mass of unwashed bodies swarmed in the pit, craning their necks and shoving at their neighbors to get a better look into the tiers above. Julian scanned the boxes to either side of them, but aside from an unusual number of opera glasses pointed in his direction, he didn't see anything worth noting.

Cam turned to him in surprise. "Why, you, cuz. You've teased London into a frenzy with your elusiveness. You've been in the city for several days without anyone catching a glimpse of you, and now here you are."

Julian stared at Cam, his brows drawn together. "That's ridiculous."

Cam laughed at this irritated denial. "I agree, but true nonetheless."

"Oh, Mr. West is quite right, Captain West," piped up a feminine voice from behind them. "All of London has been holding its breath, waiting for your first public appearance."

Julian turned around in his seat to find Ellie's three young sisters-in-law, Iris, Violet, and— well, damned if he could remember the other one's name—gazing at him, their identical blue eyes wide with admiration. Before he could reply, the eldest sister, Iris, added in a rush, her face coloring, "The *Times* called the tenth Royal Hussars 'the most gallant regiment in His Majesty's service.'"

All three girls giggled at that, and the youngest one—Cynthia? Or was it Hydrangea?—placed a fluttering hand to her breast and heaved a heartfelt sigh.

"Gallant, is he?" Their grandmother, Lady Anne Chase eyed Julian with suspicion. "Humph. It's the gallant ones who cause all the trouble, especially for foolish young girls who don't know the difference between a gentleman and a scoundrel."

Ellie's brother Robyn stifled a laugh. "Do *you* know the difference, my lady?"

Lady Chase turned her disapproving glare on Robyn. "That smirk does you no credit, sir. I know the difference well, and indeed my one regret is I was unable to impart my wisdom to my granddaughter Lily in time to save her from marrying *you*."

Robyn laughed outright at this, and turned to wink at his sisters-in-law, who did their best to smother their giggles.

Julian paid no attention to their banter, but stared at the three young ladies, horrified. *Jesus.* This absurd hero business had gone further than he realized. He'd never get any peace with every chit in London sighing over him. Why, the match-making mamas alone—

"Good God, West," said Robyn, who'd left off teasing Lady Chase. "You look as if you're ready to hurl yourself into the pit. There's no need for such desperation. London will forget you soon enough."

Robyn's wife, Lily, leaned across Ellie to give Julian a sympathetic look. "It's true, Captain West. You should be safe enough by the start of next season."

*Next season?* He doubted he'd make it through next *week*. "I feel like the bloody elephant at the circus," he muttered to Cam.

Cam shrugged. "London is an inconstant mistress. Before long she'll throw you over for someone more exciting, and perhaps—"

His voice trailed off. Julian glanced at him to find Cam's gaze fixed on a box eight or ten rows away, closer to the middle of the theater.

Ah. The Marchioness of Hadley had arrived and taken her seat, a cloud of deep purple silk billowing around her.

"Perhaps sooner than you think," Cam finished.

"Oh, she's so elegant," Iris Somerset sighed. "That gown is divine."

Lady Chase sniffed. "If you approve of a purple gown for half mourning, which I don't, and certainly not one so revealing as that."

Cam leaned over and spoke under his breath. "Are those the three ladies who accompanied her to the brothel?"

Julian looked over her companions one by one. A redhead and two blondes, one tall and willowy, the other petite and curvy. They'd worn masks last night, but he recognized them instantly. "Without a doubt."

"Just as I thought."

Indeed, it was difficult to mistake them, as their behavior at the theater was only marginally more discreet than it had been at the whorehouse. The petite blonde hung halfway over the balcony railing, her opera glasses to her eyes, seemingly unaware that a generous expanse of her lush bosom was visible to anyone who cared to look.

At least no one was gawking at him anymore. "Who are they?"

"They are the wicked widows, cuz, and each one is more notorious than the last."

"The wicked widows?" How appropriate. "I suppose the scandal sheets came up with that name?"

Ellie, who was sitting on Cam's other side, leaned over and nodded. "Yes. The tall, slender blonde is Lady Annabel Tallant. She isn't really a widow, but as Lord Tallant disappeared to the Continent four years ago and hasn't been heard from since, she may as well be."

Julian turned his attention back to the widows just in time to see the little blonde aim her opera glasses in his direction. She stared for a moment, lowered the glasses, and stared some more, then quickly brought them back up to her eyes. "And the others?"

"The redhead is Lady Elizabeth Smythe—no one is quite sure what happened to her husband. The little one with the opera glasses is the Comtesse de Lisle. The Comte lost his head to Madame Guillotine, and rumor has it she narrowly escaped the same fate. They say she fled to London with a fortune in jewels secreted away in her bodice."

Robyn snorted. "She might be able to squeeze a diamond ring or two in there, but there's no room for an entire fortune in that bodice."

"No talk of bodices if you please, Mr. Sutherland. Iris!" Lady Chase brought her fan down on her charge's wrist. "Stop gaping at their box, you silly child. That goes for you as well, Violet."

*Stop gaping.* Julian should heed Lady Chase's warning too, but he found his attention drawn toward the forbidden box, and short of hurling himself off the edge of the balcony, nothing could distract him from the little drama unfolding there.

The Comtesse passed her opera glasses to Lady Tallant, who took a long look through them, and then passed them to Lady Smythe. She peered into them, lowered them with a nod, then turned to Charlotte, tilted her head in his direction, and offered her the glasses. Charlotte declined.

They recognized him, of course, as—what had the Comtesse called him? Oh, yes. The devil who'd locked Charlotte in a private bedchamber in a whorehouse, gagged her, and tied her to the bed. Perhaps he should have done just that—tied her and left her there and gone off to enjoy the attentions of that blonde-haired doxy who'd looked so promising. Perhaps it lacked finesse, but it was one way to solve the problem Cam had dumped in his lap.

Come to think on it, it would have solved the other problem in his lap, as well. Lady Hadley and his erection, vanquished in a single move. But as it was...

As it was, his breeches were too tight.

He aimed a scowl in Charlotte's direction and shifted in his seat. Lady Chase was right. The purple gown *was* too revealing. She was a widow, for God's sake, and that was quite a generous display of enticing, creamy flesh—

"How long will you stay in London, Captain?"

Julian turned in his seat to find the three pairs of blue eyes still gazing worshipfully at him. "Not long, I'm afraid, Miss Somerset. A month at the most."

"You don't plan to settle here, then? All of London is eager to claim you as our own."

"I'm not as eager to claim London, however, so—" Julian fell abruptly silent as Miss Somerset's plump lips turned down in a perfect pout. The chit looked as if she were about to burst into tears.

*How interesting.*

If a few careless words could produce such a pretty pout, could a few more earn him a smile? "That is, I don't recall meeting such lovely young ladies the last time I was in London." He bestowed his most dazzling smile on her. "Perhaps I'll let her claim me, after all."

*Blush now, and smile shyly.*

It was as if he'd waved a magic wand over her. Her lips curved upwards and her cheeks flooded with pink. "Oh, how charming you are, Captain West."

*Charming?* She wouldn't think so if she knew what he hid under his smile, but then he'd been charming enough at one time, hadn't he? How kind of Iris Somerset to remind him that while charm might not signify on a battlefield, it was a formidable weapon in London.

Among the *ton*, charm was everything. More to the point, it was easy to fake. As long as his smile was engaging, no one would care much what lurked beneath it.

*Of course.* How had he not seen it before? A smile, a few compliments, and the debutantes were sighing. They were giggling and blushing. Their girlish bosoms were heaving, and their eyelashes fluttering. If he had to be London's bloody conquering hero, why not to turn it to his advantage? If he'd learned anything in battle, it was to use every weapon he had to gain the victory, and at the moment his supposed heroism was a weapon.

After all, every lady adored a charming hero.

*Even a wicked widow.*

He turned the full force of his gaze on Iris Somerset. "How easy it is to be charming, Miss Somerset, when one is in such charming company."

Another blush. "Well, I—"

*Rap.* Lady Chase smacked Iris sharply on the wrist with her fan. "That will do, Iris." She fixed Julian with a freezing glare and pointed. "The stage is that way, Captain West."

Julian stifled a grin and turned around obediently.

*It was so simple. So perfect.*

But the widows were hardly innocent, blushing virgins like Iris Somerset. Their jaded hearts wouldn't be touched by a few shallow compliments. Charm might get him their attention, but the widows were too cynical to succumb to tales of heroism and a practiced smile.

No. They worshipped at a different altar entirely.

But a fresh diversion? Some new amusement, the thrill of a possible scandal? He and Devon, locked in a battle for Charlotte's attentions? Ah, now that might prove too delectable to resist, and if the widows couldn't resist him, then...

Charlotte hadn't a prayer of escaping him. Every party she attended, every wager she made, every whorehouse she ventured into, he'd be right at her heels, and with her friends' blessing.

*Would it work?* He glanced into the pit. The leering faces below continued to gawk up at him. In the tiered boxes, dozens of opera of glasses followed his every move, their glassy eyes winking.

Why shouldn't it work? It was working on the rest of London.

"Bloody hell."

Cam's curse was soft, but it jerked Julian from his reverie. He turned to his cousin in surprise, but he didn't have a chance to question him before he was interrupted by another feminine sigh from behind him.

"He's very handsome, isn't he?" It was the Somerset chits—Iris again. She was whispering to avoid waking her grandmother, who'd slipped into a doze and was snoring contentedly, her head tipped back against her chair.

One of the other sisters snorted softly. "Very wicked, you mean."

"The gossips exaggerate, I believe. It's not possible a gentleman who looks so much like an angel could be so *very* wicked, is it?"

"The handsomeness likely led to the wickedness," her sister whispered back. "That's usually how it works, and I doubt Lord Devon is the exception to the rule."

Julian stilled. *Devon.* He was the rake who was dangling after Charlotte. London's murderous earl. He followed their gazes until he spotted a tall, lean man in a superbly-fitted black coat making his way toward Charlotte's box. The man had sleek golden hair and a frighteningly symmetrical, perfectly aristocratic face. Iris Somerset was right—he looked more angelic than wicked.

Cam noticed the direction of Julian's gaze. "Lord Devon. Looks harmless enough, doesn't he?"

Robyn gave a harsh laugh. "Devon's about as harmless as a flame is to a moth."

Ellie wrung her hands. "He only grows more determined."

They all watched as Devon entered Charlotte's box. The wicked widows welcomed him with every appearance of delight, and he greeted them all with the utmost politeness, but his lips lingered longer than they should on Charlotte's glove.

Robyn rose from his seat. "Shall we go and dissuade him?"

Cam rose as well. "I'd be delighted to dissuade him, by throwing him out on his arse."

"No!" This came from both Ellie and Lily at once. Lily gripped Robyn's arm and tried to urge him back into his seat. Her face had gone white. "No, Robyn. If you go, the next we'll hear of it will be pistols at dawn."

Julian stared at her. A duel? He turned to Cam. "Surely it hasn't gone as far as that?"

Cam glanced at Ellie, whose face was even whiter than Lily's, and lowered his voice. "Not quite."

*Not quite?* Christ.

"If you go to her box now, it will only end in a scene and make things worse," Ellie said. "It's too late, in any case—everyone is already staring at them. If he visits her now, perhaps he won't at the end of the evening. There's less chance she'll leave with him that way."

Cam leaned over to murmur to Julian. "Did Sarah tell you where they're going tonight?"

Julian shook his head. "No. I gather Lady Hadley was careful not to reveal her plans for the evening." No doubt she'd remain careful, but if his plan fell into place the way he believed it would, he wouldn't need Sarah at all.

Devon remained in Charlotte's box until the curtain rose on the first act. Once he resumed his seat Ellie turned resolutely back to the stage. Lily did, as well, and after another moment Cam and Robyn resumed their seats. Neither gentleman was well pleased, but even their stiff fury was easier to watch than Ellie's quiet anguish.

She kept her eyes on the stage, but Julian could see her anxiety in her clenched hands and the rigid line of her shoulders. She perched on the very edge of her seat, but as stiff as her spine was, she was trembling. Every now and then he saw her back shudder as if she suppressed a sob. Cam tried to soothe her, but even Julian could see it was hopeless.

His jaw went rigid, and the rage that seemed to be always ready to explode inside him began to claw its way to the surface. How could Charlotte put her sister through such anguish? There hadn't been a flicker of remorse in those dark eyes at the brothel, not a bat of an eyelash this afternoon in the rose garden—not even when he reminded her of her obligations to Ellie.

*Cold down to her very soul.*

But he'd be colder still. The icier she was, the less inclined he was to feel anything at all for her, and as he lapsed by degrees into a comforting numbness he gained greater control over his volatile emotions. After all, the poisonous black mass that lived inside him couldn't escape if it were frozen.

*So much more peaceful, to feel nothing.*

He did his best to concentrate on the performance, but the Merchants of Venice were no match for the wicked widows of London. His gaze returned to Charlotte's box again and again as Shylock schemed his way through the first three acts of the play, and by the time the curtain dropped for intermission, Shylock's schemes were child's play in comparison to Julian's.

He rose from his seat. "Shall we go and pay our respects to Charlotte and her friends?"

Cam squeezed Ellie's hand and he, Robyn, and Julian wound their way through the crowded corridor to Charlotte's box.

"...think it will be quite as diverting as the brothel," Lady Tallant was saying when they entered, but when she saw them her eyes went wide, and her mouth snapped close. "I—that is, Mr. West. Mr. Sutherland. What a pleasant surprise."

Cam cleared his throat. "Good evening, Lady Tallant. May I present my cousin, Captain Julian West?"

Julian bowed. "Lady Tallant. We saw each other the other night, but we weren't properly introduced." He bent over her hand.

Lady Tallant gave Charlotte a quizzical glance, but she let him take her hand. Julian pressed his lips to her glove. "A pleasure, my lady."

"This is Lady Smythe." Cam nodded politely at the redhead, then the petite blonde. "And the Comtesse de Lisle."

Julian bowed over their hands in turn.

Lady Tallant arched a brow. "Is it indeed a pleasure, Captain? I did not, alas, get the impression you were pleased to see us the other night."

"Nor did I, Annabel." Charlotte regarded him with narrowed eyes. "Rather the opposite, in fact."

For the barest second Julian hesitated. It was essential the widows find him amusing, but it might be useful if they believed him sincere as well. He let his gaze linger on Charlotte; then he leaned close to Lady Tallant and dropped his voice as if to prevent Robyn and Cam overhearing him. "Forgive me, my lady, if I appeared less than enthusiastic to make your acquaintance the other evening. At the time I was rather, ah, anxious to have Lady Hadley's company. In private."

Lady Tallant's brows shot up, but Julian could see right away he'd said the right thing. Any lady who appreciated Lord Devon must delight in a rake, and he'd been just suggestive enough to pique her interest, but not so lewd he was offensive.

Lady Tallant shot Charlotte a look of utter amazement. Out of the corner of his eye Julian saw Charlotte shake her head, but her friend ignored her. "Well, Captain, I suppose elegant manners aren't much use on the battlefield. We can hardly punish you when you so heroically sacrificed them for the glory of England. Can we, ladies?"

Julian thought he heard Charlotte make a strangled noise, but it was drowned out by the redheaded widow, who leaned forward in her chair and fixed an eager green gaze on him. "No, indeed. I read all about you in the papers, Captain West, and I won't pretend I didn't find it riveting. The tale of your regiment's bravery has captured the heart of London."

Julian tried to look abashed. "Oh well, the papers exaggerate, Lady Smythe. I don't read them myself, but I believe they make our exploits sound far more impressive than they were."

"Of course they exaggerate." Charlotte darted a look at the redhead that could only be described as scorching. "The papers are full of nonsense. Why, just last week I read the most ridiculous story about St. Giles being flooded with ale from an explosion at one of the breweries—"

"Are you not a young man to be already a *Capitaine*?"

Julian turned to the Comtesse, and she flashed him a pouting smile that no doubt rendered most men speechless. "You certainly look *très jeune*."

She didn't add *très beau*, but Charlotte's snort indicated she thought it implied.

Julian smiled at the tiny blonde. "Not at all, Comtesse. I'm certain I'm *much* older than you are."

"Yes. Well." She drew the tips of her fingers across the bare skin above her low bodice. "I'm sure England is pleased to welcome you home, Captain."

Julian let his gaze wander to Charlotte. "I'm pleased to be here."

The widows exchanged glances with each other, then turned with raised eyebrows to Charlotte, who glared back at them.

With a little laugh the Comtesse rose to her feet and curtsied to Julian, Cam, and Robyn. "If you'll excuse me, gentlemen, I must say hello to Lady Bagshot."

The gentlemen bowed to her and stayed for a few more minutes of conversation with the other ladies; then Julian made a subtle sign to Cam to retire, and they murmured their farewells. Charlotte ignored all three of them as they exited her box, but they hadn't gone three steps into the corridor before Julian heard her hiss to her friends, "You two are a disgrace."

"My God, West." Robyn Sutherland clapped him on the back. "That was brilliant."

"Brilliant," Cam agreed. "The Comtesse nearly tumbled out of her bodice. I never realized you could be so agreeable, Jules. You're certainly not that charming at home."

Julian raised an eyebrow. "Perhaps it's your banyan."

"For God's sake. What have you got against my—"

"Ah, there's the Comtesse." Julian spied the diminutive blonde just ahead. "I believe I'll have a word with her."

Robyn grinned. "Fetching little pocket Venus, isn't she?"

"Quite. I have a taste for sin tonight, gentlemen." Julian quickened his pace to catch up to the Comtesse. "And I have a feeling the fetching little Comtesse knows just where to find the wickedest entertainment in London."

# Chapter Eight

"Riveting. I believe that was the word you used, wasn't it, Lissie?" Charlotte crossed her arms over her chest and tapped one toe on the carriage floor. "You're no better, Annabel, with that speech about elegant manners and the glory of England. And you, Aurelie, what were you thinking, with your *très jeune* and *très beau*?"

A beat of silence, then, "She didn't actually say *très beau*," Lissie offered meekly.

Charlotte pressed her lips together. "It was implied."

"Come now, Charlotte." Annabel was occupied with smoothing her gloves over her elbows, but she glanced at Charlotte, her face amused. "You must admit it was diverting the way you insisted he despises you, and then in the very next breath he appears in your box, looking at you the way a pickpocket looks at a gold watch."

"*Oui!*" Aurelie cried. "That is just how he looked at her. Like he wanted to snatch her away."

Lissie cocked her head, considering. "No, it was more the way a child looks at a tray of lemon tarts right before he steals ones. He wanted to snatch her away, yes—so he could devour her in private!"

Charlotte gritted her teeth. Had Lissie just compared her to a *tart*? "For God's sake, Lissie."

Annabel gave her glove one last tug. "You must admit he admires you, Charlotte."

"I admit nothing of the sort. He doesn't admire me."

She hadn't a doubt of that, but he'd gone to a great deal of trouble to make her friends think he did. Charlotte wasn't sure what he stood to gain from doing so, but she was certain of one thing—whatever he gained, she'd lose. "You can't mean to say you believed that rot about how anxious he is for my company, for I can assure you, Shakespeare's wasn't the only performance at Drury Lane this evening."

Annabel leaned forward to pat Charlotte's hand. "The question isn't, my dear, whether or not he's sincere in his admiration, but whether or not it's likely to be amusing for us to indulge his antics."

"But you don't look diverted, Charlotte," Lissie said. "Don't say you're concerned about Captain West?"

"As concerned as any fox with a drooling hound nipping at her heels. Make no mistake, my dears. He means to chase me out of London."

"That blasted nonsense again?" Lissie frowned. "Really, Charlotte, it would be far more convenient if you had no family, like the rest of us."

Charlotte couldn't quite agree with that sentiment, so she remained silent.

"Other members of your family have tried to banish you to the country, Charlotte." Annabel ticked them off on one hand. "Your mother, and Lady Eleanor. Both of your brothers—Lord Carlisle and Mr. Sutherland—and most recently Mr. West. Yet here you are in London still. None of them has proved a match for us, and neither will Captain West."

"He proved a worthy enough match for the French, didn't he? You've all read the papers. He's not a man one trifles with."

Annabel waved this away with a careless smile. "Now don't fret, dear. It was only a visit to your theater box, nothing more. No harm done."

Aurelie hadn't said a word during this exchange, but now her face went pale, and she began to babble incoherently in French.

"What is it? For heaven's sake, Aurelie." Lissie grasped the Comtesse by the shoulders. "Enunciate!"

Aurelie wrung her hands. "Ah, well, that is…oh, dear. Charlotte, you're going to be cross with me. You see——"

"Later," Annabel hissed as the carriage rolled to a stop. "Devon's right there on the street waiting to hand us out. We don't want him to know all our secrets."

In the next instant Devon opened the carriage door. "Lady Smythe?" He held out his hand to Lissie, then one by one assisted all four ladies from the carriage. Charlotte was the last to alight. "Ah. There you are, Lady Hadley. I hope you'll be entertained this evening."

Charlotte glanced up and down the quiet street. They were on the corner of Pall Mall and St. James's Streets, several blocks south of White's. She gave Devon a bemused look. "I have great faith in you, my lord, but even you can't sneak us into White's."

Devon smiled down at her. "True enough, but what do we need with White's?" He ushered them onto St. James's Street toward Piccadilly, but they'd only gone a dozen or so steps before he stopped in front of an arched, gated entrance with a narrow passageway that let into a courtyard hardly bigger than a pocket handkerchief. There was but one gaslight fixed into the timbered roof at the end of the passage, and Charlotte stumbled a little on the uneven stones, but Devon caught her arm before she could fall. "Careful. We're nearly there."

"What an odd little courtyard," Lissie said. "It's rather darling, isn't it? What is this place, Devon?"

"It's called Pickering Place. A little off the main path, but easy enough to find if you know it's here."

Annabel gave Devon a puzzled look. "So dark and quiet. It looks far too respectable to be a gaming hell."

He chuckled. "It was notorious enough at one time, but we'll have a quiet game this evening. It's private, by invitation only."

Charlotte twinkled up at Devon. Her uneasiness was fading the farther they got from Drury Lane and that odd scene with Julian. Annabel was right, of course. He'd come to her box this evening, yes, but what of it? He had a scheme in hand, certainly, but the widows weren't a pack of cork-brained schoolgirls. They weren't likely to be seduced by a few smooth lies and a handsome face.

She gave Devon a flirtatious smile, determined to relax and enjoy his attentions, Julian be damned. "And are we invited, my lord?"

He looked down at her, his gaze lingering on her eyes, and a slow smile drifted across his face. "You are. By me."

"That's good enough for me." Lissie slipped one arm through Devon's and linked her other with Annabel's. "Shall we?"

Charlotte linked arms with Aurelie to follow them, but the Comtesse dragged her feet with every step until they fell behind. "What's wrong, Aurelie? Don't you fancy a game? I'm sure they'll have faro."

Aurelie's gaze darted around the courtyard as if she expected someone to leap from the shadows. "Oh, Charlotte. You're going to be dreadfully angry with me, I'm afraid."

Charlotte gave her friend a playful frown. "Why? Do you plan to take all my money at the tables?"

"*Non*, it's just that—"

"Is something amiss, ladies?" Devon turned and held out a hand to Charlotte. "Lady Tallant and Lady Smythe are waiting."

Charlotte tugged on Aurelie's hand. "No, nothing's amiss, my lord. Come along, Aurelie. We'll set to rights whatever is troubling you when we get inside."

Much later that evening Charlotte would remember those words, and marvel at her own blithe unconcern. If only she'd listened to Aurelie, she might have been prepared for what awaited her inside.

But she hadn't listened. Instead she'd entered the drawing room on Devon's arm, half her attention on some pleasant nonsense he was whispering in her ear and the other half on a perusal of the room—three dozen people or so, most of them gathered around the hazard table—when a dark gaze caught hers and refused to let go.

By then it was too late.

"Lady Hadley? You've gone rather pale." Devon followed her gaze. "What, is it the tall, dark-haired gentleman? Who is he?"

Charlotte moistened suddenly dry lips. "He's…West. Captain Julian West."

"Indeed? I've heard of him." Much to her relief Devon didn't fall into raptures over Julian's heroism, but said only, "Is he here for you?"

It was obvious by this point Julian was here for her, as he hadn't taken his eyes off her once since she stepped through the door, unless it was to turn his lethal scowl on Devon. "Yes, I'm afraid so. My sister is married to his cousin. He's…family of a sort."

Devon shook his head, and Charlotte saw with surprise he actually looked amused. "Ah. Your brother-in-law has sent for the cavalry, quite literally. Will you introduce me, my lady?"

She hadn't much choice, had she? Charlotte let Devon lead her across the room to Julian. "Captain West," she muttered as they joined him. "What a surprise to see *you* here. Were you invited?"

Julian raised an eyebrow at her accusing tone. "Good evening to you as well, Lady Hadley."

"*Good*, Captain? That's not quite the word I'd choose to describe it. May I present Lord Devon? My lord, this is Captain Julian West. His regiment is lately returned to London from Paris."

Julian didn't bow, but instead gave Devon a nearly imperceptible nod. "Devon. I used your name to gain entrance this evening. Worked as well as if I'd had a key to the door. I expect that's the case with every gaming hell in London, isn't it?"

Charlotte gasped. Julian's address was so inexcusably rude she half expected Devon to call him out, but his lordship only chuckled and offered Julian a careless bow. "Good evening, Captain West. Of course all of

London recognizes your name. What an unexpected pleasure to make your acquaintance this evening."

Julian's eyes narrowed, and for a moment the two men took each other's measure. They were of a height, but the similarity ended there. Every inch of Devon was golden hair and languid ease, whereas Julian was dark and formidable, his lean, muscled body vibrating with tension.

Charlotte held her breath, but after a moment Devon turned to her, all casual solicitousness. "What do you fancy tonight, Lady Hadley?"

Charlotte stared at him for a moment, uncomprehending, but then her mouth fell open in horror. Who did she fancy? Why, what in the world would make Devon ask such a question? Surely he didn't mean to imply she fancied Captain West? Because that was sheer nonsense. Other ladies might sigh over his dark eyes and wide shoulders, but she knew better than to be taken in by—

"Lady Hadley?" Devon frowned down at her. "Your game?"

Her face flooded with heat. Of course. *Her game.* "Piquet."

"Very well. Piquet it is."

He took her arm, but before he could maneuver her away, Julian stopped them. "What a coincidence. I fancy a game or two of piquet this evening, as well."

Devon studied Julian, a faint, sardonic smile on his face. "How interesting. I imagined you'd play at Hazard, Captain, or *Rouge et Noir.*"

"I don't play any game where the house takes the advantage."

"Ah. You put your trust in your skill, then? Games of strategy fascinate, I grant you, but a gentleman has only himself to blame when he loses."

"And himself to congratulate when he wins."

Devon laughed as if delighted. "Well said, Captain." He drew Charlotte's arm more firmly through his, and Julian followed them to a table in the corner of the room where a small group of ladies and gentlemen were paired off in various stages of play. "What's your wager, Lady Hadley?"

Charlotte looked Julian in the eyes. "A guinea per point." Her pockets were deeper than his. Perhaps he'd think twice on that wager.

He didn't. "A guinea per point."

Devon raised an eyebrow, but he retrieved a fresh pack of cards from a wooden box at the center of the table and handed it to Charlotte. "Will you cut for the deal, my lady?"

Charlotte cut, the edges of the cards slippery against her damp fingers. Julian won the deal, but he pushed the deck back across the table to her. "The lady deals."

"A questionable move in terms of strategy," Devon said, "but of course the Captain is a gentleman. I leave you in good hands, Lady Hadley."

Devon moved away, but behind Julian's back Charlotte saw him wander over and whisper in Lady Annabel's ear. Annabel looked over her shoulder, eyes wide, and began to nudge her way through the crowd of bodies at the Hazard table.

Charlotte frowned and shook her head. She'd handle Julian herself.

"I confess I'm disappointed," he said, before she could speak. "I thought Devon would arrange a truly spectacular diversion for the widows tonight—something to exceed a masquerade at a west end whorehouse."

Charlotte finished the deal and placed the talon in a neat pile between them. "Oh? What did you envision?"

He glanced at his cards. "Carriage races in Hyde Park at midnight perhaps, or a stroll through the rookeries in the dark. A reunion of the Hellfire Club? Which diversion would you prefer, my lady?"

"Ah well, as wicked as I am, why limit myself to just one?"

"Do you suppose I think you wicked, Lady Hadley? Or do you think it yourself?"

"Both of us, I imagine, and yet I wouldn't dare speak for you, Captain."

"But you'd dare any number of other things, wouldn't you? That's rather the problem, you see."

Her gaze shot to him over the top edge of her cards. "What I fail to see is how it's *your* problem."

"You mistake the matter. The problem isn't *mine* any more than this game of piquet is *mine*. One can't play alone, after all. The problem is yours, as well."

Charlotte plucked lightly at her cards, rearranging them in her hand, but under her heavy silk gown her spine had gone rigid. "Are you so much cleverer than my brothers, Captain? Than your cousin? You're not the first to try and take me in hand and shuffle me about like a deck of cards, and yet for all their combined efforts, here I remain."

His face hardened. "Do you boast of that? You'd tear your family apart for a bit of diversion? For wicked widows, wagering, and whorehouses?"

*Dear God.* His expression. Charlotte blinked blindly down at her cards to avoid the look of cold disgust on his face. Perhaps she deserved his loathing for being so weak, for hurting her family.

*But I can't go back there...*

"Shocking, isn't it?" She forced the words past the lump in her throat. "I can't imagine why you bother with me at all. Why not leave me in London to suffer the consequences of my wicked behavior?"

"That's not my decision to make. Or yours either, as it happens."

She made herself smile, but her face felt stiff, as if she still wore the mask from the brothel. "Forgive me if I don't take your threats seriously, Captain. I've heard this all before, you see."

"Not from me."

"No, but what makes you any different than the others? Why should you succeed when they've failed?"

*How far will you go, Julian?*

But his answer didn't matter, did it? Because as far as he'd go, she'd go further, just as she'd done in the brothel the other night. As far as she must.

Julian tossed three cards on the table and drew from the talon. "Point of five."

Charlotte barely glanced at her own cards. "Good."

Julian declared *quint*, then *sixième*, and recorded his points on a slip of paper. "You're going to lose, my lady."

"The game has just begun, Captain."

He shrugged and drew from the talon to replace his discarded cards. "I had an illuminating chat with your friend the Comtesse this evening. Did you know that, Lady Hadley? She was quite forthcoming when I asked about your plans tonight. It took no more than a minute or two to get this address from her."

Charlotte's cards swam in front of her eyes. It was just as she'd suspected. He planned to charm her friends to get to her—to make her endure his company until he made London so intolerable she had no choice but to flee the city. And what then? She had no place left to go except to Bellwood, or worse, Hadley House.

Her heart began a panicked thrashing in her chest, but she forced herself to lay a card calmly on the table. "Point of two."

"Not good, Lady Hadley."

She declared a tierce, then a trio, both of which were discounted in favor of his cards. "Perhaps the Comtesse won't be so accommodating the next time."

"Perhaps not, but she was quite sympathetic when I told her about our past tragic love affair. She kept babbling about something—a wicked widow and a war hero, I think it was. She became rather breathless with the romance of it. It's curious, Lady Hadley, but she seems to think a reconciliation might take place between us. Now, where do you think she got such an idea?"

Panic welled in Charlotte's throat, nauseating her.

*I'll go as far as Julian will, as far as I must.*

But she knew the words were a lie, because she could never go as far as he had tonight. To use what had once been such a tender love between them to tantalize her friends with the promise of a reconciliation that would never happen—such ruthlessness, such heartlessness stunned her.

Dear God, what had happened to him? She searched his impassive face, his cold dark eyes for the barest hint of the man he'd once been, but there was nothing there.

A chill settled over her heart. She didn't recognize him.

Words formed on her lips, but before she could choke them out he spoke again. "The game is over, my lady." He spread his cards across the table. "One hundred points. May I see your cards?"

Charlotte lowered her cards to the table, her hands shaking.

Julian glanced at them and made a disappointed noise in his throat. "Pity. You're unlucky tonight. Or perhaps piquet isn't your game after all?"

She looked at the cards arranged on the table, but she couldn't make sense of them. "The score?"

"You owe me two hundred ten guineas, my lady."

Charlotte groped inside her reticule with numb fingers. "My vowels—"

Julian grasped her hand, trapping it inside her reticule. "I don't think so, Lady Hadley. I'll have your coins now, if you please."

Charlotte stared at him. "You're mad. Do you think I'd carry two hundred ten guineas in my reticule?"

He didn't let go of her hand. "I'm afraid that's not my problem, but as I see you're in a predicament, I might be willing to forgive the debt entirely. In exchange for a promise from you, that is."

*A promise.* To leave London, or something equally impossible. She didn't make promises she couldn't keep.

Her face must have shown her distress, for all of a sudden she saw Devon striding across the room toward her, his mouth set in a hard line. She half rose to meet him, but Julian tightened his grip on her hand.

And that's when she felt them, the hard stones slick and cool between her fingers.

*Her choker.*

She jerked hard against Julian's grasp. Her sudden movement must have surprised him, because he released her. She seized the heavy gold filigreed clasp, drew the choker from her reticule, and tossed it onto the table. It landed with a dull thud between them, the deep purple stones glittering in the muted light.

Julian stared at it for a moment, then raised his gaze to her face.

Devon had reached her chair, and he let out a low whistle. "You'd part with Hadley's jewels?"

"No. They're not Hadley's. They're mine." Charlotte never dropped her gaze from Julian's face. "A gift."

"You brought jewels to wager?" Julian's voice was oddly hushed, his face unreadable.

"No. I intended to wear the choker tonight, Captain. I adore it, you see. It's one of my favorite pieces. Take it." She rose to her feet. Her knees were shaking, but just a little bit. "It's worth far more than two hundred ten guineas, but far less than a promise from me."

From the corner of her eye Charlotte saw Annabel, Lissie, and Aurelie staring at her from the other side of the Hazard table, their mouths open in shock, but strangely no one followed her when she turned and left the room. Not her friends. Not Devon.

Certainly not Julian.

Perhaps they thought she'd only go far enough to find a quiet space to calm herself, but within seconds she was in the tiny courtyard. She ducked into a shallow recessed doorway, pressed her back against the rough stone wall, and drew great gulping breaths of air into her lungs.

There was no calm to be found in that house. No peace. Every day there were fewer places for her to run to, and if Julian had his way, if he managed to persuade her friends…

There would be no peace for her in anywhere in London.

# Chapter Nine

Julian stared at the necklace coiled on the table in front of him and waited for it to rear up, spitting and hissing, and sink its poisoned fangs into his wrist.

Devon pushed it toward him with one finger. "You heard the lady, Captain. Why don't you take your winnings?"

*Why, indeed?* She'd wagered and she'd lost. The necklace was his now.

"Lady Hadley's debt to you is settled whether you take it or not." Underlying Devon's polite tone was a note of cold warning. "She owes you nothing now."

*You're going to lose, Lady Hadley.*

But she hadn't, because he didn't want her money, her vowels, or her jewels. All he wanted was her promise, but he hadn't realized its worth until she tossed her necklace onto the table as if her word was more precious than gold and amethysts.

*Perhaps it was.*

But the necklace—it was nothing more than a diversion, a glittering consolation prize. Julian couldn't bring himself to touch the thing.

Devon didn't have such scruples. When Julian made no move to take the necklace, he reached for it himself. Before he could grasp it, however, a slim hand plucked it up from the table.

Julian looked up. Lady Tallant was looking down at him, her blue eyes measuring. She cradled the necklace in her hand—the amethysts winked up at him from the center of her white, kid-gloved palm. "Hold out your hand, Captain West."

Strangely, he didn't think to disobey, but simply held out his hand. Lady Tallant dropped the necklace into his palm, and he closed his fingers instinctively around it. The stones were still warm.

She turned to Devon. "My lord. May I have a word?" She took Devon's arm and led him away, but before they disappeared into the knot of people around the Hazard table she shot a quick, meaningful glance at Julian and gestured with her chin toward the door.

Was she ordering him to leave, or—

All at once he understood. Lady Tallant knew Devon would go after Charlotte, and for some inexplicable reason she wanted Julian to get to her friend first.

It was what an infatuated swain would do, and as far as the widows knew, *he* was the infatuated swain in this scenario. Besotted gentlemen didn't snatch their beloved's jewels as forfeit for a wager, and then sit and stare stupidly at those jewels while their lady dashed off into the night, alone and unprotected. They charged after her, begged her forgiveness, and wrapped the ill-gotten jewels around her alabaster neck.

He lurched to his feet, stuffed the necklace into his waistcoat pocket next to Colin's watch, and stumbled to the door. He looked back once before it closed behind him. Devon hadn't yet emerged from the drawing room, but Julian had seen the man's face when Charlotte fled the room. Lady Tallant wouldn't be able to hold him for long.

The courtyard was empty. No doubt Charlotte was halfway to her carriage by now. Even if he did manage to catch her, Devon would be upon them in mere minutes, and—

Julian went still, listening. If the courtyard hadn't been so silent, he would have missed it, a quiet gasp for breath, or a muffled sob. There was an alcove to his left, a doorway set deep into the wall. He crept forward, his shadow growing blacker and more monstrous against the building as he edged closer and closer.

Charlotte darted from the alcove in a whirl of purple skirts and leapt for the narrow passageway that let out onto the street, but Julian was faster. He wrapped one arm around her waist and pulled her back into the recess. She twisted frantically in his grip, but he nudged his much larger body into hers to hold her against the wall.

"Captain West! Have you gone mad? Release me this instant."

"Quiet." In another few seconds Devon would be in the courtyard, but there was a chance he'd pass right by them if only she'd stop shrieking.

She shoved against his chest. "Dear God, you have gone mad. I will *not* be quiet—"

He grasped her wrists and held them flat against the wall to still her.

"Captain! You're hurting me!"

Julian instantly loosened his hold, but he slid one hand up her arm and wrapped his fingers lightly around her elbow, where her gloves gave way to bare skin.

"Let go of me," she hissed. "You take this too far."

*Damn it.* He covered her mouth with his hand. "Your champion is about to charge out here to rescue you, my lady. It'll be damn unpleasant if he finds us, as I don't intend to relinquish you to his care."

That gave her pause. She went still, her eyes huge, dark pools above the hand he held over her mouth.

*Her mouth.*

In his haste Julian had left his gloves behind, and now her lips, soft and half open, were pressed against his bare hand, her warm breath teasing his palm. He stared down at her, a memory tickling at the edge of his consciousness, one so sweet it made him ache with loss.

A moment with her, a lifetime ago, the night like dark velvet wrapped around them, and the sky above heavy with stars. She'd taken his hand in hers and pressed her lips against his palm, and he'd gone half mad with wanting her, loving her.

He closed his eyes against the feel of her lips against his skin, at the sight of her chest heaving within her tight bodice, but she was close, so close he no sooner denied one sensation than others overwhelmed him. Her shallow, panting breaths became deafening, her sweet lemon scent so intense he could taste it on his tongue. He moved into her, so his body pressed into hers, her breasts flat against his chest, and for a fleeting moment he felt everything he thought he'd lost forever.

He felt *her.*

On the other side of the courtyard a door opened, and the low murmur of voices reached them from the passageway beyond. Julian dimly registered the rustle of silk skirts, a female voice calling something, the click of a man's pumps against the stones, loud at first, then fading as he hurried through the passageway into the street beyond.

The courtyard fell silent again. Devon had gone.

Julian lifted his hand from her mouth and she drew in an unsteady breath, but neither of them said a word. She swallowed, and he rested his hand against her long, white throat to feel the movement.

"I—what do you think you're doing, dragging me in here?"

"Hiding you from your lover." His tongue wrapped around the word *lover,* his voice a low, hoarse whisper.

"I don't have a lover." Her own whisper was so soft he had to lean closer to hear her.

"Not yet, but you will. You'll have Devon."

*Deny it. Please.*

But she didn't. She didn't speak, only watched him with dark, fathomless eyes.

He dragged his fingertips across her jaw and down her neck. "What will he do when he finds you've eluded him tonight?"

Her throat moved against his palm again. "He doesn't need to do anything. He'll have another chance tomorrow night."

"Oh, my lady," he murmured, stroking his thumb across her cheek. "I wouldn't depend on it."

Her lashes brushed her cheeks, hid her eyes. "I don't depend on anything or anyone but myself, Captain."

He touched a fingertip to her bottom lip. "I think you do. I think you depend on Devon. I think he's the reason you won't go home."

"Home?" She laughed, but her face paled. "Which home would that be? Grosvenor Square? Bellwood? Or all the way to Hampshire, to Hadley House?"

She didn't flinch from his touch, but stared back at him with eyes so wide and dark he could see his reflection mirrored in them. And the man who stared back... Who was he? For one moment he thought he might find Julian there, but the man who looked back at him was a stranger—a man he didn't recognize.

He stared down at her. He'd known her once—the sound of his name on her lips, the caress of her fingers against the back of his neck. He'd known what mattered to her, what made her laugh, what moved her, but now...

Lady Hadley was as foreign to him as he was to himself. A stranger.

That night under the stars was nothing but a memory, a moment from another man's lifetime, and even if he could get it back, he wouldn't know what to do with it. He didn't have that kind of love inside him anymore. He'd traded it for a dark abyss of rage and regret.

And she... He didn't know what she'd traded her soul for, and he didn't want to.

He released her chin and backed away from her so their bodies were no longer touching. "Hampshire or Bellwood. Whichever you choose. It makes no difference where you go, as long as you leave London."

This time her laugh carried an edge of panic. "It makes a difference to *me*, and I choose neither."

"Neither. Now why would that be, Lady Hadley? I confess myself curious. Surely Hadley House is a grand estate, one befitting a lady of your elevated rank. A magnificent manor house, with sweeping grounds, I imagine?"

Her smile didn't reach her eyes. "Grand, yes—massive really, with rooms upon rooms upon rooms. It's an estate without an end."

An unexpected shudder chased itself down Julian's back at this description. She hadn't said anything disparaging, but at the same time she made the place sound...disturbing. Sinister. It was all nonsense, of course, an absurd fancy of hers. Cam had told him Hadley House was one of England's truly exceptional homes—the pride of Hampshire. Charlotte couldn't have any reason not to return to it.

"It sounds, ah, lovely." It didn't, but one lie deserved another. "But perhaps Bellwood suits you better. It would be the easiest thing in the world for you to travel there with Cam and Ellie at the end of next week, and stay through the winter."

Her face was expressionless. "Easier for who, Captain?"

"For everyone concerned, but particularly for Ellie. She became nearly ill with distress when she saw Devon enter your box tonight. Her health is delicate right now, or had you forgotten that?"

Her voice sounded small. "I've forgotten nothing, Julian."

*Don't say my name. Don't make me feel.*

"You've shown no concern for your family, or made any attempt at self-restraint."

Her eyes went hard. "You have high ideals, Captain, for a man with a pocketful of jewels."

Her necklace felt as heavy against his chest as if he'd stolen it, but he managed a shrug. "Perhaps you shouldn't wager what you can't bear to lose."

A strange smile crossed her lips, then was gone in an instant. "I think you'd be surprised at what I can bear to lose."

He dragged a thumb across her lower lip as if he could catch that odd smile, hold it up to the light, and study it. "A few jewels in place of a promise. Why not promise me whatever I ask, and then break it tomorrow?"

Again, that strange smile. "Because I'm not a liar."

They stared at each other until Charlotte looked away. "I imagine you wish to escort me to Grosvenor Square, to see I'm confined inside my house? Not out of any concern for me, of course, but because you told Ellie and Cam you would?"

She didn't wait for an answer, but edged to the side, careful not to touch him as she passed. He followed her out into the empty courtyard, through the passageway and down the street a short way to her waiting carriage. Once inside she tucked herself tightly into a corner and turned her face to the window.

*She wants to make herself small. To disappear.*

Somehow he knew at once this was true, and yet it was so at odds with everything he believed about her, it seemed impossible. "Why do you—"

*No.* It didn't matter why. Let her go to Hadley House if she wanted to hide. What had she called it? An estate without an end. It was the perfect place to disappear, then. "Why do you insist upon staying in London? What do you want?"

She turned her gaze from the window to face him. "Why do you want to know, Captain? Do you suppose you can give it to me? Ah, well. Perhaps you can. Perhaps all I need is a hero to save me from myself."

He gave a short laugh. "You're wasting your time with Devon, then. He sure as hell isn't interested in saving you, except for himself. He's no hero."

She turned away from him, back to the window. "I've never had much use for heroes."

*Just as well, because they don't exist.*

They rode in silence through the streets until the carriage drew to a stop in front of Charlotte's townhouse in Grosvenor Square. "The carriage will take you on to Bedford Square. Good evening, Captain."

She'd stepped down and turned away before Julian noticed the carriage—black, crested, and luxuriously appointed—waiting on the other side of the street.

*Devon.* The man couldn't seem to stay away from her.

Julian slid across the seat and through the open door. "One moment, if you would, Lady Hadley." He took her arm. "I insist upon escorting you inside."

Despite the late hour, the heavy front door flew open before they reached the top stair. "My lady, Lord Devon is here, and he insists upon seeing you at once…oh." The butler fell silent when he caught sight of Julian. "I beg your pardon, my lady."

Charlotte drew off her gloves and handed them to the servant. "Disconcerting, isn't it, Nelson, to have two gentleman callers at once, and it not even calling hours? No, there's no need to take Captain West's coat. He won't be staying."

"Very good, my lady."

She turned to Julian. "As you can see, I'm quite safe now. I do thank you for your extreme attentiveness, Captain. Good evening."

Julian deliberately leaned a hip against the wall and crossed his arms over his chest. "Oh, no, Lady Hadley. I can't possibly take my leave before

Lord Devon does. It wouldn't be proper. Your family wouldn't like it. Would they, Nelson?"

Nelson's stammering reply was cut off when the drawing room door opened and Lord Devon, who'd no doubt heard the argument, emerged. "Forgive the intrusion, my lady." He went to Charlotte and took her hands in his. "But I couldn't rest until I knew you were well."

"You're very kind, my lord. I'm sorry to have spoiled your evening—"

"But as you see, she's perfectly well," Julian interrupted in freezing tones. "No need to linger then, is there, Devon?"

Devon didn't take any notice of him. "You didn't spoil my evening, I assure you. I'm off to join our friends even now." Devon hesitated, then lowered his voice. "You'll be all right? I know you prefer not to spend time alone here."

Julian straightened up from his relaxed pose against the wall. Bellwood, Hadley House, and now Grosvenor Square? Lady Hadley, it seemed, didn't want to be…anywhere.

"You're very good, my lord, but it's all right." She smiled up at Devon—not the strange half smile she'd given Julian, but one that reached her eyes.

Devon brushed his lips across her glove. "Then I can be easy. Good evening, my lady." He turned to Julian with a correct bow, but his eyes were like a blue lake frozen under layers of ice. "Good evening, Captain West." He accepted his coat and hat from Nelson, strolled through the door and was gone.

Any trace of the warm smile Charlotte had bestowed on Devon vanished when she turned to Julian. "Are you satisfied?"

He was far from satisfied, but unfortunately he hadn't the slightest excuse to be displeased with Devon's behavior. The man had been a perfect gentleman. "For now."

"Then I'll bid you good night." Charlotte swept up the stairs without another word, leaving Nelson to show him out.

Julian half hoped to find Devon's carriage lingering in the street so he had just cause to land a fist in his lordship's excessively handsome face, but the black crested carriage was gone.

Bedford Square was quiet when he arrived. He began to mount the stairs, but then turned abruptly and made his way down the hallway to Cam's study. He couldn't face his bedchamber tonight.

He stripped off his coat and cravat, paused at the sideboard to pour a glass of whiskey, and then dropped into his chair before the fire. After a moment he reached into his waistcoat pocket, withdrew Colin's watch, and flicked open the lid. The hands remained frozen in their places. Foolish, the way he checked it every day, as if he could somehow trip time back into motion if he only looked at the watch at the right moment.

He dug into his pocket again, took out Charlotte's necklace, and dangled it between his fingers. The fire lit up the amethysts so a flame seemed to burn deep inside them.

Colin's watch, and now Charlotte's necklace.

*I adore it. It's one of my favorite pieces.*

Yet for all that she'd tossed it onto the table in front of him, her chin in the air, and refused to let him humble her. Refused to lie.

Julian closed his fist around the treasures, leaned his head back against the chair, and stared into the fire, let the flames hypnotize him with their sinuous dance. They burned lower, then lower still; their edges grew fuzzy…

He'd give the necklace back to her. He'd drape it around her neck himself so he could brush the soft skin at her nape with his fingertips, and then maybe she'd smile at him the way she'd smiled at Devon tonight.

His eyes fell to half-mast, then drifted closed.

*The glittering amethyst stones of her choker are cool and slick against his tongue. He kisses her neck, opens his lips over the stones, and takes them into his mouth. She trembles against him, turns, says something, but he can't quite hear her. His hands fill with slippery purple silk as he pulls her closer, feels her breath as she whispers in his ear… Do you suppose you can give me what I want, Julian? He wants to answer her, tries to answer, but the stones multiply, grow enormous in his mouth and lodge in his throat. Her face tunnels as the stones choke him into unconsciousness, but before the darkness can take him she tears the necklace roughly from his mouth and the amethysts cut him, slice into his cheeks and tongue and he tastes blood and then he's Colin, blood pouring from his mouth…*

He shuddered into consciousness, gasping for breath.

*Jesus. Where am I? Where…*

Cam's study. The fire was dead in the grate, and the room had gone cold.

# Chapter Ten

"Whatever it was you and those wicked widows of yours got up to last night, you can just keep it to yourself. I don't want to hear a thing about it."

Charlotte turned from her dressing-table mirror to raise an eyebrow at Sarah. "My, you're in a temper this morning, but I assure you, your snit is wasted on me. Even you couldn't find anything to disapprove in my behavior last night." Unless she happened to look in the jewel casket, that is, for there was nothing but an empty velvet tray where the amethyst choker had been.

Fortunately Sarah turned her attention to the gown Charlotte had worn the previous night instead. She snatched it up and cast a suspicious eye over it, searching for evidence of wrongdoing. When she found none, she gave it a violent shake, as if she could force secrets from its silk folds. "It's not my place to contradict you, my lady, but you were up to something, sure as I'm standing here."

Charlotte snorted. "Your place, indeed. You couldn't find your place if you had a dozen lanterns and a pack of hunting dogs at your disposal."

"Hunting dogs, my eye. That's got naught to do with whatever wickedness you got up to last night. For a lady as was such a paragon of virtue, you're awfully eager to change the subject. But like I said, I'll not hear a word about it."

"A word about what, you silly thing? I went to the theater last night, nothing more." Nothing Sarah needed to know about, at least.

The maid jabbed her hands onto her hips. "Nothing more, eh? If that's true, then why are those three fiendish females of yours waiting in the drawing room for you, and each of them looking like a cat that just swallowed a mouse?"

"My friends are here?" Charlotte jumped up from the dressing table. "For pity's sake, Sarah, why didn't you say so at once?"

"They're here all right, and all three of them look ready to burst, especially that little French one. Must be something scandalous indeed to get those three up from their beds before nightfall. Don't bother trying to confess to me, however, for I won't hear it."

"Oh hush, will you? There's nothing to confess. Now stop your ceaseless prattle and help me dress."

Sarah turned on her heel and disappeared into the dressing closet, but Charlotte could still hear her grumbling. "You may as well tell me, then. No point in hiding it from me, my lady. Whatever it is, I'm sure you've done worse."

"Much worse," Charlotte muttered under her breath.

At last Sarah emerged with a lavender gray day dress draped over her arm. "Well? Go on then, since you insist upon telling me, and don't think to skimp on the details."

Charlotte rolled her eyes. "For goodness' sake. All right then, if you must know. Once the clock struck midnight we had carriage races in Hyde Park, then a stroll through the rookeries in the dark, and finally a reunion of the Hellfire club."

*There.* Perhaps that would keep Sarah quiet.

Sarah covered her mouth with her hand. "Oh, my lady. You didn't!"

Charlotte let out an irritated sigh. It would take an act of Parliament to keep Sarah quiet. "I did, and worse too. I promise to recount it all in salacious detail later if you'll make me presentable within the next few minutes. My friends are waiting."

*And all three of them needed a good shake.* God only knew how she'd undo the damage Julian had caused last night. He'd been at his handsome, appealing best at the theater. Charlotte had seen right through him, but her friends had been one charming smile away from falling under his spell. Even Annabel's stalwart cynicism had wilted under Julian's onslaught.

He'd been far less charming at the gaming hell when he'd refused her vowels and snatched her jewels instead. Dash it, she never should have warned Annabel away from the piquet table last night. It would be far easier to convince them of his treachery if one of them had witnessed it.

Sarah quickly fastened Charlotte's gown and arranged her hair into a simple twist at the nape of her neck. "There. That'll do well enough for those three jades."

As soon as she was free of Sarah, Charlotte hastened to the drawing room. As her maid had pointed out, it wasn't every day her friends rose before sunset.

*It wasn't any day, come to think on it.*

The widows wanted details, and they wouldn't rest until they got them. Charlotte intended to oblige them too, with a thorough dose of the ugly truth.

She paused outside the drawing room and drew in a deep, slow breath. If she wanted to make her friends see sense, she must remain calm. Cool-headed. There could be no shouting and no hysterics, and above all she must refrain from referring to Julian as a false, deceitful, manipulative, ruthless scoundrel.

Surely she could manage to do that for one afternoon.

"My dears," she said as she threw open the doors and breezed into the drawing room. "I didn't realize you were aware there was such a thing as daylight hours."

Lissie blinked at the window. "I vaguely recall something about it from my childhood. It feels less wondrous now than it did then, somehow."

Annabel lifted one shoulder in a shrug. "So do most things."

"Such cynicism!" Aurelie frowned at Annabel. "It can't be good for your complexion, *ma petite*."

"Frowning isn't good for it either, and anyway, who's cynical? I said *most* things, not *all* things. Gossip, for instance."

"Did you see the scandal sheets this morning, Charlotte?" Lissie settled herself on a yellow tufted divan with the air of one who intends to stay there for quite some time. "Captain West's presence in your box last night didn't go unnoticed, and now all of London is pining for a romance between the wicked widow and the war hero. I did warn you that story was irresistible, didn't I?"

"Another day, another scandal sheet. I could write them myself by now." Charlotte pulled the bell to summon a servant. "I suppose we'd better have tea."

"*Oui*." Aurelie sat down on the settee next to Lissie. "Tea, or something stronger."

"Like smelling salts?" Annabel asked. "We may find ourselves overcome by Charlotte's tales of the delicious Captain West."

Charlotte glared at her. "You were certainly overcome by him last night. Honestly, Annabel, how can you be taken in by him? Underneath that charming smile he's a false, deceitful, manipulative, ruthless scoundrel."

*Well. That hadn't taken long.*

"Oh, you mean to say he is *un sauvage?*" Aurelie gave a little wriggle of delight. "Even more delicious!"

Charlotte threw her hands into the air in disgust. "Well, I can only hope the next gentleman who fleeces my pockets is of a less *edible* turn of countenance. Then perhaps I can depend upon my dearest friends to do more than stand by and gape at him."

Annabel glanced at Lissie and Aurelie, then back at Charlotte. "Do you mean to say he cheated at piquet? Because that would change things entirely. I can't abide a cheat."

Charlotte bit her lip. Oh, how dearly she'd love to claim he was a cheat and a liar, for he was both, but he hadn't, blast him, cheated at piquet last night. "Not as such, no, but he—"

"He didn't fleece you at all then, did he?" Lissie let out an irritated sigh. "Honestly, Charlotte, I can understand why you're so wary of him, given your past association, but you refuse to even give the man a chance."

*I gave him a chance once. He broke my heart, and I haven't another one to spare.*

"Besides, what would you have had us do?" asked Annabel. "Tackle him to the floor right there beside the piquet table and beat him senseless with our reticules?"

"That would have done nicely, thank you."

Lissie tapped a finger against her chin. "I suppose we could have done, but it would have attracted an awful lot of attention. Not quite the thing, to beat a gentleman about the head with one's reticule during piquet, you know."

Charlotte let out an irritated snort. "What nonsense. Since when do you three care about attracting attention, for any reason?" She knew her friends were right, of course—there was little they could have done that wouldn't have made the situation worse, but was it too much to ask they not refer to Julian as *delicious*?

*Even if it was true. Especially then.*

"But it had nothing to do with the attention," Aurelie said. "We didn't try and stop him, *ma chou*, because one could see from the moment you sat down to piquet nothing *could* stop him. It was *inutile*, you see."

"Quite useless," Lissie agreed. "He was determined to have you to himself no matter what."

"Determined to snatch my jewels, you mean." Charlotte scowled at them. "And you're all determined to make it sound as if he was motivated by some tender feeling, which is exactly what he wants you to believe. I can assure you, it was nothing of the sort."

Lissie leaned forward in her seat, her expression eager. "What happened after he dashed into the night after you, determined to halt you in mid-flight?"

"Lissie! Stop that. He didn't *dash* anywhere. He dragged me, with his huge bear-like paw clamped around my wrist, deposited me without ceremony in my carriage, and then dumped me on my doorstep like so much baggage. There was nothing delicious about it."

Except there had been those moments, in the courtyard…

He'd stood so close to her, close enough only a mere breath separated them, so close she could have pressed her face into his chest and inhaled his faint, clean scent of leather and starch. His voice, when he'd said the word *lover*…

Charlotte shook her head to chase away the sound of that word in Julian's hoarse, rough whisper. No. She wouldn't tell her friends he'd hidden her from Devon, his body against hers, his hand over her mouth. It would only encourage them, and besides, Julian had said other words, too—words like *Bellwood* and *Hampshire*—and whole sentences, as well.

*It makes no difference where you go, as long as you leave London.*

She didn't matter to him. She had once, a thousand years ago, and a woman didn't forget how it felt when a man cherished her. It didn't feel anything like being a fox at the mercy of a pack of slavering, snarling hounds. It didn't feel anything like being hunted.

It didn't feel anything like this.

He looked like the Julian she remembered, the Julian she'd fallen so madly in love with. When he whispered the word *lover* in her ear, he sounded like Julian. He even smelled like Julian, with that clean scent so wholly his own it made her want to climb inside his skin, to drown in him—

But he wasn't that man. Not anymore. He was Captain West, and no matter what her friends thought, this harder, colder Julian didn't care about her. He wasn't trying to help her, and if she became too lost in her memories of him to remember that, he could convince her to do anything he wished her to do. He could coax her to leave London, to go back to Bellwood or Hadley House, and God help her then.

"But if he's not motivated by passion, then what?" asked Lissie. "Why should he come to your box at all and follow us to a gaming hell? No one wants a game of piquet that badly, for goodness' sake."

Charlotte exhaled a slow, patient breath and tried to gather her wits. "Don't you see, Lissie? Cam and Ellie are convinced I remain in London for Lord Devon. They think Captain West can intimidate Devon into abandoning his pursuit. Once Devon drops me, they think I'll leave wicked old London behind and toddle obediently off to the country."

Annabel snorted. "They don't know Devon very well, do they? If that's their plan, then you have nothing to fear from Captain West, Charlotte. Devon is like a hound on a scent. An extremely handsome and divinely wicked hound, that is. He won't abandon a thing until he's good and ready."

It was true, and it wasn't even just that. Devon was her friend—a true friend, and he became more tempting by the second. He might be wicked, but he was also clever and scrupulous in his loyalties. If she decided to take advantage of his offer, he'd tear apart anyone who threatened her.

"Do you mean to say the Captain and Devon will become rivals for Charlotte's affections?" Aurelie's eyes widened. "Oh, how exciting! Do you suppose they'll fight a duel over her?"

Charlotte resisted the urge to tear her hair out in frustration. "No! Of course not. Captain West doesn't care a fig for me, Aurelie, and Devon—well, Devon is far too quick to fall for the Captain's ruse. He'll do what he will, regardless of Captain West's nonsense."

"But is it truly nonsense, Charlotte?" Annabel gave her a considering look. "Perhaps Captain West doesn't know his own mind as well as he thinks he does."

*Dear God. Now what?* "What does that mean?"

"I saw his face last night after you fled the gaming hell. He looked quite wild. He may *think* he acts only on your family's behalf, while in truth his reasons are far more...tender."

Both Lissie and Aurelie nodded.

"I'd think you'd want to know it if he does truly care for you," Annabel said. "Why not let it play out and see what happens? Perhaps history will repeat itself, after all."

Charlotte let her head fall into her hands. No matter what she said her friends simply refused to see it. Like the rest of London, they couldn't get past Julian's handsome face and the tales of his bravery and heroism.

Annabel was still talking. "Perhaps I should invite Captain West to my rout tonight? Devon will be there, and we can see—"

"No." Charlotte raised her head. "Don't you see? It will only encourage him to bedevil me further. I tell you, if we simply disregard him, he'll give up the chase soon enough—"

A quiet knock on the drawing room door interrupted her. At her summons, Nelson stepped into the room and bowed. "I beg your pardon for the interruption, my lady, but Miss Amelia and Captain West are here."

Annabel raised her eyebrows at Charlotte. "Perhaps he will give up the chase, but it won't be today."

"Not today and not ever, Annabel—not if you insist upon extending invitations to him. I shall have no peace if you do." Even now in her own home she had no peace, for as Julian no doubt anticipated, she'd never turn Amelia away. "Show them in, Nelson."

Nelson bowed out of the room, and a few minutes later Amelia darted in. "Charlotte! Oh, how lucky we found you at home. I do so want to have a ride in Hyde Park with you, for we leave for Bellwood very soon, you know, and we won't have a chance to ride together for months and months, and uncle Julian said he'd escort us, and I have my new riding habit, you see, and—oh!" Amelia spied the widows and sank into a hasty curtsey. "Good afternoon."

Julian strolled in after Amelia, and drat him, he looked nothing like a false, deceitful, manipulative, ruthless scoundrel. His tall, lean frame was made for riding attire. He was devastating in his tight breeches and bottle green riding coat. The widows were apparently struck speechless by this paragon of masculinity, for they simply stared at him without uttering a word.

The corner of Julian's mouth twitched, and he swept them an elaborate bow. "Good afternoon, ladies. I do hope we're not interrupting?"

Annabel recovered first. "Good afternoon, Miss West. Captain West."

Lissie and Aurelie managed proper curtsies, but they gazed at Julian with such avid glee they looked like two naughty girls caught giggling during the church service. "Did you enjoy yourself last night, Captain?" Lissie shot Charlotte a sly glance. "You seemed to be quite taken with, ah, *piquet.*"

"Amelia," Charlotte interrupted. "You left your gloves here the other day. I believe Sarah has them. Won't you go find her?"

Once Amelia was gone, Julian turned his gaze upon Charlotte. "I enjoyed myself immensely, Lady Symthe. Piquet is rather captivating, isn't it? I was quite mesmerized."

"But you left in such a hurry, Captain." Aurelie nudged Charlotte. "Something tore you away rather suddenly, I think?"

Charlotte crossed her arms over her chest. "Anxious to escape with your ill-gotten winnings, no doubt." He'd wagered and won fairly, but perhaps the insult to his honor would goad him into a temper, or at least an unattractive frown, and then the widows would see what he was really like—

"Charlotte!" Annabel gasped.

"It's all right, Lady Tallant. Lady Hadley regrets the loss of her necklace." Julian reached into his waistcoat pocket and drew out the amethyst choker, his face so soft with concern when he held it out to her, for a moment even

Charlotte believed him sincere. "I meant to return this last night, but if you recall I became distracted."

Lissie smothered a giggle at Charlotte's quelling look. "I don't recall anything of the sort, Captain."

"Ah, well." He gave her a suggestive smile. "Perhaps I wasn't the only one who was distracted. But I can't imagine any other lady could do justice to such a lovely necklace. I could never deprive you of it, Lady Hadley." He took her hand and draped the necklace over her palm.

The widows let out an audible sigh.

Charlotte closed her numb fingers around the choker. *Dear God. He was far too good at this.*

Annabel cleared her throat and came forward to kiss Charlotte on the cheek. "We'll see you tonight, dearest." They made their way into the hallway and collected their gloves and bonnets from Nelson, but Annabel turned back just before the butler ushered them out the door. "Oh, and Charlotte? Do extend an invitation to my rout tonight to Captain West, won't you?"

Charlotte's heart sank like a stone. She wouldn't invite him, but it hardly mattered. He'd be there, and not just tonight, but every night until he drove her out of London.

Amelia came back into the room as the widows disappeared through the front door and into Aurelie's waiting carriage. "You will come riding this afternoon, won't you, Charlotte?"

Charlotte turned to Amelia with a guilty smile. She did intend to ride this afternoon, but not with Julian. "Oh Amelia, I'm afraid not. I have an engagement this evening, and so much to do—"

"Oh." Amelia's dark eyes, so eager only moments before clouded with disappointment.

Julian snapped his riding crop against his boot. "Don't look so glum, Amelia. You'll be back in London in, what? Another six months for next year's season? I'm sure your sister will have time for you then, and you and I can still go today."

Charlotte slid Julian a resentful look. Would he stop at nothing to achieve his ends? She had all the time in the world for her young sister, and she didn't want Amelia to think otherwise.

"But Charlotte knows all about the fashions on display on the promenade. Do you know anything about fashions, Uncle Julian?" Amelia's tone betrayed her deep skepticism.

"Fashions? I can tell you all about the gentlemen's boots, if you like."

"Gentlemen's boots! What is there to know about gentlemen's boots one way or another?"

Julian looked a bit offended. "Quite a lot, as it happens, such as whether they're Hoby, or—"

"I'll change into my riding habit," Charlotte interrupted, resigned. She had no wish to spend the afternoon with Julian, but she couldn't disappoint Amelia on her last week in London, or in good conscience doom her young sister to a lecture on gentlemen's boots.

"I believe Lady Tallant said something about a rout?" Julian asked, once they were all mounted and riding down Grosvenor Street toward Park Lane.

Charlotte kept her eyes on Amelia, who rode just ahead of them. "It's nothing you'd be interested in. Just a few notables from the demimonde, along with some ne'er-do-wells from the outer fringes of the *ton*. Not your people at all, I'm afraid. Not a hero amongst them."

"It sounds delightful. What time shall I fetch you?"

"You shouldn't. I haven't extended an invitation to you."

"Ah, but Lady Tallant has, and I will attend, so you may as well let me escort you."

If he escorted her tonight, he'd escort her tomorrow night, and the next, and every night thereafter, until her last refuge became no refuge at all. "No. I want you to stop this, Captain."

"I don't know what you mean, Lady Hadley. Stop what?"

"Stop trailing about after me as if I were some kind of criminal. Stop lying to my friends."

For a long moment there was only the clop of the horses' hooves against the cobblestones, but at last Julian spoke. "Cam and Ellie are eager to have you come to Bellwood. Perhaps you should go. Put an end to this chase and simply do as they wish."

*Perhaps you should go.* So simple. The solution always was to those who didn't understand the problem, and she couldn't explain it to them, because it had become so bent and twisted inside her even she didn't understand it. She knew only that she didn't plan anymore, but acted as best she could at each given moment. She had no idea when she'd be ready to leave London. She only knew it wasn't today. "Cam and Ellie don't understand what's best for me right now."

"Do you?"

Charlotte might have been reassured if his tone were harsh or angry— she might have been able to convince herself he still had some flicker of feeling for her, some pale, ghostly remnant of what they'd once shared, but he was detached, even faintly amused.

A chill settled over her heart. She didn't want to confide in him. She didn't want him in her head, probing at her secrets, but if she told him just enough of the truth to make him understand, perhaps... "I cannot go back to Bellwood. I will not."

"Which is it? You cannot, or you will not?"

"It amounts to the same thing. I will not, because I can't. Not yet."

"Oh? When, then? Next week, or next year? Or never?"

"I don't know." She hesitated, because she didn't want to say the next words, but if they would move him at all, she had to. "If you ever cared for me, Julian, even just a little, then please—leave me alone."

Charlotte kept her face blank and her gaze focused on Amelia's back, but her breath stopped in her lungs as she waited for his answer.

*Was it enough? Enough to persuade him?*

He hesitated just long enough for her heart to leap with hope, but then he turned to her with a smile—that same easy smile that so charmed her friends. "Forgive me, but you never said what time I should collect you this evening."

*It hadn't changed, his smile. But everything behind it had.*

He wasn't going to listen to her. He wasn't going to stop, and he'd proved he could manipulate the only friends she trusted—her wicked widows.

The only friends she trusted, but one. She still had one friend who wouldn't be taken in by Julian—a friend who'd proved his loyalty to her beyond the shadow of a doubt.

She still had Devon.

# Chapter Eleven

"You haven't answered my question, Lady Hadley."

She hadn't, and she didn't now, but rode quietly next to him, her face expressionless. The dark blue ribbons on her hat fluttered in the breeze, but everything else about her was still. She looked neither right nor left, but kept her gaze fixed on Amelia, who ambled along ahead of them.

*If you ever cared for me, even just a little...*

If it had cost her an effort to say it, it didn't show on her face.

Julian tried again. "Do you object to the evening's entertainment? I grant you a rout is not as exciting as a whorehouse frolic, but with Lady Tallant as our hostess there's bound to be a scandal or two to keep you entertained."

Still no answer. She didn't look at him, but he thought he could see haughty resistance in the set of her lips and her rigid posture.

*The marchioness was not pleased.*

Well. He'd made himself perfectly clear, then. It was futile for her to stay in London. He'd follow her everywhere, attend every entertainment until Devon gave up the chase and moved on to the next widow who caught his eye. Julian doubted the man would waste much time hunting down easier quarry. Devon didn't look like the sort who'd deny himself his pleasures for long.

It was as good as done, and despite her sullen silence, Charlotte knew it as well as he did. "Or perhaps you prefer to skip the rout altogether? I doubt you'll find much pleasure in it."

At last she turned to look at him. "Oh? Why should that be? I suppose your think your presence makes that much of a difference to me."

"I know it does. Lady Tallant extended the invitation to me despite your protests, I believe."

Charlotte lifted one shoulder in a shrug. "I don't deny I'd rather not have your company, but if you think to send me scurrying off to the country to avoid you, you'll be sadly disappointed. I won't let you chase me away from my friends, Captain."

"Ah. Stubborn to the bitter end. But make no mistake, my lady. This *is* the bitter end, whether you choose to admit it or not. Lady Tallant insisted upon having me tonight. She'll insist again, and so will your other two friends. It's telling how quickly they disregard your wishes. Perhaps you're not such loyal friends, after all?"

"It's to your benefit to make me doubt them." She'd perfected that careless tone, but her fingers twitched nervously on the reins. "My friends are taken in by you. I offer my congratulations on a role well played, Captain. You set out to charm them, and you succeeded."

"Taken in? So dramatic, my lady. You make me sound a villain, and your friends dull indeed. Are they so lacking in penetration they can't tell the truth from a lie?"

"Or a hero from a liar? My friends may have more experience with liars than most, but they see you the way all of London sees you. You're a hero, after all, and heroes can't be liars, can they?"

Julian stiffened as he always did at any mention of his supposed heroics. "I've no idea, Lady Hadley. Why don't you tell me?"

"It doesn't signify. As I told you last night, I've little use for heroes, and even less use for liars. The point is my friends believe you truly care for me, and so they believe they're acting in my best interests."

"Perhaps I am. Have you even considered that possibility?"

Her gaze snapped to his face, and she let out an incredulous laugh. "My goodness. Is that what you tell yourself, Captain? That you're engaged in some heroic battle to save me from myself? First England, and now the Marchioness of Hadley. Well, the scandal sheets certainly think so, and it's a far more entertaining story than the truth."

He frowned. If the scandal sheets had picked up on this nonsense, there was a chance Jane Hibbert might hear of it. *Damn it.* Was there no limit to how far Charlotte's chaos could reach? "What is the truth, my lady? That you're better off sneaking into whorehouses in London with the wicked widows, while Lord Devon pants after you, awaiting an opportunity to make you his lover? You lie to yourself if you call that the truth."

"I don't toy with the truth anymore, Captain, but one can't say the same for you. You might want to be careful with that. Didn't you pay attention to the play last night? 'The truth will out.'"

*Whatever the bloody hell that meant.*

He didn't ask. She'd find herself bundled into Cam's carriage on her way to Bellwood soon enough, and that would be an end to the entire mess. He'd be rid of her and her endless dramas, and free to court Jane properly. After more than a year of turmoil, peace was within his grasp at last.

He urged his horse forward with a tap of his heel, intending to leave Charlotte behind and join Amelia. "Send word to Bedford Square what time you wish me to fetch you tonight."

"No need. I told you, Captain West. I don't wish for your escort this evening."

*Devil take her.* He drew back hard on the reins and his horse stopped, but it was too late to force the black anger back into its cage behind his ribs. "This evening, or any other? I'm surprised to find you so fastidious about the company you keep. I did discover you in a whorehouse not three days ago, mingling with Mrs. Lacey's doxies."

She was several paces ahead of him now, but she turned to say over her shoulder, "Mrs. Lacey's doxies have no specific interest in me. I can't say the same of you."

The poison, black as pitch, rose like bile inside him until he could taste it at the back of his throat. "I'm sorry to disappoint you, but any specific interest I had in you came to an abrupt end when you married the Marquess of Hadley."

He braced himself for her sharp rejoinder, but she remained strangely silent, her body rigid in the saddle, as if she expected to be thrown to the ground at any moment. He kneed his horse forward to catch up to her, but as soon as he saw her face his blood went cold.

Every trace of the haughty, selfish Marchioness had vanished, and in her place was Charlotte, only Charlotte, all pretense stripped away. She looked…broken, somehow. Lost. Lost inside a blank silence that nevertheless throbbed with a pain he hadn't expected, and didn't understand.

Julian stared at her, shocked. He tried to feel triumph at having managed to shake her composure at last, but as the moments continued to slip by in silence, his false smile stiffened on his lips.

"I'm not an utter fool, Captain," she murmured at last. "I don't mean a romantic interest. I know very well you only pretend to care for me to win over my friends. In truth my welfare is of no consequence to you."

It wasn't, because he couldn't allow it to be. If he let her in, if he let her make him feel anything, then God only knew when he'd lose control again. He'd explode into a rage and fail them all—Cam and Ellie, and Jane, and even Charlotte—just as he'd failed Colin.

"I suppose that answers the question of whether you think me a hero or a liar." He took care to appear indifferent, but suddenly he wanted more than

anything for her to say aloud he was no hero, because shouldn't someone—
even if it was her, or maybe *because* it was her—be able to see the truth?

Charlotte's gaze moved over his face as if she were searching for
something, but then she looked away. "I see you as a man. Nothing more,
and nothing less. I don't judge you against your heroic reputation, Captain."

He forced a laugh. "No? I hope you're not going to say you don't judge
me at all, for I find that difficult to believe."

For the briefest moment her eyes closed. His gut clenched with foreboding,
and he had to fight a childish urge to put his hands over his ears so he
wouldn't have to hear what she said next—

"I do judge you, Julian." Her voice was so soft it was more breath than
sound. "I judge you by the man you once were."

The breath rushed from his lungs. He tried to fill them again, but all
the oxygen had been sucked from the air around them. *The man you once
were.* So wistful, those words, as if he'd been so much more then, so much
better than whoever he was now—not the man who'd fallen in love with
Charlotte Sutherland, and not the hero London believed him to be.

"That man was easier to manipulate." His tone was bitter. "His naiveté
would be useful to you now, I'll grant you that."

She shook her head. "That man wasn't naïve. He was compassionate
and joyful and kind, with remarkable eyes, at once deep and dark and yet
filled with light, just like a sky full of stars."

He raised a hand to his chest as something shifted painfully beneath
his breastbone.

*Eyes like a sky full of stars.* An absurd, romantic fancy, nothing more.
But the break in her voice when she'd said it… It wasn't for herself.

It was for him, because all the wishing in the world wouldn't change
him back to who he'd once been.

*What did it matter? Starry eyes were blind. Useless.*

"Starry eyes or not, you'll have me on your heels until you agree to
leave London. But take heart, my lady. Perhaps it won't be as bad as you
fear. There was a time when you were happy enough to have my company."

Charlotte's dark eyes filled with sadness. "There was a time when your
company was worth the having, Captain."

He jerked back, but it was too late to escape a blow so powerful it left
him breathless, because he'd believed she didn't have the power to hurt him
anymore until it landed with a sickening thud in the middle of his chest.
He opened his mouth to rage at her, to hurt her in return, but strangely he
didn't have the words.

"Charlotte!" Amelia called out just then. "You must come and see this pelisse!"

Charlotte spurred her horse to catch up to her sister. Julian made no move to stop her, and in the next breath the moment was gone.

By the time he caught up to them they'd passed through the Grosvenor Gate and were riding south toward Rotten Row. Amelia was quizzing Charlotte about the fashions. "French gray silk, I think, with the buttons down the front and the lace and flounces?" Amelia gestured discreetly with her chin at a pair of ladies, both dressed in the height of fashion, who were strolling on a footpath toward the Serpentine.

Charlotte glanced in their direction. "Celestial blue, I believe. India muslin. Her bonnet is French straw trimmed with quilted net lace and an ostrich feather."

Amelia sighed with delight, but though Charlotte recited the details readily enough, she did it mechanically. Julian watched her as they continued to make their way along the bridle path toward the Serpentine. Her face was as composed as ever, so much so it would have been easy to overlook the lines of strain around her mouth and the way her shoulders sagged just slightly, as if a terrible weight were upon them.

His heart gave an odd lurch, and he urged his horse to come abreast of hers, though he had no idea what he'd say, or how he could put it right—

"Look, Uncle Julian. There's a grand pair of black Hessians, just there, on that tall man behind us. The one with the blue coat. Do tell us about his boots."

Julian couldn't help a half-hearted grin at Amelia's magnanimous tone. Clearly she'd braced herself for a lecture on gentlemen's footwear. But his smile faded as he turned to inspect the boots in question.

Black with a gold tassel, tight to the knee. Shined to a high gloss.

"Lady Hadley! How fortunate. I hoped to see you on the promenade this afternoon."

And perfectly fitted to Lord Devon's foot.

Charlotte's head snapped up at Devon's greeting. She straightened her shoulders and her face lit with a smile. "My lord, how glad I am to see you."

Julian scowled darkly at him, but Devon didn't seem to notice. He broke away from the two gentlemen he'd been riding with and brought his horse alongside Charlotte's. He removed his top hat with a flourish, then took her hand and brought it to his lips. "I thought I'd missed you. You're later than usual today."

*Later than usual?* Was Devon the reason Charlotte made such a point of riding every afternoon during the fashionable hour?

"I had callers who stayed past the usual hour. Amelia, do say hello to Lord Devon."

Devon turned to Amelia with a smile that brought a flush of pink to the girl's cheeks. "Miss West. I'm grateful not to have missed you this afternoon. Have you seen any fashions worth noting on your ride today?"

Julian ground his teeth until his jaws began to ache. *Damn it.* This wasn't Amelia's first meeting with the man either, then. It was quite the thing, it seemed, to promenade with Lord Devon.

Amelia giggled. "Oh, yes. The best so far is a French straw hat. Oh, and your boots, too, my lord. My uncle Julian is quite interested in boots, you know."

"Is he?" Lord Devon turned to Julian with a cool smile. "Captain West. I'd be happy to give you my bootmaker's name."

Julian's teeth were in danger of being pulverized into a powder in his mouth. "Hoby."

Devon studied his face for a moment; then a corner of his lip curled upward. "Just so." He didn't spare Julian a second glance, but turned back to Charlotte. "Now, Lady Hadley, these late callers of yours who were so rude as to keep you past the usual hour. Would they be anyone I know?"

Charlotte's eyes sparkled with humor. "Oh yes, my lord. I believe you do know them."

"Ah." Devon reined his horse in close to Charlotte's and led her back onto the narrow pathway, so Julian had no choice but to follow behind with Amelia.

*Perhaps a hard shove would send Devon tumbling off his horse.*

"The widows are storming London's drawing rooms now, are they?" Devon asked. "I suppose Lady Tallant was there to discuss her rout this evening."

"Yes, among other things," Charlotte murmured. She glanced sideways at Devon, as if she wished to say more but couldn't with Julian and Amelia so close.

But as close as he was, Julian may as well have been a thousand miles away for all the notice they took of him. Sweat gathered in his palms and under the tight knot of his cravat, and began to trickle down his back as the truth dawned on him.

This was no mere flirtation between Charlotte and Devon. The level of intimacy between them was far deeper than Julian—or Cam or Ellie—had suspected. Charlotte had taken Devon into her confidence, and from there it was only a matter of time before she took him into her bed.

Whatever Charlotte was hinting at, Devon understood it without further explanation. He glanced back at Julian, then leaned closer to her. "Is there some difficulty about your attending the rout?"

"No, it's only that—"

"Lady Hadley doesn't wish for my escort." Julian, who'd had quite enough of being ignored, interrupted her. "But her family does wish it, and I intend to accommodate them. Do you have some objection to that, Devon?"

Julian's voice was pleasant enough, but under his polite enquiry was an unmistakable note of challenge. Devon couldn't fail to hear it, but his only reaction was another amused curl of the corner of his lip.

Julian was starting to hate that lip.

"No objection at all, Captain. Naturally Lady Hadley should do as her family wishes. And when you arrive, my lady," he lifted Charlotte's hand to his lips again, "I'll be waiting for you."

Julian stiffened. With those few words Devon had delivered a message of his own, and it was as clear as if he'd spoken it aloud.

*She may begin her evening with you, but she'll end it with me.*

"Oh my goodness! Charlotte, look at that pelisse—pink silk taffeta with scalloped lace trim!" Amelia was staring at a blonde-haired lady riding by in a phaeton. "We must get a closer look."

Charlotte smiled. "Very well. Gentlemen, if you would excuse us?"

Devon laughed indulgently, as if he'd seen this all a dozen times before. "By all means. Never let it be said I stood in the way of pink silk taffeta with lace trim."

Amelia and Charlotte rode off in pursuit of the pelisse, leaving Julian and Devon to follow. By silent agreement they slowed their horses to a walk, both of them aware their discussion was far from over.

Julian spoke first. "Lady Hadley's family wants her out of London, Devon."

"Yes. I'm aware of that. Mr. Camden West—your cousin, I believe? Mr. West and Lady Hadley's brother, Robyn Sutherland, have made themselves quite clear on that point."

"Not clear enough, because here you are, still trying to get a hand under her skirts."

Devon made a disgusted noise. "How vulgar."

Julian chose to misunderstand him. "I agree. The decent thing to do would be to heed her family's wishes and stop giving Lady Hadley a reason to dally in London."

Devon laughed. "You think she remains in London only for me? I'm flattered."

Julian ignored this. "But then you're not a decent man, are you Devon?"

Julian sensed rather than saw Devon tense in the saddle, but the man's voice was as calm as ever. "Listening to the gossip? You disappoint me, Captain."

"Do I? I'm devastated to hear it."

"As to what's decent," Devon continued, as if Julian hadn't spoken, "it's a matter of opinion. Abandoning Lady Hadley to the tender but misguided mercies of her family hardly seems the decent thing to do."

"Misguided? Christ, you have a bloody nerve. Do you pretend to know better than her family what's best for her?"

"I don't *pretend* a thing, Captain. Her family cares for her. I don't dispute that, but none of you have the slightest inkling what to do for her."

Julian fought to keep calm. "And you do?"

"Let's just say I understand what it feels like to suffer as Lady Hadley suffers now." A mocking smile drifted across the perfect lips. "Her family's bumbling has only made matters worse, rather like a surgeon who treats the toothache with a bloodletting. Painful to witness."

"What do you mean, what she suffers? She appears perfectly content to me."

*As long as you didn't look too closely.*

For the first time Devon's cool composure slipped, and Julian got a glimpse of what lay underneath the almost unreal handsomeness of his face.

*It would be a drastic mistake to underestimate this man.*

Iris Somerset had called Devon an angel. It would be easy to see him as one—to be lulled into complacency by the golden hair and the perfectly sculpted cheekbones. But Devon's looks were misleading. The bright blue eyes, which appeared so languid at first glance, were quick and shrewd, and his dissolute manner masked a fierce intelligence.

"Jesus, West. You haven't the vaguest idea, do you? And her family assigned *you* the task of protecting her? What bloody fools."

Julian held on to his control by the merest thread, even as he pictured his fist closing around Devon's throat. "Nevertheless they *have* asked me, and I intend to fulfill my obligation. I'll escort her everywhere from now on, Devon. Not just tonight, but every night, so you may as well find some other widow to seduce, one who won't be so much trouble to bring to your bed."

Devon's lip curled again, but this time he wasn't amused. "Ah. You mean to say one widow is much like another, and I should simply exchange Lady Hadley for a similar one, as if she were a pair of Hoby boots? You insult her ladyship, Captain. There *is* no other woman like her, and you know it yourself, don't you?"

Devon waited for him to say something, but this time Julian had no ready reply.

*I knew it once, a lifetime ago.*

"Just as I thought." Devon kicked his horse into a trot, but he didn't get far before he slowed again and turned to look at Julian over his shoulder. "Oh, and West? You talk a great deal about what Lady Hadley's family wants, and about what you want, but none of you seem at all concerned with what *she* wants. Curious, that. Perhaps one of you should ask her."

With that, Devon wheeled his horse around and trotted over to join Charlotte and Amelia.

Julian watched him go. *Bloody hell. What had just happened?*

But he knew. He, Captain Julian West—the toast of London, the Waterloo hero, the man Charlotte's family had chosen to protect her fragile reputation—had just been soundly put in his place by a scandalous, licentious, ruinous earl, who, if rumor could be trusted, was also very probably a murderer.

# Chapter Twelve

It pleased Lady Tallant to call her evening party a rout, but Annabel wasn't a typical London hostess, and her routs weren't the predictable, mannerly affairs characteristic of respectable members of the *ton*. There would be cards—there were always cards—but no genteel conversation and no music, at least no music that could be heard above the din. There may or may not be a supper, but there would be enough champagne on offer to overflow the banks of the Thames. A drawing-room was not sufficiently large for such a riot of people, so guests were ushered into a ballroom ablaze with light, aside from a few corners and alcoves that would remain conveniently dim throughout the evening.

In truth, it wasn't so much a rout as a mêlée. A handy thing, a mêlée. Charlotte had two purposes tonight, and a mêlée would do well for both.

"Good God, what a tumult. I've seen calmer battlefields."

*Or not.* What good was a mêlée if one couldn't disappear into it? She glanced up into Julian's face, then down to his fingers wrapped firmly around her upper arm. She'd thought to shed him easily in this crush, but he hadn't taken his eyes or his hand off her since they'd set foot in Annabel's ballroom.

"I did warn you this wasn't your kind of party, Captain. It will only grow more debauched as the evening progresses. Perhaps you should leave now, before it deteriorates further."

As if to prove her point, Lord Ambrose sauntered by at that moment with a woman in a masque whose prominent décolletage proclaimed beyond a shadow of a doubt she was *not* Lady Ambrose.

Julian raised an eyebrow at them as they passed. "And miss all this? I think not. Unless you find yourself fatigued, Lady Hadley? If so, I'll happily escort you back to Grosvenor Square."

"That won't be necessary. I'm not at all fatigued—"

Then again, perhaps she was fatigued. So fatigued he should take her home at once. It would be a rather neat way to get rid of him. Then she could come back on her own and find Devon. "That is, I do have a bit of a headache. Perhaps you should take me back to Grosvenor Square."

"Grosvenor Square? Nonsense! We've only just found you." The widows came up behind them and Lissie linked her arm with Charlotte's. "Such a crush! Why do you invite so many people, Annabel? If I didn't know better I could swear I just saw Lord Ambrose pass by."

Annabel shrugged. "I don't invite them. They just come. But I did invite you, Charlotte, and you, Captain West, and I shall take it very ill indeed if you leave my party before you've even had a glass of champagne."

Aurelie snapped her fingers and a footman appeared out of nowhere, his silver tray rattling with full glasses of champagne. Lissie took one and drained it at once. "Thank goodness. I'm parched. How did you do that, Aurelie? I've been trying to secure a glass for an age."

Aurelie smiled. "I'm French. It's champagne. *C'est tout.*"

"Now we've had a glass together, I will ask Captain West to escort me home." Charlotte raised a feeble hand to her forehead. "Forgive me, Annabel, but I have a dreadful headache."

Aurelie patted her hand. "You only need more champagne, *ma chèrie*. It cures the headache, you see."

"The headache and whatever else ails you." Lissie snagged a second glass of champagne from the footman's tray. "After a few more glasses I won't even notice the pain in my toes, I'm sure."

"Have you a pain, darling?" Annabel asked.

"Yes. My slippers are too tight."

"My dear," Aurelie protested. "Champagne does not cure tight slippers."

"Indeed it does. Enough champagne, and one doesn't care anymore how much they pinch."

Annabel laughed and retrieved two more glasses from the footman. "Now, my dear Charlotte. Perhaps some quiet would help? I'm sure Captain West would be delighted to escort you to the library. You can have a brief rest, then return once your headache has passed. Here. Take some champagne with you."

Dispatched to the library with Julian and champagne? *How subtle.* For pity's sake, it was one thing for her friends to invite him tonight, but quite another to hold her neck between his jaws. She glared at them, but they only blinked innocently back at her.

"Oh, very well." Charlotte snatched the glass of champagne from Annabel. "Must you drag me along behind you like an animal with a carcass, Captain? Or am I permitted to take your arm?"

Lissie snickered. "Why, Charlotte, I do believe you're feeling better already."

*Wretched, wretched widows.*

Then again, the library wasn't far from the card room, and Devon had said he'd wait for her there. She only had to reach him, to tell him—

"Lady Hadley?" Julian loosened his grip on her elbow and held out his arm. "I await your pleasure."

"Indeed? I was under the impression my pleasure was the least of your concerns."

He drew her arm through his and wound his way through the crush of bodies. The noise of the crowd faded as they approached the private wing of the house, then vanished abruptly as he closed the library door behind them. "And I was under the impression your pleasure is your *only* concern, and so I need not consider it at all."

*Her pleasure.* It had been so long since she'd taken pleasure in anything she couldn't recall the last time…

A sudden, sharp pang in her chest brought her to a halt in the middle of the library.

*Dear God.*

The last time she'd felt real happiness had been with *him*—with Julian, before she discovered he'd lied to her, before he'd left London and her life had fallen apart. A year…no, longer than that. So much time, and she'd had to drag herself through every day of it, every moment, to force herself to endure it.

She gasped around the panic crowding into her throat. She couldn't keep on like this, couldn't keep struggling—

"You look pale, Lady Hadley. Perhaps you'd better take your friends' advice and lie down."

Charlotte sank onto the nearest settee before her knees could give out beneath her. "Just for a moment."

Julian cursed under his breath, strode over to the sideboard, and sloshed some amber liquid into a glass. "Here." He pressed the glass into her hand. "Drink this. It's more bracing than champagne."

"Thank you." Charlotte took the glass but avoided his gaze, focusing instead on the cold fireplace. If she looked at him now, he'd see the truth in her face, and God knew what he'd do then, how he'd use it against her—

"Devon will not give you up easily."

Charlotte gulped at her brandy, coughed. *He wanted to discuss Devon?*

"No. He won't. I suppose you asked him to?"

He sank down on the settee next to her. "No. I didn't ask. I demanded."

She smiled a little at that. Devon wasn't the type of man who responded well to demands.

"He's quite your champion," Julian went on. "He told me it was an insult to you to suggest he could simply find another widow to replace you; then he accused me of treating you like a pair of Hoby boots, or something equally foolish."

So Julian ordered Devon to quit her, and Devon refused. *Dear Devon.* If she hadn't had ample reason to trust him before, she did now.

Julian scowled at her. "He said you're irreplaceable. That there's no other woman like you."

Charlotte shrugged. She wasn't about to peel back the complicated layers of her relationship with Devon for Julian's inspection.

"Why?"

"Why?" Charlotte stared down into her glass. "Why what?"

Julian leaned forward, took her chin between his fingers, and turned her face to his. "Look at me. Why should he say that? He wants you as his lover, yes, but it's more than that. This isn't some casual flirtation between you. He *knows* you. He knows you well enough to want *you*. Not just anyone—not just any woman. You."

Charlotte stared at him, baffled. "Of course he *knows* me. Do you think I'd trust a man I didn't know, Captain? One who didn't know me?"

"How well does he know you?"

She jerked her chin from his grasp. "I don't—"

"Your marriage. Hadley's death. The difficulties with your family. The reason you won't leave London. Does he know I was your lover before you married Hadley? How much does he know?"

She took another sip of brandy. "More than anyone else does."

"Damn it. Can you explain to me why you'd tell Devon your secrets when you won't confide in your own sister? Your family?"

Because Ellie and Cam would try to fix it, to fix *her*, and she couldn't be fixed. Hadley was dead, and there was an end to it. No resolution—no way to mend it. It simply was. Devon knew it. He didn't try to resurrect the dead. He didn't pretend it was anything other than what it was.

*He didn't try to make her pretend.*

When she didn't answer, Julian shot to his feet to pace the carpet in front of her. "Well? Can you explain it?"

*Enough.* "I don't think, Captain," she said, biting off each word, "I owe you an explanation about anything."

Julian skidded to a halt in front of her, his hands clenched into fists. "You damn well owe somebody some bloody explanation. My God. Cam is at his wit's end and Ellie is nearly ill with worry over you, and you choose to share your secrets with *Devon?* To share your *body* with him? Devon, a scandalous rake, a man all of London believes to be a murderer—"

This time it was Charlotte's turn to leap to her feet. "Don't you *dare* repeat that vile rumor in my presence. Devon's no murderer." That he should be accused of hastening his brother's death even while all of London pitied her as a bereaved widow—the irony of it made her stomach heave with bitterness.

Julian closed in on her until the back of her knees touched the settee, and still he moved closer, so close she could feel the heat coming in waves off his body. "I see you're his champion, just as he is yours."

She raised her chin. "You sound surprised, Captain. I'm unfailingly loyal. Or don't you remember it that way?"

"Devon isn't a man you should trust. You're deceived in his character." His voice softened, and he brushed the backs of his knuckles over her cheekbone. "He's going to hurt you, Charlotte."

She shivered at the unexpected caress. "If he does, then so be it."

His dark eyes flashed. "You'll do nothing to save yourself? Nothing to prevent your own ruin?"

"It's too late, Captain." She tried to laugh, but the sound that escaped her lips was filled with sadness. "It's done. There's nothing left to ruin, and nothing left to save."

His body went rigid. "How can you say that?" His hand drifted from her cheek down her neck to her arm. His warm fingers closed around her wrist, and he pulled her against his chest. "Tell me what's wrong, Charlotte. You've trusted Devon with your secrets. Can't you trust me, as well?"

She tried to pull back, away from the seductive warmth of his body, but he wrapped his arm gently around her waist to still her. "Why should I? Because he's a scandalous rake, and you're a hero?"

He pressed his open mouth to her temple. "No. Because I can help you get what you need."

*How?* Beyond this day, this moment, she didn't know herself what she needed.

He couldn't help her, but even so she let her eyes drift closed. It had been so long since she'd been held in a man's arms, since she'd been touched at all. She'd been afraid to let anyone touch her, even Devon, lest she break apart.

Julian's mouth moved over her face, leaving a trail of damp, hot kisses—the corners of her lips, the vulnerable skin behind her ear, and the curve of her jaw. "Why won't you leave London, Charlotte? Do you stay for Devon, or is there something else that keeps you here?"

Charlotte's heart began to beat a wild tattoo against her ribs. Somehow, her hands landed on his chest, and she hooked her fingers into his waistcoat to steady herself. His lips were so soft against her skin. Had they always been this soft? "I have to stay here, because…"

*Because I can't be* there.

"Yes?" His lips brushed her neck. "Why do you have to stay here?"

Ah, she couldn't think with his mouth on her. The past came rushing back, memories of Julian whispering to her just like this, his lips so sweet, and his tongue painting pictures on her skin.

"Tell me how to help you, Charlotte," he murmured against her ear. His tongue darted out to taste her earlobe.

The whimper trapped in her lungs surged to her lips. Oh dear God, she wanted to tell him, to unburden herself, but she couldn't, could she? There was a reason not to trust him, but she couldn't quite remember….

"It's all right, sweet." His hand found the arch of her back and he urged her against him, so her legs were between his, his hips pressed tightly to hers. "I want to help you."

*No, he didn't…did he?*

His lips were hot, his hands like fire as he stroked her body. His mouth became more urgent, his teeth scraping gently against her throat. "Please let me help you, Charlotte."

*He wants to make me leave London.*

His other hand slid from her waist up her ribcage, palms hot and heavy against the deep blue silk of her gown. He stroked his fingertips under her breasts. "I can't help you until you tell me the truth, sweetheart."

*He wants to send me back to Bellwood, to Hampshire.*

A choked sob tore from her throat.

He touched his thumb to her lower lip. "Open your mouth for me, Charlotte." His lips hovered over hers. "Tell me."

*If I tell him, he'll leave me, and I'll be alone again, alone with the ghosts and the terrible, crushing guilt.*

She wrenched herself free from his arms and backed away from him.

He stood there, stunned, his arms still held out in front of him as if he didn't quite believe she was gone. "Charlotte." He dropped his arms to his sides and started toward her.

"No." She threw her hand up in front of her to keep him away and retreated another step, toward the closed door. "Don't touch me again. Don't come near me."

He didn't approach, but edged closer to the door. "I have to come near you eventually, sweetheart, to escort you back to the ballroom."

"I'll find my own way back."

He shook his head, his gaze never leaving her face. "No, I don't think you will. I don't think you know how to find your way back anymore."

His eyes were so dark, nearly black, and if for a fleeting moment she thought she saw a flicker of the old light there, it was nothing more than wishful thinking. "Even if I couldn't find my way out of this library, I wouldn't accept your help."

He was quiet for a moment, then "Why?"

"Why? Because instead of the ballroom I'd find myself back at Bellwood, or even worse, Hadley House. Do you think I don't know what you're doing, Captain? Such a novel idea, to try and seduce my secrets from me. Pity it didn't work."

His face closed, and his eyes went cold. "Forgive me, my lady." He swept her a mocking bow. "But it seemed to be working when you were whimpering and clutching at my waistcoat."

Fury and embarrassment made heat surge into Charlotte's cheeks. "A whimper, yes, but nary a secret."

His gaze swept over her, lingering at her mouth. "Not yet."

"Not yet? Not ever. You'll not wring another whimper from me."

"We'll see." He paused, his dark eyes burning. "You still want me. I could feel you tremble for me."

"Every debutante in London may sigh in vain over you, Captain, but I'm no innocent maiden. I know how to find my pleasures elsewhere."

His face went as hard as stone. "You want me, but you'll take Devon instead. Is that it?"

"I don't want *you*, Captain West. I want *Julian*, and he no longer exists."

She wasn't prepared for his reaction. He flinched as if she'd hit him, but then his face went so dark with pain she could no longer bear to look at him. She hastened to the door. If she could make it as far as the foyer she could lose him in the crowd—

"What's your hurry, my lady?" He came up behind her and pressed his warm body into hers, his hands flat against the door so his arms were on either side of her head. He buried his face in the loose curls that had escaped her chignon, and she felt his lips in her hair. "Off to find Devon even now?"

She would not whimper. She would *not*—

He nuzzled his face into the back of her neck and drew in a long, deep breath. "You smell of sweet lemons, just as I remember. I remember everything, Charlotte."

She fought the urge to lay her head back against his chest, to bare her neck to his mouth. "Release me, Captain."

A low groan rumbled in his chest, but after a long moment he backed away, and Charlotte pressed her hands flat against the door to steady herself.

His hand brushed her hip as he reached around her to open the door. "Shall we go find your friends?" He didn't wait for a response, but caught her hand and pulled it through his crooked arm.

Charlotte gritted her teeth as he led her toward the ballroom, away from the cardroom and back to the widows, who'd spend the rest of the evening seeing to it she never left Julian's side. She had to find a way—

"Oh, Lady Hadley! How lovely to see you!"

"Lady Avery." Charlotte disguised her impatience with a smile and a polite curtsey. Lady Avery was kind enough, but she was a dullard, and she never ceased talking—

*A dullard who never ceased talking. Of course.*

Charlotte sent up a quick prayer of thanks to whatever entity made Lady Avery cross her path just when she needed her most. "My lady, may I have the pleasure of introducing Captain West? Captain *Julian* West, that is, of the 10th Royal Hussars, lately back in London from serving with the Army of Occupation in Paris. Surely you've read about him?" Poor Lady Avery would need every detail available in order to connect the man in front of her to the stories of heroism in the newspapers.

"Captain West?" Lady Avery gave her a blank look. Charlotte held her breath as the woman's eyes slowly widened. "Oh, *that* Captain West! How wonderful!"

*God bless you, dear Lady Avery. You've done it.*

"Yes, indeed, the very one. My dear Lady Avery, I know what a patriot you are. You must have a thousand questions for Captain West, and he does so love to talk about his heroism on the battlefield!"

Julian gave her a fierce scowl as she withdrew her arm from his, but there was nothing he could do but make his bow to Lady Avery. "It's a pleasure to make your acquaintance, my lady—"

"Mrs. Barrington!" Lady Avery shrieked. She beckoned to a lady in an orange turban on the other side of the entryway. "Oh, Mrs. Barrington, do come and meet Captain West! Yes, of course you must bring Lady Euston with you!"

Julian tried to disguise his horror as two plain-faced matrons, one of them in a dreadful puce-colored gown hurried across the entryway toward them. Charlotte let out a low laugh. "Heroism truly is its own reward, Captain. Do enjoy the rest of your evening. I know I will."

He made a grab for her, but she skipped nimbly out of his reach. "You won't get away from me so easily," he muttered through gritted teeth.

"Don't be silly, Captain. I already have."

"Think carefully, Lady Hadley. I *will* find you, and when I do—"

Charlotte didn't bother to stay and hear the rest of his threat. She waved cheerfully at him, then turned and flew down the hallway like a bird who's unexpectedly found the door to its cage thrown wide open.

A few hurried steps brought her to the entrance of the cardroom. She craned her neck to scan the room, her heart pounding. Where was Devon? She wouldn't have a second chance to escape Julian.

*Ah, there.* As always, Devon was just where he'd promised he'd be. She breathed a sigh of relief as she watched the tall, golden-haired figure detach himself from a crowd of gentlemen hunched over a table scattered with discarded cards and piles of coins, and make his way across the room toward her, a lazy smile on his exquisite lips.

And just like that, she made up her mind. She would accept him.

She didn't love him. Her belly didn't leap with anticipation when she saw him. Her heart didn't pound with joy when he smiled at her, but he was her friend, and for all his wicked, scandalous ways, she cared for him. What's more, she trusted him.

A sad little smile twisted her lips. How ironic that she should feel safer with a scoundrel than with London's most celebrated hero.

"My lady." Devon took her hands in his. "You're smiling. Are you having a pleasant evening, then?"

Charlotte shook her head, but her smile widened. "No, not yet, but I have hopes I soon shall be. May I have a private word with you, my lord? I've something important to tell you."

Devon seemed to understand at once she'd come to a decision. He stiffened for a moment as he searched her face, but whatever he saw pleased him, for his blue eyes darkened and a sensual smile lifted one corner of his mouth. "Of course. Would you care to take a stroll in the garden?"

"I would, my lord." Charlotte laid a hand on his arm. "I would, indeed."

# Chapter Thirteen

"What have you done to Charlotte, Jules?"

Julian looked up from the sideboard to find Cam in the study doorway, his face grim.

"Done? Why, nothing you haven't asked me to do, cuz." He splashed a generous finger of whiskey into his glass and held it aloft in a mock salute. "To Lady Hadley's health. Care for a drink?"

"It's not yet noon. A bit early for whiskey, don't you think?"

"No." Julian tipped the glass to his lips and downed the contents in one swallow. "I don't. I need as much whiskey as I can get to survive Lady Chase's picnic this afternoon."

Cam raised an eyebrow and closed the study door behind him. "Is there any other reason you feel a need for whiskey with your breakfast? Guilty conscience, perhaps?"

"Ah. I see the problem." Drops of whiskey spilled onto Julian's wrist as he tilted his glass in the direction of the hallway. "Lady Hadley has arrived, and she's rushed upstairs to bend Ellie's ears with tales of my wickedness."

Except they weren't tales. Charlotte had no need for lies. The truth was wicked enough. Cam hadn't asked him to hound Charlotte's every step, or lie to her friends, or snatch her jewels in a gaming hell wager, and he'd damn well never asked Julian to hold her, to touch her and taste her…

*Her skin still makes my fingertips ache with want, and her sighs are still the sweetest sound I've ever heard.*

Julian sloshed another generous measure of liquor into his glass. More whiskey. Yes, that was a good idea.

Cam crossed the room, replaced the stopper in the whiskey decanter, and shoved it to the back of the sideboard. "No. She didn't mention you."

Julian snorted. "Not until you left the room."

"Amelia is with them now. Neither of them will say a word about you in front of her." Cam's eyes narrowed on Julian's face. "I can't tell whether you look relieved or disappointed to find you're not foremost in Charlotte's thoughts this morning."

"Indifferent."

*Furious.* He thought if he kept the taste of whiskey in his mouth, he could forget *her* taste, the way his tongue had traced her neck, seeking that tart sweetness, but no matter how much whiskey he poured down his throat, he couldn't drown her.

"That's a great deal of whiskey for a man's who's indifferent."

Julian shoved away from the sideboard and threw himself into his chair with a scowl. When had Cam become so bloody observant? "You accused me just now of—how did you put it? *Doing something to her.* Why should you think I did anything if Charlotte didn't say a word about me?"

"She didn't need to." Cam sank into his own chair opposite Julian's. "I could see something was wrong just by looking at her." He paused, his fingers in a steeple under his chin. "She looks drained, but she's strangely agitated at the same time. Ellie and I are concerned, so I repeat—what did you do to her?"

Not five seconds ago he'd wanted confirmation of her misery, but now that he had it, Julian's heart kicked against his ribs in protest. *Damn it.* He hadn't meant to touch her last night, but first Devon's name had dropped from her lips one too many times, and then...

*And then she'd made me feel.*

What had she meant when she said there was nothing left of her to ruin? Nothing left to save? It made sense to assume she was referring to her tarnished reputation, but something about her face when she'd said it...

It was more than that. Worse than that.

"Jules?"

Julian dragged his attention back to Cam. "What did I *do* to her? Jesus, Cam. You wanted her out of London. How exactly did you think it was going to happen? Did you suppose she'd simply skip off to Bellwood if I asked politely?"

"No, but we trusted you to make it happen without hurting her. We want to help her, Jules, not punish her." Cam ran a rough hand through his hair. "We thought you and Charlotte might... Well, it hardly matters now. This was a mistake."

Julian stared at his cousin. "You thought Charlotte and I might *what*, Cam?"

"It doesn't matter now—"

Julian slammed his glass down on the table. "You thought Charlotte and I would fall in love again and live happily ever after? Bloody hell, Cam. You're a bit old for fairy tales, aren't you? I told you. *I'm betrothed.* Or at least I was. By now Jane will have read the scandal sheets and decided to jilt me."

Cam flinched. "Has she said anything in her letters?"

"No, but it's only a matter of time. This business with Charlotte needs to end."

"I see that, but it needs to be done gently. Christ, if you knew what she's been through—"

"No!" Julian shot to his feet. "I told you, I don't want to know. It will make a mess of things."

It was too late, though, like slamming closed Pandora's Box after the demons had already escaped. He'd already begun dreaming of her, and last night when he touched her, kissed her, the memories came flooding back—the way her scent was more intense in the warm hollows of her body, the silk of her skin under his fingertips. She hadn't been the only one trembling with desire.

When he looked at her—at her red lips and dark eyes—that most primal part of him, that animal part of him, it...*wanted.* Her mouth open under his, her dark hair spilling over his hands. His body craved hers the way an addict's craved opium. Ignorant to logic or reason, it hungered for the very thing that would destroy it, and once the body became diseased, the mind would follow. If he let his desire for Charlotte poison his body again, all his plans—to wed Jane, to make amends to Colin—would disappear in a cloud of opium smoke.

Cam was staring at him. "I realize you and Charlotte have a complicated past, but my God, Julian, you're so cold. I hardly recognize you."

Julian looked away. No. Cam wouldn't recognize him, because he wasn't Julian, the man whose entire world had turned on one of Charlotte's smiles. He was Captain West now. Captain West, the man he'd become after Charlotte discarded him to marry Hadley. The man who'd held on to his limbs but left everything else behind on a muddy field in Belgium. The man who'd traded his humanity for his own private Pandora's Box, except the demons inside him were deeper, more sinister.

The man who'd left Colin to die alone on a battlefield.

*London's conquering hero.*

Cam rose to his feet. "You're still our best chance to get Charlotte to leave London, but I regret asking for your help, and I'll be relieved when this is done. I don't trust you anymore, Julian."

Julian sucked in a stunned breath. He and Cam had squabbled as children, and blacked each other's eyes as boys. They'd wrestled and argued, hurled insults and resorted to fisticuffs more times than Julian could count, but never once, in all that time, had his cousin ever said he didn't trust him.

His anguish must have shown on his face, because no sooner did the words leave Cam's mouth than he rushed to take them back. "I beg your pardon, Julian. I didn't mean—"

But he did mean it. He'd said it, he meant it, and it was too late now to pretend otherwise. "It's time to leave for Lady Chase's picnic. I'll wait for Lady Hadley in the carriage."

"Julian, wait—"

Julian closed the study door behind him.

* * * *

"But I don't understand. Didn't you already accept Lady Chase's invitation?"

Charlotte stared out Ellie's bedchamber window at the lawn stretched out below her, a lovely uniform green, velvety and lush, perfectly groomed. *Perfectly empty.* Had it been only last week she'd watched Amelia playing at bowls from this very window?

"I'm sorry, Charlotte. You'll have to give her our regrets. It's far too hot for me to be out in the sun all afternoon. Cam doesn't like it, and to be honest, dear, I don't feel up to it."

Well. There wasn't much she could say to that, was there? Charlotte braced her palms against the windowsill and touched her forehead to the glass. It was an unseasonably humid day, and it felt hot against her skin. "I don't like to go alone."

Ellie joined her at the window. "But you're not going alone. Julian will escort you."

*Julian.* Charlotte bit back a bitter laugh. The toast of London, and the only man in England who could save her from herself, or so the scandal sheets would have it. She'd managed to slip his grasp last night with Devon's help, but there would be no escape today.

Charlotte turned from the window to face her sister. "A picnic, of all things. Whatever possessed Lady Chase to have a picnic in London in the middle of July? Someone or other is sure to swoon in this heat."

Ellie gave her a hopeful look. "London will be intolerably hot for the rest of the summer, I imagine. Won't you come to Bellwood with us? You can send a note to Lady Chase excusing yourself from the picnic today so you can ready yourself to leave. I don't like you to be alone in London—"

"The carriage is ready, Lady Hadley." Ellie's lady's maid bustled into the room looking harried, and saved Charlotte from having to refuse her sister yet again. "Captain West is waiting for you in the drive."

"Thank you. Come now, Ellie. I won't have you worry about me." Charlotte gritted her teeth and forced herself to smile. "I'm hardly alone in London, after all. I daresay Captain West won't let me out of his sight."

Ellie looked anxious still, but rather than argue she gave Charlotte's arm a reassuring squeeze and turned to follow her maid out of the bedchamber. Charlotte trailed after them, down the stairs and into the entrance hall. The front door was open and Julian stood on the drive, waiting for her.

Ellie pressed her cool cheek against Charlotte's. "Promise me—" she began, but then she hesitated, and instead of finishing the sentence she simply wrapped her arms around Charlotte in a tight hug.

Charlotte's heart gave a miserable thump. Ellie didn't even bother to ask for promises anymore, for she knew Charlotte wouldn't make her one. *Couldn't make her one.*

"Your carriage awaits, Lady Hadley, as does Lady Chase."

Charlotte had to fight not to bury her face in her hands as sudden exhaustion overwhelmed her. Lady Chase's picnic was challenge enough, but an afternoon alone with Julian, with his hard eyes watching her every move… Dear God, she couldn't do it. Not now, when her chest ached with an inexplicable emptiness. By tonight she'd have gathered the pieces of herself and stitched them together again, and she'd be ready to laugh and dance and flirt like the wickedest of widows, but not today—

"You look as if you're about to beg off." Julian's voice was cold. "Are you ill, my lady, or does London no longer agree with you?"

Charlotte straightened her shoulders. *No.* She wouldn't give him the satisfaction of crying off. It was a picnic, for pity's sake. She only had to make it through the afternoon. She'd go, without her friends, without Devon, and with blasted Julian West as her escort, and she'd do it with dignity, even if it killed her.

"I have no intention of begging off, Captain. I'm ready to go when you are."

Neither of them seemed to have a word to say to each other once they were alone in the carriage. Charlotte settled back against the squabs, closed her eyes and tried to concentrate on shoring up what little energy she had for the afternoon ahead, but when they were halfway to Lady Chase's house, Julian broke the silence. "That was a neat trick you served me at Lady Tallant's rout last night."

Charlotte opened her eyes to find his gaze narrowed on her face, his expression grim. "What's the matter, Captain? Didn't you enjoy your conversation with Lady Euston and Mrs. Barrington? No? Well, think of it as another heroic service to England, then."

He stiffened as soon as the word *heroic* left her lips, and Charlotte felt a moment of uneasy triumph before she chastised herself for goading him. Whatever challenge she threw down he'd snatch up, and she didn't have the strength for a duel right now.

His lips curled in a humorless smile. "Tell me, Lady Hadley. How did Devon manage to hide you from me for the rest of the evening?"

She shrugged. "Even a condemned criminal occasionally slips the noose."

"Not without help, but then criminals are like rats—where there's one, there's a dozen. Still, you only needed the help of one criminal last night, and I presume you got it."

Despite her efforts to avoid another altercation with Julian, she could see he was already on the edge of furious. His body vibrated with anger. "You speak as if you truly believe you have a right to know about my affairs, Captain."

"I have every right. Your family has given me that right. Now answer me."

She held his gaze. If she answered him now it was as good as admitting she owed him an explanation, and once she'd given him one it wouldn't end there. In spite of her exhaustion, her chin rose in the air. "No. I don't think I will. I haven't given you any such right. I've told you before, Captain. I'm a widow, not a debutante still under my family's control. I'll do what I wish."

"Even if what you wish will be the ruin of you? My God, your heart must be encased in ice to scorn those who try to help you."

"Do you believe yourself to be among that number?" She dragged in a long, shaky breath, but her heart continued its furious thrashing inside her chest. "Ever the hero, aren't you? Had you been anyone else I might have believed you truly wanted to help me." She shook her head. "I can't understand how Ellie and Cam don't see it."

His eyes glittered, dark and dangerous in his pale face. "See what?"

"What a liar you are now." She spoke quietly, but her words seemed to echo around them. "Maybe I see it because I loved you once. Maybe that's the difference."

"Not enough. You didn't love me enough." Each word sounded hoarse, raw, as if he'd scraped them one by one from his throat.

The pain in his voice made hot tears press behind her eyes, but she blinked them back. "Oh, I did. I couldn't have loved you more, but now I think on it you lied to me then, too. Perhaps you haven't changed so much, after all. Perhaps you were always a liar."

His face went paler still, but he didn't say a word.

"I shouldn't have trusted you then. If I hadn't, maybe… But it's too late for regrets. I don't trust you now, and I won't ever trust you again. No matter how much you insist you want to help me, I will always know it's a lie. Hear me, Captain. I will not account to you or anyone else for my actions."

His voice was soft when it came at last. "I saw you slip into the dark garden with Devon last night, and you never came back the rest of the evening."

Charlotte only shrugged, but heat scalded her cheeks. "Well, what if I did? What of it?"

His eyes had gone black with some powerful emotion, but his voice was still a whisper as he leaned closer to her. "I don't know why I'm surprised at it. You have a history of similar behavior, don't you, Lady Hadley?"

Charlotte froze, her heart crashing in painful thumps against her ribs. When he said a history, surely he didn't mean…*their* history? "I— what do you mean?" Her voice sounded small in the sudden tense quiet of the carriage.

"I think you know." His eyes glittered strangely, and his black gaze never left her face. "At one time I was fortunate enough to be the recipient of your attentions in a dark garden. Ah, well. Perhaps it will work out better for Devon than it did for me. He *is* an earl, after all."

The fight drained out of Charlotte then, quickly, like blood pouring from a wound, and her body went limp against the carriage seat. She reached out to grasp the door, the edge of her seat, her shaking hand groping for purchase, for anything solid to stop the dizzying blur in front of her eyes, the roar inside her ears.

Their night in the garden—she'd fallen in love with Julian that night, and despite what they'd become, despite the anger and resentment between them, she'd cupped that memory in her palms, held on to the magic of that night as precious, as a moment she could look back upon as one thing, amidst all her mistakes, she'd done right.

Even after all that happened afterwards, she'd never regretted that night. *Until now.*

In a few cruel words he'd made it ugly, tawdry, reduced it to nothing more than a careless grope in a dark garden between two people who should have known better. For him, perhaps that was all it had been, or perhaps despite what it had once meant to him, that was all it was now. The present had a way of tarnishing the past, changing it, just as the past had a way of destroying the future.

"This ends here, Julian." Her voice was a whisper. "Whatever promise you've made my family, break it. Leave my friends alone. Leave me alone."

A long, fraught silence fell. "If I refuse? What then, Lady Hadley?"

"As of last night, you no longer have a choice."

He didn't ask her what she meant. He might have—he might have said any number of things, done any number of things, but perhaps he could see it was futile. He fell back against the squabs, and though he didn't speak a word he continued to watch her, his dark eyes filled with some emotion she hadn't seen in them before. Was it regret?

*You no longer have a choice.*

Had her words been for him, or for herself? She didn't know, but it made no difference. He didn't have a choice, and neither did she. Not anymore. Weeks ago Devon had made her an offer. Last night she'd made her choice, and that choice put her out of Julian's reach for good.

*Regret.* What a useless emotion. No matter how much one might wish to, one couldn't change the past.

Charlotte closed her eyes again.

One couldn't even change the present.

# Chapter Fourteen

Lady Chase's guests flitted around Julian in a confusing wash of colors and chatter while he remained frozen in their midst, the argument he'd had with Charlotte echoing over and over again in his head until his chest was so tight he could hardly draw a breath.

*Perhaps it will work out better for Devon than it did for me... Your heart must be encased in ice...*

Her face, when he'd said it. *Her eyes.*

He scanned the guests crowded onto Lady Chase's lawn, looking for the mauve colored gown Charlotte wore today. There, on the edge of the terrace, speaking with Iris Somerset. Charlotte was composed, smiling. He didn't see any trace of the ugly scene in the carriage on her face. Watching her now, he could almost believe it hadn't happened.

What else did she hide beneath her careful smiles? Her flirtations, her brittle laughter, and her callous disregard for her family—it all rang false now.

"Afternoon, West. Didn't expect to see you here today. Warm day for a picnic, what?"

Julian tore his attention away from Charlotte and turned toward the young gentleman at his elbow. Lord...lord... Ah, yes, he had it now. Lord Findlay. "Good afternoon, Findlay. Yes, it is rather warm."

A young lady with pale, fluffy blond hair stood next to Findlay, her face flushed with suppressed excitement. She nudged Findlay in the ribs. He looked down at her in surprise, as if he'd forgotten her, then sputtered into an introduction. "Right. Captain West, may I present my sister, Miss Lydia Fowler?"

*Fowler.* How appropriate. She looked like a baby chick struggling to burst from its shell. "Miss Fowler, it's a pleasure." Julian bowed over her hand.

"Oh, Captain West." The girl's face flushed a deeper pink; then she blurted, "Do tell me all about your heroics on the battlefield."

"For God's sake, Lydia," her brother muttered in disgust.

"What?" The girl blinked in confusion, her feathery blond lashes coming down over wide blue eyes. "What have I said?"

Julian forced a polite smile. "There's nothing to tell, Miss Fowler. I'm afraid the stories have been greatly exaggerated."

"Oh, but I'm sure that's not true, Captain, though your modesty does you credit." She clasped her hands together at her breast and gazed up at him expectantly.

"You flatter me, Miss Fowler, but I'm afraid I can't accommodate you."

"But—"

"He said there's nothing to tell, Lydia," her brother hissed. He took hold of her arm to drag her away, but before Julian could draw a relieved breath an excited screech stopped him.

"Lord Findlay! Oh, Lord Findlay!"

A rotund lady in a straw hat with an elaborate cascade of pink ribbons was bearing down on them. Three young ladies, each clad in varying shades of pink, followed in her wake, looking ready to trample into dust anyone who dared get between them and their quarry.

*Him.*

"Egads, West," Lord Findlay muttered with a sympathetic grimace. "Bad luck, that."

Exceedingly bad luck, or perhaps divine retribution. Julian straightened his shoulders and pasted a cordial smile to his lips. Either way, there was no escape.

"Lord Findlay." The lady came to a breathless stop beside them, her pink ribbons wildly askew from her trot across the lawn. "How do you do?"

Findlay had no choice but to introduce Julian. He bowed reluctantly. "Very well, my lady, thank you. Captain West, may I present Lady Wolverton and her daughters? This is Miss Wolverton, Miss Eunice, and Miss Dorothy."

The eldest, Miss Wolverton, pounced before her mother could even acknowledge the introduction. "Oh, Captain West! Is it all true, what I've heard about you? Did you really save your entire regiment from certain death?"

"Save my—no, Miss Wolverton, it would be quite an unlikely scenario indeed for one man to save an entire—"

"Of course it's true!" Miss Eunice looked offended for him. "It was in the papers, wasn't it? He shot Napoleon's horse right out from under him!"

Julian's mouth fell open. Was the girl simple? "No, I did not. No one did. As I was just saying to Miss Fowler, the stories have been exaggerated, even more so than I realized—"

"I'm sure that's not so, Captain West." Miss Wolverton fluttered her eyelashes at him. "Do tell us all about it!"

Julian stared at them. Good Lord, was he expected to trot out each moment of battle for a herd of mindless chits who looked as if they should still be in pinafores? Should he regale them with tales of soldiers with their limbs blown off, describe the smell of decaying flesh, or explain how quickly the soil could absorb rivers of blood? "There's nothing to tell."

"You're far too modest, Captain."

"Not at all. I'm sorry to disappoint you, Miss Wolverton, but it's the simple truth."

Her eyes widened at his surly tone, but then she turned and whispered audibly in her sister's ear, "Well, he's certainly as handsome as the paper claimed he was."

Miss Eunice gave a girlish giggle. "Yes, and that's more important than anything else, after all."

This was the limit for Lord Findlay, who'd been squirming with embarrassment since the conversation began. "It looks like they've just brought out more cold lemonade, ladies. Shall we go and see? You must all be parched." He didn't wait for an answer, but took his sister by the arm and offered the other to Lady Wolverton, who was more than ready to abandon testy Captain West for charming Lord Findlay.

Findlay nodded to him. "Good afternoon, West."

Julian bowed, then hastily retreated to a shady spot at the far corner of the lawn next to a bush abuzz with a swarm of fat, striped bees. Young ladies were frightened of bees, weren't they? Surely the bees would be enough to keep them away—

"Well, Captain West. We'll have you to thank for it if we get trampled in a stampede of silly chits, won't we?"

Julian started, then looked down to find Lady Chase at his elbow. He sighed. Apparently the bees had no effect on *old* ladies. "I beg your pardon?"

She eyed him for a moment, then shook her head in disgust. "It's to be false modesty, is it? Humph. I thought better of you than that. You know very well, I imagine, that all the young ladies here are angling for your attention."

Julian looked out across the lawn and barely restrained a grimace. Stampede, indeed. Even the bees weren't protection enough, for there was a staggering number of young ladies present today. He cleared his throat and changed the subject. "It's a lovely afternoon for a picnic."

Lady Chase snorted. "Nonsense. Dreadful idea, a picnic in this heat, but my granddaughters wanted it, and I am but a slave to their every ridiculous whim, Captain."

Julian raised an eyebrow at the idea of Lady Chase being a slave to anything, but he nodded politely. "You're very good to indulge them, my lady."

"Yes, well, I'm the indulgent sort, and since they're obliged to stay in town with me over the summer, a picnic seemed the least I could do for them. I'm as fair-minded as I am indulgent you see, Captain."

"I don't doubt it, Lady Chase." For God's sake, didn't anyone retire to the country anymore?

"I detest the country," she said, as if she'd read his mind. "I never go when I can help it. My granddaughters are silly enough girls, but even so I can't spare them, and so here we are, forced to picnic, and there's Lady Sutton looking as if she's about to fall into a swoon from the heat."

"I certainly hope not, my lady."

"Well, why ever not? Lady Sutton prides herself on her swoons. But I didn't come over here to talk about Lady Sutton."

Ah. So there *was* a point to this discussion. "No?"

She frowned at him. "Of course not. Why would I? No, I came because the scandal sheets have linked your name with Lady Hadley's, Captain."

Julian's back went rigid. The bloody scandal sheets again. "How curious. I can't imagine why they would."

"Can't you? I should think it was obvious. First the theater, and then some minor scandal at a gaming hell, wasn't it? Something about stolen jewels. Well, it's high time someone called you to account, so here I am. What are your intentions toward Lady Hadley, sir?"

"My intentions?" Julian choked back a sudden urge to laugh. Charlotte was a widow, and a sullied one at that. Could a man even *have* intentions toward a woman of her damaged reputation, aside from the obvious? "I'm afraid I don't understand you, my lady."

She huffed out a breath. "Well, for goodness' sake, why not? I understand you've a heroic turn. So, are you going to save Lady Hadley, or not?"

*Save her?* Christ, he'd rather be stung by bees or face a horde of stampeding chits than endure this line of questioning. "Save her from what?"

"Why, from herself, of course!"

He gaped at her. "I can't do that, Lady Chase."

The old lady scowled at him as if she'd like to sting him herself. "Well, what nonsense. You saved some soldiers in your regiment, didn't you? Why shouldn't you do the same for Lady Hadley?"

"I may have kept a man or two from being shot a second time or run through with a blade, but that's not at all the same thing."

And even if it was...

Julian searched for the mauve gown and saw Charlotte at the edge of the terrace, still engaged with Iris Somerset.

*This ends here, Julian. After today, you will not come near me again.*

"Men are useless creatures, Captain, but you're not quite as helpless in this as you'd have me believe."

"Hardly helpless, my lady. Please do feel free to call on my services if Lady Hadley should be threatened by mortar fire, though I confess I think it unlikely."

"You don't give the *ton* much credit, do you, Captain West? I assure you, they can do much more damage than mortar fire. Now, the gossip says you're the man to help Lady Hadley, and I wish you'd get on with it before she does something that can't be undone, like take up with that disreputable lord who follows her about. Lord Demon—I believe that's his name." She leaned closer and her voice dropped to a whisper. "They say he murdered his own brother to get the title and fortune, you know, and perhaps he did, because he inherited it all when his father died last year. Of course the brother died some time ago, and nothing ever came of the murder accusation, though if you ask me, he's guilty as sin."

Julian had nothing to say to that, and he was ready to put an end to this conversation. "Lady Hadley has made it clear she doesn't wish for my help, and even if she did, I wouldn't be at liberty to discuss the particulars with you, my lady."

Lady Chase dismissed this with a rap of her cane. "Certainly you would. She's my family, and I learned long ago not to turn my back on my family."

"Hardly family, is she? You've the merest thread of connection between you—"

"My two eldest granddaughters are married to her brothers, and all five of my granddaughters are excessively fond of her. That's more than a mere thread to me, Captain. Now then. Your intentions, you young rascal?"

Well. He'd gone from hero to rascal rather quickly, hadn't he? Instead of answering her, he posed a question of his own. "One might think you'd have turned your back on Lady Hadley by now, ma'am, given her reputation. That's not the case, then?"

"I don't approve of everything Lady Hadley does, Captain, but as you see, she's here as a guest in my home."

"Ah. Lady Hadley is fortunate to have so many champions."

"She has champions amongst her family, yes, but don't let the *ton* fool you, Captain. Any one of my guests here today would be delighted to indicate their disapproval by giving her the cut direct."

Ah. So the *ton* only waited for an opportunity. It was no secret they disapproved of Charlotte, but her family's wealth and social position afforded her a certain amount of protection from the more pointed sneers and cuts. But Cam and Ellie were out of the way today. If an opportunity arose to do so, Lady Chase's guests might well decide to deal Charlotte a set down, and if they did, well… Such a painfully public humiliation might be just the thing to persuade her to leave London behind at last.

Julian's chest squeezed at the thought of these people shaming Charlotte, but like a bee sting it would be quick—a moment of intense pain—and then it would be over. A sting wasn't fatal, after all.

But a drowning… That was something else.

Today in the carriage, not one hour after he'd sworn not to let his anger overcome him, he'd let it drag him down again, except this time he'd pulled Charlotte under with him, and he would have taken her down further still, until the breath left her lungs.

He'd wanted to hurt her, and he'd succeeded. He didn't trust himself not to do it again.

She must leave London at once. The further out of his reach she was, the better it was for both of them. Cam was right—he couldn't be trusted. He couldn't help her. Not without losing what little he had left of himself.

Julian's gaze roamed over the crowd. For the most part it was young ladies just out in society, each of them a more emphatic portrait of pastel-clad innocence than the last, along with a judicious selection of young gentlemen who were nosing among the prospects in the marriage mart. The rest of the party were the sharp-eyed chaperones of said young ladies, and the usual set of high-sticklers, who were no doubt friends of Lady Chase's.

Charlotte didn't exactly blend in. Aside from the Somerset girls, everyone kept well away from her. Even the gentlemen, many of whom sent her longing glances, declined to engage her in conversation. Her position in society was precarious, to say the least. Damn it, why hadn't Cam and the Sutherlands managed to put a stop to this sooner? It should never have come to this.

Julian turned his attention back to Lady Chase. "Her family tolerates her antics with a readiness that stuns me."

"*Antics?* Is that what you call them, Captain?" Lady Chase's eyes narrowed. "Antics are for children, sir, and I think we both know what Lady Hadley has been through is hardly child's play."

He didn't reply to that. He *didn't* know, and he didn't want to. He'd gone to great lengths *not* to know, and it was better for everyone if he remained ignorant.

But Lady Chase saw the truth in his face. She laid her hand on his arm as if she thought he'd try and flee. "Never say you don't know what happened to Hadley, Captain."

Julian tried to pull his arm out from under the old lady's claw-like fingers. "I do not, and I don't wish to, so if you please, my lady—"

She held him fast. "Hadley broke his neck not five months after they married. It happened on a hunt. He was showing off for his young bride, and miscalculated a jump."

*Damn it, he didn't want to know.*

"Lady Chase, I don't care to—"

"Lady Hadley doesn't talk about it, but I know from my granddaughters she was there when it happened. Saw the whole thing. Such a pity. Poor Hadley. God knows he was a fool, especially when it came to his wife, but he was a good enough sort."

Julian went still as an icy numbness started in his chest and spread, cold and liquid, into the pit of his stomach.

*Broke his neck not five months after they married…*

Charlotte was a bride, and then in the blink of an eye, she was a widow.

Lady Chase wasn't finished. "That was bad enough, but it wasn't the end of it."

He didn't want to ask, he didn't want to know, and yet he felt his mouth opening, heard the words emerge in a hoarse whisper. "Not the end of it?"

"No. After Hadley died there was some unpleasantness with the dowager marchioness. The poor old thing was practically on her deathbed when Hadley and Charlotte married, but unfortunately she outlived her son by several months. Such is the way of things, I suppose. As I said, Lady Hadley never speaks of it, but there are rumors—ugly ones. They say the dowager went quite mad with grief and blamed her daughter-in-law for Hadley's death."

*Did Charlotte blame herself?*

Julian instinctively reached for a denial, a way to make it not true. "But that doesn't make any sense."

"Grief rarely does, Captain. Charlotte stayed at Hadley House until the old woman finally passed away, though I imagine it was a dreadful ordeal for her."

Lady Chase eased her grip on his arm, and without realizing he did it Julian rubbed the heel of his hand against the center of his chest to ease the ache there.

"Charlotte was ill for some time afterwards—I'm not certain with what. She never told any of us, though likely it was nerves and pure exhaustion. She arrived in London in March, however, as beautiful as ever, and took up right away with those appalling widows and that scoundrel, Lord Demon."

Julian said nothing, but stood with Lady Chase at the edge of the lawn, the only sound the buzzing of the bees devouring their nectar, and watched as an endless parade of servants loaded silvers trays onto tables until the legs threatened to collapse under the weight. Liveried footmen appeared once the tables were laid to spread thick blankets here and there over the lawn.

Luncheon was served. The gentlemen moved in a rush toward the tables to prepare plates for the ladies, while the ladies picked their way daintily across the lawn, parasols shading their faces, and laid claim to the blankets.

"These are not quite the *antics* you anticipated, are they, Captain?"

Julian turned to find Lady Chase regarding him with a shrewd expression. "No. They aren't."

"Well, then?"

He drew in a long breath. "I can't save Lady Hadley from herself, Lady Chase. Only she can do that. Even if I wanted to help her, no one can save a person who doesn't wish to be saved."

"But she does wish it, Captain."

Julian looked away from the old woman's hopeful expression. "No, my lady. She doesn't."

She would argue with him now, or perhaps she'd simply shove him into the buzzing bush and leave him to the bees. Julian waited, but Lady Chase remained oddly silent. He glanced over to find her with her hand over her mouth, her face suddenly as white as the linen tablecloths. "Lady Chase? Are you ill?"

She pointed one shaking finger in the direction of the picnickers. "Oh my goodness. Where are my granddaughters? We're too far away to stop it…"

Julian turned back toward the terrace and saw at once what Lady Chase meant, though he doubted Charlotte herself would recognize her danger until it was too late.

Any number of things could have prevented it. If even one gentleman had claimed a blanket, or if any of the Somerset girls had been about, it would never have come to this. But the gentlemen were still at the tables filling their plates, and the Somerset girls were at the back of the terrace by the open French doors, trapped with Lady Wolverton, who was holding forth at length on some topic or other.

Charlotte hesitated at the edge of the terrace and gazed out at the crowd of young ladies scattered across the lawn. As she stood there alone, a plate clutched in her hand, the groups of young ladies drew into tight clusters on their blankets. Tight, and then tighter still...

And one by one, they turned their backs on her.

Miss Fowler, the Wolverton sisters—he could see them, smug and secure in their own places. Miss Fowler's hand covered her mouth, but even from this distance Julian could see she was laughing.

*Laughing.*

Miss Fowler, who'd never faced a greater challenge than choosing hat ribbons, she dared to laugh, to turn her back, to cut Charlotte. They all did, all these spoiled chits who'd never known a day of struggle in their lives.

What had Devon said about Charlotte? That there was no other woman like her. That she was irreplaceable. Now, as he watched her endure a public humiliation from a score of young women who hadn't half her courage, he understood this—*this* was what Devon meant.

Julian's heart shuddered in his chest as Charlotte's face grew paler and paler against the mauve silk of her dress until it simply...*folded.* There was no other word for it, for the way it fell in on itself and then tore at the creases, like a letter that's been worried over until at last it rips away at the seams. He wanted to look away, tried to look away, because to witness such despair was an obscene invasion of privacy.

But he didn't look away. He didn't think. He didn't reason. He didn't remember she'd told him to stay away from her, or recall any of the resolutions he'd made, or remind himself he'd half hoped this would happen. He didn't do any of those things.

He flew across the lawn, his long legs eating up the space between them, desperate to reach her.

# Chapter Fifteen

Charlotte stepped off the edge of Lady Chase's terrace into a nightmare. Her gaze darted back and forth across the lawn, but with every glance she sank deeper into the hellish dream. Rows of muslin-clad backs met her gaze, all of them stiff with outrage.

Somehow, she'd always known she'd end up here, and she wondered now, dimly, why she hadn't seen it would happen today. Perhaps because even in her darkest dreams, the dreams that woke her in the dead of night clammy with panic, she hadn't imagined it would happen this way. So publicly. So decisively.

But it had happened—no, it *was happening* even as she stood here, her heart shriveling in her chest.

*She had nowhere left to go.*

An anticipatory hush fell over the young ladies on the lawn as they waited to see what she'd do. Charlotte struggled to stay calm enough to think. She could turn and walk up the terrace steps and try to find Iris Somerset, but already her wrist felt ready to snap under the weight of the plate in her hand, and her knees shook under her skirts. What if her legs refused to hold her and she fell to her knees, her plate shattering on the stone terrace at her feet? It would make a terrible crash, and everyone would see, and they'd know...

She could keep moving forward onto the lawn, but what then? She'd reach the end soon enough, and short of fleeing into the gardens she'd be no better off than she was now. *No.* She wouldn't give them the satisfaction of seeing her run. No matter how much she bled inside, she'd never let them see it.

The lawn swam before her eyes, but Charlotte raised her chin and pulled her spine taut and straight.

*You've survived worse than this.*

She took a step forward, determined to put an end to the scene, but just then a high-pitched squeal broke the silence. Charlotte jerked her head in the direction from which it came, puzzled. A second squeal joined the first, sharp and malicious, and then she knew with a sickening certainty what it was. A feminine titter, still subdued, but spreading like wildfire from one blanket to the next.

Her knees began to buckle beneath her, but just when she was certain she must collapse, the plate she carried was lifted from her hand.

"Lady Hadley."

Long, warm fingers closed around her wrist and a strong forearm appeared under her fingertips. "I beg your pardon, my lady, for not being more attentive."

Charlotte looked up, dazed, to find Julian looking down at her with such an expression of grief in his dark eyes it made her breath seize in her lungs, and her own eyes fill with tears.

But if his eyes were soft with regret as they rested on her face, his mouth was pulled into such a hard, tight line his lips had gone white at the corners. She didn't know whether his fury was for her or for the ladies who scorned her, but she didn't care. All that mattered was he was here. She clutched at his arm until she was twisting the fabric of his coat between nerveless fingers. Her voice was faint. "I—that is, it's quite all right, Captain."

Without thinking, she laid her other hand over his. He went still and his gaze dropped to their joined hands, his expression unreadable. She snatched her hand away. "I would be grateful indeed if you would escort me to my carriage."

He drew her hand more firmly through his arm. "Of course."

She followed on wobbly legs as he led her toward the open doors at the top of the terrace steps. She stumbled a bit, and he steadied her against his arm as she regained her balance, but then he moved forward with quick, sure steps, as if he had every expectation the other guests would shift out of the way at once to accommodate them. He was correct. The guests lingering on the terrace took one look at his grim, set face and scrambled out of their way.

Iris Somerset and her sisters stood at the doorway, their faces pale with shock. Iris opened her mouth to speak, then closed it again as if she hadn't any idea what to say. A tense silence fell over the five of them and stretched until Charlotte thought her nerves would snap.

"Lady Sutton's swooned," Hyacinth Somerset offered suddenly. "She nearly landed face first in a large bowl of clotted cream. Her turban saved her. The weight of it threw her to the left."

Hyacinth flushed a little as they all turned to stare at her.

"Yes!" Violet grasped the thread of conversation. "She did, indeed. A shame, isn't it?"

Another silence, then Iris asked, "What's a shame? That she swooned? Lady Sutton always swoons."

Violet shook her head. "No, that she missed the bowl of clotted cream, of course."

There was another short silence, and then Julian let out a surprised laugh. "I can't think of a better use for clotted cream, myself."

Violet colored, but she gave him a sheepish grin. "Our grandmother did tell us it was too warm for a picnic. Perhaps we should have listened to her and spared poor Lady Sutton."

Hyacinth and Violet went on for a few moments longer about Lady Sutton, careful to keep their conversation light and amusing, but Charlotte could see they were appalled by their friends' behavior, especially Iris, who remained quiet until Charlotte and Julian were about to take their leave.

Iris slipped a hand into Charlotte's. "Such an unexpected blast of frigid air on a warm day. I beg your pardon, Charlotte. I never imagined my friends would—"

"Of course you didn't." Charlotte squeezed her fingers. "How could you? It's quite all right, Iris."

"No, it isn't." Iris looked as if she were torn between fury and tears. "Thank goodness for Captain West. It might have been much worse. How fortunate he was here to save you."

Charlotte's heart gave a strange, hopeful surge at Iris's words. Why had he done it? The question hardly had a chance to form in her mind before the answer was there, immediate and undeniable.

For her. *He'd done it for her.*

Not for Ellie, and not for Cam. Not because of a promise, or to get her to leave London, or for any other reason than one.

He'd done it because he couldn't bear to see her hurt. And dear God, it was so familiar somehow, the way he'd flown to her, as if the Julian she remembered, the Julian she'd loved, had emerged from the past and appeared at her side at the very moment she most needed him.

"Are you ready to leave, Lady Hadley?"

She swallowed down the ache in her throat and nodded. Iris came forward to kiss her cheek, followed by Hyacinth and Violet. "We'll call on you soon," Iris promised. "Good day, Captain West." All three girls curtsied to Julian, then turned their backs on the young ladies picnicking on their blankets, and wandered off instead toward the south lawn, where some of the other young people had gathered to play at bowls.

As soon as they gained the carriage Charlotte collapsed against the plush velvet seat. She stared down at her hands twisted together in her lap because she couldn't bring herself to look at Julian. What could she possibly say to him? She should thank him, of course, but simple gratitude felt rather like offering a plaster to someone with a gaping chest wound.

He'd appeared out of nowhere to tear her free from a nightmare that haunted her over and over again, waking and sleeping, as if he were some avenging angel fallen from the sky itself.

*An avenging angel, or a hero.*

How could she thank him for such a rescue? A cool nod and a few words of thanks were inadequate. No, worse than inadequate. Dismissive.

And yet wasn't a cool dismissal the safest course of action?

She couldn't forget what he'd done for her today, either the act or the look in his eyes when he'd taken her hand and placed it on his arm, but Julian wasn't her lover anymore. He wasn't even her friend, and she couldn't allow herself to be vulnerable to him. The past was the past, and while gratitude was one thing, trust was quite another. If she weakened toward him now she may well find herself back at Bellwood, or worse, Hadley House.

He could get her to do anything, to feel anything he wanted her to feel....

He'd made a promise to Cam and Ellie, and she'd made a promise to Devon. Nothing had changed.

Julian stretched his legs out in front of him and crossed them at the ankles, but he gazed at her with an intensity that belied his casual posture. "Are you all right, Charlotte?"

*Don't say my name. Don't be kind to me, because I can't bear it.*

She forced a laugh through stiff lips. "Of course. Why shouldn't I be?"

He stared at her for a moment, his face hard and tight. "Don't do that."

She pressed her back against the seat, but there was no escaping him in the close confines of the carriage, no escape from that gaze that seemed to see right through her fraudulent smile. "I don't know what you mean."

His dark eyes bored into her. "Don't pretend."

Charlotte made an effort not to flinch in the face of his hard stare. She forced a tinkling laugh through her lips and it rang through the carriage, loud and false. "Why should I pretend? If you think I care what they think of me—"

"I know you do."

"—a passel of cork-brained chits like that—"

"Stop it, Charlotte."

"...then you're very much mistaken—"

Without any warning his hand snaked out. His hard fingers wrapped around her wrist, and he pulled her from her bench onto his with such force she landed on top of him. Before she could think to scramble away, he wrapped his hands around her waist. "Do you think to lie to me? I saw your face when they all turned their backs on you. *Damn it, I saw you.*"

Oh, God, she couldn't be this close to him. Her heart gave a panicked thud at the sensation of his thighs under hers, his heat surrounding her. For one wild moment she started to reach up to brush away the silky hair that fell across his forehead, to cup his flushed cheek in her palm. Her gaze dropped involuntarily to his lips, and longing shot through her, so fierce it made her lower belly clench.

"Go on. Lie to me, Charlotte." His low voice rasped against her nerve endings, his ragged breath hot against her cheek. "Tell me you feel nothing. Tell me nothing matters to you."

Charlotte stared at him, half panicked, half mesmerized. It was beautiful and awful, the way he pierced through her every defense. The way he made her remember. But she couldn't afford those memories, and for all her promises to never lie again, she couldn't afford honesty. Not with him. She tried to pull her imperiousness around her again, tried to hide behind Lady Hadley's brittle mask, but the most she could manage was one word. "Don't."

"Don't what? Don't tell the truth? It's easier that way, isn't it, my lady? At first, anyway, until you can no longer tell the difference between the truth and a lie."

She forced a bitter laugh. "Do you think you know the difference?"

He ran a light, teasing finger down her cheek, but his voice was hard. "You're about to find out. Do it. Lie to me."

*No more lies.* She'd sworn it, and dear God, how easy it would be to trust him, to close her eyes, press her face into his chest, and drown in him. *So easy, and so dangerous.* "I feel nothing. Nothing matters. I don't think it ever will again."

"Never is a long time, my lady." He brushed his fingertips against her lower lip. "Can you feel this?"

She jerked her head back but his hand followed her. He touched her chin and turned her face up to his. "Ah, I think you do feel it. Tell me, how does it feel? My touch used to matter to you. Does it still?"

"No." But even as she denied it, her breathlessness gave her away.

His smiled mocked her. "I remember everything about you, Charlotte—the taste of your lips, the way your body feels when you writhe against me, but I don't remember you being such a liar."

She jerked her chin from his grasp. "You don't know anything about me anymore, Julian."

He laughed softly. "But I do. You might have left your black silk mask at the whorehouse, but you have another one—Lady Hadley, the grand marchioness who cares for nothing and no one, and you've been hiding behind it since you arrived in London."

Charlotte stared at him in horror.

"Cam and Ellie have been asking the wrong question all this time, haven't they, Charlotte? Instead of asking why you won't leave London, they should have wondered why they couldn't find even a trace of Charlotte Sutherland in the Marchioness of Hadley. They should have asked why they no longer recognize you."

*How did he see it, when no one else could?*

She pushed hard at his chest, desperate to squirm away from him, but he pulled her tighter against his body. "Do you know what happens when you hide? When you pretend you don't care for anything, and don't feel anything? When you act as if you're cold and selfish, as if nothing matters to you but your own pleasures? People believe it's the truth, and it makes it easier for them to hurt you."

She jerked her head from side to side, but she couldn't meet his eyes. "No, I never—"

"*Yes*, damn you. You did. You made it easy for *me* to hurt you."

She went still, her body going limp against him. She looked into his eyes, so dark and wild, so like she remembered them, and her words from earlier today came back to her.

*No matter how often you insist you want to help me, I will always know it's a lie.*

But she hadn't known, hadn't realized... She'd also know when it was the truth.

"I never wanted..." His hand shook as he hovered his fingertips over her face, tracing the line of her jaw without touching her skin. "I never wanted to hurt you, Charlotte."

Then his mouth was on hers, soft but insistent, his hot tongue teasing at her lips. Maybe he meant the kiss as a lesson, but to her it was a gift, one she'd received long ago, a gift she'd laid aside before she understood how precious it was.

Charlotte drew in a deep, slow breath and opened her lips under his. He surged inside with a low moan, his tongue tracing the inside of her mouth and licking delicately at her lower lip until she thought she'd fall to pieces in his arms.

He pulled away to hover his mouth over hers. "Does my kiss matter to you, Charlotte?" His voice was low in her ear, a whisper, and his warm breath tickled her cheek. He trailed his lips down to her jaw and over the soft skin of her neck, nipping at her.

Oh God, it did matter, it had never stopped, and yet she couldn't tell him so. She couldn't make any sound at all aside from a strangled whimper, but she knew as soon as it emerged from her throat, rough and needy, that it told him more than words ever could. She laid her palms against his cheeks to bring his mouth back to hers.

He groaned when her lips touched his. "Tell me. Tell me it matters."

She slid her hands into his hair, the waves so soft, so familiar against her fingertips. "It matters. It matters, Julian."

He raised his head to look into her eyes, and she only had time to trace a finger around his lips before his mouth was on hers again, sweet this time, coaxing hers apart so he could slip inside and drive her mad with each slick caress of his tongue against hers.

At last he tore his mouth away, but before she had time to sigh a protest he wrapped his hands around her back to arch her body into his. He bent his head to tease his tongue into the hollow at her throat, his mouth wide open and desperate against her flesh. "Lie back," he murmured, his voice hoarse, his breath heaving in and out of his chest. He eased her down so she half reclined against the seat. He pulled away from her, his eyes glittering. "Are you pretending now?"

She shook her head once. "No."

He looked down at her with half-closed eyes. "Don't ever pretend with me. Don't ever hide from me again. Promise it."

*Promise it.* Her last defense stripped away. If she made him a promise she'd keep it, and yet she didn't hesitate, but held out her arms to him—not to Captain West, but to Julian. "I—I promise."

He closed his eyes for a moment, his long lashes dark against his cheeks; then he slid his hands under her skirts. He opened his eyes so he could watch her face as hands moved up her stocking-clad legs until he reached the bow on her garter. He toyed with the ribbon, then slid his fingers behind her knees to stroke the pale skin there.

She sighed, but when her eyes began to drift closed, his fingers tightened on her. "I need you to look at me, Charlotte."

She opened her eyes and watched as he leaned forward and pressed his open mouth against the bare, hot skin of her thigh. "So sweet." He darted his tongue under the edge of her stocking, uttering a low, harsh growl of triumph when her back arched sharply at the caress. "Even sweeter than I remember."

Oh God, she remembered too, the feel of his hands feathering over her skin, touching her everywhere, his mouth devouring, ravenous. She cried out as he nipped lightly at her, her thighs parting as he worried her soft flesh with his teeth, then sucked the abraded skin into his mouth to soothe the bite.

"*Yes*. Open for me." His hands slid higher, higher, until his fingertips brushed the soft curls between her thighs. She threw her head back against the cushioned bench, another cry escaping her lips as he parted her folds and dragged one finger gently up her damp center, lingering to circle the tender bud that leapt to meet his touch.

He made a hoarse sound in his throat, part groan and part protest. "Don't look away." He took her chin between the fingers of one hand to hold her face still even as he worked her with the other, his skilled touch so perfect against her swollen flesh. "I need to see your face when I touch you."

His eyes met hers and held them as he probed delicately for her opening. She gasped as he slid one long finger inside her. "Do you feel me inside you, Charlotte?" The words rushed through his lips on a strangled breath. He dipped his head to kiss the insides of her knees, first one and then the other, but his dark gaze never left her face.

Her own voice emerged a choked whisper. "Yes."

He slid a second finger inside her and began to thrust gently, his thumb still circling lazily. "Will you come for me?"

Ah God, she would, she would do anything he asked of her. "Yes." Her hips rose in rhythm with his strokes, but her eyes never left his. "Please, Julian…"

A high flush of color stained his cheekbones and his chest heaved with his panting breaths. He released her chin to flick open the buttons on his falls. "Now, sweetheart. Let me see you…"

Charlotte arched against his hand as the ache between her legs began to pull tight, tighter, her lower belly clenching into that delicious tension, and oh, it had been so long since she'd been stroked this way, and yet the feeling was familiar still, and Julian too, above her, as if he'd never left her, as if no time had passed with so much despair between them, his dark eyes intense on her face and his whispered pleas in her ear to come, to take her pleasure—

A low, keening wail broke free from her lips as she shuddered into a devastating release, her body convulsing in waves around his fingers. He moved them inside her as she rode an endless climax, then slowed his thrusts as her taut spine went limp against the bench beneath her.

She lay for a long, quiet moment to catch her breath, but as the echo of her own impassioned cries faded she became aware of the growing silence between them and her face burned with sudden embarrassment. Oh God, she'd cried out for him, begged him, parted her thighs for him, and he...

She threw her arm over her eyes, but Julian leaned over her and moved it away. "No. Don't hide from me. Not now." His warm palm settled against her cheek, turned her face back to his. "What makes you hide?"

*Because if you see me, you'll know the truth about what I am.*

She wanted to bury her face in his neck, in his chest, to avoid those dark, knowing eyes. "I can't—I don't have any choice."

He cupped her face in his hands. "There's always a choice, Charlotte."

*Perhaps there was. Perhaps, after all, it had always been that simple.*

She drew his hand to her lips and pressed her open mouth to his palm.

He went still for a long time, but at last he straightened, smoothed the fabric of her skirts carefully back into place until not a glimpse of her skin was visible under the folds of mauve muslin, and moved away.

Charlotte dragged herself upright and leaned back against the carriage door. "Julian?"

He reached down and fastened his falls, then slid over to the other bench, but it wasn't enough, the space he forced between them, because she could still feel the imprint of his mouth on hers, his fingers against her skin, inside her. She pressed the back of her hand hard against her lips, surprised to find she was shaking.

He sucked in a deep breath and met her gaze. "It's been a long day." He reached up and rapped his fist against the roof of the carriage. "It's time I took you home."

# Chapter Sixteen

"Well, girls, I do hope you're satisfied. Nothing else would do but Lady Elliott's ball tonight, and now we're obliged to stand elbow to elbow with every scoundrel in London." Lady Chase's irritated flush had turned her cheeks the same dull red as her turban. "I can't think what's come over Lady Elliott, assembling such a debauched company. Why, just look! Naught but rogues and demi-reps, as far as the eye can see. Thank goodness Hyacinth was too ill to attend."

Charlotte followed Lady Chase's outraged glare to a particularly noisy swarm of said rogues, who were strutting about with puffed chests for the amusement of three demi-reps who stood in the center of the fracas, yawning delicately into their white gloves. She grinned as Lady Annabel looked over the shoulder of a dandy in a canary-colored coat, caught her eye, and winked.

Those ladies weren't demi-reps—that is, not strictly speaking. They were wicked widows.

*Rap!* Lady Chase's fan came down on her wrist. "What do you mean by grinning at them like that, Lady Hadley? Why, you'll encourage them to come speak to us!"

"Would that be so terrible?" Iris turned pleading eyes on Lady Chase. "They're so elegant. May Charlotte not introduce us?"

"Certainly not! If I'd known Lady Elliott would invite such low company, I would never have permitted you to set foot through the door." Lady Chase pointed one gnarled, shaking finger at the wicked widows. "Those three are bad enough, but wherever they go that Lord Demon follows."

"Who's Lord Demon?" Violet's brow furrowed. "I've never heard of him. What an unfortunate name."

"Ah, I believe you mean Lord Devon." Charlotte smiled at Violet behind Lady Chase's back. "Isn't that right, my lady?"

Lady Chase pursed her lips. "Demon, Devon. What's the difference? I won't introduce the likes of him to my granddaughters any more than I'd let a fox into a henhouse filled to the rafters with remarkably foolish hens."

"Oh, Lord *Devon*! Of course." Violet turned wide, innocent blue eyes on her elder sister. "Iris thinks he's terribly handsome, don't you, Iris?"

"Don't be ridiculous." Iris flapped her fan over suddenly pink cheeks. "I never said any such thing about Lord Demon—that is, Lord Devon."

"Never mind that, girls," Lady Chase snapped. "Now, Lady Hadley, I'll have your word, if you please, that we won't be overrun with demi-reps and demonic lords tonight."

"Of course, my lady. You needn't worry." *About the demi-reps, anyway.* The widows would no doubt be more entertaining company than an irascible old lady and three chaste debutantes, but for the first time in months Charlotte wasn't interested in a scandalous romp. She'd declined Annabel's offer of a place in her carriage this evening and accepted a place with Lady Chase instead.

The demonic lord, however, was another matter. She must see Devon tonight—at once, before she changed her mind again.

Devon, then Julian.

A tiny bubble of emotion rose in her breast, buoyant, familiar even, though as yet still just an echo of another, sweeter emotion, one she'd believed gone forever.

She thought it must be...hope.

She hadn't gone into the house after Julian dropped her at Grosvenor Square this afternoon. She'd slipped into the garden instead, anxious to avoid Sarah's penetrating gaze until she could piece together some explanation for what had happened with Julian in that carriage.

Those chits, at Lady Chase's picnic today... When they'd cut her, she'd been on the edge of collapse. Not from shame—the *ton* had done their best to shame her since she arrived in London, but she wasn't ashamed of doing what she needed to do to survive.

*From fear.* Fear they'd all see the scars and the ugliness hidden under the Marchioness of Hadley's glittering mask. Fear they'd see her for who she truly was—a woman who's coldness had driven her husband to his death.

The nightmare, where she had no place left to hide, no place left to go became frighteningly real today. But she couldn't hide forever. There weren't enough whorehouses in all of London to hide her from herself.

And Julian...

*I saw your face when they all turned their backs on you. Damn it, I saw you.*

How had he known? How could he have found her shivering with fear under her mask when she wanted so desperately to hide, even from herself?

He'd been so tender with her today, so passionate. Even now her heart ached to think of how he'd clasped her face in his hands, his eyes dark and soft, just as she remembered them. With one touch he'd made her believe hiding might be, after all, so much harder than simply being found.

She'd wanted to give him everything then, but when she'd taken his hand and brought it to her lips… He'd looked so strange. He'd drawn away from her, and she didn't know why, or how to close the distance between them. Even now she couldn't puzzle out what had happened in that moment.

Only Julian knew.

But as she sat in the quiet garden with the sun warm on her face, growing drunk and sleepy on the heavy, sweet scent of roses, the truth drifted over her, no less certain for all that it came softly, as if on the wings of the butterflies sipping nectar from the blooming carpet of sweet alyssum at her feet.

*It didn't matter why.*

It mattered only that he'd saved her today. Not just from Miss Fowler and Miss Wolverton and that passel of spiteful chits determined to deal her a set down, but from someone far more insidious, far more dangerous—someone she'd despaired of ever escaping.

*Herself.*

For months Ellie and Cam had tried to help her. Her mother, her brothers, Lily, and Delia—they'd all begged her to come to Bellwood, promised to look after her, to take care of her, but it was only Julian who'd *seen* her, into her and through her. It was Julian who'd torn the mask free at last. Julian, the only man who'd ever held her heart in his hands.

Her breath caught on a sob too deep to make a sound.

His hands, his mouth on her skin, his whispered pleas to look at him, to feel him, to never hide again—he'd worked the truth out of her with his touch, and it would no more go back inside her than a bird will return to the solitary prison of its cage once it's spread its wings in the open sky. She couldn't pretend anymore.

Tonight she'd find Julian and tell him she would accompany her family to Bellwood tomorrow, even as her heart throbbed with dread at the idea of giving up London's vices and distractions. Bellwood was so quiet and still, just like Hadley House.

She drew a deep breath and forced her skipping heart to calm. She'd already sent a note to Ellie to expect her tomorrow morning, and Sarah was in Grosvenor Square at this moment, packing her things. She *would* go. She wouldn't disappoint her sister now, and God knew it was time—

"Oh, dear." Violet drew close to mutter in Charlotte's ear. "I'm afraid your demonic lord is headed this way, Charlotte."

"Is he?" Iris rose to her tiptoes to see over the bobbing heads of the crowd. "Yes, just there! My goodness. He's not a gentleman one overlooks in a crowd, is he?"

"He's not a gentleman at all." Violet looked from Devon to Charlotte and bit her lip. "And you needn't sound so pleased to see him coming, Iris. Grandmamma is going to have an apoplexy. You'd better go and meet him, Charlotte, before you're forced to introduce him to us."

"Yes, perhaps that would be best." Charlotte gathered her skirts in her hand, but before she could stir a step, Iris's fingers clamped down on her arm like a vise.

"Nonsense, Violet. How rude you are. He can't be as wicked as everyone says he is." Iris raised an eyebrow at Charlotte. "Can he?"

Violet snorted. "I think you hope he's every bit as wicked as they say, and worse too."

Charlotte studied Iris's flushed cheeks and bright eyes and hid a smile. More than one innocent debutante had fallen victim to the heady combination of Devon's angelic looks and sinful reputation. "I don't believe a word of the gossip about him, if that's what you're asking. He's never been anything but kind to me."

Iris couldn't quite suppress a yearning sigh as they watched Devon approach, and Charlotte could hardly blame her. His severe black evening coat complimented his golden good looks, and his tight black breeches emphasized his long, muscular legs. He caught sight of Charlotte's gaze on him and a surprisingly boyish, lopsided smile lit his face.

This time even Violet sighed. "Oh, my."

Charlotte smiled back at him, but her heart gave a sharp, regretful tug in her chest. He'd been a true friend to her, and now she'd repay his loyalty by hurting him.

Violet and Iris stared at him with wide eyes, and Lady Chase began to sputter with rage as soon as she caught sight of him, but Devon didn't notice. He joined them and took Charlotte's hands in his. "Lady Hadley. I've found you at last. As always, you look lovely this evening."

"Lady Hadley!" Lady Chase hissed. "You gave me your word!"

Charlotte gave her an apologetic grimace. She could hardly refuse to introduce Devon *now*. "Yes, ah, that is—Lady Chase, may I present Lord Devon?"

"Lady Chase." Devon sketched an elegant bow. "It's a pleasure to meet you, madam. I know you by reputation, of course."

Lady Chase fixed him with a freezing glare. "I know the same of you, sir, I'm sorry to say, and you look even more devious than I was led to believe. Well, you may look elsewhere for your hens tonight."

Devon let out a startled laugh. "I beg your pardon?"

Charlotte jumped into the fray before Lady Chase could make the situation worse with a reply. "Miss Somerset and Miss Violet, my lord."

"My lord." Iris dipped into an eager curtsey.

"Miss Somerset." He raised her hand to his lips, then turned and bowed to Violet. "And Miss Violet. A pleasure. Now, Lady Hadley. May I take you for a stroll in the garden?"

Charlotte smiled and placed her hand into his gloved palm. "Yes, please. It's quite warm in here, is it not?"

"Exceedingly." Iris fanned herself with vigorous strokes, her feverish gaze on Devon.

Violet tittered, Iris glared at her, and Lady Chase's face flushed ominously at the idea of Charlotte walking alone in a dark garden with a notorious rogue. Charlotte, who knew an impending explosion when she saw one, began to hurry Devon away. "I'll find you again before supper, my lady."

"See that you do, Lady Hadley. And you, sir," she barked at Devon. "Take care you keep in mind what I said about the hens!"

"Hens?" Devon looked down at Charlotte, a smile tugging at his lips. "Good God. Who is that poor, mad old creature?"

Charlotte returned his grin. "Family. Her two eldest granddaughters are married to my brothers. Despite appearances tonight, she's actually quite sane."

"Really, my lady, you do have a most unfortunate family."

She let him lead her through the open French doors and out onto the terrace. She lifted her face and let the cool breeze waft over her heated cheeks. "Beautiful night."

Devon didn't take his eyes off her. "Yes. Beautiful, indeed."

Charlotte's breath hitched in her throat. Months ago he'd asked her a question, and finally, last night, she'd told him yes. Now, only one night later, she was going to take her answer back. Devon would never hurt her, she knew that, but he wasn't the kind of man one trifled with, just the same. If she meant to disappoint him, she'd best do it at once. "I can smell the roses from here." She took his arm. "Shall we walk?"

Blue heat flared in his eyes. "Are you certain you wish to stroll through a dark garden with me, my lady? I'm not quite as debauched as the *ton* likes to believe. I'm capable of waiting, as long as I'm not...unduly tempted."

Charlotte offered him a wan smile. "I only want to speak to you. Privately."

"Ah, well. That sounds far less intriguing than what I had in mind." He smiled, but Charlotte saw the sudden uncertainty in his eyes. "I'm at your service, my lady."

He let her lead him down the terrace steps and onto a dim pathway that led to the outer edge of the garden, away from the small knot of guests gathered around the fountain where the pathways converged at the center. Neither of them spoke. The only sound was the muted crunch of Devon's footsteps on the gravel pathway and the faint rustle of Charlotte's silk skirts in the breeze. As they ventured farther into the garden the light from the terrace faded, until only the starlight illuminated the pathway at their feet.

Charlotte tilted her chin to look into the dark night sky. Gardens, dark nights filled with stars—the most poignant moments of her life had taken place in gardens just like this one. That night with Julian—oh, it felt like a lifetime ago she'd lured him into a midnight garden and let him kiss her under the spreading branches of an ancient oak tree. The moment his lips touched hers, she'd known she'd never be the same again—

"You've changed your mind." There was no accusation in Devon's voice, no fury, but no question, either.

Charlotte closed her eyes. She'd accepted Hadley's proposal in her mother's garden, and Devon's last night in Annabel's garden, the scent of flowers heavy in the air, and she'd been so sure, when his mouth closed over hers, so sure...

But she'd been another person then. A person who pretended, a person who hid from herself. She drew a long, deep breath into her lungs. "Yes."

His fingers flexed around hers for a brief moment; then he nodded. "I thought you might."

He hadn't been as sure as she'd been. The thought made her heart clench in her chest, because wasn't this more proof of how well he knew her? Even better than she knew herself.

*Damn it.* A tear gathered in the corner of her eye and spilled onto her cheek, but she ignored it and continued to stare into the night sky. *Damn it*, it wasn't fair—to Devon or to her, because it would be so much easier if she could simply love Devon. So much easier than it was to love Julian.

Devon stepped toward her and brushed the tear from her cheek. "Look at me." He took her gently by the shoulders and turned her to face him. "You don't have to love me, Charlotte. We're friends, and we understand each other. We could have a good marriage, even without love, and perhaps in time—"

"No. I told myself that once before, Devon, when I married Hadley. You can't imagine how much it hurts—" Her words were swallowed by a choking gasp.

*To wish you could love someone, and to see how much it hurts them when you can't.*

This time the tears came too quickly for Devon to wipe them away.

But he tried. "Don't cry." His hands were gentle against her cheeks as he caught her tears on his fingertips. "Hush." He cradled the back of her head and eased her forward so her face was buried against his chest, and he smelled so good, of brandy and something clean, earthy, like a cedar wood after a new snow fall, before any footprints marred the pure white.

*So good, but so wrong.*

"I'm your friend, Charlotte, and I care for you." He drew back and tipped her chin up so he could look into her face. "No matter what happens. You know that, don't you?"

She gripped his upper arms, her fingers digging into the fine cloth of his coat. "I do know it. I can't imagine how I could have gotten through these months without you, Devon. You're my friend too, and you're very dear to me."

He was silent for a moment. "But it's not enough, is it? For either of us."

She held his gaze and slowly shook her head. "No. And you can't imagine how much I wish it was." Even now she wanted nothing more than to lay her head back against his broad chest and let him soothe the terrible ache in her heart.

He smiled, but even with only the starlight to illuminate his face she could see it cost him an effort. He gazed down at her for a moment, then took her face in his hands and leaned forward to press a sweet, chaste kiss to her forehead. "I wish it, too."

She covered his hands with hers and squeezed. If only—

"Well, Lady Hadley." A voice shattered the quiet around them. "You do know how to take advantage of a dark garden, don't you?"

Charlotte leapt away from Devon's embrace as if a whip had cracked between them. Devon let her go, but he stepped in front of her. "Good evening, Captain West."

Julian noticed Devon's protective instinct and his mouth twisted. "Good? For you, perhaps. Not so much for me, but then I've already had my moment with Lady Hadley in the garden. I took better advantage of it than you have, Devon."

Charlotte's mouth filled with bile at the hateful words. "That's enough, Julian."

His eyes were black, glittering with anger and pain. Charlotte's heart plummeted into her stomach and froze there, hard and cold as a stone, trapped and throbbing feebly. When would she learn? A woman like her didn't deserve a hero. She didn't deserve to be saved. That awful scene in Lady Chase's garden this afternoon—that wasn't her punishment.

*This was.*

Devon growled low in his throat and took a menacing step toward Julian, but Charlotte had just enough presence of mind left to catch Devon's arm to stop him. Julian's gaze darted to the place where her hand touched Devon; then he raised his gaze to hers.

Charlotte shivered as a cold smile drifted across his lips, then vanished. "Enough? Oh, no—I don't think so, my lady. We've just begun."

# Chapter Seventeen

*We've just begun.* A painful laugh tore from Julian's throat and fell into the sudden silence of the garden, echoing in his head in a dull, mocking roar.

Christ, what a fool he was.

He'd thought of nothing but Charlotte all afternoon, of her face when she told him his kiss mattered to her, of the way she'd opened so sweetly to his touch, her sighs when she came for him. He'd wanted her more than he wanted his next breath—had been on the verge of taking her—but then she'd dropped that sweet kiss into his palm, and it brought him back to a night a lifetime ago, a night under a sky heavy with stars and promise.

When he made love to her again, it would be as it had been that night, not with her sprawled across a bench in a carriage with her skirts around her ears, and not while he was betrothed to someone else.

But he'd been wild to see her tonight, his fingers aching to touch her again, even if it was just her gloved hand against his lips, or his palm at her waist as they whirled together in a waltz. To see her would be enough, to see her face as it had been in the carriage today.

Not her mask, but her *face.*

*We've just begun.* Dear God, how naïve it sounded. He should know by now there was no such thing as a beginning that didn't dissolve at once into an ending, like a fire that fizzles into acrid smoke when it's doused with water. He'd walked into the ballroom tonight full of a boy's illusions, but now his fantasies vanished into the night sky, leaving him empty and alone.

This was no beginning. It was an ending, and he would finish it.

*Now. Tonight.*

"Go back to the ballroom, West." Devon spoke calmly, but he looked ready to pounce if Julian so much as twitched an eyebrow. "Before you say something you'll regret."

*Regret?* An incredulous laugh burst from Julian's lips. It was far too late for that warning. Everything in him already ached with regret. He regretted he'd ever let Cam talk him into this. He regretted that night in the brothel when he'd loosened Charlotte's gown, unfastened every button all the way down to that sweet spot at the arch of her back. He regretted touching her this afternoon, her folds hot and wet on his fingers, her cries in his ears. He regretted that nothing else seemed to matter as much as her scent, her taste, and he regretted that even now, with her face flushed with Devon's kisses, she could still be so perfect to him.

He regretted that he dreamed of her.

But his deepest regret, the one that made him want to sink to his knees here in the garden, was that he'd believed, even for a single moment, he could be the man he'd once been.

He'd been so dazzled by Charlotte's courage today. She'd risked everything to tell the truth, and for the first time since he'd returned to London hope had swelled inside him, because if she could find herself again, then surely he could find Julian, hidden deep underneath all the scars, even if it meant he had to dig in with his fingernails and rip them off.

But nothing had changed. She was the same woman she'd ever been, and he'd never be anyone other than Captain West, a man of no tenderness or compassion, a man with nothing left except anger and bitterness pressing like a knife edge at his throat. Even now he could feel the blade pierce his skin, and once his neck was open there would be no way to stop the thick, black fury from gushing out.

"Don't be a fool, West."

*Too late for that, too.* Lord Devon was full of useless advice tonight. "I'm touched by your concern, my lord. I do indeed have quite a bit to say, but not to you. It looks as though your business here is finished." Julian flicked an icy glance over Charlotte. "Why don't you go back to the ballroom and join that crowd of dandies dangling after the wicked widows? Lady Hadley and I have a private matter to discuss."

Devon's lip curled with disgust. "You still don't understand, do you, West? Even after watching her every move for the past week, you still don't know a thing about her."

"Oh, I think I know more about her than you do. After all, she's still wearing her gown. I believe I got her down to her chemise during our garden interlude—"

"Stop it, Julian." Charlotte's voice was shaking.

He heard the tremor and he wanted to stop, God, he wanted to, but the knife was sharp at his throat, and he was helpless to staunch the words rushing from his lips. "Stop what, sweetheart? Stop treating you like what you are? I give you credit, my lord. You had the right idea with that brothel wager."

Devon tore free of Charlotte's grasp and charged at Julian, an outraged snarl on his lips. "Name your weapon and your second—"

"No!" The color leached from Charlotte's face so quickly Julian thought she might swoon, but even so he had to stop himself from leaping for Devon's throat when the man wrapped his arm around her waist to steady her.

"Lady Hadley," Devon said. "Please go and find Lady Tallant in the ballroom. She'll take you home—"

"No." Charlotte pushed herself upright, out of Devon's embrace. "No, I won't leave the two of you out here alone. Please, Devon—"

Julian laughed. "She begs so prettily, doesn't she?"

Devon threw him a savage look. "I warn you, West—"

"It's all right, Devon," Charlotte said. "Go back inside."

"No." Devon's hands curled as if he had Julian's throat between his fingers. "Absolutely not."

"He won't hurt me."

"For God's sake. Of course I won't." But he'd damn well say whatever he had to say to see her in a carriage on her way to Bellwood tomorrow, out of London and out of his life for good. "What kind of hero lays his hands upon a lady?"

Devon reached him in two strides. "What kind of hero insinuates a lady is a whore?" he spat through gritted teeth. "*Hero.* Bloody hell, West. You're an even bigger fool than I took you for."

"You heard the lady, Devon. Leave us."

Devon made no move to leave, but continued to stare at Julian, his face flushed with fury. The two of them stood there, each silently measuring the other until Charlotte came forward and laid a hand on Devon's arm. "Please, Devon. Wait for me on the terrace."

Devon's face softened as he turned to her. "You don't have to do this. You don't owe him an explanation. You don't owe him anything."

Julian shrugged. "You're right about one thing, at least. I don't need any explanation. I know all about Lady Hadley's garden seductions."

"Of course you do, because you know all about everything, don't you, West?" Devon sneered. "A brilliant hero like yourself needn't bother with a paltry detail like the truth."

A shiver of uncertainty drifted up Julian's spine, but he smothered it before it could grow into doubt. If he couldn't quite reconcile Charlotte's tenderness this afternoon with such a heinous betrayal, if he couldn't quite make this whole thing fit into the part of his heart that shunned logic...

*That's not your heart, you bloody fool. It's your cock.*

"If I don't return in a quarter of an hour," Charlotte said, giving Devon a gentle push in the direction of the terrace. "I give you leave to come find me."

Devon pulled a long, slow breath into his lungs. "Very well." He reached into his waistcoat pocket and drew out a gold watch. "A quarter hour, not a second more. If I have to come looking for Lady Hadley, West, you'll be meeting me at dawn."

Julian didn't answer. He was staring at the pocket watch dangling from Devon's fingers.

Colin's watch pressed against his chest, the hands motionless, forever frozen in place, but Julian wasn't frozen into this moment. Not yet. It wasn't too late to send Charlotte back to the ballroom, to get her far, far away from him before he said something he could never take back.

*Don't do this. Don't hurt her.*

"Christ," Devon muttered. "Did you hear me, West?"

Julian jerked his gaze back to Devon's face. "I heard you."

"Good." Devon turned to Charlotte. "I'll be only as far as the terrace should you need me." He gave Julian a look that managed to be threatening and contemptuous at once, then disappeared down the pathway.

Julian watched him go, then turned to Charlotte. "You did say you and Devon aren't lovers, didn't you? Hard to believe, given his fierce protectiveness. But perhaps you *are* lovers now. Such a tender scene I interrupted."

*Please. Say it isn't what it seems, and make me believe it.*

But she only pressed her clasped hands tightly against her waist as if she were trying to hold herself together. "I wanted to see you tonight."

"Oh? Well, that explains why I found you alone in a dark garden, clasped in Devon's arms. You were looking for *me*."

"This afternoon, in the carriage...I want to thank you for—"

"For giving you pleasure? Yes, you did seem to enjoy it, and it's only fair, I suppose, since I've had my share of pleasure from you. And oh, what pleasure it was, my lady. But then desire was never a problem between us, was it? It was everything else."

She flinched. "I've made a decision. I'm leaving for Bellwood tomorrow, with Ellie and Cam—"

"Do you remember our night in the garden, Charlotte?" He moved closer to her, his hand sliding up her arm. "I do. I remember the way you sighed for me, the way you moaned into my mouth and begged me to touch you."

She jerked her head as if she could shake loose the image of them together.

Agony ripped through his chest. She would *not* shake off that memory like so much dust from her boots. "And God knows I wanted to touch you, that night and for months afterward, even after you tossed me aside to marry Hadley. A few kisses and I was your willing slave. But I'm not some foolish, besotted boy anymore, and you won't make me crawl for you this time."

A tremor passed through her. "I was the slave, Julian. I was the one who ended up crawling."

He made a mocking noise in his throat. "Did you suffer for me, Charlotte? Did you weep as you walked down the aisle to Hadley? Is that what you want me to believe?"

"I—I did weep for you," she whispered.

"Ah well, a few tears perhaps, but you recovered quickly enough, likely the minute you became a marchioness. You landed on your feet just like any cat, while I spent months praying not to see your face every time I closed my eyes."

She stared down at her clenched hands. "I never recovered. I still see your face when I close my eyes. I still weep for you."

A roar started in Julian's ears and he welcomed it, rejoiced in it, for her words had a ring of truth to them he couldn't bear to hear. Her sorrow would weaken him, just as her love had done, and then nothing would matter to him except her. Not Cam and Ellie, not Colin, not Jane. Not even himself.

*Finish it.*

"Tell me, does Devon know you let me touch you this afternoon?" The words sliced between them like a blade, more horrible for the casualness with which he said them. "In a carriage, no less."

*Oh God, those words.* They echoed horribly in his head, but the monster had its hand at his throat now and there was no escape, nothing he could do but let it claw its way out of him and devastate everything in its path.

Her face drained of color, but she didn't utter a word to defend herself. She simply stood there and withstood his attack, and the horror of it made the misery rise inside him, a tide that pulled and sucked at him until he was down so deep her face swam in front of his eyes, and everything receded so he wasn't a part of it anymore, but could only watch it unfold from below, helpless to stop it.

"I could touch you again, Charlotte. Right here in the garden. Would you like that? I would. I'd love to touch you and then send you back to Devon."

"Stop this... Don't do this, Julian." She wrenched her arm free, stumbling backward, but just like the cat he'd called her, she caught herself before she fell.

God, he could almost admire it, the way she kept her feet under her while she brought everyone around her to their knees. "Christ, I almost pity Devon. He'll twist and bleed for you, just as I did. Just as Hadley did. Nothing but heartache can come from wanting a woman like you."

She froze, her body going so still he thought of a bird shot from the sky in mid-flight, the way it hovers for a moment before it plunges lifeless to the ground. Fear traced an icy finger down his back, but it was too late to stop now. He'd gone too far, and God help him, he didn't know how to stop anymore.

"This afternoon, in the carriage. Why did you help me?"

*Because once I saw the truth on your face I couldn't stand the lie anymore. Because I believed we could save each other.*

He stared down at her, into the dark eyes that haunted his dreams, and he wanted to howl in despair, because it was too late for that answer now. "Help you? I don't know what you mean. Whatever I might have done, it wasn't to help you."

"You made me tell you the truth, and I thought you did it because—"

"Because I care for you?" He forced a mocking laugh. "Yes, you would think that, wouldn't you? I hate to shatter your illusions, my lady, but I did it for myself, not for you. It's easier for me to achieve my ends if you trust me."

Her eyes were huge in her pallid face. "I—I don't believe you."

"Of course you do. I can see in your face that you do."

"But...this afternoon. I heard your voice. I saw your face. You did it for me, and now you want to take it back because you think—"

"Why would I do anything for you, Lady Hadley? Because I still love you? Your arrogance stuns me. I'm betrothed to someone else—a lady of character. Someone who deserves my attentions."

"You're betrothed?" She reached behind her as if to grasp something to steady herself, but her hand found only emptiness. "But you kissed me, touched me, made me promise never to hide from you, never to pretend."

Oh God, he couldn't look at her, at her beautiful, wounded face.

He strode forward and wrapped his hands around her shoulders. "I promised Cam and Ellie I'd get you out of London, and I mean to keep that promise, but I've grown weary of chasing a spoiled marchioness all over the city. I did it to *finish this*. You're simply a problem Cam dumped in my lap—nothing more."

She looked dazed for a moment, but then her face went so stark with misery his chest tightened like a clenched fist. Without thinking he drew her closer, but in the next moment her face shifted, went blank, as if she'd pulled down a shutter over an open window. "I see. I think… I think you'd better release me now, Captain."

He looked down at his hands. His knuckles had gone white from his grip on her. Only this afternoon he'd told her he'd never wanted to hurt her, and now…

A wave of shame washed over him, but before he could release her she touched her fingertips to the back of his hands. Hers were ice cold, but he snatched his own hands away from her as if she'd burned him. Anger, hysterics—he could bear anything but her gentle touch.

But she wasn't hysterical. She was unnaturally composed. "Perhaps you'd be good enough to deliver me back to Lord Devon? I'd like to go home. I'm certain he'll be willing to take me."

"No." His entire body went rigid. "Not Devon."

No reaction. Not even a flicker in the dark eyes. "Lady Tallant, then."

"No. I'll take you in Cam's carriage with me."

He waited for her to protest, but she only gave him a brief, polite nod. "Very well." She turned without another word and started down the path toward the house.

Devon was waiting for them on the terrace. As soon as he saw Charlotte round the tall hedge he leapt down the stairs and hurried toward her. "Lady Hadley, are you—"

"I'm quite well, I thank you, my lord. Captain West has kindly offered to escort me home. Good night." She gave Devon a vacant smile, then walked past him and disappeared through the open French doors.

Julian started to follow her, but Devon stepped in front of him. "Jesus. What the hell did you do to her, West?"

*Odd. Hadn't Cam asked him that very same question this morning?*

Julian fought off the urge to cover his face with his hands. "I don't… It doesn't concern you, but for the sake of getting you out of my way, let's just say Lady Hadley finds the truth distressing."

Devon gave a short laugh. "Which truth is that? Hers, or yours?"

"That's a liar's question. There's only one truth."

"One truth, and a thousand different ways to turn it into a lie. I wonder, West. Which lie did you tell yourself tonight? Did you convince yourself she betrayed you?"

"I suppose there's another reason I found her clasped in your arms?"

"There is. But it's none of your bloody business, and in any case I'd hate to deprive you of all that moral outrage."

"Ever Lady Hadley's champion, aren't you, Devon? But you needn't worry about her any longer. She leaves London tomorrow, and I doubt she'll be back anytime soon."

A strange look passed over Devon's face—something almost like fear. "Listen to me, West. You can't just dump her off in the country. She isn't ready—"

Julian brushed past him. "Like I said, you don't need to worry about her anymore." He didn't wait to hear if Devon replied, but strode into the ballroom.

"She's waiting for you in the carriage."

Julian turned, startled to find Lady Tallant at his elbow. She studied him for a moment with narrowed eyes. "What just happened between you and Lady Hadley in the garden, Captain West?"

"Why should you think anything happened?"

He tried to avoid her gaze, but she pinned him with a cold blue stare. "I think you've betrayed my faith in you by hurting my dear friend, and I assure you, I take it very ill, indeed."

His lips twisted in a bitter smile. "Ah, well. You should know better than to place your faith in a hero, Lady Tallant. We never quite live up to expectations."

She closed her fan with a snap. "Lady Hadley looked unwell when she passed through the ballroom. See you get her home at once."

Julian bowed. "Of course. Good evening, my lady."

He found Charlotte just where Lady Tallant said she'd be, pressed into one corner of the carriage. She didn't look ill, precisely, but there was a peculiar hunched quality to her, as if she'd pulled tightly into herself, like a child who's suffered a nightmare.

He sat on the bench across from her and the carriage pulled smoothly away from the curb. She didn't look at him as they wound through the London streets, but he found his gaze coming back to her again and again. He seemed to be always in a carriage with her, watching with helpless fascination as the moonlight moved over her face.

But this would be the last time. She'd be gone from London tomorrow—

Except she'd never promised that, had she? "Do I have your word you'll accompany your family to Bellwood tomorrow morning?"

She didn't answer right away, but waited until the carriage drew to a stop in front of her house. "You have my word, Captain, I will leave London immediately."

And then she was gone, the carriage door closing with a quiet click behind her. His last thought before she disappeared through the door was the house was very large, and she…

She was very small.

# Chapter Eighteen

*Her. The dream begins with her now, always with her. Teasing dark eyes hidden under long, thick lashes. Red lips. Such a deep red, velvety and soft. The rose petal lips smile, move, make shapes. Words. No, not words. One word only. His name. Julian. There's an entire world in that word. His entire world. His knees go weak and his heart soars, but then the thick lashes sweep down to hide her eyes, and when they rise again they've gone cold. One blink, and her beautiful dark eyes are cold, so cold his heart drops, becomes an icy stone, and then impossibly they are colder still, so cold they turn blue, and the silence is swallowed by a sudden explosion of red, such a bright red, more vivid than it should be, redder than he'd ever imagined blood could be, and what used to be Colin Hibbert's chest becomes a bloody mass of jagged metal, the flesh torn to pieces, a gaping, pulpy hole where skin and bone should be, and sightless, staring blue eyes....*

"Julian." A rough hand shook his shoulder. "Christ. Jules, wake up!"

Julian wrenched awake with a curse, his hand scrabbling for his waistcoat pocket and Colin's watch. *No pocket. No waistcoat. Damn it, where—*

"It's in your hand."

Julian cracked open burning, gritty eyes. Cam stood over him, his mouth pulled into a grim line. He gestured with a sharp jerk of his chin to Julian's hand. As always, Colin's watch was clutched in his palm.

*Where the bloody hell am I?*

"You're in my study," Cam said. "You fell asleep in the chair again, helped along by large quantities of whiskey, no doubt."

Julian struggled upright in the chair and ran a hand over his chin and jaw. He had a face nearly overgrown with whiskers by the feel of it. A quick hand through his hair confirmed it was rumpled and damp with sweat, and his eyes were no doubt bloodshot, since it felt like someone had ground glass into them.

Not a pretty sight. No wonder his cousin looked grim.

Cam strode over to the tall windows on one side of the room and yanked the curtains aside. "Something wrong with your bedchamber, cuz?"

Julian flinched as the morning sunlight fell across his face. "No."

Not unless one counted the nightmares, which had grown so disturbing he'd permanently abandoned his bed for his chair in Cam's study in the hopes he'd wake more easily if he slept in an upright position. It had seemed to work, too.

*Until last night.*

That gaping hole in Colin's chest, the coldness in Charlotte's eyes, and the blood—so much of it, and so red. Far too red—not like real blood, which was much darker, but bright, lurid, pretend blood. Julian drew in a deep breath and clutched at the watch in his palm. The blood was always the worst of it.

He fumbled for the table at his elbow until he found the glass of whiskey he'd abandoned last night. Ah, good. Still half full. "To your health." He tipped the glass toward Cam, and then brought it to his lips.

"It's not my health I'm worried about."

Julian let the liquor sear his throat, then dropped the empty glass back onto the table. "Don't say you're worried for me, cuz? I'm in the pink of health." Julian held his arms out wide. "Never been better. Just look at me."

Cam did look at him—such a long, hard look Julian had to fight to hold his cousin's gaze. What did those sharp green eyes see when they looked at him now? He'd never been able to hide anything from his cousin, not since they were boys. Maybe Cam knew he'd offered to pleasure Charlotte in the middle of Lord and Lady Elliott's garden last night.

No, not offered—*threatened.*

*What kind of hero insinuates a lady is a whore?*

No kind of hero at all. Julian did drop his eyes then, desperate to avoid Cam's searching gaze, and ran an unsteady hand down his face. Jesus. He'd been out of control from the moment he stepped into that garden last night, utterly at the mercy of the brute lurking under his skin. What else had he said to Charlotte? Damn it, he'd been so overwhelmed by his own pain and anger he couldn't remember.

But her face, pale and anguished, the tremor in her voice when she begged him to *stop*—dear God. He remembered that.

He rubbed a weary hand over his eyes. The moment she arrived this morning he'd tell her how sorry he was. He'd beg her forgiveness—

"This business with Charlotte, Julian. Its best if—"

"It's done. She'll accompany you to Bellwood this morning."

Cam's eyes narrowed. "Oh? How did you manage it? Should I expect to find her bound and gagged and deposited on the floor of my carriage?"

Julian tried to smile. "A simple thanks will do."

Cam wasn't amused. "Your tactics with Charlotte thus far have been—"

To Julian's relief, Cam didn't get a chance to finish before he was interrupted by a knock on the study door. "Yes? Come."

Phipps entered, his long face flushed with distress. "I beg your pardon, sir, but there's a gentleman here who demands to see you, and he's rather insistent."

Cam raised his eyebrows. "Insistent?"

"I'm afraid so, sir. I tried to turn him away, it being far too early in the day for calls, but he pushed his way inside. Nearly knocked me down, sir."

A strange sense of foreboding shot up Julian's spine. "Did he give his name, Phipps?"

"Yes, sir. Lord Devon."

"Devon!" Cam shot to his feet. "Send him away at once, Phipps."

"No! Wait." Julian held up his hand to stay Phipps. "Something's wrong, Cam. It must be. Devon would never come here otherwise."

Cam's face paled. "Charlotte?"

Julian nodded. It had to be Charlotte, and whatever it was, it was dire. Nothing short of disaster could induce Devon to appear on Cam's doorstep. Fear choked him as he sifted frantically through his memories of last night. What had she said? She'd asked him to stop, yes, but what else? Something about wanting to see him, to tell him something, but he hadn't let her speak, and in the end she'd said very little.

*I did weep for you. I still see your face when I close my eyes.*

Julian went still, remembering.

"Phipps, give us ten minutes for Captain West to make himself presentable, then show Lord Devon in."

"Yes, sir." Phipps bowed and left the room.

"Get dressed, Jules. Quickly." Cam retrieved Julian's clothes from the chair. "For God's sake, what did you do to them?" He cast an impatient eye over the crumpled coat and waistcoat.

Julian shoved his shirt into his breeches. "Makeshift pillow. Give them here," he snapped when Cam tried to shake the wrinkles out of them.

"Devon doesn't give a damn about my clothing, and I wouldn't give a damn even if he did."

Cam threw the waistcoat across the room to Julian. "Good thing, because it will take far more than ten minutes to make you presentable. No, forget the cravat—it's as believable as silk gloves on a cutpurse. You look a ruffian either way."

Julian had just struggled into his waistcoat when Phipps returned. "Lord Devon." The butler stood back to let Devon pass, then hastily retreated and closed the door behind him.

Julian eyed Devon. Wise of Phipps to escape before the bloodshed began. Devon looked ready to take someone's head clean off his shoulders.

No, not someone's. *His.*

Devon didn't spare Cam a glance. "What the *devil* did you say to Lady Hadley last night, West?" He strode across the room until his livid face was mere inches from Julian's. "Whatever it was, you've made one hell of a bloody mess."

Julian's heart stuttered in his chest, but there was no way he'd let Devon see his panic. "I told you last night, Devon. Lady Hadley is no longer your concern."

"Is that so?" Devon's voice was soft, menacing. "Well, I'll damn well make her my concern until you manage something more than your current pathetic efforts."

Cam shoved himself between Devon and Julian, his face dark with fury. "I don't know what you think you're doing here, Devon, but you have a *bloody nerve* coming into my home and telling me how to take care of my family."

Devon turned on Cam. "You've done a damn poor job of it, otherwise I wouldn't need to be here at all." Devon jerked his chin in Julian's direction. "Good God, man. Is *he* the best you can do?"

Julian clenched his jaw until it threatened to shatter. "You think yourself a better choice? You would have disgraced her, ruined her—"

"No, West." Devon's low voice cut through Julian's fury. "I would have married her."

Cam's mouth fell open. "*What?*"

Julian stared at Devon, searching for a blink, a twitch—anything that would give him away as a liar, but the blue eyes held his without wavering. "What's the matter, West? Have I shocked you?"

"I might be shocked if I believed a word of it." But he did believe it. He could see by Devon's face the man told the truth.

"I don't give a damn what you believe, but ask yourself this. Did you ever bother to ask Lady Hadley? To talk to her at all? You've been harassing her to leave London for a week, and in that time you never tried to understand what kept her here, did you? I suppose you thought you knew it all already. Not just a hero, but a mind reader, as well."

Julian shook his head. "No. It's impossible. She would have said something, told me—"

"Why, because you've proved yourself so worthy of her confidence?" Devon gave a harsh laugh. "You wouldn't have believed her even if she had told you."

Julian wanted to deny it, but he knew damn well Devon was right. "She'd have told her family, then. Her sister."

"No doubt she would have confided in her sister had there been a betrothal, but Charlotte didn't give me an answer until last night."

Julian's stomach gave a nauseating lurch. Last night when he'd come upon them locked in an embrace, she'd been giving Devon her answer. It hadn't looked like a refusal. Well, he bloody well wasn't going to ask Devon if they were betrothed. He wouldn't give the man the satisfaction.

But the fierce possessiveness thrumming through him refused to be denied, and in the next breath he heard himself say, "*Charlotte?* Unless you're betrothed, she's Lady Hadley to you, Devon."

Devon stared at him for a moment, an incredulous look on his face; then he made a disgusted noise and wheeled away. "Yes, by all means, Captain, let's quibble over my manner of address. Perhaps then we'll have tea and adjourn to Tattersall's for the afternoon while Lady Hadley continues her journey to Hampshire. *Alone.*"

"Hampshire?" Julian stared at him. "You're mad. She leaves this morning for Kent, accompanied by her family."

"My God. You don't even know. What did you do, West? Dump her off in front of her house and congratulate yourself on being such a hero? You haven't even bothered to find out where she is!"

A horrible suspicion began to form in Julian's mind. *No. She wouldn't have gone there, not by herself.*

But even as he shook his head he knew it was true, and in the next moment Devon confirmed it. "Last night, not an hour after you dropped her off at her house, Lady Hadley left for Hampshire. For Hadley House."

Cam and Julian stared at him, mute with shock.

"That's right. She left *in the middle of the night* with no one to attend her aside from a maid and two footmen. Whatever you said to her last night to make her leave London certainly had the desired effect, West."

The floor gave a sickening lurch under Julian's feet. "But she told me—she promised she'd leave for Bellwood—"

He fell silent as he thought back to her words last night. No, she hadn't promised that. He'd heard a promise because he wanted to hear one, but her actual words...

*You have my word, Captain, I will leave London immediately.*

She'd meant Hadley House. By the time he finished with her she no longer intended to go to Bellwood. It was too close, and she must have known at some point she'd see *him* there.

Julian groped for the mantel to steady himself. Last night when she'd disappeared into her house—God, she'd looked so small as she passed through that cavernous entryway. Hadley House would devour her, swallow her whole.

Devon was watching him. "So you do care about her, West." His face relaxed ever so slightly. "I wouldn't have believed it possible."

"How do you know about this, Lord Devon?" Despite the early hour Cam went to the sideboard and poured a finger of whiskey into each of three glasses, then crossed the room to hand one to Devon and the other to Julian.

Devon tossed his back at once. "I went to her house this morning. I was concerned after last night. When she left, she looked so...unlike herself. Her butler, Nelson, told me she gathered a few things together and was gone not an hour after she arrived home from Lady Elliott's ball. Her lady's maid, Sarah, confirmed it. Sarah is under strict orders to pack up Lady Hadley's things and come to Hampshire at once. Once she's gone, the servants will close the house."

"She intends to stay away from London for quite some time, then," Cam muttered. "This is bad. Hadley House is remote, with no neighbors nearby to speak of."

Julian gripped his whiskey glass with white fingers. What had Charlotte said about Hadley House? *It's an estate without an end.* For her to be there alone, all winter...

Devon slammed his glass down onto a table. "She's in no state of mind to be alone in that enormous house. No company, no distractions, nothing to keep her mind occupied—she may as well be locked in a tomb."

*Distractions.* All at once the truth crashed over Julian, spitting foam and spray in its wake. The scandals, the whorehouse incident, the gaming— they were what kept Charlotte in London. The widows and Devon were part of it—a convenient means by which to achieve an end—but they weren't the real reason she insisted upon staying in the city. They hadn't led Charlotte into vice. She'd come to London in search of it, to silence the voices in her head.

And what better place than London to lose oneself?

For the past week he'd chased her from one corner of the city to another, like… How had Cam put it? Like a hound after a very clever fox. But she'd begun to run long before he arrived in London. Didn't she know it made no difference whether she was in London, at Bellwood, or at Hadley House? No one could run fast enough or hide well enough to escape themselves.

He knew that better than anyone.

"We'll go after her, of course. Immediately." Cam turned to Devon. "Did Nelson say what time she left last night?"

"Midnight, or thereabouts."

"She has an eight hour start on us. *Damn it.* It's impossible for us to overtake her before she reaches Hadley House. Even on horseback—"

"I'll leave at once," Julian said. "I won't stop except to change horses. If I make good time she won't be alone at Hadley House for more than half a day."

Cam frowned. "No, Jules. I'll go after her myself. You'll stay in London."

Julian felt the refusal like a blow to the stomach. Cam looked away, but not before Julian saw the truth on his face.

His cousin didn't trust him to go after Charlotte.

Cam turned to Lord Devon with a respectful bow. "I offer you my thanks, my lord. I believe I've misjudged you. Perhaps I had reason to, given your questionable behavior with Charlotte over these past months, but it's clear to me now your intentions were honorable. I beg your pardon."

Devon looked as if he didn't quite appreciate this apology, but after a moment the white lines around his mouth eased and he returned Cam's bow. "I ask you to favor me with a line once you've located Lady Hadley. Whatever else may have passed between us, we're friends."

Devon didn't look at Julian again, but turned and left the study.

"Lord Devon. Wait." Julian followed him into the hallway. "Are you and Lady Hadley simply friends? Or are you betrothed?"

It was a dangerous question, one he had no right to ask. Whether they were betrothed or not could make no difference to him. He was betrothed to Jane Hibbert, and he wouldn't lose his one chance to make amends to Colin.

But none of this mattered. Nothing mattered as much as his need to *know*.

Devon regarded him in silence for a moment, then shook his head. "She accepted my offer, but then last night, in the garden, right before you came upon us…" Devon drew the moment out until Julian's nerves screamed in protest. "She retracted. Strange, isn't it? I can't imagine what could have happened yesterday afternoon to make her change her mind. Can you, Captain West?"

He didn't wait for an answer, but turned and took his leave.

Julian went back into the study to face Cam, his mind in turmoil. Those stolen moments with Charlotte in the carriage—

*Tell me it matters.*

*It matters. It matters, Julian.*

Was that when she'd changed her mind about marrying Devon?

Cam was waiting for him, but as soon as he saw Julian's face he began to shake his head. "No, Julian."

"Cam. Please. I have to."

"No. I should never have asked you to do this in the first place."

Julian's chest went tight. "I've made mistakes. I don't deny it, but this time I promise you—"

"I can't trust your promises anymore, Julian." Cam's mouth was hard. "I won't risk having Charlotte hurt again."

"I—I won't hurt her. Not ever again. Please. Give me one more chance, Cam."

But Cam looked away. "No."

Julian fought back the panic that threatened to close his throat, to choke him. To silence him. "You're meant to leave for Bellwood this morning. Ellie and Amelia are ready to go. It has to be me, Cam. Don't you see? Please."

Cam searched his face, looking for…what? Some trace of the Julian he remembered, perhaps. Would he find any?

"Cam." Julian's voice broke. "I'm begging you."

Cam's gaze shot back to his face. He was silent for a long moment, then, "She won't go anywhere with you if she doesn't trust you."

"I'll find a way—somehow, I'll find a way to make her trust me. Please let me try. If she won't come with me, I'll write you at once, and then stay with her until you can get to Hampshire."

"I won't have her forced or coerced or manipulated, Julian. Do you understand me? You'll have to persuade her. *Gently.*"

"I understand. I give you my word."

"Your word." Cam looked him in the eyes. "You were a man of your word once, Julian. Are you still?"

*I don't know. I don't know who I am anymore.*

But he knew one thing—a small, insignificant, paltry thing, but at the moment it was all he had. He held Cam's gaze. "I want to be."

Julian held his breath as Cam studied his face. *Please, let him find some trace of Julian there still. Please—*

Cam blew out a long breath. "Go and get her, then. But don't make me regret this, Julian."

Julian's breath rushed from his lungs and his eyes closed. "Thank you," he rasped. "Thank you for giving me one more chance."

Cam sighed. "I warn you, Jules. It won't be easy."

No, it wouldn't be easy. Rescues never were. Not even for a hero.

# Chapter Nineteen

*Darling Annabel,*

*You'll never guess where I am, my dear! I've gone off to Hampshire to visit Hadley House. Such an adventure! I expect you will convulse with laughter when you hear I sneaked away under cover of night to escape the notice of my family, all of whom wish me in Kent.*

*I couldn't, as you can imagine, countenance Bellwood for the winter. Here in Hampshire I may do as I wish, and you mustn't worry for me, dearest, for I will have a splendid time of it. I shall sleep all day and roam the gardens in the moonlight like a proper ghost.*

*I daresay you'll wonder why I've left London at all, especially without calling on you first to inform you of my intentions. I must beg your pardon for that, and ask you to convey my most abject apologies to Lissie and Aurelie. I'm a sadly impetuous creature, as you know, and once I decide on a course nothing will do for me but to put it into action at once—*

Charlotte let the quill slip from her fingers and dragged herself from her chair to the fireplace. She held the letter over the flames, watching with fixed attention as the edges of the paper began to blacken and curl.

Odd, how much easier it was to write lies than to speak them. It shouldn't be, for a paper and ink lie would last long after mere words were forgotten. Then again, with letters one needn't look into the face of the deceived.

Only when the glowing flame began to singe her fingertips did Charlotte toss the letter into the fire. These lies had flowed easily enough, yet it wouldn't serve, just the same. Annabel was no fool—she'd know this letter at once for what it was. The trouble was, the truth wouldn't serve, either.

Something between the two, then. Charlotte returned to her desk and took up her quill.

*My dearest Annabel,*

*I feel rather like a condemned criminal, sneaking away from London without as much as a word of warning. I hope you'll forgive me, and will share my regrets with Lissie and Aurelie.*

*Lord Devon will have told you by now I've rejected his suit, though it gave me no pleasure to do so. I've been contemplating a sojourn in the country for some time, and given the awkwardness likely to arise from my refusal it seemed an ideal time to go. I beg you won't worry yourself for me, but will look forward with anticipation to such a time as I may return to London and resume our friendship, though I can't say as yet how long I may linger in Hampshire.*

*Such times we had this season, Annabel! I assure you, nothing Hadley House offers can console me for the loss of your diverting company. I feel it most keenly, but I will try and console myself over the long winter months with fond memories of our many adventures together—*

Charlotte tossed the quill aside and pushed away from the desk.

It still wouldn't do. Her friends were far too clever to believe she'd fled in the night to escape Devon, and it was horribly unfair to blame him for her cowardly retreat. God knew he deserved far better from her than she'd ever been capable of giving him.

But then so had they all. Devon, and Hadley before him, and before Hadley…

No. She wouldn't think on it. She picked up the quill for the third time and bent over the paper.

*Dearest Annabel,*

*I'd thought to have time to call on you before I left for Hampshire, but circumstances with my family are such that a precipitate departure for Hadley House seemed preferable for all concerned. I think, my dear, the solitude here will do me a world of good, though I confess it's rather an unpleasant shock after the gaiety of London—*

*A world of good.* Such a glaring deception. If she couldn't write truthfully, perhaps it would be best if she didn't write at all. But what if the widows should take it into their heads to come after her? A shudder slid down her spine at the thought of her vivacious friends suffocating under the gloom of this place.

She pushed the sheet aside, retrieved fresh paper from the desk drawer, and dipped her quill in the ink.

*Dear Annabel,*

*You must not follow me here. Forgive me.*

*I am ever your friend,*

*Charlotte*

Her fingers shook as she folded the letter and affixed her seal. There. It was done, and now...

Now, nothing.

The case clock on the first floor landing struck seven times.

She glanced toward the glass doors behind the desk. Her housekeeper, Mrs. Boyle had drawn the curtains, but now Charlotte rose and pulled them aside to look out. The doors opened to a terrace with a set of shallow steps leading out into a small private garden.

Seven o'clock.

Hadley House boasted magnificent formal gardens and endless acres of parkland, but this tiny garden was her favorite. This room too, so snug, not like the other rooms, which tended toward high-ceilings and draftiness. Of course, the house had been designed to announce wealth rather than provide comfort for the hapless family who happened to live here, but this little study and the garden beyond were a small oasis in an otherwise vast desert of formal rooms and endless hallways. Why, she could slip right out these doors and into the garden without anyone taking any notice of where she'd gone. One couldn't see into the garden from the master's suite of rooms, or from the dowager's apartments, and should someone in one of those rooms be screaming, one couldn't hear it once the doors closed behind them.

Charlotte pressed her face against the glass. Perhaps she'd go outside now. It wasn't so dark yet she couldn't see the outline of the stone balustrades on either side of the wide staircase, and the shadows cast by the tall hedges in the garden beyond. Fresh air—yes, that was what she needed, and yet...

The shadows pressed upon her. She'd forgotten how deep the darkness, how profound the silence in the country. It was a shock compared to the chaos of London, but after a few weeks here she wouldn't notice the shadows anymore. The silence.

Just a few weeks, and it would be as if she'd never left Hadley House at all.

Perhaps she'd go out tomorrow, instead.

She let the curtain drop and turned back to face the room. The fire crackled and hissed merrily in the grate, but otherwise the room was as silent as the garden. The smell of burnt paper lingered, and Charlotte's stomach heaved a little in protest. It was just as well she hadn't touched the tray Mrs. Boyle had brought earlier. She hadn't taken more than a cup of tea since she arrived. Travel did tend to make her feel ill, but surely by tomorrow she'd have regained her appetite. Perhaps she'd order a large breakfast delivered to her room and dine in bed with a mountain of pillows behind her, like a grand marchioness should.

The case clock struck the half hour.

Seven-thirty. Too early for bed. If she went now, she'd wake early in the morning, and the day did seem endless when one woke too soon.

She resumed her seat in front of the fire, pulled out a fresh sheet, dipped the quill into the ink, and pressed the nib to the paper. She'd write to Ellie.

But what was she to say?

She'd begin with an apology—yes, that was right. She'd apologize for worrying Ellie, who'd no doubt been beside herself this morning when she learned of Charlotte's disappearance. And she *was* sorry—of course she was, except she couldn't quite feel the regret yet because of this strange numbness that clung to her like wet clothing.

But it wasn't a lie, for surely by tomorrow she'd feel sorry.

She'd best tell Ellie she had no plans to come to Bellwood. Yes, she should get that out of the way at once, or else Ellie would try and persuade her, and Charlotte mustn't let her, because one couldn't escape their fate forever, and Hadley House was Charlotte's fate. She'd hidden from it for a time in London, but now she saw how foolish she'd been to think she could outrun it, outmaneuver it, for it would find you and it would deal out your punishment again and again until you got what you deserved. It would have you in the end, just as this house had her now, locked in its grim embrace, squeezing the life out of her, because it was what she deserved, and London wouldn't change that, and Bellwood wouldn't change it and to pretend otherwise was utter madness—

"Lady Hadley? Pardon me, my lady. I didn't mean to startle you." Mrs. Boyle hovered in the doorway. She stared at Charlotte, her brow creased with concern.

Charlotte clutched at her quill. Surely she hadn't been talking to herself? "I—no need to apologize, Mrs. Boyle. I'm afraid I didn't hear your knock. Is something amiss?"

"Yes, my lady. Ah, that is no, not amiss exactly." Mrs. Boyle wrung her hands. "You have a visitor. A gentleman."

"At this time of night? But that's—"

*Oh, dear God.* Cam had followed her here, and at a breakneck pace to have made such a quick journey from London, and now he was going to try and make her come with him to Bellwood.

"Shall I show him in, my lady?"

*No. Send him away, back to Bellwood and his family where he belongs, and let him leave me here, where I belong.*

But she knew very well she couldn't turn Cam away. "Yes, please do, Mrs. Boyle."

The housekeeper hurried away. Charlotte came out from behind the desk and took a seat on a settee in front of the fire. She'd have to explain it to Cam, to make him understand why she had to stay here and accept the punishment fate dealt her, that for her to leave now would only make matters worse—

"Captain West, my lady."

Julian came into the room just as the case clock struck the hour.

Eight chimes.

By the fourth chime Charlotte had no air left in her lungs. By the sixth there was no air left in the room, the house—all of Hampshire. The clock fell silent at last, but by then the fear was a bottomless chasm in her chest, and she couldn't look at him, couldn't speak. Without thinking she stumbled to her feet and flew back behind the desk before he could see how badly she was trembling.

Was this what fate wanted from her?

*To make me afraid, a coward, and to make me ashamed of it.*

Julian saw it all—her trembling, her fear, even her shame, and a look of bitter regret passed over his face, a face already gray with exhaustion. He ran a weary hand though dark hair slick with sweat, then held out both hands in front of him, palms out as if to show her he had no weapon. "It's all right, Charlotte. You don't need to run away from me. I came here to help you, to escort you to Bellwood."

At last an emotion penetrated the fog that had surrounded her since last night, after that terrible scene in Lady Elliot's garden. Fury, sharp as a scalpel, cleansing. *Bellwood. Bellwood. Bellwood.* She was sick of the very idea of Bellwood. Even the word made her flesh quiver with anger, and on its heels a resentment so bitter it scraped her throat raw, gagged her.

Cam and Ellie—they'd sent *him* here after her? *Him.* Why? So she could add another nightmare to those that already haunted this house? This place offered her nothing, no relief, no protection, but she'd thought at least to be safe from *him*, and now here he was, his gaze fixed on her, the black eyes aware of her every twitch and shudder. With each tick of the clock she grew more and more transparent. Soon he'd see all the way through.

His words from last night in the garden whispered through her, just as if he'd pressed his lips to her ear. *I almost pity Devon... I don't care about you....*

No. He couldn't be here. *She* couldn't be here with his ugly words ringing in her head, growing louder by the moment, their roar deafening her—

But then suddenly, nothing. Silence.

No sooner did the pain threaten to devour her than it retreated, and the blessed numbing fog descended again, leaving her drained, listless.

Ah, yes. It was so much better this way. So much easier. "Bellwood. No, Captain, I won't be going to Bellwood."

His arms dropped to his sides. "I know you don't have any reason to, but do you think... Is there any way you can trust me? Please, Charlotte. I won't hurt you again."

Charlotte stared at him, puzzled. He didn't understand. He *would* hurt her again, and he didn't need a weapon to do it. He *was* the weapon, and his task was to punish her. "But you will. It's what you're meant to do."

His brows drew together. "I'm meant to hurt you? I don't understand."

No, he didn't, did he? But how strange. If he didn't understand, then why had he come at all? "Why are you here, Captain?"

He spread his arms wide, a helpless gesture, unlike him. He seemed not to know what to do with his limbs. "To bring you to Bellwood."

"I'm sorry you came all this way, Captain, only to have to turn back again."

He shook his head, his anxious gaze steady on her face. "No. I won't turn back, Charlotte. I won't leave you here alone."

"Not leave? But of course you'll leave, Captain. You can't stay here with me. It's not proper, and in any case I'm meant to stay here alone." She frowned a little as she considered this. "Yes, I feel sure that's right. It's not a proper punishment if I have someone here with me."

Julian's face went grayer with every word she spoke. "Is that what this is about? Punishment? Are you trying to punish me for what I said, what I did? Do it. I deserve it. But don't do this to yourself, Charlotte. You haven't done anything wrong. Don't punish yourself because I was cruel to you."

Punish *him?* Again, how odd. Why should he think so? "No, you still don't understand, Captain. Don't you see? You pretended to care for me, and I pretended, too. I pretended I could learn to love Hadley. I didn't realize it was a lie at the time, but it hardly matters. I lied to him, and then you lied to me. A liar is punished with a lie. It's all just as it should be."

She'd taken pains to speak politely, but for some reason her words made him cringe. He took a step toward her. "You think this is your fault."

*Oh.* Now she began to see the problem. He believed it was his fault she'd come to Hadley House, because he'd said all those cruel things to her in the garden. Well, it couldn't have been pleasant for him to have to be the one to deliver those truths, but someone had to do it. "And you think it's yours, but it isn't. Try and see it this way, Captain. My family struggled for months to get me to leave London, and they all failed. You succeeded because you told me the one truth I couldn't ignore."

He went paler still and... Oh dear, was that *fear* on his face? Whatever ailed him?

"The one truth." He cleared his throat, but his next words were strained, hoarse. "What truth is that?"

Didn't he remember? She remembered everything about that moment as if it had just happened. His face, and his tone when he'd said it. So much contempt. At the time she'd shrunk from him, from the disgust in his eyes, but that was before she understood it was all for her own good. "You said nothing but heartache can come—"

An odd catch in her throat suddenly stopped her words. It made no sense her heart should choose this moment to swell as if bruised, to rush into her throat and silence her. She wasn't saddened by what he'd said. Oh, she'd been devastated at the time, of course, but she wasn't…anything now. Not anymore. So much easier that way. "You said nothing but heartache can come from wanting a woman like me."

Julian went rigid for a heartbeat, but then his entire body slumped, his shoulders hunching into his chest. He covered his eyes with his hands as if it pained him to look at her, and when he let them fall, his face was slack, ashen. "I should never have said such a thing, not only because it's cruel, but because it's a lie. Please, Charlotte. I would do anything not to have said it."

Charlotte felt a slight shift in her chest, a vague twinge of sympathy. "But you had to say it, and it's not a lie at all. You, Hadley, Devon. It's rather an incriminating trail of disappointment, heartbreak, and death. Don't you agree?"

"No," he whispered. "But I can understand why you might think so, after—" He broke off, and for a moment he seemed not to know what to say, then, "You didn't make those things happen, Charlotte. Those things—they happened *to* you, not *because* of you."

Dear God, he was naïve. "You mean to say they were simply bad luck."

A glimmer of hope lit his eyes. "Bad luck, yes."

She gave him a pitying smile. "There's no such thing as luck, Captain. Only justice."

The glimmer died. "Do you really believe that?"

"Don't you?"

A strange look passed over his face then, one she couldn't decipher. He didn't answer the question, but asked instead, "Do you remember the night we first met, Charlotte? Before things went wrong. Before Hadley."

"Yes." She remembered, but she wished she didn't, because she didn't want to think on it.

Now he was looking into her eyes. "I lied to you then. I swore I didn't seduce you in the garden that night to aid Cam's scheme to blackmail Ellie into marriage. Do you remember?"

"I remember. What of it?"

"My lie set in motion this entire nightmare—our estrangement, your marriage to Hadley, his death, and every heartbreak that followed. If anyone should be punished it's me, not you. That would be justice."

*But you have been punished, in the most terrible way a person can be punished. You simply don't know it.*

The words rushed to her lips, but she choked them back. He was trying to trick her into revealing her secrets again. The minute she trusted him, the minute she revealed herself he'd hurt her. He'd say it was her fault, all her fault—that she deserved everything she got, and worse.

He seemed to be holding his breath, waiting for her answer.

She looked away from him toward the glass doors. "I suppose you'll have to stay here tonight, after all. It's too dark to travel." She pulled the bell, and after a moment Mrs. Boyle appeared. "Captain West will remain tonight, Mrs. Boyle. Please make up a room for him, and bring him some refreshment, if you would."

"Yes, my lady."

Julian stood frozen before the desk, stiff and silent, staring at her.

"Oh, and Mrs. Boyle?"

The housekeeper turned back. "Yes, my lady?"

"No need to go to too much trouble with the bedchamber. Captain West will be leaving us tomorrow."

# Chapter Twenty

She was hiding from him.

Julian slid down the wall at his back until he rested on his haunches, his hands dangling helplessly between his spread knees. He'd been hovering in the hallway outside the marchioness's apartments for the better part of three hours, but Charlotte had yet to emerge. The chamber doors remained firmly closed, and not a sound disturbed the silence on the other side.

She could be asleep, of course.

*But she wasn't.* Julian knocked his head rhythmically against the wall behind him. Somehow, he knew she wasn't. She'd slipped through his fingers again. He hadn't any idea how, unless she'd gone out a window and shimmied down a trellis to the ground, but one thing was certain. He'd never find her now.

*Like chasing a particularly clever fox through every alleyway in London.* Except Hadley House, with its endless series of rooms and haphazard hallways made the London rookeries look organized. She hadn't insisted he leave her house, after all, and no wonder. Why bother to chase him away? He may as well be at Bellwood for all the time he'd spent with her since he arrived here.

He'd wandered from room to room his first two days, fruitlessly searching for her. On the third day he rose before the sun and stationed himself at the foot of the main staircase so he could catch her before she disappeared into the complex maze of Hadley House, and he was forced to scurry after her like a dim-witted rat.

She'd frozen to a halt at the top of the stairs as soon as she saw him, but even this strange, hollow Charlotte refused to turn and run from him.

She came slowly down the stairs, her face blank, but Julian could see her knuckles go white from her grip on the railing.

"Captain West." Her dull eyes flicked over him and then away. "You're up early this morning."

His own face felt stiff, but he made an effort to produce what he hoped was a reassuring smile. "Too restless to sleep, I suppose. May I escort you into breakfast?"

She eyed the arm he offered with a frown, as if she weren't quite sure what to do with it. "No, thank you. I prefer to walk in the gardens before I breakfast, but I'll be sure to join you for luncheon later this afternoon, or perhaps for tea—"

*Gardens again.* Gardens seemed to bring out the worst in him, but there was no help for it. "I'd be delighted to stroll in the gardens with you. I'm curious about the house. Cam's told me a great deal about it, especially the grounds. He says they're spectacular."

He half expected her to refuse him, but after a moment she shrugged as if it made no difference to her what he did. She ignored his arm, but she didn't object when he followed her down the hallway and through a glass-ceilinged conservatory to a terrace at the back of the house. "They're commonly thought spectacular, yes."

"But you don't find them so?"

*Because you dread being here, because you blame yourself for Hadley's death—*

He bit his tongue before the words could slip out and forced himself to keep his tone light. "Rolling green hills and extravagant formal gardens don't appeal to you?"

Another shrug. "They're very nice."

*Nice.* A meaningless word, one that led nowhere, just as this garden did. The twisting pathways circled and doubled back on themselves, with no center and no visible end—

Julian halted on the path. No, that was wrong. Every pathway led somewhere, and every garden had a center, a heart. He couldn't see it yet, but it was there, and it only took steady, careful steps to find it.

He brushed his fingers across the pink petals of a rose and smiled at Charlotte. "Just nice? I'd call them spectacular, but then I look at them with new eyes, a luxury you don't have."

A frown appeared between her brows, but it was the wrong frown, as if they were discussing a complex scientific theory instead of how she might feel about a place that had nearly destroyed her. "What does that mean?"

There was no heat in her voice. It wasn't an accusation, only a simple question. He drew a little closer to her, until only a few steps separated them. "I mean you have terrible memories of Hadley House, Charlotte. The sorrow you endured here affects the way you see it."

Her mouth opened, but she closed it again without speaking. Her expression didn't change, exactly, but he sensed a faint shift in her, a new rigidity—a tiny fissure in the blank façade.

*Gently. Go gently.*

"Your husband's death was sudden. A shock. It must have devastated you. It would only be natural if being here caused you pain."

"I—it was sudden, yes." She gave him an uncertain look, the look of a child whose hurt herself and isn't sure whether her mother will hold her and soothe the pain, or punish her for recklessness.

God, he wanted to hold her, hold her until she was so warm and safe in his embrace she dared to reveal a true emotion, but he'd lost the right to touch her. "A tragic accident." He hesitated, but then forced the words that must be spoken past his cold lips. "But it was an accident, Charlotte, and it's time you stopped blaming yourself for it."

It was the wrong thing to say. Or perhaps exactly the right thing, because she went suddenly stark white, and he saw at once he'd struck a chord, plucked at one of the taut strings inside her chest so the pain vibrated, reverberated.

She gasped a little, and her hand flew to her throat. "I won't speak to you about him—him, or anything else that happened here. I know you don't truly care about me. Do you think I've forgotten what you said? You're a liar, Julian, and a liar will say anything to get what they want." She threw the words between them, piling them one on top of the other, hurtful words to build a wall he couldn't scale.

But he could. He would. Gently. One stone at a time.

He held out a hand to her. "I did lie to you. I lied when I said I didn't care about you. I do care, Charlotte. So much."

All the anger he felt, the bitterness and shame, the regret—it had torn and bruised him inside, so badly he hadn't believed he could find anything to salvage in that wreckage, but it was there, underneath the hurt and pain and guilt—so fragile still, like a tiny, beating heart—but it was there.

*Tenderness. For her.*

"No!" She pressed her palms over her ears. "I don't believe you."

His heart crashed against his ribs, both pain and hope at once. It hurt, God, it hurt to see her suffer, but her pain was pure, and like blood flowing from an infected wound, it would heal her. "I know you don't, sweetheart—not now. But you will, Charlotte, because I'm going to stay here with you until you do, and when you're ready, I'll take you home."

She stumbled back, away from him. "I won't ever be ready. Not for you."

She ran then, and it took everything in him not to chase after her, but it was enough—for today, for now, it was enough. If he pushed too hard all at once he'd hurt her too much. Later, he'd try again, and then again, as many times as it took to reach her heart.

But he didn't see her later. She didn't leave her room for the rest of the day. The following morning he waited for her at the bottom of the staircase again, but she never came down at all.

Now it was four days later, and today would be another day wasted. His face fell into his hands. With each day that passed Charlotte would retreat further and further into herself, and all the while the pain trapped deep inside her would continue to poison her.

He couldn't bear to watch it.

If he didn't bring Charlotte to Bellwood soon, Cam would come for her, and once he was here he wouldn't accept her refusal. Time was slipping away like sand between Julian's open fingers—slipping away with every hour, as surely as Charlotte was.

*I'm failing her.*

"Why, Captain West. What are you doing here? Are you lost?"

Julian looked up to find Mrs. Boyle standing over him, her arms full of fresh linens and her kind face creased with concern. "Lost?"

She propped her bundle against her hip and gave him a cheerful smile. "Aye. Such a large, rambling place, Hadley House, with hallways running every which way. It's quite easy to get turned around, you see."

Julian came to his feet. "No, I didn't get turned around. I was just—"

He hesitated. It was hardly proper to lurk in a hallway waiting for a lady to emerge from her bedchamber, and Mrs. Boyle struck him as the type of woman who didn't tolerate nonsense from curious gentlemen. "I thought I might escort Lady Hadley down to breakfast, but I seem to have missed her."

Mrs. Boyle looked confused for a moment, but then her face cleared as realization dawned. "Oh, dear. I see the trouble. Lady Hadley doesn't use these apartments, Captain. She's taken a much smaller bedchamber on the other side of the stairs, at the end of the hall."

Julian blinked. For God's sake, he'd spent the entire morning sitting outside an empty room? "But these are the apartments meant for the lady of the house, aren't they?"

Mrs. Boyle shifted her burden to her arms again. "Yes indeed, but they adjoin the master's apartments, you see, and Lady Hadley doesn't like... that is, ever since his lordship passed... Well. I'm sure you understand."

No, he didn't understand. That was the trouble. He didn't understand any of this, but he wanted to, and finally here was a stroke of luck. He could hardly ask Mrs. Boyle where her mistress slept without arousing the good lady's suspicions, but he didn't need to ask. Those linens in her hands could only be for Charlotte. There were no other guests, and his room was in another wing of the house. Mrs. Boyle was about to lead him to her mistress's bedchamber, and he'd sleep in front of Charlotte's door before he let her slip away from him again.

"May I help you, Mrs. Boyle?" Before she could refuse he lifted the bundle of linens from her arms. "Where shall I take these?"

"Oh no, that's not necessary, Captain." Mrs. Boyle's hands fluttered like two agitated birds. "I couldn't possibly ask you to—"

"You didn't ask." He smiled. "I offered, and I insist."

Mrs. Boyle flushed. "Oh well, I suppose that's all right, then. So kind of you. Just this way, Captain. I should have sent a maid to do this, but the silly girls refuse to enter this part of the house. They claim it's haunted. Can you imagine such nonsense?"

Julian followed Mrs. Boyle down the hall, past the stairwell, and around a corner. "Well, young girls are a dramatic lot, and Hadley's death was rather tragic, I believe?"

"Just here, Captain." Mrs. Boyle held out her arms for the linens. She didn't answer his question, and she clearly didn't intend to let him into her mistress's bedchamber.

But Julian wasn't quite finished with Mrs. Boyle yet. "Difficult for your mistress, wasn't it? Such a shock."

"Difficult, yes." The housekeeper said no more, but nodded meaningfully at the linens.

*Damn it.* Mrs. Boyle wasn't a gossip, unfortunately. Julian tried a different tack. "I wonder, Mrs. Boyle, if you might help me. Your mistress is suffering from low spirits since she returned from London. Do you have any suggestions as to how I might cheer her?"

Mrs. Boyle's face softened at mention of Charlotte's distress. "Ah, well. It's the house, you see, Captain. Not enough time has passed for her ladyship to be easy here. His lordship is gone just over a year now, and then there was that terrible business with the dowager ladyship, and what followed afterwards—"

"Afterwards?"

But his expression must have been too eager, because Mrs. Boyle gave him a wary look. "Well, the less said about *that*, the better. This house holds too many distressing memories for her ladyship, Captain. The best thing you can do for her is to take her away from Hadley House."

Julian couldn't agree more, but short of abducting her, he didn't see how it could be done. He handed the linens into Mrs. Boyle's waiting arms. "Have you seen Lady Hadley today, Mrs. Boyle?"

The housekeeper's brow furrowed. "Now let me see. No, not since this morning. She took tea in her room, quite early. Didn't eat a bite, though." Mrs. Boyle shook her head over this. "Doesn't eat enough, you know. Too thin by half."

Julian did his best to disguise his impatience. Lady Hadley was thin, but not quite invisible yet, which meant *someone* must have seen her. "And you haven't seen her since then?"

"No, I'm afraid not. She likes to walk in the small garden off the study. Perhaps you'll find her there."

He doubted it. Charlotte knew how to disappear. He'd not find her in any of her usual haunts. "Yes, of course. Thank you, Mrs. Boyle."

He spent the rest of the day scouring the house and grounds for Charlotte. He wandered from the portrait gallery to the drawing room, from the library back to the hallway outside her bedchamber, from the rose garden to the stables. He spoke to one giggling maid after another, cornered each of the footmen, and even followed the butler about until the harassed man finally ducked into the pantry to escape him, but no one had seen Charlotte.

By tea time he'd nearly gone mad, and to make matters worse, Charlotte didn't appear for tea. Julian took it alone, then retired to his chamber and threw himself on the bed, exhausted. He lay there with his arm over his eyes for a long time, lost in thought. Dusk had descended before he at last dragged himself from the bed and took a seat at the desk by the window.

He'd have to write to Cam. He doubted his cousin would be surprised to receive his letter. Cam must have known all along it would come to this, and was only waiting for Julian to admit it to himself.

*A kindness on Cam's part. One I don't deserve.*

Cam would have to come and retrieve Charlotte himself. She must leave Hadley House at once. Her happiness—no, her very health depended on it, and he could see now she'd never agree to let him take her to Bellwood. He'd hurt her too badly, and nothing he said or did would make her trust him again.

He pressed his palms to his eyes and let the emotions roll over him— each more familiar than the last, but terrible still, for all that they'd become his constant companions. Loss. Regret. A sorrow so deep his bones ached with it.

All the time he'd chased Charlotte around London he'd told himself it was for her own good, but he hadn't truly done it for her. He'd done it for himself, because every time he looked at her he was reminded of the man he'd once been. Julian. That man had embraced life, had treasured every tug and swell and burst of his heart as the sweetest thing life had to offer.

*Joyful, and kind—so kind, with eyes both dark and light at once, like a sky full of stars.*

Every time he saw Charlotte he was reminded he wasn't that man anymore, but he wanted to be—God, he wanted to be, but how could he when he had nothing left in his heart but hurt? Even now, sitting here at this desk, he still didn't know who he was.

But he knew more than he had when he'd arrived.

He knew who he wasn't.

He was no hero, and he couldn't save Charlotte any more than he could bring Colin back to life. The best he could do now was make amends by taking care of Jane. Maybe Charlotte was right and there was no luck, only justice, and he'd pay his dues with a lifetime of regrets.

He stared listlessly out the window. Below in the stable yard a groom led out an enormous gray stallion and held him with some difficulty as the horse pranced and pawed at the ground, anxious to be off.

The man called to someone behind him, someone Julian couldn't see. Damn risky time for a ride. It was nearing dusk. Who—

Charlotte hurried into the stable yard clad in a dark blue riding habit.

Julian rose slowly to his feet. *No. She couldn't possibly be so foolish.*

She mounted the block and swung herself up into the saddle.

His fist met the glass, but neither the groom nor Charlotte turned at the sound. They were too far below to hear him. The groom was speaking to her, his expression earnest. He hadn't relinquished the reins to her yet, and now Julian focused every particle of energy he had on the man as he pounded again and again on the window.

*Don't let her ride out. Refuse her—*

Charlotte tapped her crop impatiently against her boot. She shook her head at the groom and thrust out a hand, beckoning with her fingers for the reins.

*No! For God's sake, don't let her—*

Julian held his breath, but it was no use. The groom handed the reins over to Charlotte. She grabbed them, brought her crop down lightly on the horse's flanks, and in the next breath she was off, the whirl of her dark blue skirts lost in the great cloud of dust kicked up by the stallion's heavy hooves.

Julian raced for the door, his chair toppling to the floor with a crash behind him. He didn't notice the bedchamber doorways flying past him as he tore down the hallway, and he didn't hear the startled squeak of the maid he nearly trampled in his fury to get down the stairs.

Dear God, but the front door was miles away and, incredibly, retreating farther with every one of his pounding strides to reach it.

*This house truly was haunted, haunted and cursed.*

At last, at last he was through the door and flying toward the stables, his heart sinking in his chest as he realized how deep the shadows around the house had become, deep and ominous, and that horse, Jesus, he'd never seen a larger horse, and the way it twitched and stamped to be off it looked almost wild—

*No, don't think about it. Don't think about Charlotte's fragile body broken, her neck twisted...*

Don't think on it. Just get to her.

It took years to reach the stables. Decades. A lifetime, and at some point the words became an endless refrain set to the rhythm of his ragged, panicked breaths—*don't think on it just get to her*—until it became one word only, echoing over and over in his frenzied brain—

*Please, please, please...*

He began shouting before he reached the stable yard. "A horse, at once! Now, damn you! *Move!*"

The groom whirled around, his mouth falling open in shock as he saw Julian barreling toward him, but he darted into the stables and returned at a run, pulling a tall black stallion behind him. The groom tossed him the reins and Julian mounted in one quick, fluid move.

"I'm sorry, sir! I tried to go with her, but she—"

"Later." Julian's reply was tense, clipped. "Where will she go?"

The man looked up at him. "Maybe to the summerhouse? She likes to go there sometimes—"

"Are you sure?"

The groom shook his head miserably. "No, but she went off west, and that's the direction—"

Julian didn't wait to hear the rest, but set his heels into the horse's sides with one sharp jab and headed west, urging his mount into a full gallop as soon as he'd cleared the stable yard. Charlotte had a hell of a start on him—he couldn't see any hint of her in front of him, not even a telltale cloud of dust. It was too dark.

But he was cavalry. He knew how to handle a horse.

He leaned low over the animal's neck until he could see the ground flying beneath him through the horse's ears. The refrain still echoed in his head with each beat of the hooves against the turf...*please, please, please.*

And with each soundless plea came the truth, as sure as the beat of his heart in his chest. He'd never leave Charlotte here. If Cam wanted him out, he'd have to drag him out, and Julian would claw and bite and kick with everything inside him to stay. He'd never give up on her.

He would catch her. He had to.

# Chapter Twenty-one

No one could catch her. She wasn't running anymore—she was flying.

Charlotte pressed her knees hard against the heaving flanks of the horse beneath her. Sweat gathered in the hair at her temples and even through the heavy skirts of her riding habit she could feel the damp heat of the horse against her legs as he raced across the grounds like a demon turned loose from hell.

Hell, or Hadley House. It amounted to the same thing, didn't it? Except she was the demon, and she'd never truly be turned loose from her hell. Her freedom was a thing of the moment, nothing more.

She eased her grip on the reins and gave the horse his head, her gaze focused on the distant tree line, but she didn't see it. She didn't see anything, hear anything, or feel anything other than the smooth, powerful strides of the horse, his hooves reading the landscape as he sailed over the rocks and the tree roots that grew larger and thicker as they neared the forest.

She was nearly there. A steep incline into the dense ridge of trees, wide open parklands on the other side, and then, at the far western edge of the property the tiny summerhouse at the crest of a hill where she liked to stop and gaze at the sweeping views of the valley below, to remind herself there were still places she found beautiful.

But maybe this time she wouldn't stop. Maybe this time she would ride over the parklands forever, her hair flying out behind her and the wind whipping color into her cheeks—

*Charlotte, stop!*

The shout drifted over her, brushed against her, but she paid it no heed. Why should she stop? She was flying, because when the ground collapsed from beneath you, and you could no longer run, you flew.

When Julian walked into her study a week ago, the ground had trembled under her feet, but she'd pulled that lovely numbness around her like a cocoon and burrowed into it, and she'd held her footing. But then they'd walked in the garden, and he'd asked about Hadley....

*An accident... It's time you stopped blaming yourself for it.*

And the thick, dense cocoon protecting her had dissolved like spun sugar on a warm tongue. The ground had given a mighty wrench, and she was left dangling in mid-air, raw, her skin flayed from her bones and her feet scrambling for purchase.

So she ran. But running wasn't good enough. It wasn't fast enough.

So she flew.

*Charlotte! Stop, stop, stop...*

Louder this time, a shout, hoarse and panicked, borne forward by the wind. It was behind her, the sound of pounding hooves drawing closer.

*Julian's voice.*

Charlotte brought her arm down, hard and fast. Her crop sliced through the air and her horse surged so violently beneath her she swayed sideways in the saddle.

From behind her came an agonized roar. *No!*

And then in the next breath he was there, impossibly he was there, beside her, their knees almost touching as his horse paced hers. One of his hands reached for her reins and her heart stuttered to a halt, froze, her terrified gaze on his one white-knuckled hand still holding his own reins.

*One hand.*

Dear God, he would fall. "No! Let go!"

The wind tried to steal her scream, to silence her, but Julian heard her. He jerked his head hard, once. *No.*

Panic clawed at her as her horse plunged for the tree line, his head low and his sinewy legs devouring the ground at their feet. Julian couldn't hold him for long at this pace without being thrown to the ground and trampled to death under his horse, or hers.

*Please don't let him fall, please don't let him fall, not again, not this time, not Julian...*

"Let go! You'll fall!"

He knew the danger, he must know, but *he wouldn't let go.*

The tree line ahead dipped and rose crazily in front of her as it drew closer and closer, and oh, dear God, one of them would strike a tree—*him*, it would be him, she knew it, and her rein was wrapped so tightly around his gloveless hand the leather must be cutting into his flesh, and yet still he held on.

*He held on to her, and wouldn't let go.*

Charlotte wrapped her calves as far as she could around her horse's belly, threw her weight backward in the saddle, and yanked on her reins. Her horse screeched a protest and pulled viciously on the bit to loosen her hold, but she kept her elbows tight to her body and held on, and miraculously the horse began to slow. His pace slackened until at last, with a toss of his head and a sulky snort he came to a halt.

Julian dropped both reins and leapt down from his horse, but Charlotte remained frozen in the saddle, her fingers curled into claws around the leather in her palms.

*Let go. Let go. Let go.*

But she couldn't do it. She couldn't make herself drop the reins, so she sat and stared dumbly at the trees swimming in front of her. *Close. So close.* If she stretched out her arm, she could almost touch one, but something was in her eyes, black at the edges of her vision, and the trees began to tunnel....

Hands wrapped around her waist, strong and firm, gentle.

Julian slid her carefully from her saddle, but as soon as he had her safely on the ground he released her and turned away. The world titled sideways without his hands to steady her, but she said nothing, only watched as he retreated a few paces. He kept his back to her, his head down and his hands on his hips, silent aside from the great, ragged breaths he pulled into his lungs.

Charlotte gripped her skirts between numb fingers. Why didn't he say something? Anything would be better than this awful silence.

He ran a hand through his hair and made a low, rough sound, as if his throat had been scraped raw, then turned to face her at last.

The blood left her head in a dizzying rush. His skin was stretched taut over his white face, his full, sensuous lips tight and grim, and his eyes... Oh, he looked nearly wild, his eyes two burning slits of dark fire.

Dear God. *He was furious.*

Yet he'd touched her so gently just now, his hands careful against her waist as he lifted her from her horse. No matter how angry he was, he would never hurt—

Charlotte's breath caught hard in her chest as she stared at him. This man—the one who stood before her now, his eyes tormented and his face twisted with anguish—he didn't have Captain West's cold, flat eyes. This man wasn't a stranger.

*He was Julian. And Julian would never hurt her.*

"Are you hurt?"

His voice was shaking, but not only with anger. With fear. He was furious, yes, but mostly he was terrified. *For her.*

"I—" Was she hurt? She hardly knew. "No. I don't think so. Are you all right?"

He didn't look it. His hair was damp and tangled and his breath heaved in and out of his chest. He wasn't wearing either a coat or waistcoat, and his white shirt was transparent with sweat. One of his sleeves was ripped from the cuff nearly to his elbow. Oddly, this was what she focused on, and the longer she stared at it, the harder it became to tear her gaze away.

How had he torn it? He'd torn the flesh underneath, as well. She could see the blood. He was hurt. But torn flesh could be treated, couldn't it?

Not like a broken neck.

"Why are you trying hurt yourself, Charlotte?"

Her gaze darted to his face. "Hurt myself? I would never… Why would you ask such a thing?"

His shoulders went rigid. "You promised me, that day in the carriage— you promised you wouldn't pretend anymore. You promised never to hide from me again."

"I—I'm not pretending—"

"You'd have me believe this was a pleasure ride? It was almost dark when you left the stable yard. No, don't try to deny it. I saw you leave alone, on a half-broken horse and riding recklessly, as if you hoped you'd fall."

"No, I—" But no matter how she tried to force it through her lips, the denial wouldn't come, not when he looked at her with that stark panic in his face, with his torn shirt and bloody arm. Not when it could so easily have been his entire body covered in blood, or his neck broken. "When I left the stable yard I thought only of running away, of escape. I—I'm sorry. It was foolish."

A dark, bleak looked passed over his face. "Were you running away from me?"

She closed her eyes. It would be easier that way, so much easier, but the truth was never simple or easy. "No. I was running away from…me."

He stepped close to her and wrapped his hands around her shoulders. "The other night in the garden, with Devon, I thought… But you were saying good-bye to him, weren't you? I said awful things to you, called you—" He stopped, swallowed convulsively. "What I said, and the look on your face that night—it's haunted me, Charlotte. I beg you to forgive me."

*Forgive me.* But what if it was too late for forgiveness? What if there was no absolution to be had?

*Then you lived with your guilt, and you took your punishment.*

Something snapped inside her then—not into pieces, but into place, the last piece in a puzzle she'd long since despaired of completing.

All these months, since the moment she'd set foot in London—the scandals, the sneering contempt of the *ton*, the way she'd refused her family's comfort, refused to go to Bellwood—wasn't that what it had been? A punishment. Her punishment for failing Hadley. She'd wanted to hurt herself, as if her pain could somehow make amends to him, or change what had happened.

And everyone else—her family, the *ton*, even Julian—she'd wanted *them* to hurt her, too. To punish her. She shrank away from the *ton's* cruelty, yes, but even then, even as she'd been desperate to escape it a tiny part of her, a part she'd buried in the darkest recesses of her heart...

That part of her welcomed it. Because a woman like her should be punished. A woman like her deserved to be taught a lesson.

*Dear God. She couldn't look at him.*

"I—I should have stopped you from saying the things you said that night," she whispered. "I didn't, because..."

*Because I didn't know. Until this moment, I didn't know.*

He leaned closer, tried to see into her face. "Because I wouldn't listen, wouldn't let you—"

"No." She looked down at her gloved hands. "I didn't stop you because I wanted... I *wanted* you to hurt me."

He touched his fingers to her chin to raise her face to his. "Why would you want me to hurt you?"

So gentle, his hands. It was his gentleness that undid her, made the truth stir and rise from that deep, secret place inside of her, the place where she ached and bled, and she couldn't stop it, couldn't close the hole in her chest, and the truth kept rising, tearing loose until she couldn't force it back down anymore. All the pain and the secrets and the guilt shoved against her lips, gushed from her mouth, seeped from her pores—all those wet, dark, ugly truths.

"Because I... I deserve to be hurt."

He sucked in a quick, harsh breath, as if a fist had landed in his stomach. "*No.* No you don't, Charlotte."

"You don't know. You don't know what I did. What I am." She didn't want him to know, to see it, to see *her*, because once he saw that ugliness he'd leave her at Hadley House alone, just as she deserved.

He cupped the back of her head in his hand and looked into her eyes. "I *do* know who you are. It's you who doesn't know anymore. Tell me what happened here, Charlotte. To Hadley. To you."

She drew a deep breath. She'd never told anyone the entire truth, and she wouldn't tell Julian now—not the worst of it. Not what had happened to her, because it would only hurt him to know, and it was a useless, meaningless pain. There was nothing he could do—nothing anyone could do.

But she'd tell him as much as she could. "Hadley died."

Julian remained silent, waiting.

"He was about to ride to a hunt. I was standing nearby to see him off when all of a sudden he decided to take a high jump. But his horse balked at the last minute, and Hadley was thrown. The fall broke his neck."

Julian made a low, pained sound deep in his chest. He pressed his palm flat against the nape of her neck. He didn't speak, but he held her so she wouldn't look away from him.

"It was my fault. He was trying to make me look at him, to *see* him, to…to make me love him. And I wanted to, you know—I tried to. I tried so hard, but it was no use. He knew, and he kept trying to find a way."

Julian slid his hands into her hair. "It wasn't your fault. You can't make yourself love someone, Charlotte, any more than you can make yourself *not* love someone."

Tears pressed behind her eyes. "But I promised I would love him. When I married him, I swore it. I thought I could, but it became a lie. I lied to him, and then he died, and now I'm being punished."

"No." His voice was fierce. "No. You can't really believe that, Charlotte."

She gripped his wrists. "I do believe it. It's true, Julian. If it weren't, then none of the rest of it would have happened."

He stroked her hair back from her face. "What happened after he died?"

The truth tried to rise in her chest again, to tear free, but she forced it back. The whole truth of what had happened—that burden was hers to bear alone.

*Tell him what you can, but nothing more.* "His mother, she—"

She didn't want to think about it, didn't want to hear the dowager's screams in her head, but no matter what she did, no matter how many whorehouses she visited in London and how much scandal she courted, she couldn't silence it.

"The shock of Hadley's death destroyed what was left of her mind. She blamed me from the first, and she never forgave me. She wept every day after he was gone, right up until the day she died. I tried to comfort her, but whenever I came near her she'd shriek and wail and work herself into a frenzy. She said she wished her son had never married me, that I was a curse upon him. That it was my fault he'd died. That I'd killed him, and it should have been me instead."

He clasped her face in his hands and looked at her with such tenderness, such grief. "She was mad, Charlotte. You said yourself she was out of her mind."

"She *was* mad, but she wasn't wrong. Hadley was a good man, a kind man—he deserved better than to spend the last months of his life with a wife who didn't love him, could never love him. He deserved so much better—" Her throat closed on an odd, choked sound. "So much better than me."

He caught her to him, wrapped his arms around her and held her, so tight and so close she felt every thud of his heart in her own chest. "Let it go, Charlotte. Let it out, or it will keep hurting you."

No, she wouldn't let it out, wouldn't cry, because if she did, she'd never stop. But even as she denied the grief it took her, seized her by the neck and shook her like a ragdoll until there was nothing else she could do but sob against him, great heaving sobs that threatened to tear her apart.

He held her head against his chest and stroked her hair until the wracking cries subsided into quiet tears, and still he held her and murmured to her like a child, his hands warm and soothing against her back. When she was exhausted from the storm of emotion, he gathered her into his arms without a word, lifted her onto his horse, then retrieved her horse's reins and swung up behind her on the saddle. "Lean back on me."

She let herself sag against him.

"That's it." He settled her so her back rested against his chest and wrapped one arm around her waist. "Sleep."

Miraculously she did, cradled in the curve of his body, his breath a soft, steady rhythm against her back. She thought she felt his lips at her temple and his whispers in her ear, but then she succumbed to the kind of sleep that had eluded her for months, deep and dreamless.

When she awoke, the sky was dark over her head. Someone was speaking, but she couldn't quite make sense of the words. "Julian?"

"I'm here, sweetheart. Slide your arms around my neck."

She obeyed without question. The saddle disappeared out from under her and for a moment she panicked as she became groundless again, suspended, but then she felt Julian's arms under her, and her cheek found his chest, which vibrated with a low sigh as she relaxed against him. Then he was moving—door, stairs, hallways, and more doors until at last she felt a soft coverlet beneath her and knew he'd brought her to her bedchamber.

She must have slipped into another dream for a while because she lost some time. When she awoke later it was to a hushed argument taking place at her bedside.

"You can't be in here with her," a voice hissed. Mrs. Boyle? "It's not proper, Captain West. I can't allow—"

"No." Charlotte struggled to sit up, but her eyes seemed fused shut and sleep threatened to take her down again. "I want him to stay."

"Now, don't agitate yourself, my lady." A soft, motherly hand pressed her back down into the mattress. "You've been through quite an ordeal. You can thank Captain West tomorrow—"

"*No.* Julian." She forced her eyes open and grasped his hand. "Don't go."

His fingers closed around hers. "I won't. You heard Lady Hadley, Mrs. Boyle. She wants me to stay, and I'm sure you don't wish to upset her, as fragile as she is right now."

Charlotte fell back against the pillows and let her eyes fall half closed.

Mrs. Boyle huffed and fretted, but at last she accepted the inevitable. "Oh, very well." She meandered around the room, straightened a few perfectly straight objects on Charlotte's dressing table, and then closed the door behind her with an offended click.

For a moment after she left neither of them said anything. Then, because there was so much to say and no place to begin, Charlotte blurted, "You're bleeding."

"What?" Julian glanced down at the long, bloody scratch on his arm. "Oh. It's nothing."

"It bled quite a lot."

He smiled. "And now it's stopped."

"It looks deep. May I see it?"

"It's nothing, I promise you." But he sat down on the edge of her bed, obediently turned over his arm, and held it out so she could inspect the cut. The smooth skin seemed too vulnerable to belong to Julian, too fragile to protect such a muscular limb.

She hesitated for a single moment before she touched him—only a moment, a breath in time, but it lengthened, stretched, became infinite, for surely a mere moment wasn't enough to hold such emotion, such promise.

*Or such risk.* Once she touched him, she might not be able to stop.

And yet it was already too late, wasn't it? She hadn't touched him yet, and already she couldn't stop. Her fingertip met his warm skin and stroked lightly down his arm, just to the right of the gash.

His breath caught hard in his throat.

She looked into his eyes—dark and heavy-lidded—drew his hand slowly to her mouth, and pressed her lips into his palm.

# Chapter Twenty-two

As soon as her soft, red lips met his palm, those lips he'd longed for in one fevered dream after another, Julian knew he was lost. Cam and Ellie, Jane, even Colin—they all faded from his mind the instant her mouth touched his skin.

She brought his hand to her cheek and held it there. Her eyes found his, a question in their bottomless depths, but he didn't give her a chance to ask it. There wasn't any need. They both knew the answer—they'd known since that night more than a year ago when he found her waiting for him under a sky full of stars. So he simply brought his other hand up, cradled her face in both his palms, and touched his mouth to hers.

She sighed, long and low. He caught the soft exhalation on his tongue, tasted it. *Sweet.* Both familiar and new at once, her taste, like a hazy melody teasing at the edges of his consciousness, one he thought he remembered until he heard it again and found he'd forgotten how beautiful it was, how much it moved him.

"Stay, Julian." She slid her hands into the opening of his shirt to brush her fingertips over the nape of his neck. "Stay with me tonight."

Julian shivered at her touch. Ah God, nothing had changed. Her most innocent caress still had the power to send him to his knees, to make him want to stay there. He would. Tonight. He'd stay with her, and he'd love her, and he'd wait to think about tomorrow when it came.

He drew back to look into her eyes. "Did you think I would leave you?" He stroked his thumb down her cheek and brushed it across her lower lip, his groin tightening at the hint of wet warmth he found there.

She pressed her lips to the pad of his thumb, then lifted his fingers one by one to kiss them each in turn. "Kiss me again."

He took her lips with a groan. She opened eagerly for him and he surged inside, desperate to taste her everywhere. She met his strokes, her tongue as insistent as his, her mouth wet and open and so hot and sweet he feared he'd spend from just kissing her, before he could even tear off his breeches.

He should have known it would be like this. He never could stop at a taste with Charlotte. Her skin, her sighs and murmurs made him ravenous, and within seconds he was kissing her deeply, his tongue searching every corner of her mouth, the shell of her ear, her neck. His hands were rough in her hair, tugging as he sucked at the pulse point at her throat. God, he could stay here forever with her pulse fluttering wildly under his darting tongue, her breasts pressed against his chest, his hand hot against the smooth silk of her stockings, sliding higher, higher, over the bare skin above her garter, so close now, close to that heaven between her thighs....

She made the tiniest movement, almost a flinch. Julian paused, his hand going still. "Did I hurt you?"

"No. It's nothing. Just a bruise from the saddle."

A bruise, on the tender white skin of her thigh. Where else was she bruised, hurt? He pulled back slightly and let his gaze move over her. She'd lost her hat somewhere during her mad dash for the forest. Most of her hair had come loose, but a few pins were still tangled haphazardly in the long dark strands, and one of them had scratched her cheek. Some buttons had been torn from her riding habit, and her hands...

"Let me see your hands, Charlotte."

She hesitated, but he took her wrists and turned her hands up. Her gloves had protected her from being scraped raw by the reins, but the tender skin at the heart of her palms had already begun to swell and purple with bruises.

He pressed his face against her neck and inhaled. Her skin was so soft here, the curve where her neck met her shoulder so fragrant. She might have broken her neck today. Her skin might be cold by now, with no pulse there for his tongue to caress, and he was so desperate to get between her thighs he'd nearly forgotten—

"Julian?"

He wanted her, so much his blood scorched him as it rushed through his veins, but though her body had survived today's ordeal, she was fragile still, with wounds and scars beneath her skin. She'd lost so much—everything, even herself—and now he wanted to take more from her.

He traced a gentle finger over the swollen skin of her palm. The bruises would fade, her body would heal, but what of the lacerations inside her, under her skin? The deep gashes in her heart, her soul—would they heal, or would they bleed forever?

"Julian? Are you all right?"

He raised her hands to his lips and pressed a soft kiss into each of her palms. "Yes, sweetheart. I just want to slow down."

Flesh and bone, a body—it was alive or it was dead, and nothing in between. Not like a heart, which could keep beating even after everything else that made a person who they were was gone.

*If you touched a body with love, could you heal a heart?*

"Julian?"

Charlotte was looking up at him with such big, uncertain eyes he couldn't resist taking her mouth again, but then he set her gently away from him. She made a protesting noise in her throat and clutched at his shirt to bring him back to her, but he captured her hands and lowered them gently to the coverlet. "I won't leave you, Charlotte. I couldn't, even if I wanted to."

He rose, crossed the room, and locked the door. When he turned back, she'd moved to the middle of the bed, her knees curled under her. God, he was going to bare every inch of her, slowly, kiss each bit of creamy flesh as it was revealed, worship her with his hands and his mouth and pray it was enough to heal her heart.

"How slowly do you wish to go?" She bit her lip. "That is, do you think you might come back to the bed?" Her cheeks heated in a furious blush.

Julian couldn't help his grin. She was part temptress, part innocent, with her teeth caught in that plump red lip and that blush. "I think..." He tugged off his boots and tossed them into a corner. "Nothing could stop me"—he pulled his shirt over his head and let it drop to the floor—"from coming to you in that bed."

"Oh, my."

Her eyes were like the stroke of a hand against his bare skin as she watched him approach the bed. She crawled across the coverlet to the edge and wrapped her arms around his waist, sighing with pleasure as he pulled the remaining pins from her hair.

He caught his breath as the dark tresses spilled into his hands. "I dreamed about you like this, with your hair loose in a cloud around you."

She laid her cheek against his belly and traced a finger around his navel. "So much fuss is made over a woman's figure, but a man's body is just as beautiful. Or is it only your body I want to taste?" She pressed her open mouth against him, her tongue following the path her finger had taken to lick delicately around his navel.

Julian threw his head back with a gasp, his hands moving instinctively to clasp her head and hold her to him, to feel the wet warmth of her mouth on every hot inch of his skin. "Charlotte, wait."

She slid a finger under the waistband of his breeches. "I can't wait any longer, Julian."

He looked down at her, at her earnest, beautiful face and his resolve slipped at the desire he saw there. "I want this to be for you—"

He wrapped his hand around the long length of her hair and tried to ease her head gently away from him, but she curved one hand around his hip to draw him closer and gazed up at him, her dark eyes luminous, her face flushed. "There is no you and me. Not now. There's only us."

For him there was only her, and God she was lovely, kneeling on the bed before him with his hands buried in her hair, her red lips open and eager and her fingers just a little clumsy as she unbuttoned his falls. He brushed a few dark tendrils back from her face and curved a hand over her cheek. "Ah sweet, I just want—"

She looked up at him, an impish grin on her lips. "Don't say you want to slow down again."

A defeated groan slipped from his lips. "Men's bodies are greedy, love. I'm not sure I can slow down now."

She gripped his waist to hold him still and kissed her way down his stomach until she was dangerously close to the edge of his breeches. "I don't want you to slow down. I want you to be greedy."

His hard length strained against his falls, demanding her hands, her mouth. He looked down at her with heavy-lidded eyes, at her plump lips curved in a secret half smile. God, he knew that smile, and his cock jerked with anticipation at the memory of what followed it.

And then she pushed his breeches aside and her mouth was on him, hot and wet and perfect.

"Ah God, Charlotte." Julian's knees buckled at the exquisite torment of her lips sliding over his aching flesh. His hips moved helplessly as her slick tongue circled and teased. She took him deeper with each of his panting breaths and loved him for long, hot moments, her mouth sweet agony, until Julian felt the delicious tightening in his lower belly and drew away from her with a groan.

She grasped his hips to bring him back, but he resisted. "No, sweet. I want to be inside you." He'd waited for this moment with her, dreamed of sinking into her soft, welcoming body, her arms tight around him and her breathless cries in his ears. Now it was here. For tonight she was his, and he would savor it.

He shucked his breeches, climbed onto the bed, and went to work on the buttons of her riding jacket. "How is it you're still clothed?"

"Am I? I hadn't noticed. I did notice you're *not*." She smoothed her hands over his shoulders with an appreciative sigh, then teased her fingertips down the arch of his spine.

"No, you don't." He tossed her jacket over the side of the bed, then sent her riding skirt sailing after it so she wore only her thin muslin riding shirt and underclothes. "It's my turn to play with you." He nudged her onto her back and stretched out on his side beside her.

Her eyes went wide. "*Play with me?* How—"

"Like this." He turned her face toward his and nipped lightly at her lips, his tongue darting and teasing until her breaths came short and fast. "Yes." He took the lobe of her ear in his teeth and bit gently. "I want you breathless."

She gave a shaky laugh. "I *am*."

With a single tug he released the tie at the front of her shirt and slipped his hand inside the loose material to caress her breast. "I want you hard and aching for me, *here*." He ran a thumb across her nipple until it strained for more; then he rolled the tender bud between his thumb and forefinger. She cried out and the high, needy sound shot straight to his cock.

*No. Slowly.* He would work her slowly, build her up until she was mindless, begging for release. He held her hips flush against the bed and took her other nipple in his mouth, biting it gently. "Do you need more, sweetheart?" She didn't answer, but writhed against the bed as he continued to stroke her. "I think that's a *yes*."

He moved to her other breast and circled her nipple with his thumb, his touch slow, feather-light, torturous, then bent his head and took the dark pink bud into his mouth to suckle her, his lips gentle at first, then more insistent, his tongue darting roughly over the tender peak as his hunger grew.

He drew back to gaze at her, at her dark pink nipples so hard and tight against the transparent white muslin, wet from his mouth. He blew on the peaks and watched them tighten even further, but his gaze darted to her face when she whimpered in response. Her hips rose from the bed, tempting him to slide a hand down her belly and run his fingers through her damp curls.

She cried out again and her back arched sharply. "*Please*, Julian."

God, he was greedy, greedy and desperate, because with that one breathless plea all his plans to tease her evaporated in the heat of his own desire. He tore off her shirt and chemise and fumbled with her drawers until he slid them off at last and she lay bare before him.

"Charlotte." He pressed a lingering kiss between her breasts. He could feel her heart throbbing against his lips. "You don't know, you can't know how lovely you are to me, how much I want you."

Her fingers twisted in his hair. "No more waiting, Julian. I want you, too. I'm ready."

He groaned as his fingers found the weeping center of her desire and circled the tiny nub with his thumb, once, again—

She let out a strangled cry and urged herself against his hand. "Julian, *now*."

"Let me just… I don't want to hurt you, sweetheart." He held her open, his thumb caressing still in slow circles as he pressed one finger inside her, and God, she was ready, her damp flesh yielding, her body melting for him.

"Yes, love. *Now*." He came over her and kneeled between her thighs, gasping as her hand reached out to caress his cock. He rocked into her fist, unable to stop himself, but then she pressed him against her damp heat and he surged inside her with one deep, hard stroke.

She sank her fingernails into his back as he began to move, his neck corded with the effort to keep from plunging wildly into her like some untried schoolboy with his first woman. Sweat broke out across his brow and his breath came in harsh, panting gasps, but he kept his strokes deep and steady for her.

"Oh, yes. Oh please, Julian."

She wrapped her legs around his waist and rose to meet him with every thrust, pleading with him, begging him, her sighs and moans driving him so mad with desire it took everything in him to hold on, to wait for her. "Come for me, sweetheart."

At last she cried out and her body convulsed around him and ah, God, the sweetness of her, the beauty of her… He couldn't get enough. His back arched and he buried his harsh groan in the soft skin of her neck as his pleasure took him.

They were both panting when he rolled to his side and gathered her into his arms. She moved to lay her head on his chest and he held her against him, both of them silent, because if they didn't move or speak, tomorrow might not find them, and they could stay here forever, where there were no doubts and no unanswered questions.

He came awake a while later, his eyes opening to a dark, quiet room… somewhere. His chamber at Bellwood? No, that was a place of nightmares, and there were no nightmares here. Here was deep, even breathing, a hand on his stomach, and something soft and warm against his neck.

*Charlotte.*

She was asleep, her cheek pillowed on his chest. He tightened his arms around her and relaxed back against the bed. What had woken him?

A dream.

Not Colin this time. Not a nightmare, but something so sweet he stayed as still as he could to hold on to it, because in this dream he could touch one of the tiny glimmers of light pinned to the midnight blue sky. He could touch a star.

*Charlotte.* In the dream he traced her smile so the shape of it would be always on his fingertips—more than a memory. A part of his skin.

*Julian. I knew you'd come.*

*Did you hope I would?*

*You know I did. You already know.*

And he did know. He's always known. He was born knowing.

The next time he woke there was the faintest trace of light in the eastern sky. He rose from the bed, tugged on his breeches, threw his shirt over his head and wandered over to look out the window.

Tomorrow had found them. His dream from the night before grew fainter with every finger of sun curling over the horizon, and in its place...questions.

Questions with no answers.

*Jane.* He was betrothed to her. He couldn't change his mind now without loss of honor, and if he did, he'd lose something even more precious, too. His one chance to make amends to Colin. Jane would be left alone, with no protection—

"You're dressed."

Julian turned away from the window. Charlotte was propped against the pillows, her eyes sleepy, her dark curls spilling wildly over her bare shoulders.

If ever there was a moment he wanted to keep forever, this was it.

"Not really." He crossed the room and sat down next to her on the bed. He would leave soon, before he couldn't make himself leave at all, but not now. Not yet. "I can't properly be said to be dressed in this shirt." He stuck his fingers into the rip and wiggled them, hoping to amuse her, to see her smile.

She didn't. Instead her face went alarmingly pale. "It could have been so much worse."

"But it wasn't."

"If you'd fallen, I never would have forgiven myself."

*No. Not this. Not with him.* "Don't do this, Charlotte."

"You could have broken your arm, or your leg. You could have broken your neck—"

"If I had, it would have been my own fault." He took her chin in his hand, stunned at the fierce tenderness inside him. "I'm a grown man. I made the decision to come after you, to grab your reins."

Her gaze darted away from his. "You came because you had to come. I was reckless and foolish. What else could you do but follow me? I gave you no choice."

"*No.* Look at me." He waited until her gaze met his. "I made my own choices, and so did Hadley."

She was quiet for a moment, then, "You mean to say it's not my fault he died."

"Ah, sweetheart. A tragedy like that is no one's fault, no matter what Hadley's mother said. It just…is. You must know he never would have blamed you."

"No. He wouldn't have. But I blame myself."

The break in her voice cleaved his heart in two. "You have to make peace with it. Don't you see, Charlotte? Nothing will ever be right again until you forgive yourself."

She curled her fingers into his palm. "How do you know so much about forgiveness?"

*Because I've denied it to myself, just as you have.*

That hopelessness in the face of unbearable pain, that crushing guilt—he knew it as well as she did, and he couldn't outrun his demons any more than Charlotte could. He'd realized that yesterday when he'd flown across the grounds after her, his panicked heartbeats echoing in his head as she wobbled in her saddle, one breath away from being crushed under her horse's hooves.

He drew a deep breath and met her eyes. "You were right all along, Charlotte. I'm no hero, despite what all of London thinks. The soldiers I dragged from the battlefield to the field hospital? I left someone else behind."

She said nothing, only squeezed his hand.

"My best friend," he said after a moment. "Colin Hibbert. He was killed by a French Dragoon—the sword passed clean through his chest and out his back. If I'd been there, I might have done something, fought beside him, but I was too busy being the hero. I left him to die alone on the battlefield."

Tears rushed to her eyes, and Jesus, it was bitter to see her cry tears for him after all she'd had to bear. Tears he didn't deserve.

"You blame yourself for his death."

He ran a weary hand down his face. "I do. Or I did. I hardly know anymore."

"Young men die in war, Julian. They die, and it just…is," she whispered, giving his words back to him. "It's no one's fault."

Fault, blame—the words felt meaningless to him now, even selfish. What did it matter who was at fault? It didn't change anything. "Colin's dead either way, and I'm still London's conquering hero."

He heard the bitterness in his voice, and she did too, because something flickered in her dark eyes. She reached for him, but after a breathless moment he gently pulled away from her. "My betrothed." He cleared his throat. "Her name is Jane. Jane Hibbert. She's Colin's sister. Aside from an elderly aunt she's alone, and I—"

"You have a chance to make amends."

"Yes."

She let out a long sigh, then reached out and took his hand. "Julian? You weren't being a hero when you saved those soldiers."

He flinched. It was true, but it hurt like the devil to hear *her* say it. He looked away. "What was I, then?"

She turned his face back toward hers. "Don't you know? Don't you recognize yourself? When you saw those men struck down, you couldn't have behaved in any way other than you did. In that moment you were, down to your soul, just who you are. You weren't a hero that day—you were more than that. You were Julian."

Her faith in him, her kindness, after all he'd said to her, all he'd done— it shamed him. His throat went tight and he reached blindly for her. She opened her arms to him and drew him down beside her, touched her lips to his forehead, his cheeks, his eyelids, and he didn't think of Jane, or what he owed to Colin. He thought only of Charlotte, of finding her mouth with his so they both could know what forgiveness felt like.

They woke much later. She was cradled in his arms, her back pressed to his chest, their legs entwined. He tightened his arm around her waist and cupped his hand over her belly. "Charlotte? Will you let me take you to Bellwood?"

She hesitated, then threaded her fingers through his. "Yes."

There was more to say, but he didn't say it. He buried his face in her hair, inhaled her sweet lemon scent, and he couldn't even remember what it was.

# Chapter Twenty-three

As the carriage slowed Charlotte roused herself and pushed the curtain aside to glance out the window. Sometime during the past few hours while she sat in her solitary corner, daylight had given way to a dusky purple twilight. She watched out the window as the carriage drew to a stop in front of tonight's inn.

The Liar's Arms. Well, that seemed appropriate.

They'd reached Oxted, then. They'd arrive at Bellwood by luncheon tomorrow. The familiar panic began to well in her throat, but she took a deep breath and swallowed it back down. She couldn't stay at Hadley House—she saw that now. Later, yes, in the future, but not yet.

She let the curtain fall back across the window. Three days to make the journey from Hampshire to Kent. It was more than they needed, but Julian insisted on setting a leisurely pace to Bellwood so as not to exhaust her—frequent stops for rest and refreshment, no travel after the sun set—yet despite his careful attentions, weariness gnawed at her bones.

Three days. She leaned her head back against the squabs and closed her eyes. Three days ago she'd lied to Julian. It felt like an eternity had passed since then.

She'd been calm enough at first, riding next to him in the carriage, his warm thigh pressed to hers. It became more difficult when he wrapped an arm around her and urged her to rest against him, but she managed to keep her peace, even when he stroked her hair to soothe her into sleep. But as the miles disappeared under the horses' hooves she felt the faintest tickling behind her lips, and soon afterward it became painfully clear that…

*The truth will out.*

The tickle became an itch, then a sting, then a burn, and then such a raging conflagration nothing but the most violent effort on her part could keep the truth from blazing forth and burning to ash everything in its path.

*And the main thing in its path was Julian.*

So she'd done the only thing she could think to do. She'd retreated behind pleasantries and careful smiles. By mid-morning on the second day she'd stopped smiling and lapsed into monosyllables. This morning she'd pressed her lips together and gone utterly silent. At last, unable to bear the hurt look in his dark eyes, she'd opened her mouth long enough to say she preferred to ride in the carriage alone. Julian hadn't said a word, but at the next inn he'd procured a mount and left her to her lonely fate.

A liar's fate.

*But she hadn't lied. She simply hadn't told the entire truth. It wasn't the same as a lie.*

She'd been telling herself that since they left Hampshire, but three days later it still felt like a lie, and now here they were at the Liar's Arms.

Which seemed appropriate.

A light rap sounded on the carriage door. "Lady Hadley?" Julian's voice, cool and distant. "I've secured rooms for us. Will you alight?"

Charlotte winced at the formal address. "I beg your pardon, Captain." She wiped her eyes with her gloved fingers, took a deep breath and opened the carriage door. "I must have fallen asleep."

Julian held out his hand to assist her from the carriage. He released her the instant the toe of her slipper touched the ground, but his gaze narrowed on her face. "You do look fatigued. Are you well?"

"Yes, quite well. You said you secured rooms?"

"Yes, and I ordered you a bath."

She fixed one of the meaningless smiles onto her face. "That will be lovely." Against his wishes she'd declined taking a maid with her on the journey. Hardly proper, but at the moment Sarah was on the road somewhere between London and Bellwood, and if she couldn't have Sarah, she chose not to have anyone. "You'd make a wonderful lady's maid, Captain."

She meant to lighten the mood and perhaps wipe the grim look from his eyes, but Julian's face remained stiff. "I'll order dinner delayed for an hour, then. Will that do?"

She wilted like a flower under a boot heel at his cold tone, though it was nothing more than she expected. And dinner—dear God, the very idea of a stilted, near-silent dinner with Julian made her throb with exhaustion, but she didn't want to hide in her room like a coward, either. Perhaps she'd feel better after her bath. "Yes. Thank you."

But she didn't feel better after her bath. The warm water eased the aches from her sore limbs, but any illusions she'd cherished about her deceit vanished into the curls of steam rising from the tub.

The Liar's Arms. She kicked listlessly at the cooling bathwater. It wasn't as if the name of the inn was a sign of some sort, or a condemnation of her actions. It was nothing more than a simple coincidence. And anyway, she hadn't lied. She hadn't revealed everything to Julian about what happened after Hadley died, but that was a lie of omission only, which wasn't the same as a true lie.

Charlotte rose from the bath and reached for the length of toweling a maid had placed on a chair. A chair from The Liar's Arms.

Which was an appropriate name, because she was a liar.

*And she'd remain one.*

That is, as long as she could keep from blurting out the truth before they reached Bellwood, and to do that she'd have to avoid Julian as much as possible. One more reproachful look from his dark eyes was all it would take to break her.

She pulled on her night rail and wrapper, yanked on the bell to summon a servant, then paced from one end of the room to the other until a maid appeared at the door. "Take a message to Captain West, if you please. Tell him I'm too tired for dinner tonight and will retire at once. He should dine without me."

"Shall I have a tray sent up, your ladyship?"

Charlotte's stomach rebelled at the thought of food. "Nothing to eat, but a glass of port will be welcome."

The maid bobbed a curtsey. "Yes, my lady."

Charlotte leaned back against the door and stayed there until the maid returned with a tray holding a single a glass of port. As soon as the door closed behind the girl Charlotte sank into the chair before the fire. She curled her legs underneath her and sipped at her port while she watched the flames dance in the grate. They seemed too bright, somehow, so bright they made her eyes burn and tear.

It was better if Julian didn't know. It wasn't as if he could change it. He'd said it himself, that morning at Hadley House after they'd made love.

It just is.

She turned her hand and watched the ruby red liquid swirl and cling to the bowl of the glass. It was in the past, and God knew it had taken all the strength she had to leave it there. It had nearly destroyed her, and if she let it back into the present, there was no telling what it would do to Julian. She wouldn't steal his chance at happiness from him—

*Slam!*

Charlotte jumped up from her chair and spilled half the glass of port down the front of her white night rail.

"Charlotte! I know you're not asleep. Open this door. *Now.*"

Charlotte clutched the night rail to her throat. What in God's name was Julian doing out in the hallway, shouting—

"I will not leave until you open this door!"

No, not just shouting, but pounding against the door until the wood threatened to splinter. She hurried across the room and pressed her mouth into the gap between the wall and the door frame. Had it grown wider since he started pounding? "What do you want? Didn't the maid deliver my message?"

"Oh, I got your message." He gave the latch a violent wrench. "Now open this door."

"I will not," she hissed into the gap. "I told you, I've retired for the evening. I'm not decent."

"Decent?" He gave a disbelieving snort. "It's a bit late for you to worry about that now, when just the other night I had my mouth on your—"

Charlotte threw open the door, grasped his arm, pulled him inside the room, and slammed it shut behind her. "For God's sake. What's the matter with you? Do you want the entire inn to hear how you…"

Well. There was no way she was going to finish *that* sentence.

He smirked. "How I what?"

"Never mind what." She crossed her arms over her chest and glared at him. Every innocent traveler within shouting distance didn't need to know he'd put his mouth on her—

Well. There was no way she was going to finish *that* thought. "What do you want, Captain West?"

An angry growl tore from his throat. "Don't call me that."

*He was growling at her?*

"Don't call you Captain West?"

"You heard me."

She gaped at him, and for the first time noticed he looked a bit disheveled. His dark hair fell over his forehead in a tousled mass of waves, he'd left his coat somewhere, and his cheekbones were flushed, as if he'd—

"For pity's sake. You've been drinking, haven't you?"

He waved a hand at her night rail. "So have you. Either that or you've stabbed yourself."

Charlotte glanced down at the red port stain on her night rail. *Damn it.* "That's your fault. You made me spill my port when you tried to smash my door to bits."

He leaned a hip casually against the door. "I wouldn't have had to smash your door to bits at all if you'd simply come down to dine as you said you would."

"Is that what this is about? My not coming down to dine? I beg your pardon. I didn't think you'd mind, and I confess I find the extremity of your disappointment surprising."

"Do you?" In the blink of an eye he abandoned his relaxed post to prowl toward her. "You think I don't care if you eat? You can't afford to miss another meal, Charlotte. You're already too thin."

"Is that so? Well, I don't recall you complaining about my figure the other night!"

*Oh, for pity's sake!* She hadn't truly just said that, had she?

He ran a finger across his lips as his hot gaze raked over her. "Oh, I'm not complaining, sweetheart. On the contrary. Your figure is all I've been able to think about for the past four days."

Charlotte shivered at the heat in his eyes. He was looking at her as if he could see through her night rail. Could he? She pulled her wrapper tighter around her waist.

He laughed. "Do you think that's going to do any good? You don't even need to be in the same room for me to see your body, to hear your cries and gasps—"

"Stop it, Julian! Why are you saying these things to me?"

"You'd prefer I didn't? Ah, that must be why you hid from me tonight." He closed in on her and pulled her against his chest. "Because you don't want me to look at you? Because you want me to call you Lady Hadley, even though it chokes me? Because I can't bear to be confined in a carriage with you without touching you?"

Charlotte's knees buckled at the wild look in his eyes. "No." Her voice was a whisper. "Because it's better this way, Julian, for both of us. You're betrothed—"

"You think I don't know that?" He pressed his face into the curve of her shoulder and inhaled desperately. "I swore to myself I'd stay away from you tonight, and I tried. Ah God, I tried, but I can't."

Her eyes slid closed as he kissed and sucked at her neck as if she were a feast laid out only for him. With every moment that passed she vowed to push him away, but her fingers refused to obey. Instead they tangled in his hair to hold him more tightly against her.

*He's not yours, and he never will be.*

But he was. Not to keep, not to hold forever, but tonight, just for one more night he was hers, and she could no more refuse him now than she could rip her heart from her chest.

A harsh breath tore from his throat. "I won't let you go so easily, Charlotte. I lo—"

"Hush." She pressed a finger to his lips. She didn't want his declaration—not now, when it didn't belong to her. He would be another woman's husband and another child's father, and she...

She would lose him again and again, every time she was compelled to see him with his wife and—*dear God*—eventually his children. She'd never marry again, not without love, and she'd never love anyone but Julian. Her heart would fall into pieces every time she looked at him, and she'd never be able to see that as anything other than a punishment.

She wouldn't see him again after he left her at Bellwood. This wasn't a beginning between them. It was an ending.

But not yet. Tonight she'd lie in his arms and love him and try to forget she'd lose him tomorrow. She leaned her forehead against his for a moment, laid her hands against his chest, and felt his muscles tense under her fingers, then slowly, tenderly she found his lips with hers.

*Oh, God. So sweet.*

And after all, endings didn't have to be bitter, did they? They could be sweet, sweet enough to be mistaken for another beginning.

His gathered great fistfuls of her night rail into his hands. "I won't say it, then." He held her gently with a hand against her throat and looked into her eyes. "But it's no less true for my silence, Charlotte, and you know it, just as I do."

He didn't give her a chance to speak, to deny it, but kissed her deeply, his mouth open, his tongue seeking hers, and she knew there could be no denial, not with the taste of him on her lips, and she met him eagerly, her mouth clinging to his, ravenous, every thrust of his tongue chasing the breath from her lungs.

Her breath, her heart—they were his.

She tore away with a gasp and grasped his wrists to stop him when his hands shot out to cradle her face and bring her lips back to his. "No." She twined her fingers with his, raised his hand to her mouth and touched her open lips to his knuckles. "I want to watch your face this time."

Julian's lips parted in a sigh as she pressed a brief, hot kiss to the inside of his wrist. She lowered his hands to her waist and held them there for a moment to let him know not to move.

"Charlotte…"

"Shhh." She traced a finger around his lips. "Soon."

His skin was hot under her fingertips, the heat of him burning her hands through his shirt as she slid them over his chest and leaned forward to taste the hollow of his throat. He shuddered as her tongue played against him there, his hands squeezing her waist.

She tugged the hem of his shirt from his breeches and admired each inch of his skin as it was revealed, his stomach, corded with muscle, his skin darker than hers, olive-tinted, and so smooth under that seductive trail of dark hair low on his belly. She sifted it through her fingertips so she could hear his breath come short and feel his chest heave, then she took his hands from her waist and held his arms up to lift the shirt over his head, so his chest was bared for her.

"Let me touch you." He dragged his hands from her waist up her rib cage. She shivered as they brushed the sides of her breasts. He noticed, and a faint smile touched his lips. "Or do you want to drive us both mad?"

"Am I driving you mad?" She raised herself to the tips of her toes to press her lips behind his ear, against his neck, his throat, soft, brief, open-mouthed kisses, just a taste until she opened her mouth against the center of his chest, felt his heart leap up to meet her lips as she licked him there and teased at his nipples, circling first with her fingertips, then the tip of her tongue.

His sharp indrawn breath made heat bloom in the secret place between her thighs. "Touch me then, before we both go mad."

She felt his smile against her neck as he ran his teeth lightly over the sensitive skin there. He moved down her body, his hair tickling her chin. She gasped as he opened his mouth over her nipple, hot and wet against her straining flesh. A sigh slipped from her lips as he suckled her. How could his lips be so soft and so demanding at once? She wanted to ask, but when she opened her mouth all she could manage was an inarticulate moan. "*Julian…*"

He didn't give her time to say more, but tossed aside her wrapper, dragged her night rail over her head, and lifted her into his arms. He lowered her onto the bed, then stood there for a moment, his hands on his falls, his eyes dark and hot as he looked down at her. "Do you want me, Charlotte?"

She gazed up at him. The firelight caressed him, trailing glowing fingers over one side of his face and burnishing his shoulders and chest to a deep gold. His hands hesitated over the buttons on his falls as he awaited her answer.

*Want him.* Didn't he know everything in her ached for him? Not just for his body, but for *him*, body and soul, for everything he was, and everything he would become. She wanted him beyond reason, and beyond any right she had to want him. "Yes. So much, Julian."

*So much it breaks my heart.*

Some emotion flitted across his face—pain, almost as if she'd spoken the words aloud, but there would be time for pain later, a lifetime, and she wouldn't give it a place here and now.

She held out her arms to him. "Come here."

And his face, ah, her heart did break then, for there was such yearning there, and she knew it was mirrored in her own face just as desperately, but hopelessly.

He came to her, moved over her, and she pushed the thought from her mind. Nothing else mattered but this moment, his legs twined with hers, his skin under her fingertips as her hands roamed over his back to his hips, his thighs—

"Ah Charlotte, *yes*," he groaned as her hand closed around his cock. His hips surged forward as she stroked him. Triumph darted through her as she tightened her fingers around him and he gave another guttural moan and arched into her caress. Dear God, she wanted to make him shatter *now*, with just her hands on him, his magnificent body so much stronger than hers, but a body she'd rendered weak with desire as he panted and strained for his pleasure—

"Inside you." He covered her hand with his own to still it. "Inside you, here." He slipped his hand between her legs, slid a finger inside her, and brushed his thumb over the aching center of her, once, then again, until she abandoned any thought to bring him to pleasure with her hand and wrapped her legs around his waist to urge him closer, gasping when the head of his cock nudged inside her.

He hissed in a sharp breath and sank into her with one urgent thrust. "Ah, you're so wet for me...always this way, sweetheart," he murmured to her as he moved inside her, whispering words of passion and desire tangled with love. She clung to those words, hoarded them greedily, deep in her heart as she held him deep inside her body, his surging strokes taking her higher and higher until, with a low moan she found her pleasure and Julian followed, burying his face in her neck with a hoarse cry as he shuddered over her.

He gathered her close against him and eased over onto his side, his arm wrapped around her waist and his face buried in her hair. "I'll find another way to take care of Jane," he murmured after a moment. "I won't let you go, Charlotte. I can't. I love you."

She said nothing, but watched the fire and listened to his breaths grow deep and even. Just before he drifted off to sleep he sighed, long and low.

Charlotte turned her face into the pillow.

# Chapter Twenty-four

Even in the dim light of the room, with the curve of his lips lost in shadows and his exquisite dark eyes closed in sleep, Julian's face could still break her heart.

She'd woken hours ago. For a long time she lay next to him and listened to the sound of his deep, even breathing, but at some point she'd risen in the dark and quietly moved the chair to the side of the bed, and now she sat, fully dressed, her arms wrapped around her knees, and watched his chest rise and fall under the white coverlet.

*I won't let you go, Charlotte. I can't. I love you.*

He loved her so much he was about to sacrifice everything for her. His chance to make amends to Colin, his chance to forgive himself.

And his love was based on a lie.

She had to tell him the truth. All of it. Whatever it led to, whatever might happen afterward she would tell him, because if she didn't tell Julian, she'd never tell anyone, and she couldn't live that way. She couldn't live a lie.

She loved him. She'd never stopped loving him. Even when she didn't trust him, even when she hated him, she'd loved him. For her, it would always be him.

*And now she was going to break his heart.*

She pressed her hand against her lips but a sound escaped—a sigh, a quiet sob—and Julian stirred and reached an arm across the bed, groping instinctively for her sleeping form even before he'd fully awakened. When his hand met only cold sheets, he rolled over and squinted into the dark. "Charlotte?"

She eased onto the edge of the bed and stroked the unruly dark curls away from his forehead. "I'm here."

"What are you doing out of bed?" He caught her hand and tried to pull her down beside him. "You must be freezing. Come here, and I'll warm you."

Charlotte gently freed her hand from his grip and wondered if she'd ever be warm again. "Not right now. There's something…I need to tell you first."

Julian hesitated, then rubbed a hand over his eyes. "Why are you dressed?"

"I—I thought it would be best."

"It's never best for you to be dressed, sweetheart." His tone was light, but some of her dread must have communicated itself to him, for he struggled upright against the pillows, his shoulders suddenly tense. "All right. What's so urgent it can't wait until sunrise?"

Charlotte opened her mouth, closed it again. How could she tell him now, like this, with his naked body still warm from sleep and his hair tousled like a boy's? Dear God, she felt like a criminal, as if he'd tried to wrap her in his arms only to find she'd plunged a knife into his chest. Perhaps she should wait, tell him when they were in the carriage on the way to Bellwood—

"Charlotte." A quiet command.

*The truth will out.* Here, and now.

She drew a quick, hard breath. "I didn't tell you everything about what happened at Hadley House, after Hadley died."

His shoulders relaxed. "I know that, love, but Lady Chase told me already."

Charlotte froze, all except her foolish heart, which leapt into a single beat of wild hope before it plummeted into despair again. Lady Chase couldn't have told Julian the whole of it, because she didn't know. No one but the staff at Hadley House knew, not even Ellie and Cam, because Charlotte had never breathed a word of the truth to any of them. Whatever Julian thought he knew, he didn't know the worst of it.

If he did, he'd already despise her.

She twisted her fingers together until her knuckles ached. "What did Lady Chase tell you?"

"That you stayed with the dowager until she died, despite how difficult it must have been for you, and you were ill for several months before you came to London. Exhaustion, she said." He took her hand. "Whatever it was it doesn't matter, Charlotte—"

"It does matter." She withdrew her hand, because if he touched her, she'd never be able to force the words out, and it had to be now, before she found another excuse to keep the truth from him forever. "I wasn't ill, Julian."

"What, then? It's all right, Charlotte. Just say it."

"I wasn't ill. I was…carrying a child, and I—I—"

*Oh God, she couldn't say it. She couldn't tell him.*

But of course he knew. He went motionless against the pillows. "You lost the child."

"Yes." She gulped in air to push the rest of the words out. "I lost her, and there was a great deal of blood, and the doctor said I may never be able to—"

"Don't say it," he whispered. "You don't have to say it."

But she did, and now she'd begun she was desperate to get it out, the worst of it, and there was no way to warn him, to make it easier, to make it hurt him less. "The child, Julian. I was carrying her when I married Hadley."

For a single moment he looked perplexed, but then in the next breath the truth crashed over him, and she knew the exact moment when he understood, because it was the same moment her heart shriveled in her chest. He would hate her now, he'd blame her, just as she blamed herself—

"My child? A daughter. Oh, no. Oh, Charlotte, no. No, sweetheart." He slid his arms around her and his warm palm cupped the back of her head to press her face against his chest. She let him hold her, but her body was taut against his as she waited for the moment—as inevitable as the rise and set of the sun—when he'd push her away.

She felt it seconds later, the slight stiffening of his arms, a catch of breath in his lungs, and then his hands were on her shoulders, gentle still, but inexorable, pushing her away so he could look into her eyes. "Did you… Did you know you were going to have my child when you married Hadley?"

She heard the pleading note under the forced calm of his voice, and for one wild moment she nearly denied it, but she couldn't bear to carry such an awful lie with her for the rest of her life, and she wouldn't deceive him into carrying it, either. Her eyes closed and she bowed her head. "Yes. I knew."

Silence. Julian didn't move or even appear to breathe, but the air in the room shifted somehow, became thinner, colder. When he spoke at last, it was one quiet word only, but it shattered the silence like a bullet. "Why?"

*Why.* Oh, God, so many reasons. She'd been terrified when she found she was with child, and so ashamed—too ashamed to tell her mother or even Ellie the truth. She remembered little from that time except the agony of a tender first love crushed into oblivion, and a blinding fury at Julian, because despite his lie she'd loved him madly still, and his betrayal had shattered her heart into a thousand pieces. Those weeks had blurred together in a kaleidoscope of rage and heartbreak, and by the time she found herself again, it was too late.

By then she wasn't Charlotte anymore. She was someone else. A wife. The Marchioness of Hadley. Mistress of Hadley House.

She struggled to find the right words to make him understand, but when she opened her mouth to give voice to the crushing welter of emotions she'd felt at that time, all that emerged was, "I was afraid."

It wasn't enough. As soon as her words fell into the silence between them, she knew it wasn't enough.

"I begged you to see me before you married Hadley, but you wouldn't talk to me." Julian's voice was low and hard. "You sent back all my letters unopened, you refused to see me when I called, and all that time you knew about our child, and you never told me."

Charlotte covered her face with her hands. "I was afraid, Julian. I'd just found out you lied to me, and I thought... I didn't know what to do."

Julian didn't answer. He didn't say another word, but slid out from under the covers and rose from the bed. She heard him fumbling in the darkness for his clothes, the rustle of cloth as he donned his breeches and shirt, and it was odd, wasn't it, to hear such normal sounds when her world was falling apart? The ring of his boots across the wooden floor as he walked toward the door, away from her—that sound made more sense in this moment, each of his steps heavy, portentous.

Final. The way an ending should sound.

She didn't want to look at him and see his back turned on her, but as the silence continued to stretch between them her gaze was drawn to the door. Julian's head was down, his gaze on the floor. "It's best if we don't... I can't ..."

*I can't even look at you anymore.*

He didn't say it, but he didn't need to. Charlotte heard the words echo in her head just as if he'd said them aloud. Her heart gave an agonized lurch. She couldn't bear to see his pain, and she felt her mouth open, heard herself offer him the words he needed, the words that would let him leave her behind. "I'll make the remainder of the journey to Bellwood alone."

"No. I'll take you the rest of the way. I made a promise to Cam." He waited, but when she didn't answer, he opened the door. "I'd appreciate it if we left as soon as possible. If we make an early start, I can be in London by this evening."

"Yes, of course." Charlotte's voice was faint. "I can be ready in half an hour. I'll meet you in the carriage, if that's acceptable."

"Half an hour, but I won't ride in the carriage. I'll travel the rest of the way on horseback."

Before she could reply he slipped into the hallway and closed the door behind him, taking all her hope with him. Charlotte clenched her hands into fists, suddenly furious with herself, because a part of her had thought—

what? That he'd gather her into his lap and cradle her head on his shoulder for the remainder of their journey? No. She'd never again feel his lips on hers, his arms around her, his hands buried in her hair, and the sooner she accepted it the better. Before the year was out he'd be betrothed, and she...

She wouldn't stand in his way. He had a chance at redemption, and no one knew better than she how precious that was. To wish for him to turn his back on Jane Hibbert would be to wish he wasn't Julian, and that—that she could never wish for.

She squeezed her eyes shut. No more tears. She'd cried enough tears to last a lifetime.

If she'd found Julian at last only to lose him again, well, life was made up of such moments, wasn't it? Such heartbreaking ironies. Not just her life, either—anyone who'd ever loved had suffered. She mustn't look on this as another punishment. She'd had one final night with him, and that was a gift. It was more than she expected, and more than she des—

*Deserved.* More than she deserved.

She stared down at her clenched fists. Hadley's foolish trick on that horse—he'd *died*, damn him, and left her with nothing but a heart full of regrets—but she'd forgiven him for it. She'd forgiven his mother, too, though the dowager's mad rages had left her with wounds that still bled.

But never, in all this time and amidst all this forgiveness, had she ever tried to forgive herself. She wouldn't wish her bitterest enemy to suffer the agonies she'd endured these past months, and yet somehow she believed she deserved it all.

*Deserved to lose her child.*

Despite her promise to herself tears rushed to her eyes, and they were bitterer than any tears she'd ever cried, because these tears were for Julian, for all he'd lost. A child, gone before he even knew he had anything to lose.

Her breath caught on a sob. He didn't deserve to lose his child.

*And neither did she. No one did.*

If she could only believe that, if she could somehow find the faith and the strength to believe she didn't deserve the one thing in her life that nearly broke her, then surely, surely she could believe...

She didn't deserve any of it. If she could believe that, perhaps, just perhaps she might find a way to believe in herself again.

\* \* \* \*

If the first three days on the road from Hampshire to Kent felt interminable, the last leg of the journey passed in the blink of an eye.

Before she knew it, the carriage had turned into the long drive that led to the front entrance of Bellwood.

The silvery ash trees arched toward each other from either side of the drive, one crown of spear-shaped pale green leaves indistinguishable from the next. Charlotte leaned her head against the window, just as she had done when she was a child, and watched the carriage pass under their sheltering arms. Those trees had stood guard over the drive for as long as she could remember, and like all of Bellwood, they never changed.

Home never did, did it? When one thought of home, they saw it with a child's eyes, and it lived as such in their memories, forever the same. Every time she came home it was like walking through a dream into the past.

But the people—they changed. She'd changed.

A sad smile crossed her face as she conjured an image of herself as a child—a regular hoyden, with wild black curls, dirty frocks, and ripped stockings. Oh, Ellie was forever scolding her when they were young, plucking her out of one scrape after another, and hiding Charlotte's many transgressions from their father.

The carriage came to a halt in the circular drive in front of the house. They'd arrived much earlier than expected, but Ellie must have stationed a servant to watch for them, for there she was, standing in the drive, Cam's arm around her shoulder. Waiting.

Charlotte's heart swelled with gratitude. *Oh, Ellie.* Always waiting, always ready, her arms open and stretched toward Charlotte, ready to catch her when she fell.

Perhaps people didn't change as much as she thought.

And now, at last, she was ready to let her sister catch her. "Ellie." Charlotte didn't wait for the coachman, but wrestled the door open herself and stumbled onto the drive. "*Ellie.*"

Something in that one word told Ellie all she needed to know, and the pinched lines of her face relaxed at once. "Oh, Charlotte," she murmured as she came forward to close her sister in her arms. "Oh, thank God."

Charlotte let her head fall onto Ellie's shoulder and thought how lovely it was, just for a moment, to feel like a child again.

After a while, Cam cleared his throat. "Charlotte."

She disentangled herself from Ellie's embrace and Cam gave her a fierce hug. She stood on her tiptoes to kiss his cheek. "It's all right now," she whispered, and gave his hand a hard squeeze. "Thank you, Cam."

He kissed her forehead. "Thank Julian. He's the one who brought you home at last."

Charlotte looked over Cam's shoulder. Julian had dismounted and now he stood silently beside his horse, one hand on the reins still, his face turned away, and in an instant everything else around her faded until there was only him, the sun limning his profile and the breeze tugging with playful fingers at his dark hair.

He must have felt her gaze on him because suddenly he raised his head and their eyes locked, and she'd never forget how lost, how desolate he looked in that moment. Everything inside her squeezed tight, and oh, she yearned for him then—yearned to brush his hair back from his face, to take away the hurt in his eyes so when she looked into those depths she saw not only the darkness, but the light.

He went stiff as she came toward him across the drive, and stiffer still when she took his hand, but she wouldn't let him pull away. He didn't want to speak to her, didn't want her touch, but maybe someday he'd understand she couldn't leave it this way between them. They'd both spent too much time living with regret.

Afterward she didn't remember what she'd meant to say to him. Perhaps she wanted to thank him, or beg for his forgiveness, but in the end she simply said what was in her heart. "You'll always be a hero to me."

She didn't give him a chance to reply, but only pressed his hand briefly between hers and then ran back to her sister before he could see the tears gathering in her eyes.

But Ellie saw them and she rushed forward, wrapped an arm around Charlotte's shoulder, and led her up the walkway toward the house. "What did you say to Julian, Charlotte?"

*I told him I was sorry. I told him I loved him.* "I said good-bye."

Ellie's brows drew down in a puzzled frown. "Good-bye? What, you mean he's not staying at Bellwood, even for a few days?"

"No." Charlotte glanced back out to the drive just in time to see Julian mount his horse. Cam said something to him, but Julian shook his head. "He's going on to London at once to see his betrothed."

"I thought...that is, I'd hoped..." Ellie fell silent.

Charlotte took her sister's hand. "I have so much to tell you, Ellie."

Ellie searched her face, nodded, and led her toward the stairs.

Charlotte didn't want to look back and see the empty space where Julian had been, but even as she promised herself she wouldn't, her gaze was drawn toward the drive.

Julian was gone.

# Chapter Twenty-five

"For God's sakes, Jules. Why the infernal rush? If I didn't know better, I'd think the Bow Street runners were after you. At least stay for luncheon."

Cam's voice was light, but he kept a firm grip on the horse's reins, and Julian could feel his cousin's penetrating green eyes on his face, assessing him, peeling back his layers.

"Sorry, cuz." Julian tried to match Cam's light tone and failed. "My betrothed is waiting for me in London. Remember?"

"Ah, yes. That. But surely this young lady would rather you didn't collapse from hunger and fatigue on her doorstep. It's another half day's ride to London."

"I'm cavalry. We're used to long rides."

"Jules." Cam's voice was soft.

Julian stared straight ahead. "I said I'd bring Charlotte to Bellwood, Cam, and I have. I never promised anything beyond that."

"No, you didn't," Cam agreed. "You've fulfilled your promise. The one you made to me, that is."

Julian let out a harsh laugh. "You think I made a promise to Charlotte? I assure you I didn't. I told her just this morning I'd take her as far as Bellwood, and that's all."

*And last night you told her you'd never let her go. Hadn't that been a promise?*

"I'm speaking of the promise you made to yourself, Julian. Before you left for Hampshire, you told me you wanted to be a man of your word."

Julian blew out an irritated breath. "I suppose you're saying I'm not."

Cam was never one to mince words. "Yes. That's what I'm saying."

"Jesus, Cam." Hot anger rushed over Julian. "What do you want from me? I kept my promise to you, and I haven't lied—"

"You *have* lied. You're lying right now by charging off to London to marry a woman you don't love, and leaving behind the one you do."

Julian jerked on the reins to loosen Cam's hold. "You'll have to forgive me for not delivering the happy ending you asked for, cuz, but there's another story between me and Charlotte—one you don't know about—and it's no fairy tale."

"I've never known a true love that was. You love Charlotte—you have since the first moment you laid eyes on her. What else is there?"

Julian couldn't bear to look into Cam's knowing green eyes. "What else? Lies, Cam. Betrayals. Distrust. Love doesn't matter."

"It's the only thing that matters, Jules. The rest? That's what forgiveness is for. Whatever it is, find a way to forgive Charlotte. Not just for her sake, but for yours."

Forgiveness—so easy, like snapping his fingers. Maybe it had been that easy for Cam and Ellie, but Julian had no forgiveness to offer anymore. This morning, when Charlotte told him the truth about his child, the dark thing with claws and teeth that lived inside him had leapt from his chest. That blackness, that anger and pain—he'd never be able to crawl free of it.

"Maybe I could have forgiven her once, but I can't now." Julian took in a deep breath and met his cousin's eyes. "I'm not the man I used to be, Cam. Something inside me, it's...broken."

Cam's gaze turned fierce. "Bent perhaps, but not broken. Dig down under the rubble, Julian, and you'll find you're the same man you've always been."

Julian shook his head. "You see what you want to see, cuz. I'll be in London for some weeks," he interrupted when Cam tried to speak. "If you've no objection, I'll stay in Bedford Square. When Miss Hibbert and I have settled the details, I'll send word."

Cam hesitated. "I've no objection," he said after a moment, his voice subdued. "Stay in Bedford Square as long as you like."

Julian nodded his thanks, then kicked his horse into motion before Cam could say another word. Within minutes he was at the end of the drive, Bellwood behind him.

*Charlotte behind him.*

He rode hard for London. He didn't look back, as if he were afraid to find she was chasing him. He'd reached the outskirts of the city before he admitted the truth to himself.

*She was.*

With every mile he put between himself and Bellwood he thought of her. Of her face this morning, the shadows not quite deep enough to hide her despair when she told him about their child. His chest hurt now, thinking of it, of all she'd endured, all she'd lost.

*No.* Damn it, he wouldn't think of that.

She'd lied to him—taken something precious from him. He'd begged her; he'd haunted the street outside the Sutherland townhouse night and day just to catch a glimpse of her. He'd sent letter after letter, pleading with her to give him one more chance, but she'd turned her back on him, and all the while she'd known his child was growing in her belly.

But hadn't she been justified in believing herself the victim of a ruthless rake? He'd been a rogue when they met—not quite a despoiler of virgins, but a rogue nonetheless—and she'd been an innocent. He'd seduced her, and not long afterward she found out he'd lied to her, as well. Was it any wonder she'd turned to Hadley?

The black, ugly thing in his chest gave a few half-hearted twitches of protest at these fevered thoughts, but strangely there was none of the suffocating swell of pain he dreaded. He prodded at it, stabbing harder and deeper to provoke it into a rage, but every time he tried to think of how she'd betrayed him, he could only conjure her face as it had been this morning, her hand as she'd swept his hair back from his brow.

But damn her, what if his child had lived? What if Hadley had lived, what then? If it all had been different, would Hadley be raising his daughter right now?

*If, if, if...*

Jesus, the insidiousness of that word, the treachery of it. It would drive him mad, imagining what might have been.

Why had she confessed at all? Why not hide the truth from him forever?

*Because she wouldn't live a lie.*

Even when it was easier, even when she stood to lose everything, she told the truth and bore the consequences. Her strength, her courage—Jesus, it was a miracle she'd even survived the past year. She could have bled to death when she lost the child, or lived through it only to be worn down by Hadley House, slowly, one day at a time, the regret and guilt scraping away at her until there was nothing left—

*She could have died.*

Without warning the black thing roared to life inside him, ripping through his chest with such force he doubled over in agony, as if he'd stabbed a blade into a bloody, gaping wound. He tried to twist free of it, gasping with fury and pain, but there was something else, something that held him fast in a relentless grip. Not the ugly black rage so familiar to him, but something softer, gray, blurred at the edges.

*Grief.*

As soon as he gave it a name it poured through him. He tried to stop it, to fight it, but it was like trying to hold back the ocean with nothing but his bare hands. All he could do was close his eyes and let it take him, let it gush into his chest and drown his heart. Grief for a child who'd never had a chance at life, and for Colin, who'd been cheated of his before he could live it. Julian covered his eyes with a shaking hand and let the grief flood through him until his heart was ready to burst and he was gasping, suffocating.

It would overflow, and he'd drown in it—

But he didn't. It began to recede, draining away gradually, never disappearing entirely, but enough so a space opened inside him for something else, something tender and green that rose in place of the grief over all he and Charlotte had lost.

Gratitude, for all they hadn't.

And then at last came the sweetest thing of all, the one thing that made everything else possible. His love for Charlotte.

*It's the only thing that matters, Jules.*

Damned if Cam hadn't been right.

Every muscle in Julian's body tensed with the need to fly at once back to Bellwood, to take Charlotte in his arms, but this time when he held her, he'd never let her go. When he came to her, it would be without any barriers between them.

Julian gritted his teeth, set his horse's head in the direction of London, and headed west, away from the woman who held his heart, toward London, and Jane Hibbert.

\* \* \* \*

"Captain who?" The elderly lady who answered his knock glared at Julian through the narrow crack in the door.

"Captain Julian West, madam. I beg your pardon for calling so late, but it's urgent that I see Miss Hibbert at once—"

"My niece doesn't know any Captain West, and neither do I." She began to close the door in his face. "I'll thank you to leave my doorstep at once."

"Wait. Madam, please. I assure you she does know me, though we've not yet been formally introduced. If you'll only ask her—"

"I certainly will not ask her!" The old lady looked scandalized. "No respectable gentleman calls at this time of night—"

"Aunt?" Light footsteps approached the door and a low, musical voice asked, "What is it?"

"He says his name is Captain West. He claims to know you, dear, but I don't recall—"

He heard a gasp. "Captain Julian West? Please do let him in, Aunt. He and Colin were in the same regiment. He was Colin's friend."

"Colin's friend?" The door flew open. "Why didn't he say so at once?"

Julian stepped through the door into the tiny entryway. "Thank you, madam. I know it's not a proper time to call, and I do beg your pardon...."

Julian's voice trailed off into silence when Jane Hibbert came forward and took his hands in hers. "Captain West. How happy I am to meet you at last. This lady is my aunt, Mrs. Wilton."

Julian managed an awkward bow for Mrs. Wilton, but his chest had gone so tight with emotion he couldn't say a word. Jane Hibbert had Colin's light brown hair, his kind blue eyes and the same sweet, guileless smile. Looking at her was like looking through a window into the past, to a time when Colin was still alive. He tried to clear the lump from his throat, but his voice remained hoarse. "Miss Hibbert. Forgive me—"

"There's nothing to forgive, Captain." She gave his hand a friendly squeeze. "You look fatigued. Won't you come sit by the fire? Aunt, you'll excuse us?"

Mrs. Wilton bustled off and Julian followed Jane down the hall into a small parlor with a warm fire burning merrily in the grate. She smiled, took a seat on a chair near the fire, and gestured for him to take the one across from her. "Well, Captain West. This is an unexpected visit. I think you must have something quite important to say to me."

Julian looked at her for a moment, sitting there with her hands folded calmly in her lap. She was pretty, her eyes gentle and intelligent, just as her brother's had been. He knew instinctively a life with Jane Hibbert would be peaceful, that she'd make a perfect wife for any man. She'd make a perfect wife for *him*, except for one thing.

*She wasn't Charlotte.*

"I do wish to speak with you on an urgent matter, yes, but I hardly know where to begin." In truth, there was no delicate way to say what he must say to Jane Hibbert, so he simply plunged blindly ahead. "After Colin's death we exchanged letters in which we formed an understanding of sorts between us—"

"Our betrothal, you mean."

Julian stared at her, amazed. Miss Hibbert, it seemed, *did* know where to begin. "Our betrothal, yes. I feel …that is, I think…I wish to discuss…"

"You wish to be released from your promise to marry me."

His mouth dropped open at her frankness.

She smiled. "There's no need to look so shocked, Captain. We entered into our agreement at a time when both of us had suffered a great loss. One can't be held to a promise made in distress. Of course we won't marry—once I'd recovered from the first shock of Colin's death, I saw that clearly enough. I've been expecting your call for weeks, you see."

Julian's head was spinning. "But you continued to write to me, while I was in Paris. I thought—"

"Yes. I know it wasn't proper, but I couldn't quite make myself…" She paused, and for the first time her composure slipped. "You're my last connection to Colin, Captain West. I couldn't bear to sever it by dropping the correspondence. I hope you understand." Her eyes grew bright. "I miss him terribly."

Julian only nodded, because he wasn't quite sure he could speak. For a moment they sat in silence, each of them lost in their memories; then Julian cleared his throat. "Colin worried for you. He didn't want you and your aunt to be alone, with no protection. If we're not to marry, you must allow me to—"

"Please don't worry, Captain. My aunt and I are not unprotected. I've, ah…" Her face turned a becoming shade of pink. "I've had an offer of marriage from another gentleman—the deacon at our local church. He was a great comfort to me after Colin's death. He recently received a living from his uncle, making it possible for him to marry."

Julian's heart lightened at her revealing blush. "And you're fond of him?"

Another flood of pink suffused her face. "Oh yes. Very fond," she said, in a tone that left Julian in no doubt as to her affections. "And you, I think, are also fond of someone?"

A startled laugh escaped him. "How do you know that?"

"You're here after dark, Captain, calling on a young lady you've never met, and—forgive me—but you look as if you've spent the entire day in the saddle. You show all the signs of a man addled by fondness."

Julian shook his head. *Clever, just like Colin.* "Addled is a good word for it, isn't it?"

A tiny dimple flashed in her cheek. "Indeed it is."

They sat in silence for another moment; then he reached into his waistcoat pocket, pulled out Colin's watch, and held it out to her. The thought of giving it up made his heart sink again, but he couldn't keep it now. It belonged with Colin's family. "Before I take my leave, I want to give you this."

She didn't move for a moment, but then she reached out a trembling hand. He placed the watch in her palm, resisting the urge to snatch it back.

"Colin's pocket watch." She ran one finger over the case. "He had it from birth, you know. My father was so proud of his son that he went out the day Colin was born and purchased matching watches, one for each of them. Colin treasured it."

Julian drew in a deep, unsteady breath. "I know he did. The key is lost, so I'm afraid you can't wind it anymore."

Jane didn't answer, but rose and walked to a small desk in the corner of the room and removed something from one of the drawers. When she returned, she was holding a tiny gold key. "The key to my father's watch."

She inserted the key and turned it, and Julian had the oddest sensation he'd been holding his breath since he first tucked the watch into his waistcoat pocket, and could only exhale now, as if its faint ticking had tripped his lungs back into motion.

Jane took his hand, placed the watch with the key in his palm, and closed his fingers over it. "Colin thought the world of you, Captain West. He would have wanted you to have it."

Julian stared down at his closed hand. He should refuse to accept it—he should give the watch back to her so she could give it to her own child someday, but he couldn't make his fingers open. His waistcoat pocket would forever feel empty without it.

He looked up at Jane. "Thank you," he said, his voice husky. "Thank you."

\* \* \* \*

Bellwood was dark and silent when he arrived, which was not a surprise as it was only a few hours shy of dawn. It was a surprise, however, when he reached the end of the walkway and Cam opened the door.

His cousin leaned against the doorframe and crossed his arms over his chest. "You could have saved yourself a great many hours in the saddle if you'd only listened to me this morning. When will you learn, cuz?"

"Good Lord, Cam. What are you doing up?"

"Oh, I've been awake for hours. I knew you'd be back, sooner or later."

A wry smile touched Julian's lips. "You've been awake for hours, and you still answered the door in that ridiculous banyan?"

Cam raised an eyebrow. "Is that why you're here? To malign my banyan?"

"As a matter of fact, it's not."

"I didn't think so. Up two flights, right at the stairway, last door at the end of the hallway on the left. I trust you to behave like a perfect gentleman, of course."

"Of course." Julian hesitated, then found Cam's eyes with his own. "Thank you, Cam."

He was halfway up the stairs when Cam called up to him. "Jules?"

Julian looked over the railing at his cousin standing in the foyer below. "Yes?"

"Welcome home." Cam didn't wait for an answer, but turned and shuffled off in the direction of the library, the hem of his banyan flapping around his calves.

Julian's smile faded as he neared Charlotte's bedchamber. He didn't want to frighten her by suddenly appearing in her dark room. Worse, what if she didn't want him there? There were still so many unanswered questions between them.

But he wouldn't think on that. He'd let himself into her room quietly, so as not to wake her, and he'd spend the night on the settee. He just wanted to see her, be in the same room with her and breathe the same air—for tonight that would be enough.

But Charlotte wasn't asleep. She was at a window looking out at the last remaining stars still visible in the sky. His heart leapt at the sight of her standing there in her billowing white night rail. She looked like a star herself.

He closed the door with a quiet click. "Charlotte."

She whirled around.

Julian leaned back against the door, suddenly uncertain. "Did you know I'd come?"

Her hand fluttered to her throat. "No."

He took a step toward her. She was trembling. "Did you... Did you want me to? Do you want me here?"

"You know I do." Her voice was choked. "You already know."

He did know. With her, he'd always known. He took a deep breath. "I'll never leave you again. I love you, Charlotte. I never stopped."

She hid her face in her hands for a moment, and when she looked up, her cheeks were wet with tears. "I love you too, Julian. So much."

He was across the room in three strides and then she was in his arms, her head against his chest, her shoulders shaking with sobs. He gathered her against him, carried her to the bed, and lay down next to her, and as he stroked her hair and murmured to her, he let his mind wander into a waking dream, one both bitter and sweet, a dream and a wish at once, for something he'd lost before he'd ever had it.

A child, a little girl, with long dark tresses and thickly-lashed dark eyes, an impish grin and a face—oh, a face so beautiful it could break a man's heart.

*Her mother's face.*

He gave his mind and heart up to the pain, such a world of pain for a child he'd never known, a little girl who'd never been his. He lay still for a long while, then eased Charlotte onto her back and slid down the bed so he could rest his cheek against her belly. He stayed there, tracing slow, gentle circles over her abdomen with his palm, and let the sorrow flow through him and dampen the soft skin under his cheek.

After a while a hand touched his head and tender fingers threaded through the locks of his hair. "Catherine Mary," she whispered. "Or Mary Catherine. I hadn't yet decided."

Catherine—her mother's name, and Mary...

He nodded against her, but he couldn't speak.

*Mary.*

His mother's name.

He turned his head and pressed a tender kiss against her belly. She drew in a deep, slow breath, let it out in a soft sigh, and tugged gently on his hair to draw him up to her, but without a word he crawled to the floor and fell to his knees before her.

He slid his hands up her calves and then higher, until his palms found the inside of her knees, her thighs, and—*gentle*—he nudged her legs open, not much, just enough for him to slip between and take her hips into his hands and move her down the bed, closer to him, closer to his mouth so he could open his lips over her belly—*Skin like silk*—then open her gently, taste her—*at last*—just the lightest touch with his tongue, gentle at first until she whimpered—*hush love I'll take care of you*—then a little more, a little faster, his strokes firmer, over and over again where she needed him until she began to arch and twist—*no let me, I want to do everything for you*—and he held her against the bed, held her thighs open and loved her, loved her until her body went rigid and she broke apart for him with a cry—*yes let your body know joy again*—and she fell panting back against the bed. He crawled up next to her—*just hold her*—but she took him in her hand and he was so hard for her—*want you so much*—and she moved on top of him and then he was inside her, his hands gripping her waist, holding her hips to steady her for his thrusts—*so good can't stop*—stroking into her again, again until she gave a low moan and collapsed on top of him, and he held her and shuddered his release into her.

He waited for their breathing to calm, then turned her gently onto her back and shifted on top of her so he could feel her warm, silky skin against every part of his body. He touched his forehead to hers. "Did you see the stars tonight?"

She took his face in her hands, stroked her thumbs softly over his cheeks, and looked into his eyes. "I see them now."

# Epilogue

*Hadley House, December 1816*

"My goodness, Aurelie. Why did you insist on smoking the wretched thing when you knew it would make you ill? You look quite green."

Aurelie waved the smoke away from her face and gave Lissie a wan smile. "But it's a lovely, flattering shade of green, *non?*"

"No." Lissie rose from her seat, took the cheroot from Aurelie and tossed it into the fire. "You look like you're about to disgrace yourself all over Charlotte's lovely Aubusson carpet."

Lady Annabel studied Aurelie through a cloud of smoke, then turned her gaze on Charlotte, who was sitting facing the fire, her cheeks flushed, and a soft smile playing about her lips. "Such a satisfied smile you have this evening, Charlotte. You look as though you're thinking pleasant thoughts."

"Or wicked ones." Lissie gave Charlotte a playful nudge with her toe. "For your sake, my dear, I hope they're wicked, because those are ever so much nicer."

Charlotte roused herself from her contemplation of the fire, and turned to her friends, her smile widening. "I was thinking how happy I am to have you all here."

There was a short silence; then all three of her friends began to laugh at once.

"What?" Charlotte frowned at each of them in turn. "Why should you find that so amusing? I *was.*"

"No, you weren't!" Lissie gasped out another laugh, then wiped her eyes with the sleeve of her gown. "You were thinking of that handsome husband of yours, and wondering how much longer it would be before you could bid us good night, hurry off to your bedchamber, and pounce on him."

"Well, *mon Dieu, cherie*," Aurelie drawled. "Do you blame her?"

"I don't blame her a bit. If ever a gentleman was made for pouncing upon, it's Captain West." Annabel studied her for a moment. "He was always sinfully handsome, but I fancy he's even more so since you settled at Hadley House for the winter. Does the country agree with him? He looks much more rested and peaceful than he did when we met him in London."

He was. They both were. Julian still had occasional nightmares about Colin, and every now and again a painful memory would come upon Charlotte as she wandered the house or grounds of Hadley House, but they had each other now, and they were building new memories together.

"He does look very well." Lissie grumbled, a little crossly. "I suppose you'll never come back to London *now*."

"Of course we will, Lissie, next season, and I'll expect you all to be as entertaining as you've always been when I arrive."

"Well, perhaps not *quite* as entertaining. I don't suppose your husband will approve of another brothel wager."

"No, I think my brothel frolics are over." Charlotte laughed, but after a moment her smile faded. "Speaking of brothel wagers, what's become of Devon? Julian and I invited him to come stay with you all, but he declined."

"Devon's gone off to Cornwall on some mad adventure or other." Annabel took a last draw on her cheroot, then rose and tossed it into the fire. "Cornwall, of all places. Can you imagine?"

"Poor Devon." Aurelie shuddered. "It's quite wild there, *non?*"

"Devon's from Cornwall, and it's not a mad adventure, for goodness' sakes. He's gone to close down his ancestral estate. He thought his father shut it down after his brother died, but it seems the old earl never quite got around to it. Devon was furious when he found out."

"Close it down?" Charlotte frowned. "But… Didn't he grow up there?"

"He hasn't been back in several years. It's out in the wilds, much too far for an easy trip from London, and Devon told me once he despises it there." Lissie paused. "He didn't go into details, but I gather his childhood wasn't a happy one, and there was that business with his brother.…"

"Poor Devon," Aurelie said again, but her voice was subdued this time, and for a moment no one spoke.

"Perhaps there will be another brothel frolic, after all," Annabel murmured. "To keep Devon amused."

"Not for Charlotte. Husbands tend to look with disfavor on brothel frolics." Lissie shook her head. "Much more amusing to remain a widow, Charlotte."

Charlotte only smiled. She wouldn't trade Julian for every wicked entertainment London had to offer, and her friends knew it well.

"My goodness, there's that wicked smile again. I can see you'll be useless to us for the rest of the evening, Charlotte. Off you go to your husband, then." Annabel waved a hand toward the door. "I feel quite sure Captain West will keep you amused for the rest of the evening."

Lissie snorted. "The rest of the night, you mean."

"*Bonne nuit*, Charlotte." Aurelie blew her a kiss. "You will show us the gardens tomorrow, *oui?*"

"Yes, of course." Charlotte kissed each of her friends on the cheek, then made her way upstairs to her apartments. Julian was stretched out on the bed with a book open over his chest, wearing a dark blue banyan.

"My, you look comfortable." Charlotte closed the door behind her and approached the bed. "Is that a new banyan?"

"It is. A gift from Cam." Julian grinned at her. "Ridiculous, isn't it? Take it off me at once, please."

"But you look so dashing in it." Her gaze moved over him and her body flushed with heat, as it did every time she looked at Julian. "Very handsome indeed, Captain."

He let out a low growl, and tugged her onto the bed and into his arms. "What took you so long? I've been waiting all night, and I'm…lonely." He rolled her onto her back and slid his leg between hers.

Charlotte wrapped her legs around his hips, a smile rising to her lips at his helpless groan. "I've been trying to come up this past hour. I adore my friends, but…" She slipped her hands into the open neck of his banyan to caress his bare chest.

"You adore me more?" He was pulling the pins from her hair with one hand and tearing at the buttons on her gown with the other. "I know there's bare skin under here somewhere. Ah, here it is." He pressed his lips to the hollow of her throat, then dragged his mouth lower, to kiss between her breasts. "Dear God, you smell good, and you taste even better."

She sank her fingers into his hair and tugged gently to raise his face to hers. "I adore you above all things, Julian. You know I do."

He nodded, his dark eyes going soft as his gaze moved over her face. "And I adore you. I love you so much, Charlotte."

"Show me how much." Charlotte dragged his banyan down his back, then arched up to nip at his bare shoulders and whisper, soft and low in his ear. "Show me, Julian."

And he did.

*When a headstrong beauty clashes with the man she once loved, she's determined that the spirit of Christmas will open his mind, heal his heart, and perhaps give them a reason to celebrate—for many seasons to come...*

As far as Ethan Fortescue is concerned, his family's seat in Cornwall is only a source of torment, one that he's managed to avoid for two years. Now that he's the Earl of Devon however, he can close the door on his haunted past by locking up the cursed place for good. But upon arriving at Cleves Court, he's shocked to find the house aglow with Christmas celebrations, and filled with music and laughter. And right at the center of the holiday madness is the infuriating—and eternally tempting—Theodosia Sheridan...

Thea has always loved the town of Cleves, especially at the holidays. As a girl, she also loved Ethan with all her heart. It's painful to see how his brother's tragic death has embittered him. Still, she will do anything to make sure the town thrives—even if it means going to battle with Ethan to save Cleves Court. Now she has only until Twelfth Night to make a Christmas miracle happen—by proving that his childhood home can be a source of love and wonder. But before long, she finds herself wondering if she's trying to save the house—or its handsome master...

**Please turn the page for an exciting sneak peek of Anna Bradley's**

**TWELFTH NIGHT WITH THE EARL**

**coming soon!**

# Chapter One
Cornwall, England
*Christmas Eve, 1816, 7:00 p.m.*

Somewhere between the Duke's Head Inn and here, he'd fallen off the edge of England and into the deepest pit of hell.

Hell, or Cornwall. Same bloody thing.

*The Duke's Head.*

Ethan snorted. Pity he wasn't in the mood for a laugh, because that was damn amusing. The Duke's Head was the only inn in the tiny village of Cleves, and it was the last place a duke would be caught dead, with or without his head.

His horse stumbled as Ethan led him around another of Cornwall's endless muddy puddles. Christ, it was dark here. He wouldn't have believed any place in England could be this dark if he hadn't seen it himself. Or not seen it, as it happened, because it was too bloody dark to see bloody anything. Well, except for his flask. He could see that because he had it clutched in his hand, and a bloody good thing too, because a man doomed to spend Christmas in the wilds of bloody Cornwall bloody well better keep a flask to hand at all times.

He paused to count, the flask hovering in front of his lips.

*Six bloodies in less than a minute.*

There was a chance—just the merest possibility, of course—he wasn't overflowing with the joys of the season.

Ah, well. At least he was overflowing with whiskey.

He tipped the silver flask to his lips and took another swallow. What he lacked in Christmas cheer he more than made up for in drink, and it wasn't as if any of the servants left at Cleves Court were in a position to scold him for his drunkenness. He was the Earl of bloody Devon now, and in the year since he'd become his lordship, he'd discovered earls were permitted to behave rather badly, indeed. Not as badly as marquesses and dukes, but badly enough, and no one seemed to trouble themselves much about it.

Perhaps that's how his father had become such a wastrel. Too much... Earling? Earlishness? Lordshippery? Ethan frowned. It was one of those, but it didn't matter which. Whatever you called it, it amounted to the same thing—some earl or other had behaved badly, so the new earl was obliged to ride to bloody Cornwall in the cold and dark to clean up the disaster the previous wastrel of an earl had left behind.

That it *would* be a disaster, Ethan hadn't the slightest doubt. The last time he'd been to his country seat it was teetering on the edge of disreputable, and that was two years ago. He hadn't the faintest idea why his father hadn't shut the cursed place down altogether as he'd promised he would, but whatever whim had moved the old earl was no doubt fleeting, like most of his whims.

God knew once his father abandoned something, he never looked back.

He'd have forgotten all about the place the moment he returned to London, and by now the old pile would be collapsing into rubble. With only a handful of servants left to tend to it, it would be dark and freezing, and likely damp as well, with cobwebs thick enough to smother Ethan in his sleep, and servants who hadn't the faintest notion how to look after an earl.

What if they led him to some godforsaken room with damp walls, uncarpeted floors and mice-infested sheets? What if they didn't even *have* sheets, or proper lamps or candles? Or, dear God, what if he should run out of whiskey while he was trapped in that old tomb, and was forced into tedious sobriety?

Damn it, perhaps he should have dragged Fenton with him to Cornwall, after all. He'd considered it, but Cleves Court was barely civilized. His fussy London valet would be in fits of horror over the savagery of it all, and Ethan didn't want another useless servant about, wringing his hands and making things difficult. This visit was bound to be unpleasant enough without Fenton's hysterics to contend with.

No, it was best to keep things simple. Wrestle his way through the wilds of Cornwall to Cleves Court, issue orders for the house to be closed at once, stay long enough to see those orders carried out, then get back to London before his supply of whiskey was depleted.

But he'd have to see to it he had a proper bedchamber. He was an earl, after all, and accustomed to his comforts. He'd need something with sheets and without mice, and he'd prefer better music, as well, instead of that incessant picking on the pianoforte keys, but he supposed it was too much to ask if anyone at Cleves Court would know how to play the pianoforte—

*Music? What the devil?*

Ethan brought his horse to a halt and stared down at the flask in his hand. Good Lord, how much whiskey had he drank? He was so far in his cups he must be hallucinating, because there wasn't a blessed thing for miles around here aside from Cleves Court, and the music couldn't be coming from *there*.

Could it?

It was damned odd, but it seemed as if someone at Cleves Court was playing the pianoforte. If you could call it playing, that is. *Pick, pick, pick.* He couldn't quite decipher the song, but it was something irritatingly festive. Without realizing he did it, he began to hum along under his breath, trying to place it.

*Four calling birds, three French hens...*

Oh, Christ. It was the Twelve bloody Days of bloody Christmas. Christmas music in general was intolerable, but he loathed this song in particular. A man might be partial to milkmaids, and eight of them at once could prove amusing, but what the devil was he to do with French hens and a partridge? They'd only get in the way.

Ah, well. It was nothing more whiskey couldn't cure.

Ethan drained his flask and urged his horse forward, but once he crested the hill he stopped a second time, his gaze frozen on his ancestral estate nestled at the notch in the hill just below him.

Light spilled from every downstairs window and cast a cheerful glow onto the drive in front of the house, which was crowded with wagons and carriages. Even from this distance he could see people passing to and fro in front of the windows, and hear voices and an occasional shriek of muffled laughter. The delectable scent of sugared apples and roasted meat drifted through the air, and Ethan's stomach let out an insistent growl.

Laughter, music, and sugared sweets? He might be in his cups, but he wasn't so foxed he couldn't see what was right in front of his eyes. Some presumptuous devil was running amok at his estate, without his knowledge or permission.

Ethan tucked his flask into his pocket, kicked his horse into a run, and shot down the hill toward the house. *Damnation.* He'd only just arrived, and already he was being thrown headlong into sobriety.

A few coachmen were loitering in the drive, but they were distracted by cups of ale, so he dismounted and tied his horse himself, grumbling at the neglect. What bloody good was it being the earl if he didn't get to shout orders, and then stand back like a proper aristocrat while the servants rushed about in a panic to do his bidding?

He strolled through the front door, squinting at the sudden light. It appeared they did have candles and lamps at Cleves Court, because the place was brighter than a London ballroom. A dozen or so people hung about, and the entire entryway was smothered in kissing balls and evergreens. It looked as if Christmas had gotten foxed, and then cast up its accounts all over Cleves Court.

But there was a rather nice-looking Christmas punch on a table at his elbow, so Ethan snatched up a glass. Whiskey was preferable, but he'd drunk it all, so the punch would have to do.

He raised the glass to his lips, took a healthy swallow, spluttered, and then stared down at the glass, aghast. For God's sake, who made a punch without brandy? It was a disgraceful waste of perfectly good fruit—

"Who d'ye think ye are? That's my punch ye just drunk."

Ethan dropped the glass onto the table and turned to find a thin, dark-haired boy at his elbow. "Who the *devil* are you?"

Instead of disappearing as a figment of one's imagination should, the boy jabbed his thumb into his chest. "Why, I'm Henry Munro." He announced this as if everyone in their right mind should know who Henry Munro was. "Who're *you?*"

"The Earl of Devon." Everyone in his right mind *should* know who that was, but if Ethan expected the boy to blanch with terror to find the master of the house had suddenly appeared in his midst, he was disappointed.

"What, yer a lordship? I've not got much use fer lordships, meself." Henry took in his depleted glass of punch, and gave Ethan a disgusted look. "'Specially those what drink my punch."

"That's *my* punch. Didn't you hear what I just said? I'm Lord Devon." Ethan waved a hand around the room. "*Lord Devon.* This is *my* house. Every glass of punch in the bloody place belongs to me."

He sounded like a two-year old whining over a toy, but for God's sake, who was this demonic imp, and what was he doing here? And didn't anyone in this house recognize the name Devon?

"Aw right then, guv. No need to take on like that."

The boy grabbed what was left of his punch and tried to dart away, but Ethan snatched him up by the collar and hauled him back. "Who's in charge here?"

"I thought ye said this was *yer* house."

"It is, but—"

"Ye don't know who's in charge of yer own house?" Henry eyed him, looking less impressed with every passing second.

Damnation. As much as Ethan hated to admit it, the boy had a point. "I've been away. Is it Mrs. Hastings still?"

It seemed unlikely Mrs. Hastings—or Mrs. Hastens, he couldn't quite recall—was the authoress of all this offensive merriment. A vague image of a gray-haired lady with lace collars and dozens of iron keys at her hip rose in Ethan's mind. She had to be at least sixty years old by now. Perhaps she'd gone senile.

"Mrs. *who?* Never heard of 'er."

Ethan's eyebrows shot up. What, the boy hadn't even heard of Mrs. Hastings? What had happened to his bloody housekeeper? "Well, who then, Henry? If it's not Mrs. Hastings, then who's responsible for this house?"

"Same person what's always been responsible, guv."

Ethan tightened his grip on the boy's collar, ready to shake the answer out of him. "And who would that be?"

Before Henry could reply, a maid appeared and held out a tray to Ethan with a smile. "Punch, sir?"

"No! No bloody punch. I'm Lord Devon, just arrived."

"Lord Devon? Oh, no. That is…oh, dear, the earl himself." The maid's face went white and she sank into a hasty curtsey, still clutching the tray. "I, ah—welcome home, your lordship."

Cleves Court wasn't his home anymore, and in another few weeks it wouldn't be anyone else's home either, but the maid would find that out soon enough. "What's your name?"

"Becky, sir—that is, my lord."

"Becky, you will tell me at once who's responsible for this madness."

Becky shifted from foot to foot, looking uncomfortable. "Um, our housekeeper, your lordship, just as she is every year."

*Every year?*

Ethan gritted his teeth. "Would you be so kind as to tell me where I might find the housekeeper?"

"Let's see. The last time I saw her she was in the kitchens, but I think she may have gone back to the drawing room. I'd be happy to take you to her, sir—"

But Becky got no further, for at that moment a child darted through the drawing-room door, his head down, and slammed right into the back of her, sending the tray in her hands to the floor with a crash of shattering glass. Becky let out a despairing wail as punch splattered everywhere.

The floor, the walls—Christ, even the kissing balls were dripping with it.

Ethan might have laughed if it hadn't been for his boots, which were now splattered with sticky punch. He'd managed to make it through every muddy inch of bloody Cornwall with the pristine shine still on his boots, but the second he set foot in this godforsaken house, they were ruined. Damn it, a man's boots were sacred—

"George Munro! You naughty boy! Look at what you've made me do!"

*George* Munro? Ethan stared at the child who'd come to a screeching halt in the middle of the hallway. He was an exact replica of Henry, who'd taken one look at the mess and doubled over with laughter.

*Dear God, there were two of them.*

George Munro was no fool. He took one look at the mayhem he'd caused, turned on his heel, and fled. Becky made a grab for him, but the boy, who looked as if he'd perfected his escape technique, leapt nimbly out of her reach.

"Come back here this instant, George!"

George did not come back, and Becky chased after him, leaving Ethan standing in a puddle of brandy-less punch and a pile of broken glasses. Such a scene would have reduced Fenton to tears, but Ethan simply stepped over the mess, made his way toward the drawing room, and found a place at the back of the crowd, near the door.

The housekeeper would have to appear eventually, and when she did, she'd find one furious earl in ruined boots waiting for her.

There were a great many servants rushing about—far more than he'd expected to see at Cleves Court—and a great number of guests, as well. A few of them looked vaguely familiar, but damned if he could say what any of their names were. They were all having a grand time of it, and looked quite at home, as if they spent every evening at Cleves Court, drinking his liquor and smashing his crystal to bits.

Not that he gave a damn about the crystal, or anything else in this house. He didn't intend to take so much as a teaspoon from here back to London with him. Tomorrow he'd order everything packed away forever. They were welcome to smash every glass in the house until then, and the windows too, if they liked.

"Oh, here comes the housekeeper with the bowl of brandy," a lady next to him whispered to her companion. "It's so pretty when it's lit, isn't it, with the blue flames?"

A flutter of excitement passed over the knot of people gathered in the drawing-room, and a hush fell as the servants lowered the lamps and doused the candles. Every head turned to the door, the faces alight with anticipation. The children were wriggling with excitement, and the adults were nearly as enthusiastic.

Despite himself, Ethan felt a twinge of anticipation. They'd played Snapdragon in this very room when he was a boy. He straightened from his slouch against the wall to get a better look, but the servants had plunged the room into near darkness, and he couldn't see a bloody thing.

"Over here, ma'am!" George Munro, who'd evidently escaped his pursuer, was hopping up and down and waving his arms in the air. "I've been a very good boy!"

Ethan snorted aloud at this blatant falsehood, but the sound was swallowed by another childish voice, this one raised in outrage. "Ye *haven't* been a good boy, George. Ye made Becky drop the glasses and they all smashed to bits! Ye're naughty, and ye don't deserve any raisins!"

"Quiet, Henry, ye tell-tale!"

A furious shriek followed this insult, and Ethan turned just in time to see Henry leap upon George's back and the two tumble to the floor in a tangle of limbs. He watched them with a grin, because a brawl was good fun—especially one so indecorous as to happen in the midst of a Christmas Eve party—but this one was even more impressive because the two boys looked so much alike, it was impossible to tell where one ended and the other began.

"Henry, George, you will stop that scuffling at once."

A tall, slender woman with dark hair passed near Ethan, carrying a large glass bowl in her hands. She was looking down, and he couldn't see her face, but one thing was certain.

She wasn't Mrs. Hastings.

His memories of that good lady were indistinct, but he was damn sure her scent hadn't made his mouth water. This lady smelled of warm, rich brandy, with a faint hint of cinnamon and vanilla, and her voice—low and faintly husky, but utterly feminine—tugged on him, as if a hook had caught at the memories buried deep inside him and was trying to drag them out through his chest.

They two boys climbed off each other, but Henry couldn't quite hold in his ire. "Aw, but Miss Sheridan, he called me a—"

"At once, Henry, or no raisins for either of you."

Ethan might have laughed at the chastened expression on the boys' faces, but he wasn't looking at them anymore.

He was looking at *her*.

*Miss Sheridan.*

He went still, his mind reeling with shock. There had only ever been one Miss Sheridan, and there'd never be another—not for Cleves Court, and not for him.

*Thea was here.*

Theadosia Sheridan, his childhood playmate, then his dearest friend, and then, when he was fourteen, the year Ethan was sent away from Cleves Court for good, his first love.

His only love, though he couldn't have known it at the time.

He never thought about her—he wouldn't let himself think of her, because thinking about Thea was like floating to the surface and sucking in great gulps of air when you hadn't even realized you were underwater. Once you got that air, once it filled your lungs you realized again that you needed it, that you couldn't live without it ...

*It was so much easier just to drown.*

He stiffened as she drew closer, so close he could reach out and catch a handful of her silk skirts in his fist, but he forced his arms to his sides, and she passed by without noticing him.

"Here we are!" She set the large bowl carefully on a wide table that looked as if it had been brought in for that purpose. She touched a cloth to the candle on the table and lit the brandy, then raised her beaming face to the crowd gathered around her. "There are plenty of raisins for everyone this year—too many to count!"

Ethan sucked in a breath as blue flames rose from the bowl and shone full on her face, and he could see every graceful line of her features, every curve of her smile ...

*And those eyes.*

Wide and green, long-lashed, and still with that touch of cheekiness that had driven him mad as a boy, before he was even old enough to understand what it meant to be driven mad by a woman.

Theadosia Sheridan. A termagant, a sharp-tongued hellion, a scapegrace—yes, she was all of those things. Bold and fearless, too, and if her eyes were any indication, she hadn't changed.

What was she doing here? As far as he knew she'd left Cleves Court two years ago. When had she come back, and why—

Ethan froze as all the pieces snapped into place.

*Of course.*

Thea was at the bottom of this madness. This was *her* fault. The music, the guests, the games, and those two fiendish boys—she was responsible for it all. It made such perfect sense he couldn't imagine why he hadn't realized it at once. Who else but Thea would dare to take over his house as if she were mistress of it?

She'd brought Cleves Court back from the dead. Instead of the cold, empty house he'd expected, the old place was warm and alive again, *and as long as it was alive, he couldn't bury it.*

He'd come here to shove Cleves Court as deep into the ground as it would go, to cover it with dirt and bury it forever, and his memories right along with it. It should have been a simple enough thing to do, but now ...

Now *she* was here, and nothing was simple anymore.

Thea was a complication waiting to happen—chaos in silk skirts, with a tempting smile and devastating green eyes. No sooner would he have everything in its proper place than she'd sweep in like a hurricane and send it all into disarray with a snap of her pretty fingers.

Simple things had a way of becoming complicated around Thea.

An adolescent flirtation, a single kiss… They were simple things, and yet somehow, without him knowing when or how it happened, Thea had become the woman against which every other woman was measured.

All at once, Ethan was furious.

He didn't stop to think. If he had, perhaps he wouldn't have done it, but he'd drunk an entire flask of whiskey, and his heart was pounding, and the blue flames were dancing in front of his eyes, and damn it, the geese and the French hens made no sense at all, and what was he supposed to do with eight bloody milkmaids?

Before he'd even made up his mind to move, he was standing in the middle of the drawing-room, bellowing and frothing like an inmate at Bedlam. "What the *devil* do you think you're doing with my house, Theadosia Sheridan?"

There was a moment of shocked silence, and then everything happened at once.

Henry and George were in the midst of snatching raisins from the bowl and licking their fingers, but the minute Ethan's voice rang across the drawing-room, they came to a dead stop.

"He cursed!" Henry nudged his brother. "He said a curse, right 'ere in the drawing-room!"

"He did." George looked as if he couldn't decide whether to be impressed or offended by such a thing. "And 'e did it loud, too."

"Look at 'im, George. A right swell, in't he? He's a lordship, ye know."

"Don't care if 'e's a swell, or even a lordship. He shouted at Miss Sheridan." George took a step toward Ethan, his hands balled into fists. "No one's s'posed to shout at Miss Sheridan."

"That swell right there did!" Henry pointed at Ethan, appealing to the rest of the party, all of whom were standing around watching the scene unfold, still mute with shock. "That's not right, it's not, but then 'e's a lordship, and in his cups. That's what lordships do when they're in their cups."

Ethan ignored them, his gaze never leaving Thea's face. "I asked you a question, Miss Sheridan, and I'll have an answer at once."

"Ethan? My goodness, is that you?" One shaking hand came up to cover her mouth, but when she lowered it again her lips were curved in the same smile that still haunted him, the one that made his heart leap in his chest. The smile that said she couldn't imagine it being anyone but him, as if he were the only person in the world she wanted to see.

*But he didn't deserve that smile. Not anymore.*

"Ethan, what are you doing here? I can't believe it's—"

"Not Ethan, Miss Sheridan. I'm Lord Devon now, and I'm here because this is *my* house. Or perhaps you've forgotten that?"

She stared at him in silence for a moment, then, "No. I haven't forgotten ... your lordship." She paused before she added his title— not for long enough to be accused of outright insolence, but just shy of it.

"I'm pleased to hear it. Given you do recall I'm the master of the house, perhaps you'd favor me with an answer to my question. What do you think you're doing?"

"Having a Christmas Eve party, my lord." Her voice was calm, but Ethan didn't miss the flicker of temper in her eyes.

"Did you get my permission to have a party at my house, Miss Sheridan?"

"No."

Ethan's temper rose at this blithe dismissal. She didn't sound the least bit repentant, damn her. "Well, why not? I believe it's customary for servants to ask the earl's permission for such things."

"My apologies, your lordship. I've never done so in my tenure as housekeeper here, but I should have realized *this time* you meant for me to write to London for permission to have guests at Cleves Court."

Christ, the sting of that tongue. Only Thea could make an apology sound like an accusation. "You've stolen from me, Miss Sheridan. I could bloody well have you taken up by the law if I chose."

Henry sucked in a gasp. "Oh, 'e did it again, George! He said..." he lowered his voice to a whisper. "He said *bloody*."

Thea held up a hand to quiet the boys, but her gaze remained fixed on Ethan. "Very well, my lord. I believe our magistrate, Mr. Williamson is in the entryway even now, helping himself to a glass of punch. Becky, if you wouldn't mind fetching Mr. Williamson? His lordship wishes to have me taken up for theft."

"Do you suppose I won't?" Of course he wouldn't—Thea could march out the front door with every silver teaspoon in the house secreted away in her bodice, and he wouldn't move a muscle to stop her—but devil take her, her stubbornness could drive a saint to the flask, and he was no bloody saint. "I warn you, Miss Sheridan—"

"No!" A high-pitched wail pierced the room, and a tiny child with wild black curls tossed all the raisins clenched in her chubby fists to the floor, rushed forward, and threw her arms around Thea's knees. "No! George, that lordship there said 'e's going to have Miss Sheridan taken up, and then she'll have to go to jail, and we won't ever see 'er again!"

"Hush, Martha. I won't be taken to jail." Thea gathered the girl into her arms and glared at Ethan over the child's head. "I've done nothing illegal, no matter what *that lordship* says."

"Um, Miss Sheridan? There's a—"

"I hope you aren't teaching these children stealing isn't illegal." Ethan pointed to Henry and George. "Those two in particular need a lesson on proper morals and behavior."

"Miss Sheridan!" George tugged at the sleeve of her dress. "Martha's raisins are still—"

She waved him off. "I'm not teaching them anything of the sort. I'm simply telling them I'm not a thief. But thank goodness your lordship is here, because I can't think of anyone more suited to give a lesson on morality to young boys than a man who wagers on a marchioness's virtue!"

Ethan crossed his arms over his chest. Well, it seemed rumors of his London exploits had reached Cleves. Not so bloody remote after all, was it?

"Sir? That is…lordship?" Henry was starting to look panicked. "Hadn't we better—"

"As it happens, the gossips had it wrong. That wager didn't have anything to do with the marchioness's virtue at all. It was about a West End whorehouse."

There was a shocked gasp, but Martha's excited voice drowned it out. "Miss Sheridan, look!" She tugged at Thea's skirts, her face filled with glee. "The carpet's on fire!"

# ABOUT THE AUTHOR

**Anna Bradley** is the author of The Sutherland Scandals novels. A Maine native, she now lives near Portland, OR, where people are delightful and weird and love to read. She teaches writing and lives with her husband, two children, a variety of spoiled pets, and shelves full of books. Visit her website at www.annabradley.net.

Printed in the United States
by Baker & Taylor Publisher Services